TROPHY LIFE

TROPHY LIFE

A NOVEL

LEA GELLER

LAKE UNION

PUBLISHING

Published by Lake Union Publishing, Seattle

www.apub.com

Amazon, the Amazon logo, and Lake Union Publishing are trademarks of Amazon.com, Inc., or its affiliates.

ISBN-13: 9781503904200
ISBN-10: 1503904202

Cover design by Kimberly Glyder

Printed in the United States of America

To Mich, who makes it all possible.

PART ONE: SUMMER

-1-

When you're making your husband's green smoothie and forget to put the lid on the blender, and you're crouched on the counter staring up at the oozing ceiling when the housekeeper shows up and is standing under you, it's a good idea to be wearing underwear. I was not.

"Why don't you let me make Mr. Jack's breakfast?" Sondra asked, her eyes, thankfully, fixed on the ceiling.

"I'm fine," I said, desperately swabbing away at the green juice that had started to drip down while trying to keep my knees pressed firmly together. "I've got this." I looked over at the clock: 7:55. I had five minutes to clean it up before Jack walked in. Seven years ago, when I first saw this kitchen, Jack's kitchen, I thought it looked like heaven. Everything was white on top of white, adorned with more white. At first, I didn't understand why a compulsively neat person would want to decorate in white. But I soon realized that white kitchens and white bathrooms allowed people like Jack to eradicate dirt before it got too comfortable, before it settled in.

The green glob was doing more than settling in—it was threatening to take over.

The mop was useless, or perhaps I was, because all I was succeeding in doing was moving the smoothie around the ceiling, increasing the downpour of blended kale (handful), cucumber (one-quarter), almond milk (half a cup), shelled hemp seed (two teaspoons), and blueberries (one dozen). I wiped some juice out of my eyes, wincing as I remembered adding the pinch of cayenne that Jack said was good for memory.

Sondra forced herself to look at me. She often had to force herself to look at me. "You OK, Agnes?" she asked as I stood on the counter, my eyes now squeezed shut, mop overhead.

Drip.

"I'm fine," I moaned. Damn, that cayenne burned.

"I'm here early anyway," she said. "It's no problem for me to make it."

"Yeah, I get that." Drip. It might not have been a problem for Sondra to whip up Jack's daily green smoothie in addition to all the other cooking she was doing for us, but I wanted to make this smoothie. I needed to make this smoothie. I needed to do one thing in this heavenly kitchen other than sit at the island and eat what was given to me.

"You don't have much time," she said, unspooling a heap of paper towels. She began mopping the counter and floor, then motioned to the clock on the wall with her head. "He'll be down soon, and I don't think you want him to see this."

She wasn't wrong. I didn't want Sondra cleaning up my messes, but I *really* didn't want Jack seeing them.

"Fine," I said, lowering the mop in defeat. I took stock of myself. My oversize tank top was covered in green juice, my eyes still crusted with sleep, my hair unbrushed. The wrinkles I had apparently gifted myself for my thirty-fifth birthday were screaming for a tub of spackling paste. There was a lot about this Jack didn't need to see. I squatted as demurely as possible and handed the mop to Sondra.

"Thank you," I said.

"I keep telling you," she replied, helping me off the counter and looking up at the ceiling, "stay away from the kitchen."

~

By the time Jack came looking for his smoothie, the kitchen was once again a scene of white-on-white order and serenity. Sondra handed him a glass. I watched him take a sip, my eyes moving from the silver at his temples to his perfect jaw and then resting on the shoulders of the suit that I knew would be just as pristine at the end of the day as it was now. I briefly wondered how someone so put together could choose a woman who just minutes ago had been standing on the counter waving a mop around. Jack may have been the older man, but I was the one out of my league.

"Delicious, Sondra," he said, smiling at her. Sondra was no less taken with Jack than I was. She beamed and managed to give me a healthy dose of side-eye without even looking at me. Whatever. I'd earned it.

I sat in front of Grace's high chair and began feeding our six-month-old a bowl of pureed organic pears. I had neither purchased the pears (Sondra) nor pureed them (Alma, our nanny).

"Is Alma late?" Jack asked, finishing his smoothie and putting the empty glass in the sink.

"Yes," I said. "It's just me and Grace for breakfast."

Always happy to disapprove of Alma, Sondra tutted loudly and placed her hands on her hips. I looked over at her small, round, compact body and wondered how much tutting she did when I wasn't in the room. She was still disapproving audibly when Alma ran in.

"So sorry I'm late," Alma said, throwing her purse down on a barstool. "Bad traffic this morning." She swooped in and took the bowl of fruit from my hands. I had no choice but to yield. This was, after all, why Alma was here.

Now that order had been restored in his kitchen, Jack bent down and kissed the top of Grace's head and then moved over to me and put his lips on my neck. He'd just showered after spending an hour with his trainer. I breathed in the scent of his cheek. I could spend all day smelling that man.

"I'll see you at the spa," he said in my ear, reminding me that this was the last Tuesday of the month and therefore time for our monthly massage. "We can grab dinner after," he added. I also knew what that meant. It was Tuesday. Tuesdays were sushi.

~

Later that day, when I first realized something was wrong, I was naked and facedown on a table, my arms pinned down by my sides, my head shoved into a spongy doughnut pillow. The beds in the couples' massage room were placed in a V formation, so if I lifted my head, I was staring directly at the empty pillow of what should have been Jack's bed. But Jack, who set all the clocks in the house ten minutes ahead, was now thirty minutes late.

"We could try him again," said Lynne, my masseuse. She and Misha had been giving us our monthly late-afternoon massage for ten years. It had been an engagement present from Jack. "The gift that will keep on giving," he'd promised.

"No," I said, staring down at the creamy tile floor. Jack didn't answer calls from numbers he didn't recognize. "I should probably call him from my phone." I was starting to feel queasy and worried that I'd drool through the hole in the pillow, so I flipped over onto my back and stared up at the ceiling, which was painted a very light blue and layered with gauzy white clouds.

Lynne looked down at me, her face leaning over mine. She ran her fingers through her cropped hair. Both women were blonde and tan, their faces smooth. But Lynne was fifty-five, old enough to be my mother.

I needed to get up off the table and call Jack, but I couldn't move. Lying there, sensing that first small, almost imperceptible shift in my fortune, I was frozen, my clothes and phone stashed in a locker in another room. In hindsight, I would have liked a phone. In hindsight, I would have preferred to be clothed and upright.

I forced myself to sit up, pulling the sheet to my chest for coverage.

"I have to go," I said, swiveling and swinging my legs off the table, pulling the sheet with me.

"Agnes," Lynne began. There was something about her voice that told me I didn't want to hear what she had to say. "Agnes," she repeated, reaching for me, touching the sheet, which was now acting as a toga.

"Listen." She took a deep breath, a look crossing her face. I knew this look. This was the look of the bearer of really shitty news.

"Jack hasn't paid us in a while."

"Yeah," added Misha.

I blinked and Lynne continued. "You know, it's not like him. He's usually on time with his payments." I shifted my eyes to Misha, but she looked away. She hadn't been touching me monthly for the past ten years. She didn't owe me anything.

I wanted to tell Lynne that there was probably a perfectly good reason that Jack would suddenly stop paying, but I couldn't think of one, and although I opened my mouth, nothing came out.

I clutched the sheet and eyed my robe hanging on the back of the door. I was freezing.

Lynne took a step closer to me. "There's more," she said.

Of course there is.

"Roger called him a few times, but Jack hasn't returned any of his calls."

"Yeah," Misha chimed in. She nodded, her ponytail swaying with her. I wanted to tell her that if she didn't want people to know that Misha the Santa Monica masseuse was really Michelle from somewhere in New Jersey, she probably should say "yeah" a lot less often. But I just turned and looked back at Lynne.

"I have to go," I said, standing up and pulling the sheet around myself. I shuffled to the door and looked back at Misha, née Michelle,

7

and Lynne with her mommish hair, and although I wasn't sure what exactly was going on, I did know that my monthly late-afternoon couple's massage would be a thing of the past.

~

I called Jack as soon as I got outside, doing my best impression of a wife who was concerned but not panicked. I leaned on the wall, dropped my purse at my feet, and watched the contents spill out onto the sidewalk. I took a few deep breaths before I spoke, swallowing back the bitter taste in my mouth.

"Hey, it's me. Just wondering where you are. Call me when you can." I didn't need to remind Jack that you don't stand someone up with a history like mine. I thought about calling again, but instead I sent a text—What's up? No massage today?—and walked the three blocks home as quickly as I could.

When I got to the block before the beach and turned onto our street, I found Alma sitting on the wraparound deck with Grace. They were perched on a blanket playing with painted wooden rings. You had to look pretty hard in Santa Monica to find a toy made from plastic. I walked up the front steps and onto the deck and sat in a chair at the large table, my arms resting on the thick planks of reclaimed wood. Grace looked up at me, her one clump of thin blonde hair gathered in a clip above her forehead.

"Alma," I began, "has Jack been home?"

"Not yet," she said. "No massage?"

"No. No massage." I slid down off the chair and sat on the deck with them. I picked up Grace and put her between my legs. She was not yet sitting up on her own, so she leaned against me for support.

"You want to give her the bath tonight?" asked Alma. Jack never understood why I bathed Grace while Alma was on duty, but I often did. The bathroom off her nursery was one of the smallest places in a house full of large, open rooms. It was manageable for me. I knew where to sit, where to be.

"No, you do it," I said. "I need to figure out where Jack is." Alma shrugged, took Grace from me, and carried her inside. I tried Jack one more time, but when the phone went to voice mail again, I hung up and texted him. I didn't trust my voice.

Home now. Call when you can.

I looked out at the ocean and saw the sun starting to make its way down to the horizon. Maybe this was nothing. Maybe something came up at work and he really was just running late. But Jack didn't run late. Jack never ran late. I thought about what Lynne said about missed payments and unreturned phone calls, and an awful, familiar feeling that I could not shake off started moving up through me.

Sondra always cooked a light dinner and left it in the fridge, even if we were eating out. Often there were notes: bake at 350 degrees uncovered for forty-five minutes, serve at room temperature. Jack wanted his food to taste as fresh as possible, which was hard when someone was cooking it hours before he ate it. Sondra and I had worked out various ways around the problem—none of them requiring me to cook from scratch. (Before Jack, in my cooking days, I understood "from scratch" to mean "pour a can of condensed mushroom soup over rice and bake," just as I did not know the word *source* could be used as a verb, as in "sourcing the freshest coffee beans" or "sourcing kale that is both local and organic." That might explain why cooking was still Sondra's job.) I pulled out tonight's dinner and put it on the counter.

I sat in a kitchen that was mine, but not mine. Each appliance was professional grade, and while there was no microwave in this kitchen, there were items I hadn't known existed, including something called a warming drawer. (What is an oven if not a warming drawer?) There was also an enormous faucet over the industrial stove so that when making soup, one did not have to lift a pan heaving with water from the sink to the range. I had never made soup. Sondra made soup and complained regularly that for all its bells and industrial whistles, this oven did not self-clean and had no timer. I nodded in mock agreement. Despite my recent forays into smoothie making, when Sondra was not cooking, the kitchen spent much of its existence looking abandoned. It was a pretty kitchen, and sometimes I felt bad for it.

I heard Sondra walking in to get her jacket before she left. I didn't want her to catch me appearing to nap or rest. I quickly sat up and peeled the aluminum foil off the dinner dish. She had made some sort of grilled chicken. There was a finely chopped salad in a glass bowl with plastic wrap clinging to the top. I made a mental note to remind Sondra that Jack had put a kibosh on plastic wrap. Something about plastics and foods. It was hard for me to keep track. We were now to use something called beeswax wrap.

"Sondra, do you know where Jack is?"

"No. He didn't go to the massage?" she asked, pulling on her jacket.

"No, he missed it." I heard the worry in my voice. "I haven't heard from him all afternoon. He's not answering his phone." At that moment, Alma walked in, carrying Grace on her hip.

"He still not home?" asked Alma. I could feel Sondra's eyes narrowing. *Crap,* I thought. I needed Sondra's help now. What I did not need was her to feel turfed out by a baby nanny who knew before she did that Jack was mysteriously late, or even worse.

"She knew first?" Sondra asked me, sticking her thumb out at Alma. Sondra believed this house was hers as well as Jack's and that I was no more than a childbearing arriviste. She had even less patience for Alma, partially because she did not understand why I would need someone around all the time to take care of one child, but mostly because she wrongly suspected Alma made more than she did. When Grace was born and Alma came on the scene, the two women wasted no time establishing and defending their territories. It grew so unbearable that I went to Jack for help. I was tired of listening to them gripe about each other, and I was even more tired of watching them circle each other like feral dogs, teeth bared, often in front of guests and other help. (Carlos, the gardener, seemed to delight in their rivalry. I believe he had a bet with the window washers on who would quit first.)

Jack had told me to leave it be. "Oh, this is good," he'd said, sitting shirtless in bed one night, checking email. "The less they like each other, the better it is for you."

"Seriously?"

"You want them competing for your attention and approval. The minute they team up, you're through. They'll start asking for more days off and another two weeks of paid vacation."

"That seems counterintuitive," I told him.

"Are you kidding?" He sat up straighter and leaned forward, his broad shoulders pressing into his knees. "Why do you think I hired two women from different countries? You do *not* want these women to be cohorts, darling. You want them to be rivals." When he said this, it occurred to me not only how little I knew about the workings of household staff, but also that I had no idea which countries Sondra and Alma came from. (I asked Sondra the next day. She was from Mexico, Alma from El Salvador. Sondra could not even bring herself to say the *El*, only spitting out the word *Salvador*. Apparently it was a thing and Jack knew all about it, intentionally hiring a nanny from a country Sondra could not stomach, let alone say aloud.)

I wanted to avoid a brawl between the two women, so I ignored Sondra's question. I just looked at her imploringly. "What should I do, Sondra?" I asked. She smiled a smug but nervous smile and put her hands on her hips.

"Call Don," she announced, leaving me to wonder how the hell she'd figured that out before me.

Jack did not have friends, and the people he socialized with mostly serviced him—the secretaries in his office who presumably fought for his attention, his tennis partner, his car guy, his trainer. The only real friend Jack had was Don.

Don was Jack's college roommate, and an accountant as well as a lawyer. (I always suspected neither one alone would have been enough for Don.) I was never really sure if he was our accountant and lawyer, but I knew that he and Jack did some business together.

Don and his wife, Cheryl, a real estate agent, had three school-age children, all much older than Grace. Their lives were full of travel team games, recitals, and swim meets. We always went to their house for Christmas Day. I had to sit and smile while their children tore through the wrapping and complained openly at the insufficiency of their gifts.

Don had always been very nice to me, but Cheryl winced when talking to me, as if she'd taken a sip of rancid milk. I knew why. Jack wasn't the only fiftysomething man in Los Angeles to marry someone almost twenty years younger. But as far as trophy wives went, I was a disappointment. I was educated, reasonably well read, and I knew what happened in the seventies, even if I hadn't been born then. It would have been far easier for Cheryl had I been a Pilates instructor or, even better, a life coach, but I once made a literary reference and poor Cheryl almost burst into tears. Maybe she thought that in another life I could have been her—someone with her own career and a wall of calendars, each for a separate but incredibly busy child. *Busy* was Cheryl's favorite word. She wore her full life as a badge of honor and she resented anyone who wasn't as busy as she was, even if her busyness was a choice. She wasted no opportunity to mention how much she had on her plate— how much work was piling up, how much driving she was doing. There was nothing busy about my life, and Cheryl couldn't stand it. Each time she looked at me, with her bad-milk face, all she saw was wasted opportunity and time. Lots and lots of time.

What Cheryl didn't know was that I wasn't looking to never be busy, to have nothing but time on my hands, my only job to look after myself and pretend to be busy with my house and child. Had she bothered to ask me, Cheryl might have known that this was the first time in my life that I didn't have at least one job, plus the gnawing fear of staying on top of my money. If she'd bothered to ask, Cheryl might have known that a full scholarship was the only reason I was able to go to college. She did not know that when the college meal plan points ran out and I was between paychecks, I ate tuna and corn out of the can. To mix things up, I ate cereal, but the off-brand kind. I don't know if Cheryl had ever had a bite of Krispy Rice Bits or Flaky Bran. She did not know that when the last of my foster mothers pressed fifty dollars into my hands on the day she dropped me off at college, it was the very last time anybody would give me money until Jack.

I wasn't looking for Jack. He found me. I fell in love with him and happily took what he was offering. My parents had died in a car accident right before I started middle school, and with no other family around, I went to live with a series of foster families, because nobody wants to adopt an adolescent, or because nobody wanted to adopt me. I had been orphaned and shuffled around. Jack didn't just offer me money. He offered me order and structure and the one thing I wanted most, even if I didn't know it at the time. He offered me family.

I never bothered explaining this to Cheryl. She never gave me the chance.

Because they were so very busy, Don and Cheryl were ordered and efficient in a way that was dull rather than impressive. But when you have no idea where your husband is and you don't even know where the checkbooks are kept, you need order and efficiency. I pulled my hair into a bun and called Don.

"Don," I said, racing to get it all out. "It's Jack. I don't know where he is." My heart was pounding in the back of my throat.

"Agnes," he began, "take a deep breath. You need to calm down." Don was the kind of older man who had never learned that telling a woman to calm down actually has the opposite effect. I had nothing to say in response that did not involve hysterics.

"Are you there?" he asked.

"Yes," I replied, as calmly as I could. "I'm here."

14

"When did you last see him?" he asked. His voice was unsurprised, as though he knew it was just a matter of time before he got a call like this.

"This morning," I said. "Breakfast."

"He didn't come home from work?"

"No. He didn't show up for our massage," I said, hating that I had to reveal this to Don. "We have a standing appointment. I've been calling and texting him all afternoon, but he's not answering."

"Does he have his car with him?" he asked.

"Yes," I said.

"How about his passport?"

"I don't know," I said.

"Did he take any of your jewelry with him?"

"What? No. At least, I don't think so. Don, Jack's just a little late. Why are you asking me this? Why are you making it sound like he's done something wrong?" But Don wasn't answering questions, he was just asking them.

"Has he emptied the bank accounts?"

"Emptied the bank accounts? Of course not! Well, I don't know. I'm not actually sure where to look . . ." That metallic taste returned to the back of my mouth. I found a glass and spat into it.

"I'll check all that," he said, without asking me for my Social Security number or any bank account numbers—nothing. I thought there was only one bank account, and I didn't even know the account number.

"One more thing, Agnes," he added before hanging up. "Don't call the police."

"What?"

"Don't call the police," he repeated, his voice calm and flat.

"Why? What if something has happened to him?"

"Agnes, he's fine. He's OK."

"How do you know?" I didn't wait for Don to answer. I just kept spitting out saliva and questions.

"I just know that he's all right. That's all," Don repeated, his tone hardening. "You can't call the police. Do you understand?"

"Yes," I lied.

"I need to be certain you get it." His voice was finally taking on a nervous tone. "If you call the police, Jack could be in real trouble."

"I get it, Don. No police."

"Be at my office tomorrow night at eight. I have to go now." Don hung up, without waiting for me to reply, without waiting for me to ask him how he knew Jack wouldn't be home by then.

"What the hell is going on, Jack?" I spat into his voice mail a few seconds later. "I have no idea where you are or what you've done, but I just had the worst conversation with Don, and that's saying a lot. You should know better. You should know me better."

- 3 -

When your husband has been missing for more than twelve hours and his only friend tells you not to call the police, there isn't much you can do. There are some things you should not do, however, and one of them is sit in an armchair near a dark window in the middle of the night and look through old pictures.

Jack kept meticulous albums. There was an album for each year we had spent together. The albums were all an identical navy leather with the year embossed in gold on the spine. His life before me was also laid out in albums, but those were red. Pictures of my life before Jack were in a hodgepodge of mismatched albums. Some were glued onto pages of spiral-bound notebooks, some taped into journals, and some in plastic bags from unique stores, or uninteresting stores that just happened to have a shopping bag worth saving. They all lived in a box in my closet.

I crept into Jack's study and sat in the deep, brown leather armchair near the bookshelves. I would often sit in this chair and read or nap while he worked. Jack was not territorial about his space in the way that some of my friends' husbands were. I knew nothing about our finances, but I was never physically shut out. After years of being on my own, I wanted him to be in charge, to take care of things, and of me. I was allowed into the nerve center, and I chose for that to be enough.

The rain was coming down hard against the window. I pulled the first album off the shelf, sat down in the chair, and there I was, a pony-tailed twenty-four-year-old preschool teacher, standing proudly in front of the shabby beachside bungalow that housed Sunny Day Nursery. I grinned, leaning against its chipped white fence. Jack lived in a house—this house—only two blocks off the beach, several blocks north of the school. Within three months of our first date, I had moved out of my dusty, crowded apartment, waved goodbye to my roommates and my life of chore wheels and marked food in the refrigerator, and into Jack's house. Views of the Pacific replaced views of a Korean deli, and chore wheels were replaced by Sondra.

I ran my fingers over pictures of us on the beach, out to dinner, on vacation, and then to the picture of me standing in the same spot in front of Sunny Day, on my last day of work, just before Jack and I were married. I was surrounded by teachers, students, and Marge, the eighty-year-old woman who'd run Sunny Day for over fifty years. On that last day, she told me that she would always have a place for me, should I ever decide to come back. She also told me, as I got up to walk out of the sunroom she used as her office, that I was to make sure I kept a space carved out for myself. I smiled indulgently at her, but she pressed on.

"Keep it," she warned me, "even if it is so small you can barely see it. It will be all yours."

I knew what she meant, just as I knew what the other teachers, as well as the mothers at school, were talking about when they thought I could not hear. In my future life as the younger wife of a wealthy man, they said, I didn't know what I was really giving up. I didn't know what price I would have to pay for those large diamond stud earrings or that house near the beach.

But I knew the price. I knew that when you couple with someone your own age, someone in the same stage of life as you, you get to grow up together, you get to form each other. I knew because people around me were doing it—other teachers, college friends, roommates. When you marry someone who is older and richer, someone who wants to take care of you, even if it is not sinister or calculating, as those women all thought it was, it was different. I was marrying someone who was twenty years older and already formed, whose ideas about money, time, and personal space were set without any influence from me. Jack was not a Svengali, a term I overheard two moms using when they thought I wasn't listening. But he had a head start on life and adulthood, and because we now shared a life, it meant that I walked into an adulthood that was already formed for me.

I skipped to the album that included pictures of my thirty-fourth birthday and Grace's arrival. Jack had wanted to wait to start a family. "I want you for myself, at least for now," he'd said. In many of the pictures, I sat in baby-group circles with other new moms. We all sported the same diamond studs, we all wore our skinny jeans weeks after giving birth—even to twins, as several had. When you had a personal trainer and a postpartum doula who also doubled as a chef, the weight didn't stick around for long. Peppered in between our blonde-streaked, blow-dried hair were the other moms. These were the moms who had married men they met in college, in graduate school, or at work—men their own age. Their husbands were not rich, or at least not yet. They did not have large diamonds in their ears. They took many months, even well over a year, to lose all their baby weight, if ever. Their hair was pony-tailed and frizzy, and their strollers and diaper bags were not fabulous. One by one these moms dropped out of our overpriced, moderated baby group because you could not make a mortgage payment on your first house and pay sixty dollars an hour to sit with other moms and get advice you could read for free online. But we all smiled in those photos, as if we were one happy group of cohorts, even if we were not.

I kept flipping through albums, watching Grace grow. Jack smiled at the camera, at me, at Grace, his arms around us protectively. I wasn't stupid enough to look for clues in his face. If I hadn't seen any of this coming in real life, how could I expect to find clues in the curated pictures of the past?

I stared at the most recent pictures. Some of them had been taken only a month ago. It wasn't Jack that I was looking at anymore, or even at Grace. Now I was looking at me, something I rarely did. The me in these pictures felt safe and cared for. The me in these pictures had few worries, other than canceled reservations, missed naps, or Alma calling in sick.

I got up out of the chair and walked around the study. I circled the desk and moved in front of Jack's chair. I could smell his cologne on the seat as I looked down at the desktop. I ran my hands over the wood, leaning on it for support. I closed my eyes and breathed him in, and suddenly, for the first time in over a day, I felt his presence. I could hear his voice in my ear—"We're your family now, Aggie, me and Grace." I felt his arms circling me, I smelled the base of his neck, and I could almost feel the weight of his body as I fell on him for support. I felt safe and cared for and loved. It was not a cynical love, like those nursery school moms thought it would be, and it was not a purchased love, as I suspected those lumpy, ponytailed moms in my baby group thought it was. It was real and I could feel it, surrounding me, keeping me warm.

When I opened my eyes, it was gone.

-4-

I didn't have parents or siblings to tell. Sitting alone at my kitchen table long after Grace had gone to sleep and hours after I should have followed suit, I called the only other person I had in the world besides Jack. I called Beeks.

I met Beeks the summer after high school while we were both scooping ice cream. She had gone to a different high school, but we were both headed to the same college. At eighteen there is meaning to everything, even nothing, and we took our chance meeting as a sign that we were to be friends for life.

"It probably doesn't matter if we even really like each other," I remember Beeks saying, her long, curly hair tucked up into her Fairy Freeze hat. "But what are the odds that we'd be the only two people in this godforsaken town going to Lewis, and that here we are, scooping ice cream together?"

Oh, but I did like Beeks. I liked her instantly. I liked that she knew what she thought, that she didn't speak in questions—the ends of her sentences were firmly grounded, while mine raised into a question even when I wasn't asking one. I liked that she was funny, but mostly at her own expense, and that she could spot a phony a mile away. Mostly, though, I liked that she thought I was terrific. To everyone else—my foster families, my classmates, my teachers—I was bumbling and insecure. To Beeks, I was brilliantly undermining, observant, and, for the first time ever, funny. It was my job, at the end of each of our shifts at Fairy Freeze, to provide her with a list of the five dumbest things that Amy, our shift manager, said or did. Often it was hard to narrow this list down to five. We'd sit on the floor in the storeroom, where we were supposed to be doing a final count of supplies for the night, our bright-orange wings removed from the backs of our Fairy Freeze T-shirts. (It was one thing to serve ice cream in a fairy costume; it was another entirely to sit on the floor of a glorified supply closet in one.)

From that summer on, Beeks was my lodestar. So it was Beeks I called at 1:00 a.m., which was 4:00 a.m. in New York City.

"What haffened?" Although she'd been out of braces for years, Beeks was a creature of habit and she still slept in retainers. For me, she didn't need to take them out. I'd spent years conversing in nighttime Beeks talk.

"He's missing, Beeks," I whispered. If I said it aloud to Beeks, if I announced it to her, then it would be real and unchangeable. For Beeks, the words only deserved a whisper.

I heard her spit out her retainers, and I pictured her wiping the spit off her mouth with the back of her sleeve.

"Who's missing? What's wrong? What happened, Aggie?"

"Jack. Jack is missing."

"Can you speak up? I can barely hear you. Where are you?"

I looked down at the kitchen table. I wasn't sure I had the strength to say the words to her again, let alone to say them louder. I felt my eyes grow moist and hot.

"Jack is missing. He went to work this morning and never came home."

"Have you called the police?"

"Not yet. Don told me not to."

"That idiot? Why would you call him?" She had a point. I often called Beeks after spending time with Don and Cheryl and debriefed by complaining endlessly. The first time I mentioned them to Beeks, she shrieked, "Don? What the hell kind of name is Don? Who has that name anymore?"

"I had to call him. Don is Jack's closest friend."

"By closest you mean only," she said and then caught herself, softening her tone. "I'm coming, Aggie," she announced. "I will be there by lunchtime." As always, there was no question in her voice. I pictured her sitting up straight on the edge of her bed, her eye mask pushed atop her mass of hair.

"Please don't," I said. "Beeks, if you come, then this is all really happening." I could hear her breathing more heavily as she jumped out of bed and ran somewhere else in her apartment where she could talk privately and possibly start yelling at me. Many conversations with Beeks involved what she called the yelling portion. She would announce the portion by saying to me, "Aggie. This is the point in the conversation in which I am going to yell." This time, she didn't announce it first.

"YOUR HUSBAND IS MISSING!" she roared. "HIS CLOSEST AND POSSIBLY ONLY FRIEND HAS ADVISED YOU NOT TO CALL THE POLICE! THIS IS HAPPENING!"

"Beeks—"

She cut me off, speaking in a somewhat quieter voice. "This doesn't sound sketchy to you?"

"No, Beeks," I said. "It all sounds just fine. I'm totally cool with it. Did I also mention that Don asked me if Jack has his passport with him, or if he took my jewelry or emptied our bank accounts?"

"WHAT?"

"Please, let me just meet with Don tomorrow. He'll have more information for me, maybe even some answers." My eyes stung and were suddenly full of a searing liquid that had started to spill down my cheeks. I shivered, and before I knew it, a sob had escaped.

"Aggie," she said in her best attempt to be gentle, "just say when and I'll be there. Brian's whole family is visiting and we're going to be spending the rest of the week arguing publicly about which brother his mother loves best and privately about which sister got the ugly genes. Please give me an excuse to get out of here. By then you'll know more, and you'll be doing me a favor."

"Lindsey," I said.

"Huh?"

"Lindsey got the ugly genes."

Beeks laughed. "And that's what I love most about you, Agnes. At the depths of despair, you can still take down an ugly sister-in-law."

I wished she were next to me so I could put my head on her shoulder and cry in between jokes. The kitchen felt even more cavernous and hollow. The whole house, already too big for three people, felt vast and empty.

-5-

I must have dozed off for an hour or two on the living room couch. When I heard Grace calling out to be rescued from her crib, I looked down at my phone on the floor. Zero missed calls. Just a few texts from Beeks and one from one of Jack's secretaries, whom I'd called earlier: Any word?

It never seemed unusual that Jack had no friends. He worked a lot, investing money for people, and he worked alone, except for the office "ladies." There were no boys' nights, no golf trips, and I therefore didn't need the equivalent girls' dinners and movie nights. We had each other and the people who worked for us. Speaking of which, as I got up, I calculated how long it would be before Sondra and Alma arrived.

I got Grace from her crib. She was crying, her wet face pressed against the railing. We had decorated this room months before she was born. I had taken such little interest in the rest of the house, and so much of it had been done before me, but this room bore my mark. Three walls were a pale mint, the fourth a deep turquoise. Although the furniture and bedding were shades of white, there were murals of flowers and birds on the walls. All of it, even though more muted than I would have liked, amounted to the only real color anywhere in the house.

I picked up Grace and buried my face in her neck. I breathed her in, hugging her tight. Her diaper was soaked, tugging at the crotch of her pajamas with its soggy weight. I suspected the diaper was what had woken her so early, but I couldn't bear to put her down on the changing table just yet. I sat in the rocking chair and held her to me.

~

Grace had only recently started solid foods, so breakfast was apple and pear sauce mixed with some yogurt. She took a few bites and then proceeded to raspberry out the rest, sending it all over the front of my shirt. I thought about Sondra meticulously stewing and blending all those organic apples and pears from the farmers' market, most of them never making it into Grace's mouth. While I was wiping the sauce from the folds of Grace's neck, I heard keys in the door. I froze and looked at Grace. I felt my heart beating faster and my breath quickening. Then I heard Sondra call out, "I'm here early. He home yet?" I exhaled loudly, the force of my breath taking my head down with it, my chin touching my chest.

Sondra walked into the kitchen and looked at me nervously.

"Nothing yet," I said, looking up. "Nothing at all."

She put down her purse and reached for Grace. "Why don't I take Grace and you go into the office. Maybe you find something."

Was there something Sondra knew about, something I would find if I looked?

I handed Grace to her, washed my hands, and reluctantly walked up a flight of stairs to the office.

~

A few months ago, I picked up a copy of *Marie Claire* while getting a pedicure and read an article called "The If-I-Die Folder: How to Make

Sure You Are Never in the Dark." The article detailed the folder spouses should make for each other, with all sorts of personal information a surviving spouse would need to carry on, alone. The folder included a copy of a will, maybe even a living will, passport numbers, mortgage and car information, documents about life insurance, and bank accounts. When I read the article, I realized I knew none of this. I didn't know where checkbooks were kept, or if we had any accounts other than the one I used regularly. I didn't know which bank our mortgage was with, if we even had a mortgage, and I wasn't sure how to access any life insurance information or, again, if we even had it.

I came home after that pedicure and asked Jack if he had made me an If-I-Die folder. We were sitting on the deck off our bedroom, drinking wine, watching the sky turn. In Santa Monica, sunset was just a prelude. All the action happened once the sun dropped into the ocean and the sky turned a million shades of pink.

"A what?" he asked, grinning at me. "Is this the latest thing from baby group? Do you talk about this once you're done with all that cosleeping nonsense?"

"Funny," I said. "No. I read about it in a magazine. It's a folder with all the information I'd need if anything ever happened to you."

"I'm not even going to ask which magazine you read it in," he said, swinging his legs around and sitting up in his lounge chair. "What I really want to know is how soon are you planning on something happening to me, or, better yet, what exactly are you planning on happening?"

"You guessed it," I mocked him right back. "I am planning on killing you in your sleep, but before I do, I want to know where the money is hidden."

"Good to know," he said, lying back down in the chair and closing his eyes. Conversation over as far as he was concerned.

"Jack, pay attention," I pleaded. "Make fun all you like. But when I read that article, I realized I wouldn't know where to start if something happened to you, and I know what that feels like. I've already done that. I don't want to do it again."

He paused, not looking at me. He took a breath and folded his hands on his chest.

"You just need to know, my darling, that I have taken care of everything. Should anything happen to me, you and Grace will be provided for."

"That's not what I—"

"I know exactly what you're asking, and if you want one of those little folders, I'll make you one. All right?" He dropped his head to the side and forced a smile at me.

"All right," I answered. He reached for me, pulling me out of my chair and onto his.

I shook away the rest of the memory and returned to the task at hand. Now, months after that conversation, months after he'd promised to make sure I was never in this position, I had to scour his office for clues.

Jack's laptop was with him, wherever he was. I sat in his chair, breathing in his smell again. I brought in my laptop and tried to log in to Jack's email. I failed at every attempt to guess his password. I tried my name, Grace's name, all sorts of combinations of the two, birthdates, names of our favorite restaurants, but came up empty each time. I closed the laptop and started opening desk drawers.

The desk was large and dark, one of the few accents in a room that was endlessly layered in cream. I opened the center drawer and found pens, pencils, paper clips, phone chargers, and some batteries—all separated into square Lucite cubes.

I opened the next drawers and found stacks of paper held together by shiny gold binder clips. I pulled out the stacks and flipped through them. They seemed to be client reports, full of bar charts and pie charts and sections detailing gains and losses. As I paged through them, my eyes glazed over. I wasn't sure what I was looking for, and frankly, if there was something in these reports, or in the pages of bank statements that were in a separate pile underneath, what made me think I'd be able to find it? Not only did I not have an If-I-Die folder, not only had I ceded control and was completely in the dark about the details of our financial life, but if there were any clues at all in these pages, I didn't think I'd be able to find them, and if I'm being perfectly honest, I wasn't sure I wanted to.

6

That evening, Alma stayed late and I drove twenty minutes to Don's office in the skyscrapers of Century City. I sat in the car for a moment before I went up. I pulled out my phone and called Jack.

"I am about to meet Don in his office. I do not want to meet Don in his office. Please, whatever is going on, don't make me do this."

I got out of the car and walked to the elevators. The secretaries had gone home for the night, and Don greeted me as I walked off the elevator onto the twenty-third floor. Like Jack, Don was in his midfifties, but unlike Jack, Don looked his age, his hair thinning on top, his body thickening in the middle. I often wondered if this was what Jack would look like if he didn't have to keep up with a wife in her thirties. Don led me to his office in silence, and I stood facing his wall of diplomas and awards. There were so many, and they were hung in a large pattern, each side of the pattern mirroring the other. I suspected that each time he added a new distinction, throwing off the wall's symmetry, he had to find another to even things out. Don waited for me to sit and then sat himself in the chair next to me, perhaps so he could also face his accolades. He moved his chair closer to mine but made sure to line his left armrest up with my right armrest so that neither was sticking out past the other.

"The good news is that Jack is fine. At least, he's not in any serious physical danger." He spoke as if he were ordering a coffee.

I leaned forward. "Have you spoken to him?"

"You have to trust me when I tell you that he's fine," Don said flatly, answering me without really answering me. "That's the good news." He paused. "The bad news is that he's gotten himself into some trouble."

"Ya think?" I said, then remembered that Don didn't do sarcasm. I tried again. "What kind of trouble?"

"Jack lost a lot of his clients' money. He's trying to pay them back before it gets bad. He's had to clear out your bank accounts and sell whatever assets you had. Agnes, you have no money." Again, spoken as if he were simply ordering a skinny latte.

I was suddenly glad for Don's lack of social skills. No amount of small talk could make that statement any less devastating. Don repeated it, this time in an even lower voice. "Agnes, your bank accounts are practically empty, you have no savings, no investment accounts, nothing."

Sometimes I need to see words to really understand them. I closed my eyes and gripped the arms of my chair, picturing Don's words in white letters on a black background: *No Money*.

I opened my eyes and stared back at Don's baffled face. I was sure he had played this scene out in his mind, but he probably had not expected having to sit while I actually visualized the bad news.

"What about the house?" I asked. "We could sell the house."

Don looked down at his large feet and lined them up with each other. He took a breath and looked back at me. "You're underwater on it. You can sell some of the furniture, but I think some of your newer appliances are rented."

Rented appliances? I paused, almost laughing at the idea of someone coming to repossess my enormous, almost empty fridge.

"OK," I said. "No money. No money." At this point I had taken to repeating the phrase as well as visualizing it, in the hope that at some point it would not only sink in but start to make sense.

"Actually," he began, his voice dropping another octave so that now he had to move even closer to me for me to hear him, our legs touching, "actually, it's worse than that."

I took my head out of my hands and looked up at him. "What?"

"Jack is in debt. Serious credit card debt. There are several cards I know of, and there may be even more. And that's only the beginning . . ."

"I looked in his office," I started.

"What did you find?" he asked.

"Nothing," I said. Nothing I could understand. Nothing I wanted to understand.

Don moved even closer to me so that the sides of our bodies were almost touching. He lowered his voice. "You need to forget everything you saw. Do not go digging any further. Do you understand me, Agnes? You have to forget all of it."

"Why? What's going on? What has Jack done? And why isn't he calling me? Why are you telling me all this?"

"What exactly Jack has done is the least of your problems," he said. "As of now, you have no money, and once the bank repossesses the house, you'll have no place to live. You need to focus."

Suddenly, the office, Don's detached yet threatening tone, the fact that he felt the need to practically sit in my lap to deliver the news, was suffocating. I gasped for breath and scraped my chair back, pulling away, its legs tugging at the rug in his office. We sat almost five feet apart. I didn't want him breathing on me, lining himself up with me, or even consoling me. I also didn't want to stick around for the part of the conversation where he offered to help me. I stood up and gasped again, as if more air awaited me the higher up I got.

I backed up toward the door. Don stood up, lining up the empty chairs, and then reached out for my arm, as if to hold me in place. "Wait. There's more," he said. I was beginning to understand that there would always be more. Maybe I should have stayed and let Don rain more bad news down on me, but I was desperate to process his first news dump.

"I'm sure there is, but this is all I can take right now," I said and then stumbled away from Don and his office, took the elevator down, and climbed into my car. I got off the freeway in Santa Monica but didn't remember driving home.

7

Later that night I walked out onto the porch off our bedroom. We always ended the day here, and sometimes started it, having breakfast while Alma fed Grace, passing sections of the newspaper back and forth. At night, we'd sit in our midcentury lounge chairs, drinking whatever wine Jack had brought home that day. I'd listen to Jack's stories about his secretaries, and he'd ask me questions about my day—whom I'd met for lunch, which yoga teacher I'd had, if Grace had napped on schedule. I slid open the door and stood at the doorway.

I replayed the scene in Don's office in my mind. As was so often the case, I thought of a million things I should have said, questions I could have asked. Why would Jack disappear just because he lost money for his clients? How much money did he lose? Where did he go? Mostly, though, I couldn't believe I'd left Don's office without an answer to the one question that hung over everything else: Why wasn't Jack telling me all this himself? How could he let me wonder what had happened when he knew that I was always waiting for the other shoe to drop, for something to happen to him to take him away from me?

Looking out at the water, I called Jack again.

"Please," I begged. "This isn't right. Come home and let me help you, but don't leave me in the dark like this. Don't make me depend on Don for information. Don't make me sleep alone, wondering where you are. It's just not right." I wiped my soggy face, hung up, and walked inside, into the closet we shared. My chore-wheel apartment might have been smaller than this closet. When I moved in, a woman arrived with a clipboard in hand and asked how I organized my clothes. I had to laugh when she asked how I liked my shoes arranged—did I store them in their boxes with a photograph of each pair on the outside, or did I prefer clear plastic boxes so I could see the actual shoes? I didn't tell the woman with the clipboard that at the time I only owned five pairs of shoes and that two of the pairs were flip-flops. I didn't see myself taking pictures of shoes and pasting them onto boxes, so I told her plastic would be better and then left the rest up to her.

I walked to the back of the closet to the shelves of shoes and opened a plastic box on the top right. Inside was a pair of flats I hadn't worn since I moved in. I stuck my hand in the right, then the left shoe and pulled out two plastic bags full of cash. I was pretty impressed with myself for hiding what I called the "shoe-drop fund" in an actual pair of shoes. This was the cash I had slowly siphoned off—twenty, thirty, sometimes fifty dollars a week (depending on my anxiety level)—just in case something happened. I always knew the other shoe would drop. I just didn't think Jack would be the one to drop it.

~

I shuffled through the next day in a fog. Sometime after Grace's morning nap, I buckled her into her stroller and left the house just to get some air. I passed the yoga studio and waved to the girl behind the desk. Her name was Shanti, and I often wondered whether, like Misha, Shanti was really Shelly. I walked past the restaurants I lunched at with my baby-group friends and realized that I hadn't told any of them Jack was missing. But this was LA, and I knew that nobody would just pop in to check on me. Nobody wanted to invade my personal space or fold impromptu house calls into their scheduled but unproductive day. I walked past the juice bars and cafés, and I realized that if I didn't want to be seen, I had to stay away from these places. I yanked my hood up over my head. I needed to see the ocean, so I walked three blocks to the beach as quickly as I could and sat down on the first bench I saw. I called Don, but he didn't answer, so I hung up without leaving a message. I pulled the stroller so Grace was facing me. My eyes were closed and I was breathing deeply when Don called back.

"Where are you, Agnes?"

"On the beach," I said, gazing out at the vast blue, watching some birds dive down and then rise up again.

"Are you alone?" he asked.

"Grace is with me, but otherwise I'm alone." Those last words stuck in my throat. I coughed them out.

"You left my office without the full story," he said.

"OK," I said, inhaling sharply, preparing myself for the full story. Whatever the full story was, I was pretty sure I didn't want to hear it.

"Jack wants to tell you the full story himself," he said quickly, rushing to the end of the sentence.

"What?"

"Jack. He's here. He wants to talk to you."

I heard some shuffling, and then I heard Jack.

"Agnes?" He sounded tired, raspy.

When I heard his voice, I realized that there was a piece of me that hadn't been sure I'd ever hear it again. I closed my eyes and let the relief wash over me.

"Yes," I said, the word catching in my throat.

"I'm sorry this is happening," he said. "I'm sorry I let you down."

"Why?" I asked, because really, I could only get out one word at a time.

"Why?"

"Yes. Why are you hiding from me? Why are you doing this?"

"I'm embarrassed," he said. "I told you I'd take care of you, and I don't want to see you until I've made this right."

"Bullshit," I said, surprising myself. I looked around, as if the person who said that word was not me but another more assertive person, possibly standing behind me.

"What?" he asked, sounding as surprised as I was.

I closed my eyes and concentrated on getting the words out. "I don't know why, but I find it really hard to believe that you're nowhere to be found, or at least nowhere that I can see, just because you're ashamed."

He paused for a few long seconds. "Fine," he finally said. "You're right. People may be looking for me. I'm calling to tell you that you need to get out of town."

Bolting off the bench as if it were suddenly on fire, I heard myself screaming into the phone, "Out of town? What the hell are you talking about? To where? I don't have another town to go to." Grace started to cry. I reached down and lifted her out of the stroller.

"Agnes . . ."

"Am I even safe?" I shouted, quickly looking around, although I wasn't sure what I was looking for. "Is Grace safe?"

"Yes," he said. "You are safe. For now. It's not really about safety. Things could get ugly here, and the house is about to go. You need to leave town."

"This is crazy," I said, jiggling Grace on my hip. "I can't hear this right now." Then I did something I'd never done before. I hung up on Jack. I stared at my phone and then threw it in my bag. Seconds later, I fished it out and tried calling him back, but I got no answer.

Grace stopped crying, but she refused to go back in the stroller, making herself rigid whenever I tried to fold her into the seat. I had no idea how Alma did this, so I carried her in one arm and pushed the stroller with the other.

I walked in the front door to find Sondra and Alma in a rare moment of concert. They both looked up at me.

"Agnes," Sondra began. "You find Mr. Jack?"

Jack had gone missing on Tuesday. It was now Thursday afternoon. The people who presumably had been hired to look after me were looking to me for answers. The man who'd promised to look after me so that I never had to worry about a single thing had just told me I needed to get out of town.

"I don't know what to do," I began. "Jack is gone, and we have no money. I'm scared, and after this week, I don't even know how I can pay you or where I will be living."

Sondra blinked. "There," I said, handing Grace to Alma. "Now you know as much as I do."

8

I was sitting on the floor of my closet counting out my shoe-drop money when Jack called.

"Agnes, we don't have much time. I need you to listen," he said. "The house and everything in it will be gone soon. Sell whatever jewelry you have in the next couple of days. Ask Sondra. She knows people."

"What?"

"Don will send someone to pick up your car because you won't be able to make the lease payments."

"My car?" Jack had bought—or I thought he'd bought—the SUV for my birthday. Sometimes it was hard to believe there was a time when I thought ribbons on cars were just something in commercials.

"Yes, the car," he answered. "Don just put his mother in a nursing home and was about to sell her Honda. He'll drop it off. It's nothing fancy, but it will get you where you need to go."

"I don't understand . . ."

"Then you're going to leave town."

"Where am I supposed to go?" Surely I wasn't expected to figure this out on my own.

"New York," he answered.

"What the hell, Jack?" I dropped the cash. Spit flew out of my mouth. Luckily, I was alone.

Silence. I wondered if I'd pushed too hard. I couldn't risk him short-circuiting, and I needed information, so I softened my tone. "Wait," I said, squeezing my eyes shut. "I have a question. I want to know why I have to get out of town if you only lost money. Don't investors lose money sometimes? Isn't that part of the risk? What's really going on?"

Once again, my question was met with silence. I'd summoned all my courage to ask, and I wasn't sure I had anything left in me. "Jack?" I whispered, opening my eyes tentatively.

"You need to leave town because I didn't just lose my clients' money," he said. "There's more."

"How much more?"

"To cover up the losses, I had to take money from other clients. I made some bad calls and I made things worse. I need to go underground for a while and get the money back to the people I took it from so that I don't end up in jail. Is that enough information?" He didn't wait for me to respond. "Now you need to listen to me and follow my instructions. Understood?"

"Understood." But really, I didn't understand. What the hell was happening? Jail? "Why New York?" I asked.

"A friend of mine, Ruth Moore, is the head of school at St. Norbert's, in the Bronx. There's a teaching job for you with faculty housing and day care." Jack paused.

"A school? The Bronx?" I asked, not quite soaking in all the information.

"It's a boys' boarding school. You will be teaching English in the middle school." He spoke slowly and loudly, as though I were hearing impaired. "This means you will have a source of income, a home, and day care for Grace. Most importantly, you will both be safe."

Now I was the one short-circuiting. "I can't teach at a middle school, let alone a boarding school! I can't live in New York! Jack?" More spit. I took my phone and quickly wiped it on the bottom of my shirt.

"Please, Agnes," he said, sounding desperate for the first time. "You'll be safer there, and frankly, there's nowhere else for you to live once the house is gone."

"You're telling me that I'm on my own?" I said. "That I have no choice?"

"You're not on your own," he whispered. "The last thing I want is to send you away, but you just can't be near me right now. You have to trust me to fix the mess I've made and to keep you safe." His voice cracked. "I need to know that you're both safe."

"Then come with us," I said in between sniffles. "If we have to go, then so do you."

"That's not practical."

"So me moving across the country and working at some random school is practical, but you get to stay here?"

"I don't get to stay, I have to stay," he said. "I can only fix this mess if I'm here. For now."

"Yeah, well, I need some time to let this all sink in," I said, mopping up the mess of tears and snot on my face. "I don't understand how you can be in so much trouble and not want me around to help."

Jack cleared his throat and swallowed. "Actually, you'll be able to help me more if you're in New York."

"How? How can I help you from the other side of the country?" I sobbed.

"Ruth Moore isn't just the head of the school, she's also an investor. At least, she was."

"I don't understand . . ."

"She used to invest some of the school's endowment, as well as some of her own money, with me. She pulled out of my fund, and I'm worried other big investors are going to follow and this is all going to get a lot worse. I need to know why she pulled out—if the school is in trouble, I need to know."

"And you can't just ask her?"

"That's not how it works, Agnes," he said.

"And me teaching at this school is going to help you find out . . . how?"

"If the school is strapped for cash, you'll know pretty quickly. Besides, you'd be surprised how much you can learn just by being in the right place."

"This is all so much," I said.

"I know, but I need an answer, and you don't have much time," he said. "I'll call you tonight. I love you, Aggie." His voice broke again. "So much."

"Me too," I said back before I hung up. "Me too."

I lay on my side on the closet floor, pulled my knees up to my chest, and called Beeks. She was in the middle of yelling at her children, who were always up way too late. "If I stop now," she said, "I'll forget what I was yelling about." She promised to call me back. That gave me just enough time to do some research on this mystery school. I was ready for Beeks when she called.

"This East Coast–West Coast time difference is really coming in handy," she began. Beeks never said hello. She just dived in. "I'm so frickin' happy to hear your voice. Don't get me wrong, I'd let you call every night at four a.m., but I'll take earlier any day. What's up?"

"The good news is that I've spoken to Jack. The rest is bad," I said, lying down on the closet floor. (Yes, I was back in the closet.)

"How bad?"

"Bad. Stolen money bad. Have to get out of my house bad."

"Shit."

"Pretty much."

"No money at all?" she asked, cleverly sidestepping the questions about Jack I knew she was dying to ask.

"Nope. Nothing. Apparently I don't even own the stove."

"I never liked that thing anyway," she said, not missing a beat. "I mean, how many burners does one woman need?" I laughed. Of all the noises I'd made in the past few days, laughter had not been one of them.

"There's more," I said.

"There's always more," she followed.

"He says I need to leave town. I'm coming to New York." I didn't finish the sentence before she started whooping with joy. Beeks, Brian, and their boys lived in a small apartment on the Upper West Side.

"Beeks," I said, "remember, this is bad news."

"Oh," she said, chastened. "You're right. Bad news. OK, tell me more of this bad news and I'll try to control myself."

"I'm supposed to go live at a boarding school called St. Norbert's. I'm apparently going to teach English in the middle school. Oh, and there's day care for Grace and free housing for us." My God, this sounded worse each time someone said it.

I rolled over and looked up at the shelves of T-shirts that Sondra neatly folded and organized by color. It was still hard for me to believe that I had more than one yellow T-shirt.

"And they want you?" she asked.

"I guess so. I looked online, and I don't need credentials to teach at a private school in New York. Anyway, you now know as much as I do," I said.

"Oh," she said again. "A middle school teacher? At least you'll be prepared."

"How so?" I asked.

Beeks and Brian had four boys. Stevie was thirteen and was Beeks's stepson, a product of Brian's first, early, and very brief marriage. Kyle and Alec were five, and Jimmy was three. "I live with a middle schooler. They're moody, impulsive, and they smell awful. How different can it be from teaching preschool?"

"Beeks, I think it's going to be really different," I said. "I don't feel prepared, not at all."

She ignored me. "Tell me again," she said. "How does Jack know this place? What's his connection? Who does he know there?"

"I thought you wanted me close," I said, listening to her click in her retainers.

"Aggie, I'm just asking questions. Do not take any of them to mean that I do not want you to get on the first flight to New York. I do. It's just all a little fishy and, frankly, a little neat."

"I know. But this is my only choice right now." I was convincing myself as well as her. "I'm scared, Beeks, and I don't have any other options." My voice began to crack. I hoped that Beeks would hear it and go a little easy on me. "I know he did something horrible. I get it. But I also know that he'll fix it, whatever it is. Don't you see that?"

I knew Beeks did not see that, and I was annoyed with myself for asking her. I ended the call and walked down the back stairs into the kitchen.

I sat at the kitchen table clutching a mug of tea I probably wouldn't drink. "New York," I said aloud. "Middle school." I closed my eyes and tried to picture the words but only saw black. What other choice did I have? I could look for a place to live and a job here, but that wasn't easy. I thought about calling Marge at Sunny Day, Marge who would always have a place for me. The thought of her was warming, but the thought of facing all those teachers and moms who knew something like this would happen was terrifying. Maybe they hadn't predicted that Jack would steal money and go underground, but they knew I'd be back. I'd be back when Jack traded me in for a newer model, because that's what happens to trophy wives. And what of the other trophy wives, the other moms in my baby group? What would they say when they thought I was out of earshot? That they knew I'd be the first to go? That it was only a matter of time?

I felt my stomach convulse, and I ran to the sink and threw up. I didn't know what exactly made this sink a farmhouse sink, but I would have traded anything to be on a farm somewhere. New York, on the other hand, did not sound like a place to which one escapes. Don't people leave New York when they are in trouble? Still, the only person I had besides Jack was Beeks, and Beeks was in New York. With Jack gone, maybe this made sense. I could be near Beeks and still help Jack get the information he needed.

My phone buzzed with an incoming call. Jack.

I dumped out the mug of tepid tea and picked up.

"I'll do it," I said before he could even speak. "I'll take the job."

9

A week later, a company called Happy Home Furniture Resale came and took all our furniture. I asked Sondra to pack up the contents of Jack's desk along with some of my old schoolbooks. As for the few things that were left, what I couldn't quickly sell fit into a few boxes. Sondra gave me the name of a pawnbroker downtown where I sold all the jewelry Jack had bought me. I kept my wedding band but parted with the engagement ring. I also bade farewell to those diamond earrings.

I pressed some money into Sondra's and Alma's hands. Not as much severance as I should have given them by local standards, or by decency's standards, for that matter, but enough to let them know that I knew that they were also giving something up.

The day after I told Jack I'd take the job, Don had parked a sedan in front of our house. I packed up the sedan, the car that took the place of my shiny BMW. When I first sat inside the white Honda, which was at least fifteen years old, and inhaled the stale smell of cigarettes, dust, and coffee, it was as though this past decade of my life had never happened. Sitting in that car, I could have been in my first car, a used Mazda into which I could easily have fit all my possessions. I had worked two jobs in college, three over the summers, just to buy that car. Here I was, once again, sitting in a used, pungent car, a car that other people had driven and tired of.

On the day I left California, I packed that car with what remained of my earthly belongings. I strolled down to the beach with Grace for a final look at the ocean. We lived up on the cliffs in Santa Monica. If I looked left, I could see the pier punctuated by the Ferris wheel. If I looked right, I saw the mountains. From up on the cliffs, I often felt like I was on the deck of a ship. The sand below was invisible, as were the beachgoers, mostly families who lived miles east of here and were willing to brave legendary traffic on the freeways.

Many East Coasters found the Pacific Ocean surprisingly cold and unwelcoming. It made little sense to them that California's waters would be unswimmable unless you were brave or in a wet suit. To me, the Pacific, or at least this part of the Pacific, was my mooring. As far as I drove, once I saw the ocean rise up in the distance as my car dipped down over the hill, I knew I was minutes from home.

I closed my eyes, saw the word *goodbye* in my head, sucked in all the air I could get, and opened my eyes for a final look.

~

Even though I could have used the air and was desperate for my last breaths of the ocean, I kept the car windows up so nobody on the road would see me weeping over the wheel. When I got a final glimpse of the beach behind me, and when I lost the LA radio stations and then the desert stations of the Inland Empire, I sobbed. There are few things that feel both more permanent and transient than crossing from one state into another. When the WELCOME TO NEVADA sign came into sight, I felt my roots being torn out of the ground.

Grace sat rear facing in her car seat, with a mirror in front of her, so that if I looked in the rearview mirror I could watch her sleep. I quickly learned to time big chunks of driving with Grace's naps, and I was never so grateful for her rigid, reliable sleep schedule, courtesy of our sleep consultant, baby nurse, and Alma. Watching her head nod to the side, her eyes flicker, then close, and listening to her breathing grow slower and deeper, I found it odd that Grace had learned to sleep from women who were not me.

During one of her naps, I let my mind wander, back to a night not so many weeks ago. I had woken up and realized Jack wasn't in bed. I sat up and saw that he had stepped out on the deck. His back was to me as he faced the beach, his back bent slightly, his arms resting on the railing. When he turned, I saw him from the side, wearing an expression I hadn't seen on him before. He looked anxious, possibly even scared. I told myself it was a private moment, one I shouldn't interrupt, but I knew otherwise. I chose not to see him this way, wearing a face I didn't recognize.

I shoved that memory where it belonged, in the back of my mind, with all the things I didn't want to think about. Instead, I focused on the road.

When Grace was awake, in the moments between her naps and cries for food and a clean diaper, I played her songs on my phone and sang along with them. By day three, I had memorized all the words to every *Sesame Street* song ever written. It was just as well. The radio stations continued to shift as the car drove through the states in the middle of the country and only served as a reminder of what was happening to me.

Jack and I spoke on the day I left, and he told me that from now on, at least for a while, Don would be my contact. Jack was going to be incommunicado.

"It has to be this way," he said to me as I drove through many miles of desert.

"Does it?" I spoke calmly but loudly so the speaker on my phone would pick up my voice. The Honda predated Bluetooth.

"You have every right to be angry," he said.

"Oh, really?" I snapped, no longer making any attempt to mask my feelings. I didn't have to worry about angering Jack or incurring his silent treatment, because I was about to receive the mother of all silent treatments. "That's good to know."

He didn't take my bait; he left it dangling on the line.

"I love you, Agnes, and I need your help," he said.

"About that . . . ," I began. "If Ruth Moore has pulled her money out, why is she hiring me?"

"Because she's an old friend and I asked her to."

"And it's not weird?" I desperately needed fresh air and thought about rolling down the window, but I wasn't sure he'd be able to hear me with the windows open on the freeway.

"Hardly. Business relationships are deep and complicated, and one thing has nothing to do with the other."

I loved that Jack wanted my help. He never wanted my help. I just wished he'd wanted my help locally. He must have read my mind, because he said, "I am not sending you away. I love you, and it's my job to keep you safe. I promise you that this will all work out. I will get all the money back, and you will come home."

"You can't get a new phone or some prepaid burner phone?" I asked. I honestly had no idea what a burner phone was, but I'd heard the term tossed around casually on procedural crime shows. Besides, just saying "burner phone" made me feel a little tougher, and I needed all the help I could get.

"The less you hear from me, the safer we will all be. I promise—I'll be in touch when I can. For now, we'll communicate through Don."

That was just what I wanted to hear. That from now on, my in-hiding, money-stealing husband and I would communicate with his emotionally challenged business associate slash only friend. This was getting better and better. Luckily for me, I wasn't thinking too much about any of this. Thinking was too hard. I just kept moving forward, one mile at a time.

Somewhere in Nevada, or possibly Utah, Grace and I pulled into a motel to spend the night. The night air was dry and crisp, all its moisture having been sucked out. I felt tired, as though I'd run all the way here rather than having spent hours sitting and staring ahead.

I carried Grace and a few of our bags into our room. I immediately closed the blinds and got us both ready for bed. Without Jack, if I was able to fall asleep with Grace, I often did. Now that the bed was mine alone, I brought her into it. Jack had believed that the bed was just for the two of us. This wasn't an easy position to maintain in Santa Monica. At the Sunday-morning farmers' market, both moms and dads wore their babies in carriers and slings. According to some of the baby-group moms, the market parents went home and napped with their children in one giant bed, or even on a series of mattresses on the floor so that they could all climb in and out with ease. But to Jack, a marital bed was just that—marital. Family snuggles were for the morning, or better yet, for the couch.

Now I didn't even bother to bring a portable crib for Grace, nor did I request one from the motel. Now I kept her close. It felt better to have someone else in the bed, even if that someone else was six months old and weighed little more than a backpack. When I woke in the middle of the night, gasping for air, desperately trying to remember my dream, sure that it would give me some clue as to where Jack was, I reached out and Grace was there. Sometimes I'd swear I heard a sniffle or a whimper from her, and I would pull her close and sleep with her in the nook of my arm or on my chest. I was never able to nurse Grace (practically grounds for capital punishment in Santa Monica), and she certainly took no bottle at night (our baby nurse had set all that up for us before she left), but in those days on the road, I prayed she'd cry out for a nighttime feeding.

As I lay with Grace snuggled perfectly into my side, the crown of her head just under my chin, I thought about the farmers'-market parents. Maybe they were onto something. There really was something about a baby in your bed—a warmth, a smell, a security, all of which would be gone in a matter of months. I had been so sure of myself when I sat in that baby-group circle and announced that our nurse had trained Grace to sleep through the night in a room that was not ours. I had been so sure and so proud of the husband whose territory I worked so hard to preserve. All the younger wives had. We were so damn sure. But my husband and his territory were miles away, and now all I had was his baby. Those other moms in their drawstring pants and nursing bras, did they know something I didn't? Did they know that the reason younger wives of older men keep their babies out of their beds is because they're desperate to keep their husbands' attention? As I lay with Grace on that lumpy motel mattress, I wondered—had I been desperate, or now, abandoned and unmoored, had I not been desperate enough?

-10-

I was hungry. In preparation for the trip, I'd emptied out the contents of the fridge into a cooler. This did not get me far; our fridge was never very full. I wasn't planning on packing Jack's store of probiotic morning drinks or the thirty-six glass bottles of mineral water that occupied the bottom shelf. I took whatever fruit and cheese I could find, noting that this might be the last organic fruit and cheese I'd be eating for a while. I asked Alma to use some of the fruit to make little baggies of fresh puree for Grace. I ran to the store and bought several boxes of Grace's organic rice cereal as well as her organic formula—that much I could do. I also bought a loaf of bread. I didn't remember the last time I had brought bread, but I assumed I'd be eating sandwiches on the road, because Sondra and her quinoa bowls weren't coming along for the ride.

After the first couple of days' driving, I had run through most of my food. Grace still had some baggies left, and I wondered if I'd take the plunge at some point and buy baby food. I swung into a gas station to refill the car and took Grace inside the minimart for food. Just getting Grace in and out of the car was a challenge. I remembered some of the baby-group moms talking about how long it took them to leave the house (or in their cases, the apartment) with the baby and how hard it was carting a crying baby around in a car. These poor moms looked completely bedraggled, overwhelmed by the thought of leaving their homes with their babies. When they started down this discussion, one that could go on for a good thirty minutes, their words turned to white noise. I only ever took Grace in the car to go to the pediatrician, and even when I did, Alma came with me. I sometimes took her out on short walks, but never long enough for her to get hungry, lose her mind, and start howling like a car alarm, as these other babies seemed to. I wished all these moms had an Alma, even if it only meant they could go to the supermarket alone. Truth be told, I didn't go to the supermarket much, either, but when I did, I certainly didn't have Grace in tow.

Now I had to make sure she was full, burped, and in a clean diaper before I put her in the car. I'd learned my lesson on day one when I drove for too long and couldn't find a rest stop when she started to moan. By the time I pulled over, somewhere in the California desert, she had drenched herself in tears, sweat, and possibly the biggest poop I'd ever seen. Lesson learned.

My search for food led me to a minimart somewhere in the middle of Nebraska. I hadn't realized how little geography I knew until I had to keep googling maps of the country to figure out where I was. The woman behind the counter was large, so large that I was sure someone was standing behind her, pressing herself close, but in fact it was all one deep woman.

She smiled at me. "Can I help you?"

"Do you have food here?" I asked.

"All here on the right." She waved an arm in the direction of some graying hot dogs, deli sandwiches, and a pot of what I assumed was soup.

"Do you have fresh food?" I asked.

"This is all fresh." She continued to smile. "Made it myself this morning or late last night."

"Oh," I said. "I guess I'm wondering if you have salads." As soon as the words were out of my mouth, I heard how ridiculous I sounded. Who did I think I was? Not so long ago, I would have known that you can never get a salad at a highway rest stop. I began to bounce Grace on my hip as she, too, moaned in hunger.

"Nope, darlin'," said the woman, suppressing a laugh. "There's a Taco Bell in about fifty miles, and they have a pretty good salad bar." She paused. "I think we have some tuna salad in the fridge," she said. "It has celery in it."

By now a line had formed behind me, and the woman was no longer smiling. I shuffled toward the fridge. I could not bring myself to buy the tuna. It was grayer than the hot dogs, and I saw none of the promised celery. Then I turned around and found myself face-to-face with something called a baby puff. It seemed that in the middle of the country, babies, even babies as young as Grace, liked to snack. I had been warned about such snacking from Deirdre, the woman who ran our baby group. She said we might encounter these snacks, snacks that were no more than processed wheat, sugar, and air. We were to avoid these snacks at all costs. But these snacks didn't look so evil. There was a smiling baby on them, and they even came in vegetable flavors. There was also a banner across the front of the can that screamed "All-Natural Ingredients." How bad could they really be? Grace was starting to pull at my hair, which had fallen out of the messy bun in which it now lived.

I grabbed a can of sweet potato puffs and ripped off the top, shoving a puff into Grace's mouth. She immediately stopped braying, grinned, and reached for more. The kid was just learning to reach for me, and now she was reaching for these poison puffs? I gave her one and stuck one in my own mouth so I could see what all the fuss was about. A burst of sweet potato melted onto my tongue. It was sweet and satisfying, and I wasn't sure how I'd live without another. I jammed a fistful into my mouth, gave one to Grace, and grabbed a bunch of cans—including one promising mixed veggies. Carrot sticks and salads would have to wait.

The next day, in another state, I fell upon a bag of yogurt chewies, which were apparently designed for older babies and their hungry and cash-strapped mothers. I took it upon myself to test the entire genre of baby and toddler snack food and choose the winners for when Grace was ready to eat them. I found some snacks in the shape of wagon wheels. I wasn't so excited about the cheesy corn wheels, but the rice wheels with cinnamon were heavenly. These snacks sustained me as I drove east, and with each purchase of a yogurt chewy or a cinnamon rice wheel, I told myself that by the time Jack found us, I would have gotten rid of all the evidence.

I realized that I was also running into something of an underwear problem. While I was packing my clothes, I'd made a separate pile of underwear, intending to put it all in a small bag I'd be able to access easily. I had stood in front of the dresser inside my walk-in closet and held up some of my lacy thongs, all gifts from Jack. There's something wonderful about being married to a man who loves you so much that he wants to buy your underwear. Each pair was expensive, beautiful, and if it was not comfortable, it was not so uncomfortable that I spent the day counting the moments until I would be able to tear it off. I had never worn thongs much before Jack, but a month or so after we began dating, he presented me with one. It was the color of my skin, he said. I imagined this well-dressed, established man walking into a lingerie department and buying a thong for a twentysomething preschool teacher who bought her underwear in packs of six or eight. I was flattered. That's how Jack made me feel so much of the time: honored to be the recipient of so much attention and time, warmed by his appreciation and involvement in the details of my life. I loved the attention. I was happy for it.

Perhaps I'd been caught up in the underwear moment when I was packing, because once I got on the road, I realized that I didn't have any of it with me. I just had the one thong I'd put on the morning I left California, and I'd been washing it out at night in the sink of whatever motel we were staying in. It wasn't until I reached the halfway point that I finally grew tired of the lonely, overwashed thong and found a Super Walmart right off the highway. I stocked up on snacks and bought two eight-packs of women's briefs. I took Grace into the Walmart bathroom and checked the stalls to see if anyone was around. The bathroom was empty. I strapped Grace onto the changing table. I'd long since abandoned Jack's advice (OK, instructions) to swab down the changing table with baby wipes before she went near it. I quickly unpeeled my jeans and removed the thong, replacing it with a roomy, cottony pair of briefs.

The briefs were like an old, comfortable T-shirt, wrapping around me and my midsection. They rose up high, almost to my belly button. I looked at the pack and realized I'd just bought sixteen pairs of grandma underwear, underwear that had enough fabric to actually be one of my T-shirts. I shrugged. I hadn't been this comfortable in a long time. I stashed the thong in my diaper bag for when Jack returned, and took Grace off the table.

I sat down in the car and felt a noticeable difference. It was like sitting on a pile of fresh laundry. I was shifting around in my seat, marveling at the wedgie-proof underwear (no matter how I sat, it always stayed in place!) when Beeks called.

"How are you?" she asked.

"I'm better now," I said. "Did you know that when you wear granny panties you never get a wedgie?"

"I know that all too well," she said. "My underwear are so big I could hide a turkey in them. I never understood your thongs." There was so much Beeks never understood. My thongs were just the tip of the iceberg.

"How's the road trip?" she asked.

"Lonely," I said. I had been driving for five days and still had about five to go.

"Isn't it a little bit romantic? You and your daughter, out on the open American road?"

"I'm pretty sure Jack Kerouac didn't travel with burp cloths and wipes," I said, eyeing the floor of the car.

"Fair enough." She paused. "Have you heard from Jack?" Beeks's tone changed when she asked questions she didn't want to ask but had to.

"No. He's gone underground," I said. "I won't be hearing from him for a while."

"WHAT?"

"Beeks . . ."

"Underground? What is this, a mob movie? How are you not furious?"

"Because if I'm going to be furious, I wouldn't know where to start. Am I furious at Jack for putting me in this position, or furious at myself for letting him do it?"

"Aggie . . ."

"Don't. If you're going to make me talk about how I feel, then we're done talking. As soon as I start to think too much about this, it all falls apart." I paused. "I fall apart. And if that happens, I could just end up losing my shit and camping out somewhere in the middle of the country, and New York won't happen."

"Fine," she relented. "Message received. Loud and clear. From now on, we will only discuss your new underwear."

"You mean my fabulous new underwear?"

"Exactly."

Although Jack had said he needed to disappear, even from me, he never told me not to call him, so I continued to leave him voice mails from the road. I was trying not to think too much about New York and just concentrating on getting there. Every time I thought about the job, I started to sweat and the metallic, bilious taste returned to my mouth. I quickly learned to keep an empty plastic cup in the car just in case my mind started to wander. But with the new job days away, I needed information. I had no choice—I called Don. Grace had fallen asleep in the car, so I left the engine running (I learned that lesson pretty quickly) and stretched out on the hood, soaking in some non-Californian sunshine. I had to take what I could get.

"I need to know more about this school, Don. Tell me what you know." I slid off the hood of the car and stretched my legs.

"I just know that it's a boarding school for boys. That means it's not just a job, but it's also a place to live."

"I would have somewhere for us to live if we end up in a halfway house. Surely you can tell me more."

"Fine," he replied. "It's a middle school and a high school, both on the same campus."

"I know that already," I said, brimming with impatience. "Anything else?"

"What else do you need to know?" he demanded. "Honestly, Agnes. There's not much more to it." For the first time he was beginning to sound irritated, almost angry. He just wanted me to follow his directions and go. He hadn't planned on more questions.

"Just tell me something, Don, anything."

But Don had either lost signal or hung up on me, because my questions were met with nothing but silence.

~

"It's a private school," Beeks said when I called her later. Don seemed prepared to give me no more information and was now forwarding all my calls to voice mail. "That's all you need to know," she said. "More specifically, St. Norbert's is a private school for rich kids who have been thrown out of other private schools. It's a last-ditch effort for rich parents to keep their kids out of public school. And if you're in the middle school, you're really scraping the bottom of the barrel. That would explain why they hired a woman who has only taught preschool, who hasn't done any creative writing since high school, and whose résumé was likely written by her husband's shady lawyer."

I had no response for this. Once again, I was reminded that with Beeks, I had to be careful when asking for the truth, because she'd gladly lay it out for me in all its unflattering glory.

"Oh." Sometimes that was all I could say to her.

"By the way," she plowed on, "the school is in Riverdale, which is technically the Bronx, but it doesn't feel like it. It's pretty green. Oh, I also found out that St. Norbert's sounds Catholic but isn't Catholic."

"Huh?" I asked, wondering why Beeks had done more research on this school than I had.

"Yup. I spoke to a friend who writes about education for the *Journal*. When the Catholic Church had to make payouts to settle some of the child abuse cases, they sold some of their low-performing colleges. St. Norbert's was bought by a private boys' school looking to relocate. They kept the name. Maybe because it's on all the buildings."

I heard her clicking in her retainers.

"Listen," she said, "I can't believe I'm saying it, but this may be perfect for you. You have somewhere to go, something to do, somewhere to live, and you can do it all without anybody breathing down your neck. Nobody is paying much attention to these kids. I speak from personal experience. Middle schoolers are moody, awkward, and uncomfortable in their own skin. They are unpleasant as a rule. This means that people prefer to look away while middle school is happening. Don't you see? It's perfect!"

I shared none of her enthusiasm until she said, "Plus, and most importantly, you will now be closer to me. We get to have conversations in the same time zone. Even if they won't be keeping an eye on you, I will."

~

We bypassed Manhattan and drove to the very top of New York City, to the leafy north Bronx neighborhood of Riverdale. I rolled down the windows. Even in the very last days of August, the air was thick and heavy, and I learned to keep the car windows up to keep out insects—insects that seemed to have crawled out of a nuclear meltdown. I had never seen bugs this size, this ferocious. They could not be swatted away, at least not permanently, and when they returned, they did so with a vengeance. They bit and they stung, and a day before, at a park somewhere in Pennsylvania, a mom cautioned me to check Grace for ticks after she had been rolling in the grass.

"Excuse me?" I replied. "For what?"

"Ticks," said the Pennsylvania mom. "You know, Lyme disease?" No, I did not know. I had just mastered the art of bug spray, not to mention the art of timing our park visits with the mosquitoes' naps (or whatever it was they were doing when they weren't biting). How could I possibly be expected to take on Lyme disease? Still, sure enough, there I was, combing Grace's chubby pink arms for insects that burrowed and left behind illness. Wasn't it New Yorkers who came west and complained of the lack of amenities? ("What do you mean, you don't deliver?") At least in California we didn't have swarms of enormous, pissed-off, disease-carrying insects.

But California now lay on the other side of the world, or at least of the country. I couldn't be like those New Yorkers in college. ("You call the *LA Times* a newspaper? This is a bagel?") I couldn't see everything through a rosy, beachy Californian lens. I had to take off that lens and put it somewhere else. I needed a drawer for it, and I needed to tuck it away.

PART TWO:
FALL

I reached Riverdale on the first day of September. I spread out a map of St. Norbert's on the passenger seat, obscured by a lifetime supply of veggie puffs and a stack of organic, dye-free burp cloths. Pieces of my old and new life, mingling right next to me in the car. I reached over and shoved the puffs and cloths to the side so I could read the map and find my way.

I drove in from the highest point of the campus, and as I learned later that week, from what was also one of the highest points in the Bronx and in all five boroughs. Campus was a tall, thin spiral. From what I could see on the map, faculty housing and the student dorms were at the bottom of the campus, down along the Hudson River. What used to be a convent sat at the very top of the spiral. When the convent closed, years before the actual university shut down, it was converted into dorms. I'd learned this and a score of somewhat useful facts when I'd googled "St. Norbert's" every night since Beeks had shamed me with all her knowledge. I also learned a ton about this Norbert, who seemed to have lived a charmed, royal life in Germany until he got thrown off a horse and gave himself to God. He now had a couple of colleges named after him, even if one of those colleges had been forced to close down when the Catholic Church was scrambling for cash.

As soon as I'd passed the guard booth, I saw a statue of Norbert. He was not what I had expected. When I read that he was German, I envisioned an angelic-looking Augustus Gloop—a smiling, stocky, greedy boy with shiny cheeks—a piece of schnitzel in his right hand and a cream puff in his left. This Norbert was not a Roald Dahl character. Humor had never crossed his path, especially at his own expense. While there was a doughiness to his cheeks, he was unsmiling and severe. He seemed to look right at me and at all the contents of my car. I became self-conscious of my tank top and shorts and stared ahead, driving down the steep hill in search of faculty housing.

None of the buildings seemed to match. I didn't know enough about architecture to identify them, but looking around it seemed that campus was like a bag of hand-me-downs from unrelated people. There was a lot of brick, probably more brick on this one campus than in all of California. A few of the buildings looked like the architect couldn't decide whether to build a castle or a villa and just settled with a building that looked like both but, really, neither. A few buildings were cement, but not in a breezy, modern Palm Springs way. No, this cement was about as far from a palm tree as it could get.

Grace started to stir. She'd soon be up and hungry. I turned a corner, and at once the Hudson River lay before me. It was not vast like the ocean. Cliffs lay on the other side, topped by dense trees, not a building in sight. No, you couldn't disappear into the enormity of this river. The other side was near enough to see, and the river was moving quickly, on its way somewhere, as if in a hurry. But the water itself was a reminder that I had traveled from one end of the country to the other. I drove to a dead end and into the parking lot in front of a cluster of buildings marked FACULTY HOUSING.

It was bright and my sunglasses were lost in the morass of the passenger seat. Squinting, I pulled into a faculty parking spot and saw a woman headed toward me. She was tall, with broad shoulders, and wore gardening gloves, a faded blue apron, and a big, floppy, flax-colored sun hat.

"Hello!" she boomed, extending a gloved hand into my open window. I took it, wiping some of my clamminess on her glove.

"Ruth Moore, head of school!" More booming. "Who are you?"

I opened the car door and climbed out, peeling my legs from the seat. I stood close enough that I could still lean on the car door for support. I looked down. There were a handful of sweet potato puffs stuck to my right thigh, just above what appeared to be some crusted peach yogurt. I wiped away the puffs, scratched at the yogurt, and quickly stuffed my clamminess into the pockets of what now felt like exceedingly short shorts. I gripped the pocket seams in search of an answer.

"Agnes," I spat out, looking at my shoes, one of which had a glob of yogurt settling into its laces. "Agnes Parsons."

"Agnes Parsons," she repeated, taking a step back to see all of me. Grace was braying in her car seat. I tried to look up, but Ruth was in front of the sun. I closed one eye, taking her completely out of focus. "You must be Jack's wife, then," she said.

I suddenly opened both eyes, almost blinding myself. Had I given this any thought, I might have anticipated that someone at St. Norbert's, especially Ruth, would mention Jack. After all, he'd sent me here. I suddenly felt short of breath and dizzy.

"Yes," I stuttered. "I am. Jack's wife." Just saying his name made my chest ache and my stomach sink. There was that strange taste forming in the back of my throat again. I prayed that I wouldn't mark my arrival on campus by throwing up a combination of veggie puffs and yogurt sticks all over the head of school.

Before I could stutter out any more of a response, another voice rang out from behind a bush. "Yoo-hoo!"

I squinted and saw a short, thick figure, clad in black, emerge from the shrubbery behind Ruth. I scanned the woman, who looked like a spandexed garden gnome, but couldn't tell if she was wearing a skirt and top, a dress, or just a large piece of stretchy fabric that she had wound around herself. Her thick brown hair was shoved into a twist and looked like it was bursting to escape. In fact, all of her looked like it was bursting to escape.

"This," said Ruth, sounding slightly annoyed, "is Stacey Figg. She likes to help me garden. She likes to help in general." Ruth raised an eyebrow. "Stacey will be your coworker and neighbor." She smirked slightly, as if to say to me, *Aren't you the lucky one?* "Stacey, this is Agnes Parsons. Agnes will be joining the faculty of the middle school. I'm sure you'll make her feel very welcome."

Stacey Figg climbed clumsily over some flowers, many of which she seemed to be crushing under her short, wide feet, and shook my hands. Both of them. "So happy to meet you." She smiled through all her teeth. "I don't know how I didn't know about you." She shot a quick look at Ruth. Before I could say anything, she dodged right by me and pressed herself up against the car window.

"Is this baby yours?" she asked, not looking at me.

"Yes," I said. Apparently I was only capable of one- or, at most, two-word sentences.

"When do we get to meet your husband?" Stacey asked, turning her head to me, her eyes narrowing.

"Her husband travels for work," Ruth interjected.

"For work," I repeated, nodding at Ruth. I was getting very good at this.

"How often?" Stacey asked.

"How often what?" I said, pleased to have moved on to three-word sentences. Stacey was going to have to work harder for her information. From what I could gather, this didn't bother her at all. Working for information was the lifeblood of the Stacey Figgs of the world.

"How often does he travel?" she said, planting her hands on her middle.

"Never you mind," said Ruth. "I think you can save some of your interrogation for later on, once Agnes has settled in."

Stacey Figg was not backing off so easily. "What do you teach?" she asked, taking a step toward me and assessing me, my outfit, and all the food stuck to me.

I looked at Ruth for an answer. I couldn't bring myself to say English, not now that I was here on campus. Coming from my mouth it would have sounded like a question, or even worse, a joke. I needed Ruth to say it.

"English," she said, not taking her eyes off me. "Agnes is an English teacher."

Hardly, I thought to myself. *But maybe if enough people say it, I'll start to feel like one.*

"Does your baby have a name?" Damn, this Stacey Figg was relentless.

"Grace," I said, putting a hand flat on the car window.

"Grace?" she asked. "And you're Agnes?"

I was sure I knew where this was going. "We're not Catholic," I continued in my wholehearted determination to be as awkward as humanly possible. "My husband named the baby. I mean, my mother's mother was Catholic, and I am named for her, but I am not Catholic. My baby isn't Catholic. We're not anything. We're from California."

My response was apparently not what Stacey Figg was looking for, because she seemed very confused by my verbal unraveling. Before I could say anything else, Ruth plunged into the conversation and saved me.

"Stacey, dear," she said, more firmly this time, "we really don't need to be asking so many questions, do we? Let the woman unpack. She's just driven across the country." Stacey Figg nodded dumbly, but I wasn't fooled. She'd find me and squeeze more information out of me, I was sure of it.

Ruth pointed me in the direction of a row of brick town houses, singling out mine, and with a secret wink pointed to Stacey Figg's, which was next door. She then waved herself off and dragged Stacey Figg with her. Before Ruth got too far, she turned back and called out, "Oh, I forgot! There's a key in the mailbox. I'll have someone email you the curriculum and some sample lesson plans later today! Good luck and welcome!"

I turned and looked over at the town houses, a long red row of homes, all attached to each other. Each town house had a large bay window to the left or right of the front door, and each had an identical mailbox on the other side of the door. I freed Grace from her car seat and walked up to the matte-black front door of our new home.

2

The house was narrow but deep. Before I stepped inside, I could see all the way through it, past a small dining room, through an even smaller kitchen, and out a back door onto what looked like a small patch of cement. I entered into the cramped, linoleum-tiled foyer and dropped my purse on the floor. On my left was a compact living room, complete with a dark-brown couch for two, possibly three, a single bookshelf, and an outdated deep television. I poked my head into the living room but kept walking straight. I moved through the dining room, past a dark, scratched-up table for four and into the kitchen. Once inside, it was clear why a house this small needed a separate dining room—because there was no room in this kitchen to sit. I scanned the beige cabinets, which seemed to have a fresh coat of gloss paint and the white appliances, and looked down at my feet on the cream linoleum floor. I chuckled to myself. *At least this kitchen is kind of white.* Actually, it was as if white had gotten really dirty and never bothered to wash. Standing in the tight galley kitchen, I was a long way from Jack's cavernous white rooms. I stood in a room in which, by default, I would be alone. Even if Sondra had stowed away in my luggage, the two of us would barely fit in this kitchen together.

There I was, in my new home, not mourning the loss of my husband. Instead, I was mourning the loss of a woman with whom I'd spent most of my days, a woman I knew did not like me much, and a woman I was not sure I even liked myself. But over the last six months, it was Sondra with whom I'd spent many hours, and it was Sondra, and Alma, to whom I turned for help during the day. Alone in this house, which was small but daunting, my first thoughts were of her. How would Sondra clean this kitchen? How would she unpack the few items I'd brought with me?

It was also possible that I was not thinking about Jack because I could not picture him, could not even imagine him here. Despite the bay window in front and the glass back door, the house was dark, walled in by the houses on either side of it. I imagined Jack walking through and running his finger along the windowsills and countertops, searching for dust. I envisioned him opening the fridge, the oven door, hunting down crumbs and mold. I thought about him breathing in the mustiness of a room that smelled like it hadn't been aired out in generations. I imagined his beautiful bronze face wrinkled in disgust, his nostrils flared.

I especially could not picture him as I walked up the staircase, with its low stucco ceiling and small cloudy picture window. On the second floor of the house were two tiny bedrooms, one with a full bed for me, another with a small crib for Grace, and a bathroom in between them. The entire floor was smaller than Grace's nursery. In fact, like the houses I grew up in, this whole house could have folded several times into the ground floor of our home in Santa Monica. No decorator had ever been in here. No furniture had been custom made to fit the space. In fact, what little furniture there was seemed to have been collected from a variety of uncoordinated but equally cheap sources, and I briefly wondered if the crumminess of my surroundings was a sign that St. Norbert's was having money troubles.

Still, it was immediately clear that in this dark, musty little house, I knew where to be. I knew where to sit. I knew where to stash the few things that I owned. I felt alone and daunted beyond belief, and if given the chance I'd have run home to my life of help, comfort, security, and what I had once thought was predictability. But I did not feel out of place. In fact, I felt quite the opposite.

~

Grace had starting sitting but not yet crawling. Looking back, I know now that she was in that remarkable but short period of time where she could sit and play and I could be free of the worry that she'd crawl off and disappear down a flight of stairs or out a back door. I put her down in the living room with some chewy, squeaky toys and unloaded the car. I put everything in the foyer and dining room. Looking at the few suitcases and boxes, I saw how very little I had brought with me.

That night, Grace slept in a crib and I slept alone for the first time since I'd left Santa Monica, and I dreamed about Jack. We were dancing on the deck off our bedroom. It was dark and we were alone, as we often were. We weren't really dancing, more like holding on to each other and moving slowly to music. In the dream, I could smell and taste him. I don't know what I was wearing, but Jack was wearing only pajama pants. I ran my fingers over his chest and put my lips on his neck, taking in his musky scent and the clean, salty taste of his skin. When I looked up at him he turned; his face clouded and turned dark. I tried to pull away so I could get a better look, to make sure it was him, but he just pulled me close and held me tighter. I said his name, but he didn't answer. Finally, he looked back at me. Half his face was still dark and clouded, but the other half was normal, just as it always had been.

When I woke up, I instinctively rolled over in bed, a bed Jack had never slept in, to see if he was there. When I realized where I was, I lost my breath.

This is real. You are in New York. You are in New York and Jack is not.

I grabbed the empty pillow next to me, wrapped myself around it, and for the first time since Jack disappeared, I let myself ache for him.

Looking around the room, at the solid but dingy furniture, I felt far from home, and even farther from Jack. I was in a bed he had never seen, in a room he wouldn't recognize. *You are here, and he may never be.* I woke up feeling so alone and so desperate that I called Jack. The call, as did all the ones I'd made from the road, went straight to voice mail, but Jack's voice made no appearance. He didn't like personalized messages; he found them juvenile—his word, not mine.

"It's me," I said. "I'm here. But I don't plan on staying long. I want to come home. I miss you." I hung up and threw down the phone. The call was supposed to make me feel better, closer to Jack, but it only left me feeling more helpless and alone.

I hadn't seen Beeks yet. She, Brian, and the boys were finishing up the summer on a beach somewhere in Massachusetts. I felt untethered and alone in New York. I wasn't sure how I could let Beeks see me like this, in this house, but I also needed to see the only person here who knew me before all this happened.

- 3 -

I spent the Sunday before Labor Day unpacking and preparing myself to start teaching on Tuesday. Grace was upstairs taking her morning nap and I was in the kitchen putting things away when I heard a knock on the door. Instinctively I froze, and my mind flashed back to the conversation I'd had with Jack on the beach. I'd asked him if I was safe, and he'd said, "For now." In theory, I could have been followed here by whoever it was that Jack was hiding from. I don't know why, but it wasn't until the moment when I heard the first knock on my New York door that I actually worried about my safety. Jack was hiding out, and I had been sent away. What made me so sure that I was safe here? I looked at my phone, unable to even reach for it. I had no way of seeing who was at the door without walking into the foyer and peeking through the window, but my feet were frozen to the already dirty kitchen floor. I could not make them move. I had no choice but to call out.

"Hello?"

No answer. I tried again. "Hello? Who's there?"

"It's me! Your new neighbor!" sang Stacey Figg. My shoulders slumped down with relief, and I walked to the front to find Stacey Figg standing there, wearing what I think was a jumpsuit, a basket of tomatoes in her hands. "I grew these," she said, thrusting the basket at me. "In my window box. You'd be amazed what you can grow in a window box."

"Wow, thanks," I said, actually pleased to see some produce that wasn't under several layers of truck-stop plastic wrap.

"You settling in?" she asked, craning her neck to see what was happening behind me. Like an overeager dance partner, she lunged toward me, forcing me to take a step back. If she kept doing this, eventually I would have no choice but to let her in. I did not want to let her in. I did not want anyone to see the inside of this place. Once anyone else saw this, once someone else bore witness to my new situation, then it would all be real. After a few steps, I placed my arms on either side of the doorframe.

"Actually," I said, with a firmness that surprised me, "it's a mess in here, and Grace is about to wake up."

"Oh," she said, crestfallen. "Another time, then. I just wanted to let you know that the people who lived here before you complained a lot about the air and the heat, because, you know, this unit hasn't been updated yet." Pause. "Not like mine." She gazed triumphantly at her own house, which was only feet away but apparently far superior. "They also said something about a mouse population." She lingered over the word *population*, as though she were getting points for saying it as slowly as possible.

I shuddered, and Stacey Figg took notice, crossing her arms in victory. "Don't worry, though. I'm here to help. You know, if you need me." I prayed I would never need a reason to invite anyone in. I thanked her and almost wept with joy when I heard Grace cry out for me. I ran inside and slammed the door before Stacey Figg even had time to turn around.

I fed Grace a jar of applesauce for lunch. With each jar I opened, I thought wistfully about the days of homemade purees and trips to the farmers' market. Grace didn't seem to notice the difference, even if I did. Using her stroller as a high chair (I got an email from the facilities office informing me that one would be delivered to me by the end of the week), I watched her polish off a jar, wiped her face, and walked her around the house, from the foyer through to the kitchen and back again, until she fell asleep. Once she was asleep, I parked her in her stroller in a dark corner, a blanket draped over it to make sure she stayed sleeping. Hungry myself, I made a cheese and tomato sandwich, using the bounty from Stacey Figg's window box. I'd eaten more sandwiches in the past week than I had eaten in the past five years. I was nearing the end of the organic, grass-fed, free-roaming cheese (the cows roamed free, not the cheese) that I'd stocked up on before we drove east. I layered the cheese and tomatoes on an everything bagel. I would like to be able to say the bagels tasted better here than they did in LA, but I don't remember the last time I ate a bagel in LA. I definitely didn't remember eating a bagel that wasn't hollowed out, the fluffy, tastiest white bread pulled away in the hopes of enjoying the bagel but avoiding the carbs. Ah, California.

Later on, when Grace was asleep for the night, I sat down next to the bay window in the living room on the box of books I'd asked Sondra to pack. They were texts on education and child psychology, relics of my college days. I wasn't sure what was in them that could possibly help me teach English to middle schoolers. I would be more likely to get any information I needed from Google rather than a textbook I'd been dragging around since college. But I hadn't brought the books for the information they contained. I brought the books for luck or security or both. Maybe I brought them just to have something to bring.

I heard another knock on the door. I assumed it was Stacey Figg again, this time with homegrown squash, but then I heard a male voice. I froze. I thought if I said nothing, maybe the voice and the man to whom it belonged would leave. I also wondered if I'd misheard the male voice. Maybe it was Stacey Figg. *Please let this be Stacey Figg and I'll never have another nasty thought about her again.*

"It's Gavin Burke," said the voice. When I did not answer, he spoke louder. "The middle school principal."

I skipped into the foyer with relief and yanked open the front door, beaming a little too eagerly. As I tugged at the door, it was also being pushed open by the hairless arm of a tall man with a shaved head. He wore a faded T-shirt, cargo shorts, and sneakers. He was older than I was, but not as old as Jack. His eyes were two very different colors—one a bright blue, the other a deep brown. Even though I was still grinning with relief, I couldn't look directly at them.

"Hey there," he drawled. "I guess I'm happy to meet you, too." He was thick, a big guy who looked like he could have played football at some point, but as he raised an arm to lean against the doorframe, I saw that he also worked out. I could have sworn his muscles were twitching, moving independently. He saw me gaping at his arm, then looked at it himself and smirked proudly.

We stood there, smiling at each other for different reasons, when his eyes shifted. He looked down at my feet and then surveyed me, starting there and moving up.

I'd always suspected that one of the first things Jack had noticed about me was that other men notice me. I'm blonde, lightly freckled, cute in a nondescript way, and in California shape. But it had been a while since I'd been leered at. This guy was smiling as though he'd heard a joke about me but didn't want to let me in on it. He managed to look at all of me at once without moving his head. I felt his mismatched eyes move up and down, and I was self-conscious of my sweatpants, my stained T-shirt, my enormous—if extremely comfortable—underwear. I instinctively took my hands, cheese sandwich and all, and crossed them over my chest. I waited for him to say something, but when he didn't, I had no choice but to start talking.

"Hi," I chirped. "I'm Agnes Parsons. I'm teaching English in the middle school." I stood in the doorway, trying to figure out how I could offer to shake his hand while still having my own hands cover what I now realized was my braless chest.

"I know who you are," he said, raising an eyebrow. "I'm Gavin Burke, and I run the middle school." He leaned forward, as if letting me in on a secret. "I'm the principal, remember?"

"Did we have a meeting? Did I forget something?" I shuffled back into the doorway, but I didn't want to invite him in.

"No," he said, still smiling, taking a cue I hadn't meant to give and walking a step forward. "I just thought we should meet before school starts on Tuesday. Honestly, I kind of had to check out this mystery teacher I'd been ordered to hire." A bigger smile this time, but more forced.

"Ordered?" I asked, immediately wishing I hadn't. I knew Jack had pulled strings to get me here. I didn't want to know more.

"When Ruth Moore tells you to hire a teacher, you know, when you get the command from on high—" He had now straightened up and waved his hands in the air, making a strange, jazzy motion. "When that happens, you don't ask questions." We were both standing in the cramped foyer. I couldn't figure out how we ended up there when I'd been so determined to keep him out.

"I don't really know Ruth," I said, a little too forcefully.

"Well, you know someone," he said, no longer smiling. "But I guess we all know someone." He walked right past me, into the living room.

I followed him in and stood with my back to the bay window. Without any curtains to cover the window, the light poured in from behind me and the glare bounced off his forehead. I could only squint at him, as I'd done with Ruth. I moved to the side, to see him better, so that I wouldn't be caught off guard, even if it meant getting closer to him. The room wasn't big enough for both of us and all my boxes and suitcases, without us standing in very close proximity. Gavin looked down at me, and I felt myself shrinking. He clasped his hands behind his neck and rolled his head around, his gaze finally resting on me.

"Don't you want to introduce me to your family?" he asked, his eyes moving from my face and chest to the ringed finger on my left hand.

"Huh?"

"Your family, your husband, kids."

"I have a daughter, but she's asleep," I said. "And I have a husband . . . but he travels for work."

"Really," he said, leaning in. "What kind of work would be worth leaving you behind?"

I swallowed nervously. Honestly, I'd never been able to really say what Jack did, even when I knew where he was. I'd always just said that he worked for himself, or that he invested money for people. It never seemed weird that we didn't talk much about it, or that I didn't know more. Frankly, in LA, unless you worked in the entertainment industry, people never asked too many questions about work. They weren't interested. As I was learning, though, in New York, no matter what you did, people wanted to know all about it. I was going to have to have better answers. In the meantime, I mumbled, "He works for himself. It's just me and my daughter here now, and like I said, she's asleep."

"Interesting," he said.

"Not really."

"Huh?" he asked.

"Me," I said. "I'm not interesting, not really. You know all there is to know now."

"Oh," he said, grinning, his mismatched eyes bearing into me, "I highly doubt that. Everybody has a story."

Perhaps, I thought. But I didn't want to know his. As for mine, that had to stay as quiet as possible. The fewer people who knew me here, the better.

Gavin started walking to the door. "Before I forget, lesson plans are due on the first of every month."

What?

"And I'll ping you later about office hours and study hall."

What and what?

"And I'll expect you to be available for both."

My head started to spin. I had only really thought about being in the classroom. My brain had not registered that teaching middle school came with add-ons like lesson plans and study hall. "Sure," I said, swaying slightly and blinking to bring him into focus. He just stared at me, unflinching.

"You OK?" he asked.

"Sure," I said, taking a step back.

"I live across campus, on the other side of the cafeteria." He gestured with his shiny head, his eyes still piercing me. "In case you want to stop by and ask me questions, or if you need me to come by and help lift some of these heavy things." He nodded to the boxes behind me.

"Of course," I said quickly, desperate to cut this off. "Thank you. I actually have a bunch of stuff to get done."

"A bunch of stuff?" he asked, laughing. "You certainly don't talk like an English teacher."

That's because I'm not an English teacher. I'm a former preschool teacher whose husband stole some money and then sent me here. "Yeah," I said, "well, I'm saving all my big words for Tuesday. Wouldn't want to use them all up."

"You're funny," he said. "But maybe a little too funny. Remember, these kids are like horses. They can smell weakness."

"I—" I started.

"I have somewhere to be," he said. He walked to the door and turned back to me. "At least I know where to find you now." He grinned again before letting himself out.

I locked the door, unlocked it, and then locked it again to be sure. Then I ran upstairs to shower and wash off the whole encounter. I made a mental note to buy more soap, because I had unwittingly used half a bar trying to do so.

- 4 -

On the night before school started, I locked the front door, unlocked it, and locked it again. I looked through each window and made sure they were all closed. When I was sure nobody was standing outside the house, I put Grace down, took a bowl of cereal to bed, and texted Don.

I'm playing the part of a middle school teacher tomorrow. For how long? When do I get to come home?

Don't know. Stay there. Do your job.

The principal stopped by to say hello and I thought he was coming to kill me. Am I even safe here?

Yes.

Did Don really think that a simple yes would be enough? Unplanned house calls didn't happen in LA, and I wasn't enjoying jumping out of my skin with each knock on the door.

Not feeling satisfied, I decided to make things worse. I called Jack. "Hi," I said. "It's me. I'm still here. But I wish I wasn't." I half expected the voice mail lady to say something to me, anything, but she didn't. I hung up and looked at the picture of Jack in his contact. *Really? Nothing?*

I'd tried calling Beeks a few times since I'd been on the East Coast, but bedtime for Grace was hours before things quieted down for her. She was back from the beach, so I tried her again. Finally, I got through.

"I was hoping you'd call," she started, "to distract me from the thirteen loads of laundry and the six buckets of sand I inadvertently ran through the washing machine."

"Was it fun?" I asked.

"Sure," she said. "It's fun getting out of the city and being on the beach. It's just a little less fun spending most of the vacation feeding children, cleaning up after you've fed them, only to realize it's time to feed them again. It's a good thing the beach house had a good kitchen, because I think I spent most of the day in it. And then there's the laundry and all that sand. But enough about me," she said, stopping herself. "I'm boring. All the good stuff is happening to you. How is St. Norbert's, and are you ready for tomorrow?"

"It's fine," I said. "It's weird living in this house, you know, being without Jack. It's weird being so far away."

"Give it time," said Beeks. "You just got here." She paused. "Have you heard anything from California?" Beeks wanted me to walk away from Jack and the mess that came with him. But she had to ask. A best friend doesn't not ask about a missing husband, even if that friend never really liked him.

"Nothing," I said, finishing the cereal and putting the bowl on the pile of books and papers that would now be my nightstand. "I checked in with Don. Nothing new has come up." I didn't want to tell her that I'd been calling Jack's phone and leaving him pathetic messages.

"Crap!" she yelled. "I think I just washed a diaper. Do you know all that gel inside that is supposed to soak up pee? Well, now that shitty gel is everywhere." I could not even begin to imagine Beeks's life in a small apartment with four boys. "The super will kill me for messing up the washing machine."

Her voice was muffled, trailing off. "Beeks?" I said. "You there?"

"If you can't hear me," she yelled, coming in and out of range, "it's because I have climbed into the washing machine to remove the gel by hand. Jealous?"

I laughed, grateful for the convenient, if minute, washer and dryer that were stacked in a closet in the upstairs hallway. It was one thing to leave the luxury of Santa Monica; it was another to have to deal with a shared laundry room.

"By the way," I said, "I met the middle school principal, Gavin. He's a total creep. He showed up here."

"What?" she asked.

"Yeah," I said. "He wanted to meet me, or so he said. He really looked like he wanted to eat me for dinner."

Now it was Beeks's turn to laugh. "As if. There's not enough meat on you anymore to make a light snack. Besides, don't worry. You're good with men."

"What's that supposed to mean?" I asked, sitting up.

"Nothing bad. Anyway, he's not the one you should be worried about. Come tomorrow, you'll have to charm a room of adolescent boys."

"That's right," I said, slumping back in my bed. "Beeks, what the hell do I know about teaching middle school boys?"

"Nothing. That's why you have me," she said. "Living with a middle schooler is like watching a train wreck in slow motion. They are awkward, clumsy, impulsive, and they can't decide if they want you to do everything for them or if they want you to take a hike. It's dizzying."

"You're right," I said. "They do sound a lot like preschoolers."

I had no idea.

-5-

If anyone had ever asked me which period of schooling I'd want to revisit, my absolute last choice would be middle school. Yet here I was, hours away from my return to middle school, trying not to think about what those years were like for me. There were the big things—my parents dying suddenly, being completely without family, taking my first steps of the foster home dance. I spent most of middle school with the same foster family, a nice enough couple, who kept me until I became too much work. They gave me a free-range adolescence, not because of a particular parenting philosophy but because even though they opened their home to me, they didn't really want to parent me. I was on my own in middle school, on my own to deal with the seemingly unimportant but devastating things like staring at a mirror full of frizzy hair and zits for the first time and having to wear clothes several sizes too big to hide my suddenly bloated, pubescent form.

That morning, almost twenty-five years after I'd started middle school in Modesto, I woke up on the first day of school in New York. I had left the countertop espresso machine behind in California. I wasn't sure I even owned it, and I couldn't see it making the trip with us across the country. In its place stood a cheap French press I'd bought over the weekend. I plunged a full pot of coffee—ready to drink the six to eight cups I would need to face my first day of work in several years, and my first day ever teaching someone other than a four-year-old. The coffee was thick, oily, and delicious. The first sip took me back to my college days, when I'd first learned to drink coffee with my sophisticated roommates. This was how I drank coffee before Jack, and it was how I would have to drink it without him.

I thought about Jack and started to smile, but something stopped me. I felt uneasy. It wasn't a warm, comfortable feeling. Instead, I felt something else, something closer to sadness, frustration, and anger. But I didn't want to be angry. Not now, anyway. Now I had a job to do—a job for which I was neither ready nor equipped. *Go back,* I told myself, leaning on the kitchen counter. *Go back to when it all made more sense.*

I remembered sitting with Beeks at the bar in the Tahoe hotel the night before my wedding. Beeks was my entire wedding party. She was my entire family by then. But Beeks was Beeks. Even if she had wanted to be restrained, she was incapable of restraint. We sat leaning over our drinks, and she came right out and asked me, "So Jack. This life. This is what you want, Aggie?"

I looked down into my glass. I knew what she was asking me. "One hundred percent," I answered. "I want this, Beeks. I want all of it."

"You know," she said, "you don't have to marry Jack just so you don't have to eat beans from a can."

I cut her off. "There are plenty of rich guys in LA. If all I wanted was money, I could have gone and found myself one."

"But you did," she said. "You did go and find yourself one. You went and got engaged to the very first rich man you found. Maybe you could wait a little, shop around, and then find a rich guy who's a little less . . . I don't know . . . controlling." She paused and leaned in to me. "I get it. I get that you were tired of being ignored. I get it that you want someone who sees you. But do you really need someone who manages you?"

I reached in and fiddled with the lime in my glass. "Here's the thing—all the stuff that irks you about him, those are the things I love.

I love that he cares what milk we drink, how we grind our coffee, which light fixtures we buy. Have you ever considered that?" I looked up at her. The bartender, sensing this was a conversation he shouldn't interrupt, quietly replaced the gin and tonics we had emptied.

"I love that he sweats the small stuff," I said. "I love that the stupid, insignificant details like dish soap matter so much to him. I want that, Beeks. And the predictability, the routine? I love that, too." Beeks furrowed her brow, but I pressed on before she could say anything. "I love knowing what next week, next month, even next year is going to look like. I love that Jack plans for things that I can't even see. I love that he makes restaurant reservations weeks out. I love that he has a rule about having the next vacation planned before he finishes the vacation he's on. All that unpredictability, the uncertainty, I want it gone."

We never had that conversation again. We had others, and there were moments during her visits to LA when she looked at me and she didn't have to ask, "What happened to you, Aggie?" because it was scrawled all over her face. She'd comment on how much blonder I seemed, not to mention how much thinner I looked. But Beeks knew enough to know that I wasn't just tired of eating beans out of a can. She was on the other side of the country, and I was tired of being alone. Tired of being the only one looking out for me. Tired of watching all those preschool kids go home to families I never had but desperately wanted.

The next day, hours before our wedding, Jack found me crying in my hotel room.

"You're not supposed to see me," I sniffled, sitting on the edge of a very large bed, wearing the hotel robe over some expensive but uncomfortable underwear. Every time I shifted, the underwear would lodge itself in a different yet equally excruciating position. I was hoping I wasn't going to be the first bride photographed picking out a wedgie.

"Yeah, well, you're not supposed to be crying on your wedding day," he said, coming over and sitting next to me. He took my hands in his and kissed them. I couldn't look at him, though. Looking at him might only make me cry harder, and I wasn't sure I was ready to reveal my blotchy, puffy face to him. I also wasn't sure what tricks the makeup artist had in her arsenal, but she was going to need every one of them. It would take a trowel of makeup to make me look like someone who hadn't been up all night crying.

"Yeah, well, a girl is supposed to have someone give her away other than her best friend. A girl is supposed to have actual family at her wedding."

Jack slid down onto the floor and knelt in front of me, my hands still in his. "Look at me," he said.

I could not look.

"Aggie," he whispered. "Look at me. Look at my face."

I looked.

"You have family now. You have me, and at some point in the future, we'll have children, and one day we'll dance at their weddings. I promise you, you will never be lonely again, and you'll never have to worry about what's coming next." Then he reached up and took my face in his hands, kissing me until I nearly forgot why I was crying in the first place.

Jack knew. He knew that even when I wasn't worried, I was worried that one day he would disappear like my parents. I was tired of being lonely, but I was also tired of surprises. Jack offered me love and family and an orderly, planned life that was supposed to free me from surprises. Beeks may have seen it as claustrophobic, but I welcomed it.

Now I was bathing in the unknown. I was sleeping in a strange bed, in a strange house, in a strange city. I was due to teach in a couple of hours, and I had no idea what lay before me. So much for predictability.

I drank the entire pot of coffee standing at the shallow counter, because there was no sitting in this kitchen. Eventually, I'd have to put down the coffee and put on some clothes. I hadn't fully unpacked yet, so I riffled through the few suitcases and boxes I'd brought with me. The small collection of designer clothes Jack had bought for me—without me, without ever asking my size, in time I didn't know he had to spare, the clothes that just showed up hanging on the closet door or spread out across the bed—those clothes were in separate boxes. I had sold my jewelry to drive here and set myself up until paychecks arrived, and the designer clothes were all I had left should stuff really start flying at the fan. Those clothes were an insurance policy.

I stared at the pile I'd unpacked on my bedroom floor, and I wished I'd saved clothes from my preschool days. Over a period of our first three months together, Jack had slowly gotten rid of all my Old Navy sundresses, the brightly colored pants that were on sale at the end of the season at J. Crew (What? Nobody wanted tangerine capris?), the gauzy T-shirts I wore until they practically disintegrated on me like the biodegradable paper plates I would be instructed to buy as a new wife. Now all I had was a box of ridiculously expensive tight jeans that cost as much as a week's salary, and that were off-limits, according to the school dress code. This left only a few boxes of what I quickly discovered was glorified yoga gear.

In hindsight, I could not have picked out a less appropriate outfit had I tried. I settled on a dress that, when I'd bought it, was billed as just the sort of thing you could throw over yoga clothes and wear to meet your friends for lunch. I once went to such a lunch and found that three other women were wearing the same dress, but only one of us had actually come from a yoga class. One of the women had spent the morning choosing fabric for the cushions of her outdoor furniture; the other had been watching an episode of *Ellen* she'd taped the day before. She explained that she was watching because her trainer was on it, giving Ellen's audience tips on how to stay in shape during the holiday season. She was watching out of loyalty, she said. She'd never normally watch daytime TV, she said. We knew she never missed an episode.

I looked down at my legs, which seemed precariously exposed without the requisite yoga pants. I couldn't wear yoga pants to class under the dress, so I found a pair of faded black leggings I wore when Jack wasn't home and threw them on underneath. Determined to do something about the mess of hair on my head, I wrapped it in a bun and made a note to ask about a nearby hair salon. When Jack came for me, I'd just have to explain that I had no time to blow-dry it and no money for highlights or keratin treatments to keep it straight and manageable.

I squeezed a packet of applesauce into my mouth and called Jack. I wanted him to tell me that I would be all right, that I could do this, that it would all be worth it. But all I got was the voice mail lady.

"Hey there, random, anonymous voice mail lady. If you happen to speak to my husband, please let him know that even though I'm completely unqualified and not at all ready, I'm about to be a middle school teacher. Tell him I need to talk to him. Tell him I need to hear his voice." I hung up, stared at Jack's picture, and slammed my phone down on the kitchen counter a little too forcefully.

I closed my eyes and took a couple of yoga breaths but struggled to focus. With my eyes closed, I needed something to think about. I couldn't think about being in a yoga class or sitting cross-legged by the ocean, because I couldn't go there. I couldn't wonder if I'd ever be in another yoga class, or, worse, if I'd ever see the Pacific Ocean again. I quickly pictured Grace and began to breathe. I didn't have room for sadness, and I had even less room for anger and frustration, so I breathed it all out, and when Grace called out for me, I was ready for her.

I fed Grace and packed her some formula and a lunch (pear sauce, a yogurt stick, a baggie of some sort of puffs, and a banana) as well as a lunch for myself (identical). I dressed her and strapped her into her stroller.

"You're right," I said to her as I tried to jam the little silver bars into the snap between her legs, "this stroller is ridiculous. Maybe we should trade it in for six months of groceries." I knew Grace couldn't understand me, but I could have sworn she nodded. I nodded back, and we walked to day care.

6

Day care for St. Norbert's employees was conveniently located in between my town house and MacReady, the building that housed most of the middle school classrooms. As I pushed Grace across campus, I tried not to think about what was in store for her. Honestly, I wasn't sure what to expect. *Day care* had been a dirty word in Santa Monica. The moms talked about it in hushed tones on barstools in coffee shops and in the corners of baby group. It was one thing to have a baby and hire a team of people to care and cook for her. It was another thing entirely to drop your baby off in an infected room with forty other neglected babies, crawling around with runny noses, crusty eyes, and filthy, saggy, dirty diapers, all while playing with grimy toys and snacking on lint. There were a few moms, the ones who lived in the rental apartments down near the beach, the moms who had to go back to work and couldn't afford full-time nannies, nannies who were forever in high demand and full of expectations. These were the day-care moms. Their kids got sicker, riding the welcome wagons for the new germs that came to town. What did they think when they looked at the nannied babies, whose fine baby hair was in intricate braids, who ate homemade food and spent their mornings in luxury strollers at Starbucks and their afternoons in the park?

This day care was in a building called Blackwell, halfway up one of the many hills on campus. It was a small, unimpressive stand-alone one-story building and looked like something of a mistake or an after-thought in a sea of buildings all trying to outshine one another with mismatched pillars, random statues, and elaborate moldings. The front door was locked, so I picked Grace up out of her stroller and knocked. I was about to knock again when I saw a woman ambling down the hallway toward us. I leaned away from the window, not wanting to look too eager. When I did that, I realized that it had been a little while since I'd tried not to look eager—and that I'd probably spent a quarter of my days in Santa Monica trying not to appear too anything—too lonely, too desperate, too afraid, too needy. Cool and confident wins the race out west, but in New York, I hadn't given it a thought until now.

As the woman inside approached the door, I squinted to bring her into focus. She had long gray hair pinned in a bun atop her craggy face, and wore a large, shapeless, sleeveless denim dress. Under it was a long-sleeved red T-shirt. I would soon learn that the dress was a daily staple and that only the shirt underneath would change. Red shirts were for Mondays. There were all sorts of things hanging around her neck. The door swung open, and I stood back quickly to make room for her.

"Hello!" she announced, holding out both her arms. I wasn't sure whether she wanted me to shake her hands or hug her, but I wasn't ready to do either. I tried to take another step back, because she seemed to be unnaturally close to my face. I forced a smile and tried not to think about the fact that I could smell her breath. I thought back to my encounter with Gavin. What was with these people? Hadn't anyone heard of personal space?

"Dot!" she said loudly, extending her arms out by her sides, announcing herself.

Dot. A perfect name. I saw not a stitch of makeup on her face. This was a woman for whom lipstick was for weddings and blush was some-thing you did, not something you wore. I blinked away at my eyeliner, feeling incredibly self-conscious. It didn't matter, though, because Dot had no interest in me or my eyeliner. She made a beeline for Grace and stooped down to make eye contact with her.

"Hello, Grace," she said quietly, leaning back to give Grace space to take her all in. She lowered her voice. "We are so very thrilled to have you join us. I am Dot." Grace gave her the same nod of faux comprehension she'd given me earlier.

Dot led us into the building, chattering to us as she showed us around. Day care turned out to be not what I had expected. First of all, Grace was only one of sixteen children, who ranged in age from eight weeks to three years old. Any older children were already in preschool. These were the babies and toddlers of teachers who were coming back to work after maternity leaves that were as short as six weeks. The children were divided into four groups so that Grace and three other babies shared Dot. Dot explained that the day care was housed in what used to be a carriage house, where the school's caretaker had lived with his family. The building was old but scrubbed clean. The floors were dark wood, the walls mostly white with glossy moldings. The main playroom in the center of the house had sloping dormer ceilings. At either end of the room were enormous windows. Along the other two walls were handprints in all sizes and colors, with the name of the child who made the handprint underneath it. There was a small but sparkling kitchen, a bathroom, and four small rooms with cribs and mattresses for rest time. I didn't see a square of dingy carpet, only dark, shiny wood and the occasional brightly colored rubber play mat. Who knew day care could be so clean and appealing? Certainly not my squad of baby-group moms, who might've taken it upon themselves to raise funds for Grace had they heard she was headed to day care.

I kissed Grace goodbye and walked to the door, but something stopped me from waltzing out in that carefree way I'd left her so many times before. Partly, it was because I knew frightfully little about this place. I knew absolutely nothing about Dot other than her name and her love of denim. Jack had vetted Alma so carefully, you'd have thought she was applying for a job with the FBI counterterrorism unit. But there was more going on here than a lack of a background check on Dot. Even when she was a newborn, I'd left Grace at the blink of an eye—exercise classes and massages called, and I answered. Something was different now, and I felt queasy when I walked out of day care. I leaned on the outside wall of Blackwell, closed my eyes, and saw the word *Grace*. I breathed slowly until I was ready to open my eyes again, only to discover an enormous bug was coming straight for me. I ducked and ran to class.

7

MacReady Hall, or Mac, as I later heard the students call it, was a tall brick building with four white pillars in the front. My first class was on the fourth floor, and Mac, like most of the buildings on campus, had a small elevator that never seemed to arrive. Boys were running up and down the staircases.

I climbed up the four flights of stairs, not at all surprised that years of yoga, Pilates, and simulated bike riding had not prepared me for actual stair-climbing, and stopped at the top to catch my breath. My dress had ridden up and was now barely covering my backside. I yanked it down with my free hand, the other hand carrying my bag, a water bottle, and a last-minute box of yogurt chewies, which, for reasons I did not want to think about, did not need refrigerating.

Two boys rushed past me, almost knocking me over.

"I bet she's hot," said the first, a chunky boy with frizzy hair and what looked like a slick of hair gel perched atop his head. "You know, California hot!" he added, cupping his chest with his hands, each about a foot away from his body.

"Ugh. Gross," said the second, a shorter, skinny boy with glasses and a large swath of feathered bangs. The boys did not look the same age. Both ran past me, leaving a burning smell in their wake, unaware that I was right in front of them. I briefly wondered if I was still "California hot"—with my frizzy bun and smudged eyeliner—and then remembered I would be spending my days in the company of middle schoolers. My physical appearance was the least of my problems. How was I going to teach these boys English? Or better yet, how was I meant to breathe through the fog of whatever it was these boys just left in their wake?

The odor pushed its way up into my nostrils, burned my eyes, and, at the same time, dripped down into the back of my throat, forcing me to gag. What was that smell, that taste? It was tangy, musky, and vinegary, and it was getting stronger the closer I got to my classroom. I tugged at my eyes and tried to cough the taste out of my throat.

"Oh, that's just the Wall of Axe," said a voice from behind me. "You'll get used to it."

I turned around and looked down. Stacey Figg. "You'll get used to it," she repeated, "but it takes a while." She was wearing a lime-green wrap dress. Once again, she seemed to be ready to burst forth from her clothes. Her thick hair was blown straight and sat patiently on her shoulders. She planted her arms on her waist, her eyes glittering. She leaned in, as if letting me in on a secret. "It doesn't wear off, so you'll be taking the smell home with you." She blinked, and I noticed several shades of eye shadow.

"What's Axe?" I asked. "And why is there a wall of it?"

"It's a deodorant brand," she said. "Some product people decided that they could market deodorant to kids who don't really smell yet. You know, make them feel older and cooler than they are." She rolled her eyes.

"That smell is deodorant?" It didn't smell like any deodorant I'd ever smelled, even on a guy. It certainly didn't smell like Jack. I quickly blinked the thought of him out of my mind.

"Well," she said, "you haven't smelled Axe before. Each kid uses a different smell, and each uses about half a can in the morning. If you can believe it, the stuff has names like Anarchy and Vice. Last week I confiscated a can of something called Provocation!" She snorted, unsmiling, while bobbing and weaving as boys ran through the hall to their classes. She looked like a squat lime-green bull in the ring. Finally, she stopped and took another step closer to me so that our noses were almost touching. "When a whole class of boys is coated in the stuff," she whispered, "it creates the Wall of Axe."

I smiled. Despite the stinging in my eyes and throat, there was something endearing about the idea of a boy thinking half a can of deodorant called Anarchy was going to make middle school easier. Stacey Figg was having none of my smiling. She wheeled herself around, and before I knew it, she was clomping down the hall.

I crossed the hall and froze at the threshold of room 408. I looked down at my feet, willing them to move forward. After a few seconds, they got the message and dragged me into the classroom, a large white room with several large windows and bare walls. If someone had asked me to describe the room afterward, I would not have been able to. I was so terrified and overwhelmed that I was unable to absorb any information that day. I entered, breathing in another eye-watering dose of body spray, and saw about a dozen boys sitting at or on their desks. Some were looking at laptop screens or down at their phones, and some were looking right at me. I smiled weakly and walked to the desk in the front of the room. I pulled out the chair and, leaning on the desk, scanned the room.

"Hi," I said, as though I were picking up clothes at the dry cleaner and not communicating with my students for the very first time.

"Hey," said a kid from the back of the class. I couldn't tell who. My first impression was that I was standing in the front of a sea of thick dark hair. I hadn't seen so little blond in one room before. Without thinking, I put my hand on the bun at the back of my head. Perhaps it'd be safe to let my highlights grow out here. It's not like anyone would notice.

"Are you the teacher?" said a voice from behind a screen.

"What's your name?" asked another.

Crap, I thought. *Where were these coming from? Where were these kids' faces?*

"Agnes," I replied. "You can call me Agnes."

"Mrs. Agnes? That's your last name?" I pegged the voice to a boy with a bright-red buzz cut in the middle row, whose face was only partially obscured by a laptop screen.

"No, it's my first name."

"Uh, yeah," said red buzz cut. "We can't call you that. Too dis-re-spect-ful," he said, sounding out each syllable.

Before I could reply, Aretha Franklin's "Respect" came blaring out of a laptop at the very back of the room. Behind it sat a kid with green eyes, a shock of black hair, and a nose full of freckles. He said nothing. He just raised his right eyebrow.

"Agnes," I persisted. "You can call me Agnes. If you're uncomfortable with that, call me Ms. Parsons."

"Parsons sounds like Watsons," said the red buzz cut.

"Huh?"

"You know, *The Watsons Go to Birmingham.* They made us read it last year. It sucked."

Two kids in the front row made retching sounds, another stuck his finger down his throat, and a fourth fell out of his chair, lay on the floor, and convulsed. At some point he got up, and they all high-fived each other.

"Oh, OK," I plowed on. "I think you have some great books on the reading list this year."

"Like what?" asked one of the kids who'd been retching.

"Oh."

"You don't know?" asked his neighbor.

"I do so," I said, sounding like a five-year-old. I dug my hands deep into my pockets and thought quickly to the email I got from Gavin with an outline of the syllabus. "*Roll of Thunder, Hear My Cry,*" I blurted out.

"La-ame," said the red buzz cut.

Before I could say another word, the freckly kid hit a key on his laptop and we were all listening to the booming sounds of a virtual thunderstorm. It was loud and it was all I could hear.

I plopped down into the chair. Surely I could get on the right side of this. I was about to make an effort when the thunder stopped. In its place I heard Darth Vader's march. I looked up and turned to the door. Gavin walked in. The music stopped.

He strode to the front of the class, surveyed my outfit, and then rounded my desk and sat on it. "Boys, I see you've met Ms. Parsons," he drawled. He perched on the edge of my desk, his legs stretched out in front of him. He was wearing a short-sleeved button-down shirt, and he stretched his thick arms out behind him. The class was silent, and the room felt different. The confidence and cockiness I'd felt from the kids evaporated, and in their place was compliance, silence, and possibly even fear.

"I said," he repeated, "I see you've met Ms. Parsons."

"Yes, sir," said the kid in the back with the freckles. "We've met her. She's met us."

"And Ms. Parsons," he said, presumably to me, even though he was facing the class, "I see you've met my boys . . . my *special* boys." I could tell from the way he said it that he didn't think there was anything special about these kids. The red buzz cut slunk down lower in his seat. I could have sworn I heard a fart sound come from him. The freckles behind the laptop also sank lower so that only the top of his dark head was visible over the screen.

"You see," he started in again, "I love a good challenge, and that's what these boys are—each and every one of them. A good challenge." He paused and scanned the room. Nobody moved an inch. With his back still to me, I could not see Gavin's face. All I could see was the spreading back of his Dockers and his bare arms. "Each of these boys, Ms. Parsons, will be applying to high school in exactly one year." I saw his ears twitch, which I assumed meant he was smirking. I studied the boys, whose faces remained frozen in the positions they were in when Gavin entered. "High school is a real competitive process here in the city, and these boys are going to need *a lot* of help to get in." He turned around and looked at me. "You're not on the beach anymore," he said, grinning, something halfway between a smirk and a smile.

What I wouldn't give to be on the beach right now. Although it sickened me, I smiled back at him.

"We've got to make sure these boys are not only ready for high school, but that each of them can actually get in somewhere, including this high school," he said, pointing down, almost implying that St. Norbert's high school happened right here on my desk. "You see," he went on, "most students who have been with us since elementary school have automatic admission to the high school." Another pause. "Most students," he said. "But some students are on academic or behavioral probation, and they have to go through the regular application process to stay at St. Norbert's for high school." He stood up and faced the class. "Every day and every grade counts, boys. Every one." His ears twitched again, signaling a fresh smirk. "I'm sure you will all do just fine. I'm sure of it." Nothing about his tone sounded sure.

I was nervous for the boys. I could see their faces falling, one by one, into panic. I looked at my wrist and saw some of Grace's rice cereal caked on my sleeve. I immediately brought it to my mouth and tasted it. With my other hand, I gripped my chair, willing Gavin to leave us alone. Perhaps some cosmic message was relayed to him, because he abruptly clasped his thick hands behind his back, swiveled, and turned to me, winked, and walked to the door. I could have sworn he clicked his heels like some smarmy Bavarian prince. Now it was my turn to slink down into my seat. I was at eye level with the boys. The laptop in the corner was silent, even though I had fully expected it to play out a song of joy in relief.

I leaned forward and put my elbows on the desk, resting my chin on my hands. "I am sure you're all going to get into high school." I smiled. "Each and every one of you," I said, winking and doing my best imitation of Gavin's nasal drawl. If I had sensed fear with Gavin in the room, once he left, I sensed shame. These boys were trying to show me who was boss, wanted to play with me a bit on my first day here, and Gavin had walked in and sucked all the wind out of their sails. I saw a few smiles in the back of the class, so I kept going. "I don't buy it. I think you guys are probably the cream of the crop," I said, using one of Jack's favorite expressions. I was about to go on, but I was quickly interrupted by Stevie Wonder. "Isn't She Lovely" poured out of the laptop in the back corner.

I didn't know this kid's name, this freckled boy with thick dark hair and a taste for retro music, hiding behind the laptop screen. I didn't know any of their names. I hadn't asked, and I wasn't sure if I'd remember them anyway. But these kids had just given me my first vote of confidence in two months. I gladly took it.

Later that day, I spotted a small cluster of parents outside Blackwell waiting to pick up their children from day care. Maybe if I were planning on sticking around, this would be my new baby group, but for now, I held back. When they were inside the building, I went in and made a beeline for Dot. Grace's first day of day care had been a quiet, uneventful success. I hushed the baby-group voices in my head and congratulated the both of us on getting through it. I walked Grace home, fed her, bathed her, and put her down to sleep. Then I fell into bed and called Jack.

"I think I can do this. I just wish I didn't have to." I hung up and slept with the phone under my pillow.

8

Day two was a setback.

At Sunny Day, Marge warned us about day two. The young kids often separate easily on day one, because they have no idea what's happening. It's day two that bites you in the ass. True to form, Grace howled when I dropped her off at day care. She clung to my shirt as I tried to pass her to Dot. I never remembered her doing that before. At home, she had gone to Alma and Sondra willingly, almost too willingly, and it eased the rhythm of my life. Gym class—handoff. Manicure—handoff. Massage—handoff. Now I actually had somewhere to be, somewhere that was not a pedicure or a facial. I had to be at a job, and Grace chose this as the time to broadcast her recent attachment.

Eventually Dot pried her off me, calmed her, and walked her inside. I leaned on the outside wall, taking deep breaths to steady myself. Another mom with a short brown bob stumbled out of the building, closed the door behind her, and stood next to me. "It's a bitch," she said. "Which is why I like the gum trick," she added, offering me a stick of gum. "By the time the gum loses its flavor, your kid will have forgotten all about drop-off." I took the gum and thanked her as she walked off.

Sure enough, Dot texted me moments later that Grace was happy and had all but forgotten about the separation. I, on the other hand, was still a hot, jittery mess. I closed my eyes, saw the word *Grace*, and took myself briefly back to Santa Monica. I thought about a chilled glass of wine on the porch. I thought about our lounge chairs. I thought about the beach. I thought about Jack. He was never involved in the day-to-day of Grace. Hell, I barely was. But today I needed to tell him how hard it was to leave her, how unsettling it was to pry her off me and hear her crying. But I had gone too far. The thoughts that were meant to comfort me were about to swallow me whole. I quickly opened my eyes and took a sharp breath. I had five minutes to get to MacReady. That porch, the wine—they were far away, and if I was going to make this happen, they'd have to stay there.

My classes didn't go much better than drop-off. None of the boys I taught would be winning any awards for academic achievement, but my first-period crew was an unpleasant combination of difficult and unpredictable. Still, I knew the teaching drill—win over the difficult kids and the rest would follow.

Yesterday the boys had been confident, almost buoyed, by my newness. Today they were lethargic and unresponsive. I sensed this immediately when I walked into class, to the sound of no music and no raised heads.

"Hello, boys," I began, sitting on the edge of my desk, my legs crossed out in front of me.

I'd decided to abandon the après-yoga gear and was wearing a dress that Jack had bought me for Valentine's Day. It was gauzy and bohemian, but it had sleeves and came to my knees. I thought it would be more professional, but I hadn't realized how sheer it was until I looked down at my thighs and saw the outline of my enormous white underwear. I quickly ran behind the desk and plopped down into my chair, shoving my legs under the desk. I breathed in the Wall of Axe but remembered to keep my mouth open, letting some of the fumes pass through my head.

"Hey," sounded a voice from the back of the class.

I turned around and looked behind me. Rose, one of the school administrative assistants, had tried to explain the smart board to me in a series of rambling emails. From what I could gather, it was some sort of computer screen, and the kids could sync up their iPads and laptops to it. The very sight of it terrified me. I assumed I'd ignore the board and do things the old-fashioned way, even though for me, old-fashioned meant a chalkboard. I looked around but didn't see any chalk, only a whiteboard and some markers. I wondered if chalk was suddenly unhealthy. I wondered if it had gone the way of plastic wrap and cheap sunscreen. For a second I wondered what Jack would make of it, or if he even knew about it.

I shuddered, shaking off Jack, and grabbed a thick green marker. Immediately, I took a whiff of a strong smell. This smell was no match for the Wall of Axe, but it was powerful and artificial, and it made my eyes water. Still seated, I turned and wrote on the whiteboard, *If You Had a Superpower, What Would It Be?*, feeling pretty pleased with myself. Last night, I'd read through the syllabus Gavin had sent me and picked out some writing prompts I thought would best speak to the boys. I wanted to spend the first couple of weeks getting to know them, so I'd decided to hold off on assigning any reading. Smiling, I swiveled around and faced the class. Some boys looked at me. Some looked out a window. Some looked down in their laps, presumably at their outlawed-in-class phones.

"OK!" I chirped. "Why don't you all take ten minutes and write a handful of sentences. When you're done, we can share."

Nothing. Not a single move. Apparently, this prompt had prompted nothing.

"OK!" I sang, trying again. "Let's go! Come on!" A couple of the boys started to snicker. They were looking behind me, not at me. I whirled around, and there on the smart board was a picture of what could best be described as the slutty stripper version of Supergirl. The horns of the *Superman* soundtrack belted from the back of the class. I tried to make eye contact with the boy behind the computer, but he looked down. As the laughter grew more raucous, I turned back to the board and saw the same Supergirl stripper from behind, bending down, a red *S* on the back of her incredibly small underwear—underwear that looked like the kind I had abandoned on my road trip. I ran to the board and started pushing keys and buttons, hoping to take the image down, but a paper airplane hit me in the side of the face. As it fell to the floor, the airplane opened and I saw the words *Go Back to California* written on the inside.

I willed myself not to cry. *Surely this could be worse.*

"Fine," I muttered. "Fine. Don't write. Just tell me. One of you just tell me—which superpower would you like to have?"

"I wouldn't mind flying out of this place," said the red buzz cut.

"What's your name?" I asked.

"Why?" replied the red buzz cut.

"Because I don't know it. I don't know any of your names."

"Caleb," he answered. I heard more snickering.

"I'm Caleb," said the freckles in the back, the music mastermind, the boy who wouldn't meet my eyes. "*He's* Art."

"But we call him Fart, and you can, too."

"Really?" I asked, looking at Art.

"Yup," Art said, his face blushing to match his hair. "Because of my name."

"That's not the only reason," said the freckles.

"Oh, and because I fart when I'm nervous," Art admitted. "Think you can call me that?"

I refused to miss a beat. "Nice to meet you, Fart," I said. Hell, in preschool we let some kid wear a tutu and a pilot's cap every day. The least I could do was call this kid Fart.

"And you?" I asked the freckles. "You're Caleb?"

"Yup. In the flesh." He ran his hands through his thick black hair until it stood up on its own.

"OK, then, Caleb," I said. "Tell me about your superpower." I looked right at him, right into his very green eyes.

"I'm a mind reader," he said.

"Oh, really?" I asked.

"Yup."

"Well, then," I said. "Tell me what I'm thinking."

Caleb's large green eyes narrowed. "You can't believe you left sunny California to spend your days with losers like us. You're stuck here with us and these dumb writing prompts that aren't gonna make any of us good writers."

I blinked at him. Was it the pain of the paper airplane hitting me earlier, or did this kid just verbally smack me in the face?

"You're wasting your time with us," said Art.

"Yeah," echoed the short, skinny, spectacled kid I'd seen in the hall on the first day. His voice cracked, and he looked at me nervously.

"What's your name?" I asked.

His eyes grew wide. "Um, Guy . . . ?" Was he asking me or telling me his name?

The chubby kid who had been with Guy in the hall, the one who had assumed that because he'd heard I was from California I'd be really hot, so hot that he needed to cup his hands to his chest, chimed in. "I'm Davey, and we think teachers who pretend to like us are lame." He took extra time with the last word, stretching it out—*laaaaame.*

"It looks like you've been voted off the island," Caleb announced, his eyes staring right through me. "Pack your bags and go home."

As if, I thought, staring back at the boy who, just yesterday, had been my only ally. As if I could leave this muggy hole, with its bugs and its smells and these kids who didn't even want me here. I'd have done anything to click my heels and go back to California, to have woken up from this awful, interminable dream. I felt sick and scared and almost naked in front of them (or as naked as you can be in underwear that practically reaches your chin).

"Fine," I mumbled. "Do whatever you want. I'll just sit here."

"Huh?" said Guy.

"Go for it," I said, not looking at them. "Check your phones, watch a movie, I don't care."

Guy's face crumpled. "Are you mad at us?"

These kids made no sense. I wanted to run, to get out of there. But I knew better than to walk out on a paying gig. So I just sat with my head on the desk. I could hear them, and occasionally I could sense a couple of them hovering near me, whispering, "Is she OK?" I didn't raise my head until the bell. When it finally rang, I raced out before a single one of them could stop me, pulling my bag close to me to cover as much of my backside as possible. I remembered I had a sweater in the bag, so I pulled it out and tied it around my waist. As soon as I got out of class, I ran down the hall and leaned against the wall, my eyes closed: *Stay put.* Before I knew it, Stacey Figg was upon me.

"Rough class?" she asked, jingling. Her arms were elbow-high in bangles.

"Kind of," I said. I was annoyed with the boys, but more annoyed with myself for not being able to take it. "I think I could've handled it better," I added.

"You get used to it," she said knowingly. "Kind of like the smell."

"I'm not so sure about that."

"I don't know what happened, but you'll see soon enough." She leaned in as if letting me in on a secret, except that she didn't whisper. "These kids are awful." She looked around then back at me. "Awful," she breathed.

I didn't know what to say, so I just laughed nervously.

Stacey didn't need me to say anything. She kept talking. "These are the kids that other schools didn't want, so we took them. Congratulations. Your first class is bad, but you'll see soon enough.

Your others won't be much better. You just won yourself a troop of disruptive, disrespectful private-school rejects." She snapped in my face when she finished her sentence.

Beeks had told me that St. Norbert's was the kind of place kids went when they ran out of options, but I was still surprised to hear Stacey talk this way.

"Don't be fooled by a good day, and don't be manipulated by some kid you think is sweet. None of these kids are sweet."

I guess I didn't look convinced, because Stacey took another step in, so that our noses were almost touching. "These poor, 'misunderstood' kids," she said, crunching her fingers in air quotes, "these kids do things like set off fart bombs in the lunchroom and take embarrassing pictures of us while we're teaching, doctor them, and send them around to the whole grade. These kids break into supply closets and even hack into our email accounts. One got into mine and sent a fake email to his parents about how well he was doing here. The thing is, not one of these kids is doing well here." She paused to catch her breath. "The secret is boundaries and consequences," she said.

"Thanks," I said. "I'll try to remember that. I guess you can tell I'm new to all this."

"Yeah," she said with a nod, pulling back. "That's why we have the teachers' lounge. That's where we all go to commiserate."

"That's good to know," I said. "I think I'll be needing that."

"Honey," said Stacey, putting a hand on my arm, "you can come and talk to me anytime. We teachers need to stick together."

"Gavin mentioned the lounge in an email," I said. "I just don't remember where he said it was."

"Gavin." She sighed girlishly, flashing me a big, garish smile and shivering in delight. "Such a hero to come here and lead us all. You should have seen what it was like before he got here." She shook her head and looked down.

I needed to get out of the hall before the boys came out and saw me, and I wasn't sure I could hear much more of her singing Gavin's praises. I made an excuse and backed away from Stacey. As I walked off, she called out, "Remember, you can always come to the lounge! There's popcorn on Fridays!"

If Stacey Figg was right about these kids, I was going to need a lot more than popcorn on Fridays to get me through the week.

9

I tried to recharge at home that night. Dinner with Grace was hard. She rejected whatever I fed her, pursing her lips and turning her head. If I could manage to shove in a single spoonful, she sprayed it out all over the two of us.

I sat at the table coated in chicken and pea mush, which, I had noticed, was the color of neither chicken nor peas, and I willed myself not to think about my former life. If I wanted to puree food for Grace, I wouldn't know where to start. Even if there were farmers' markets in the Bronx, I was in no shape to go looking for them. Besides, I hadn't brought the machine Alma used to make the food. Hell, I didn't even know what that machine was called. I quickly shut Alma out as well, banishing all thoughts about how glorious it had been to call her name and have her take over whenever I ran into trouble or felt the need for a break. I wondered about those tired-looking moms in baby group. *This is relentless, and this is why they all looked so damn exhausted.*

"Just one more bite," I begged. With the jar of food in one hand, I waved the spoon around, made some frenetic airplane noises, and rammed it into her pursed lips.

"Gracie, eat!" I yelled, slamming the jar of food down on the table and cracking the bottom. I looked at the jar. Could the mush inside be salvaged, or had the crack released minuscule shards of glass? I had no idea. I just knew I'd wasted a dollar fifty on something that would never get eaten.

I started to cry, and because I'd just yelled, Grace cried along with me. At some point I gave up on dinner and let her eat Cheerios and suck down a bottle of formula, Santa Monica be damned. I needed to collapse on the couch, and I couldn't do that if she was awake. I bathed her and put her to sleep, both of which seemed to take forever. Once she was down, I thought about getting myself in the bath, a grim-looking tub that Jack would have had ripped out and replaced with a newer, glossier, whiter model. Instead, I took a long, hot shower and sat in pajamas on the little brown couch. It was still muggy, even inside.

Stacey Figg had been right. The town house had no central air-conditioning. Instead, each room had a hulking air-conditioner box attached to the outside of the window. The boxes were ugly and blocked out what little light managed to sneak in. They made a loud blowing noise and dripped puddles of water onto the floor. I could not believe these things even existed anymore.

I couldn't deal with the noise, so I opened a window, even though the air was heavy and thick. I closed my eyes and took a sip of the wine I'd bought over the weekend. The local grocery store was narrow, grimy, and only seemed to have one of everything. I'd bought the only bottle of red wine on the cramped shelf, officially depleting the store's reserves. I had been waiting all day for a glass, but it tasted to me not like a glass of dry red wine, but more like I was sipping from the Wall of Axe. I would have cried then and there had I not leaped three feet into the air when an enormous shiny roach crawled over my foot. I screamed and kicked and the creature landed on its back, flipped over, and scrambled under the couch. Honestly, I can't say for sure if it was a roach. I'd seen some roaches before, but this thing was the size of my hand. Each of its evil antennae was spinning in a different direction, and its shell was so thick and shiny it looked almost lacquered. I ran into the kitchen, grabbed a bottle of Windex, and began to spray under the couch. As I did this, I was 100 percent sure that this enormous persevering bug was not going to meet its end at the hands of a bottle of Windex.

I didn't see the roach again that night, but I shoved a towel under the door, closed all the windows, and slept with the Windex next to me. If those things were coming in from the outside, then I sure as hell wasn't going to make it easy for them.

10

This is how I spent my first days at St. Norbert's: I taught, or at least, I'd try to teach. Often I'd be wearing something wildly inappropriate, like a sundress with a cropped jacket on top and leggings underneath. Most of my sundresses were apparently completely sheer, and I thought it best if the giant underwear were for my eyes only. Sometimes I'd wear a brightly patterned wrap dress with a cardigan, pinned shut, because I quickly learned that middle school boys won't pay attention to you if they can see even a hint of your cleavage. I hadn't gotten a paycheck yet, so I didn't have any money for new clothes, and I wasn't sure I was ready to buy anything, anyway. Buying a teacher's uniform would mean that I had accepted this new reality. Still, I made a mental note to ask Stacey Figg when and how often we got paid.

Living paycheck to paycheck was neither new for me nor hard. My parents had believed their best defense against a lack of money was a near-religious commitment to organization. They knew exactly how much money was coming in and how much was going out, and it was all written down in a spiral notebook we kept in the kitchen. And here's the thing—as an only child, I had a seat at the kitchen table. I knew what was in that notebook. I knew how much and when they got paid and what we spent on things like rent, food, and clothing, as well as what we had in our emergency fund, a stash of money we kept in a jar under the sink.

Our weeks were organized by our commitment to the spiral notebook. On Sunday mornings, we'd cut coupons and make a meal plan for the week based on what coupons we'd found. On Sunday afternoons, we shopped for the whole week and rarely went back to the store to refresh. My parents were never short and were seldom caught by surprise, because they always made sure they were one step ahead of their money. But all their devotion to planning, all their lists—none of it had protected them from the car crash that ended their lives. None of that had kept them, or me, safe.

Still, in those first few weeks, I was thankful to my parents for teaching me how to stay on top of my money, what little there was of it. Instead of a notebook, now I kept all my information in my phone, and I made note of everything I spent. No, living paycheck to paycheck was not a problem for me. I knew how to worry about money. Some mornings I would wake up and wonder if my life with Jack had even existed or if it had all been a dream. But then I would hear Grace's voice on the monitor, and I would know. It had all happened.

Grace. She and I technically had fewer hours together, but we had so much more time. At the end of each school day, I'd pick her up and we'd spend our evenings together, evenings that were fulfilling but also exhausting.

Often, we'd see a bug. Sometimes we'd see more than one. Once I'd done my kabuki dance with the front-door lock and all the windows, I'd fall asleep, but never before I'd checked in with Don, hoping to hear news of Jack. Don was pretty much sending me variations on the same text:

Jack is fine.

Stay where you are.

Do your job and wait.

Don was nothing if not consistent. Circular and consistent.

I kept calling Jack and leaving messages. One night, the voice mail lady was no longer there. Instead, there was just another message, from another detached lady, possibly a cousin, announcing that the number was no longer in service. *Funny,* I thought when I first heard the message, *Jack isn't, either.*

I fell back into the couch and threw down my phone and spoke to someone who wasn't just not here, but who wasn't even available. "I don't know what I did to let you think that this would be OK with me, that you could send me here, make me wait, and not send a word. But it isn't OK. None of it is."

~

After a few days, Stacey Figg abandoned the pretense of bringing me vegetables, and I agreed to let her inside one evening.

"Want company?" she asked, standing on my doorstep.

I did want company. I just wasn't sure I wanted hers.

"Sure," I said. "Come in." I stood back and let her walk into the foyer.

Like a dog sniffing out a new home, she quickly began working her way through the first floor.

"This couch," she said, pointing at the brown couch. "You should call facilities and see if they have something better." I did not want to tell Stacey Figg that I was not going to be sticking around long enough to need better, so I just smiled and nodded.

"When will your husband be here?" she asked, walking into the dining room and eyeing the mess on the table.

"Soon."

"How often does he go away?" she asked, continuing on into the kitchen, as though this were her one and only chance to see the inside of my house and she had to make sure to see as much of it as possible. I trailed behind.

"It's hard to say," I said.

She stopped and turned to look at me. Her eyes narrowed. "When did he last see Grace?"

"July," I mumbled.

"July? And you're OK with that?"

No, Stacey Figg. I am not OK with that. I am not OK with any of this. I am especially not OK with you leading yourself on a self-guided tour of my home and interrogating me in the process.

"I don't have a choice," I said. "End of story." I shrugged and walked out of the kitchen and back into the living room. I fell back onto the brown couch and waited for her to come in. She wasn't done asking questions, but she was smart enough to shift gears.

"So how long have you been teaching?" she said, sitting next to me on the couch, putting her hands on her lap.

"A few years."

"Why English?"

"It was always my strongest subject, so it seemed like a no-brainer."

"Why did you choose middle school?"

"I didn't. It kind of chose me."

Stacey Figg kept coming back and peppering me with questions. I got better at answering without really answering. At some point she relented and went home.

~

I had been dodging calls and texts from Beeks. After two weeks of classes, I finally answered one of her calls.

"You're not going to believe this," she said. "But you have once again found me in the laundry room."

"You called me," I said, but I appreciated that she was giving me the chance to pretend I'd called her. Beeks was generous this way. No hard feelings.

"It's early for you to be doing laundry," I said. I knew from Beeks that laundry usually happened after bedtime.

"Yeah, well, let's just say I didn't have a choice this time. The little boys tried to prank Stevie by putting plastic wrap on his toilet seat. He's a teenager, so he's completely irrational and impulsive and was therefore unable to stop himself from pouring an entire jar of crushed garlic all over their bunk beds. And by 'all over,' I mean even inside their pillowcases."

"My God," I said. "That's insane. How do you even live with that? And why don't you sound angrier?"

"That, my dear, is an excellent question," she said. "Remind me to ask my therapist that."

"Well, when you see your therapist, maybe you could also ask her a few questions on my behalf," I said, not joking at all.

"How is it?" asked Beeks. "How are you?"

"Jack is nowhere," I said, eating a handful of spinach-and-apple puffs. "The job sucks. The kids hate me. It's muggy, even though it's the middle of September. Everything around me is dirty, and the bugs are huge and mean." I stopped myself because I knew where this was going, and then I went directly there. "I want to go home, Beeks. I'm done." I hadn't said any of this aloud yet. I missed Jack desperately, but I couldn't say that to Beeks, not now. I couldn't tell her that the only way I fell asleep at night was by closing my eyes and imaging our bedroom in Santa Monica and conjuring Jack in bed beside me. I'd been waking up each day and plodding along, sleepwalking through the motions and waiting for it to get better. But it wasn't getting any better. Saying the words to Beeks, hearing them come out of my mouth, it was all too much. Before I knew what to say next, I was sobbing.

Beeks let me finish before she said anything. "Can we replace the yelling portion of this call with the 'I'm sorry' portion?" she asked.

"Huh?" I sniffled and fished a puff out of my bra.

"I'm sorry, Aggie," she said. "I'm sorry I haven't just shown up uninvited. I knew you needed me, but I wanted to give you some room."

"That's silly," I said. "I told you not to come yet. You were being a good friend. That's all."

"I'm not so sure about that," she said. "When I broke my leg, you just showed up, even though I told you I didn't need help."

"It's not the same," I said.

"And that time you faked pneumonia so I could get out of skiing with Brian's family?"

"Beeks, it's different. I'm not ready for you to see me."

"Jeez, Aggie," she said. "Can I have the yelling portion back?"

"If you see me, this is all real. And I just can't deal with that now. Please understand," I begged.

There was a long pause. "OK," she said. "Whatever you need."

"I love you, Beeks. I just need a little more time."

"You can have it then. But don't make me wait too long. I can wait to see you, but you've got my unofficial niece there as well. You know how I feel about patience—it's somebody else's virtue."

11

Beeks called again the next evening.

"I'm glad you didn't send me to voice mail," she said. No hellos.

"Why's that?"

"Because I'm wandering around campus searching for what looks like a place you'd live in."

"What? You're here?" I jumped up off the brown couch.

"Yup," she said proudly. "You sounded positively dreadful last night. I may be a bad friend for not coming immediately, but I'm not a downright shitty friend."

"Beeks," I said. "I told you not to come." I regretted the words as soon as they were out of my mouth.

"Yeah, well, I came anyway." I could hear the hurt in her voice. "So tell me where you are or I'll start asking people. I know how much you like it when people start talking about you, and I can promise they're all going to talk if some crazed woman with frizzy hair and a gigantic mom purse is wandering the campus trying to track you down."

"Fair enough."

I gave Beeks my address and some directions. I stuck my head outside quickly to make sure Stacey Figg wasn't around.

Grace was not yet asleep. Bedtime had turned hairy in the past few days. Although she once went down quietly in her crib, she now howled until I'd gone into her room multiple times. One night I did the unthinkable. I rocked her to sleep in my arms and put her down only when her limbs were floppy and limp. I tried not to think about my baby nurse or the baby-group moderator and their admonitions. Grace and I were on the brown couch when Beeks knocked on the door. I carried Grace to the foyer and opened the door to see Beeks standing in front of me, wearing black capri pants and a white button-down shirt and, as promised, carrying an enormous overstuffed purse with a newspaper sticking out of it.

I hadn't gotten the door fully open before she jumped into my foyer. I stuck my head out, and sure enough, there was Stacey Figg looking through her window. I ducked back inside.

"Let me look at you!" Beeks said, pulling me to her. "Wow, do I spot roots up there?" She stood on her tiptoes and peered down at the top of my head. "Be careful or I'll call the highlight police."

And that is Beeks. Right there. I just smiled. Even though she'd surprised me, not really giving me time to prepare for her visit, I knew exactly what she'd say when she saw me. She reached over and scooped Grace out of my arms.

"Gracie, darling," Beeks said. "Remember me? Aunt Beeks?" Grace just stared and then reached for the mass of Beeks's hair. "She's your mother," she said, pointing at me. "But I'm your aunt. That means we both love you, but when you're older, I'll like you even when she doesn't."

"That's right," I said, finally speaking. "And you should know, Grace, that your aunt Beeks is also very forgiving."

Beeks looked at me.

"I'm sorry," I said. "I'm sorry I wouldn't let you come sooner."

"Enough," Beeks interrupted. Before either of us could say another word, we fell into each other. I don't remember who moved first, but I hugged her, almost flattening Grace in between us. I smelled the coconut oil she piled into her big, coarse, curly hair, the oil she swears keeps the frizz at bay. I breathed it in. When we finally pulled away, loosening our grip on each other, I saw that we were both red-faced and blotchy. Our mascaras were in a competition to see whose could get farthest down our cheeks. I was still using pricey mascara that I'd brought with me, so I suspected Beeks's was winning. We grinned at each other, and at Grace, and before I could say anything, Beeks had launched herself on a tour of the town house.

She pushed past me and walked into the living room. "You're not planning on unpacking?" she said.

"I dunno," I replied. "I could be leaving at any moment, and I don't want to get too comfortable."

"Right," she said, barely concealing her disapproval. She walked into the kitchen and opened my fridge. Damn, her instincts were good. We both stared inside. I saw a half gallon of milk and a lot of baby yogurts. Before I could say anything, Beeks whirled around and surveyed the kitchen. I wished I'd washed the dishes. I wished I'd bought some food to put in the pantry, even if I wasn't going to cook it.

"Where's the rest of your food?" Beeks asked, picking up an empty can of veggie puffs, her eyes darting to a shelf of replacement puffs, stacked up in all the colors of the rainbow.

"Huh?"

"Where's your chicken? Where are your eggs? What are you guys eating? Are you a vegetarian now?" She reached for another can of puffs. "And what the hell are these things?"

"We're eating fine, Beeks. We don't need much."

Just then, before I could stop her, Beeks fixed her eyes on some small jars huddled behind the microwave. She waltzed across the tiny kitchen and swept the jars up in her hands. They were baby food jars, and inside each one were what appeared to be very little fingers. Baby fingers, almost.

"Aggie, what in God's name are these?" She held the jars up to her eyes to look inside them.

I mumbled a response.

"What?"

"Sticks," I mumbled again, slightly louder. "Meat sticks."

"MEAT STICKS?"

I leaned back on the dirty counter and braced myself for an in-person yelling portion.

"LAST TIME I SAW YOU, YOU WERE BUYING A FIVE-DOLLAR APPLE AND HAVING SOMEONE MAKE IT INTO FOOD FOR GRACE. NOW YOU'RE FEEDING HER THIS SHIT? WHAT HAPPENED TO YOU, AGGIE?"

"Beeks, they're not for Grace. They're for me. I eat them."

"WHAT?"

"I discovered them on the road. I eat them."

"Aggie, I know you can cook! I've eaten your food, remember? That tuna bake with cereal may have been revolting, but at least it was technically food. What about that fancy chicken dish with the olives and canned corn? What happened to you? I know you know that glorified corn pops and these revolting toddler fingers aren't really the staples of a solid diet."

"Please tell me you didn't come here just to criticize me, because if that's the case, you'll be really busy. I'm a mess," I said. "I'm a hot mess. My roots are showing; my child and I are living on puffs of sugary air and sticks of processed meat." I looked at her defiantly. "Anything else I'm missing?"

"Yeah, well, this may be temporary, but you need to unpack. It looks like you're just stopping here for the night, and by the sound of things, you may be here for longer." Beeks glared right back at me. "One more thing. This baby," she said, making an upward motion with the hip that held Grace, "this baby is up way too late. She needs to go to sleep. She needs to go to sleep because babies should not be up at nine. She also needs to go to sleep so we can drink." Before I could say anything, Beeks went looking for the crib.

I wanted to stop her from taking over. I wanted to show Beeks that I could put Grace down on my own, that I didn't need her help. But I was so relieved to hand her off, to have someone else put her sleep, that I didn't protest. I didn't even mock protest. Beeks found Grace's crib and slowly lowered her into it after kissing her good-night. Grace moaned, and Beeks went in and rubbed her back. She did this a couple more times until Grace fell asleep. Beeks walked out of her room and gave me a look. *This is how it's done,* her face said. *This is how you do it.*

I wanted to be angry. But even more, I wanted to have a glass of wine on the couch with my best friend, even if she was pushy and opinionated. I let Beeks lord over me some more. I had it coming, anyway. She left once we polished off a bottle of wine she'd pulled out of her sack. It was much better than anything I could get at the local supermarket, even if it wasn't Jack quality. Beggars can't be choosers. Hell, beggars can't even have opinions. Beggars just drink whatever wine is in front of them.

12

Some days the boys were unresponsive, almost drugged. Other days I spent the entire class trying to get them to sit in their seats. The morning after Beeks stopped by, they were bouncing off the walls. Guy was standing on his desk. He had rolled up a piece of loose-leaf paper and was shooting spitballs at his friends.

"Geeeeeee!" they called, begging for spitballs to come their way. Some of the boys were using their iPads as shields. Others used their hands. (Nobody used a notebook or a binder as a shield, because nobody used notebooks or binders.) One boy sat in the back with his mouth open, waiting for a spitball to fly in. I assumed my unproductive position in the front of the class. A spitball flew over my head and landed on the smart board. "Geeeeeee!" they continued to yell. I looked over at Caleb, who got out of his seat and made his way over to me.

"Guy's father is French," he explained. "That's how they pronounce his name at home."

"Oh, I see," I said.

"Yeah, his father is also kind of an asshole. But we don't talk about that much."

"Language! Boys, please!" I begged. Nothing.

"Boys!" I said, this time even more loudly, but still getting no response. I turned around, held my skirt down, and climbed onto my desk. I summoned all my dormant yoga skills and balanced, facing them.

"Boys!" I yelled, surprised at the volume in my voice. I am not a yeller. Beeks is a yeller. Jack, on occasion, is a yeller. I do not yell, but here I was, standing on a desk in a skirt, yelling at a group of twelve- and thirteen-year-olds who were now engaged in a full-on spitball war.

"Don't shoot spitballs!" As the words came out of my mouth, I remembered Marge at Sunny Day, telling me that you should never tell a toddler what not to do. If you say, "Don't throw your food," the toddler hears, "Throw your food." If you say, "Don't bite your sister," he hears, "Bite your sister." If that applied to adolescents, and I was beginning to suspect it might, then all these kids were hearing was "Shoot spitballs." I needed another tactic.

"Outside! Now!" I yelled. "All of you! Outside!" One or two of them looked at me. I realized I needed to use names. I could not address the group, because as a group, these boys were unable to hear me. As a group, they were a spinning mass of chaos. To get their attention, I needed to make a dent in that mass. I needed to pull them apart.

"Guy! Caleb! Fart! Outside!" Nobody moved much, but one by one, I got their attention. "Davey! This way!" I pointed to the door. Davey, who always seemed to be rocking in his seat, standing on a desk, or running down a hall, paused, still moving his feet, and looked at me.

"All of you," I said. "Follow me outside." I did not wait for them. I walked to the door and ran down the four flights of stairs. The boys were rowdy and they filled the halls with their noise, but I didn't hush them. I needed to save what little capital I had for what was going to happen once we got outside.

I walked out of the building and onto the small patch of grass in front of MacReady. I stood at the base of a statue of St. Norbert, his round, bloated face glowering down at all of us.

"Davey," I said. "Do ten jumping jacks and tell me what you had for breakfast."

He looked at me blankly.

"Now!" I barked, surprising myself.

Davey began to jump. After a few jumping jacks, he yelled out, "Froot Loops!" The old me would have wrinkled my nose in disdain, but I had eaten canned corn for dinner and washed it down with Rice Krispies. I was hardly in a position to judge.

"OK," I yelled. "Guy, do fifteen push-ups and tell me the name of your kindergarten teacher."

Guy giggled, dropped to the grass, did some of the lamest, wobbliest push-ups I'd ever seen, and panted, "Mrs. Loom!"

I looked over at Caleb, who was leaning against the statue of poor old Norbert and scowling. "Caleb, jog in place and tell us your grandparents' names."

"Nice try," he said. "I think I'll pass." He looked at me, daring me to challenge him. But I didn't see him. I suddenly saw the four-year-old he probably was. I remembered one of my first students, Ronan, a four-year-old who tested every boundary, a four-year-old who did exactly what he was asked *not* to do and did nothing he was asked *to* do. I knew what a power struggle with a Ronan looked like, and it was a struggle without a winner. It was a struggle for struggle's sake. I thought back to Marge again and I remembered one of her first pieces of advice: "Ronan wants to be asked to do something again and again, just so he can have the pleasure of saying no each time. So stop asking." I decided to stop asking. "Whenever you're ready, Caleb. I'll be here," I said, looking away and giving someone else my attention.

One by one, I went through all the boys and had them doing a variety of ongoing exercises while singing nursery rhymes, answering questions, reciting their addresses. The air around me smelled like deodorant, grass, and clammy middle school armpits. When most of the kids were worn out, I sat down on the grass.

"If I had a superpower," I said, looking up at them, "it would be to get food in my daughter's stomach without actually having to feed her. You know, bypass her mouth. I'm kind of tired of having her spit applesauce all over me. I probably have some of it in my hair right now." I ran my fingers through my ponytail, and sure enough, I landed on a clump of hardened puree.

Some of the boys giggled.

"Anyone else?" I asked.

"X-ray vision," giggled Davey, looking at the boys. "I think you guys know why." Several boys hooted around him. He bowed to them.

"I would want a power that made me taller," said Guy, looking around nervously to see what his friends would say. "Much taller."

Davey shouted, "Yeah! No more growth hormones for Geeeeeee." Guy smiled at him in appreciation.

Art announced that he'd like teeth that never needed brushing, and then he blushed to match the color of his hair. A few more boys chimed in, and one by one they sat down around me. They did not sit in a circle, because they were incapable of forming a circle. I thought back to the boys in preschool who could not sit crisscross applesauce and how we just had them sit however they could, on their knees, on their backs, or not at all. These boys were *all* like that. A lot of my students were. Some boys needed to sit unreasonably close to the boys around them, almost touching. Others needed to sit far away, with a mile of space around themselves, often with some sort of physical barrier—a book, a backpack, a removed sneaker.

"Are you gonna ignore me again?" Caleb called from the back. "Or don't you care what I think?"

I could see from looking at his face that he was completely serious. Everything this kid said sounded sarcastic, but he didn't do sarcasm. None of them really did.

"I'm interested in what you have to say," I said. "Do you wish you had a superpower, Caleb?" I waited, looking right at him.

"No," he said. "Not that I can think of. I'd just like to be a lot better at everything. That's all."

The boys all turned to look at him. I could have sworn I saw his eyes fill a little. I wanted to say something more to him, but the bell rang.

"This was good," announced Davey. "Outside is good." He got up and bounced back into the building. We passed Stacey Figg, who gave me a quizzical look. She mouthed a question to me, *What's going on with you?* Her glossy lips formed a perfect circle at the end of her question. I quickly looked away, pretending I didn't see her.

I didn't feel like getting cornered, so I followed the boys. I spotted my third-period boys throwing their water bottles in the air to see if they'd land upright. I hated this trick.

I watched the boys open their lockers, shove things in, then pick up the mountain of things that fell out as soon as the lockers were opened. I never got to see them out of class. I was curious about what they were like when no teacher was around. I walked a little closer to a back I was sure belonged to Art—there were not many red buzz cuts around. As I neared him, he whirled around, and before I knew what happened next, I got a face full of Axe. I choked on it, coughing up talc and chemicals, wrenching my eyes in pain. I couldn't see anything. I could only taste and smell. I fell back into a pair of thick arms.

"Whoa!" said Gavin as he propped me up. "What do we have here, boys?" My vision was starting to come back. I still had a nose full of Anarchy, but I could see the boys, and I wrestled myself out of Gavin's meaty hold. The boys looked terrified. Art, still holding the can of Axe, started to stutter, and true to his nickname, farted nervously.

"Sir, we really didn't mean to get her. It was an accident." Art looked at Gavin pleadingly.

"Sure. An accident," Gavin sneered.

"Really, sir," Caleb added, nervously running his hands through his hair. "We didn't know she was here. We were just playing around."

"You can tell me more about this little *accident* of yours," he said, looking at Caleb and Art, "when you're in my office, which is where you'll be spending some time." He stood right in front of us, his feet spread wide, his arms crossed against his chest.

"Really, Gavin," I said, smiling as sweetly as I could. "It was an accident. I kind of snuck up on them." I laughed nervously, shuffling toward the boys.

Gavin looked me up and down. "Agnes, remember," he said, "don't be fooled. Fools don't last here." He raised his eyebrows. "Got it?"

I thought about my days of off-brand cereal. I thought about marking down all my expenses in a little notebook, just to make sure I had enough money each month. I thought about Don's instructions—"Stay there and do your job." I thought about Grace. I had to do this for her. Gavin stared at me, waiting for a response.

"Got it, Gavin," I said, my stomach sinking.

"I thought so," he said. Then he altered his tone and spoke loud enough for all the boys in the hall to hear.

"You are not their friend, Agnes," he said. "Friends can't take away recess. For a week." The boys groaned.

I nodded dumbly, unable to look at the boys. I should have stood up for them, but all I could do was nod at Gavin.

"It's good to have you on the team, on *my* team," he said. "Right?"

"Right," I mumbled, giving him the best conspiratorial smile I could muster. I needed this job and this place to live. I just wished I could have needed them out of earshot of the boys.

-13-

October began much the way September ended. The air was crisper, less sticky. The bugs had migrated somewhere else. I turned off the air-conditioning units and opened some windows. When I saw a mouse under the dining room table, I closed the windows again. I heard Stacey Figg's words in my head: *mouse population*. This mouse was tiny, too small to be anything other than a baby. Some mother mouse's baby. I shuddered when I thought of the mouse mother, with whom I was presumably sharing the town house. If I was going to get rid of these mice, I needed something stronger than Windex. The local supermarket, which still seemed to only carry one of everything, had a solitary glue trap on its sad shelf. I ran into Ella, an eighth-grade social studies teacher and a day-care mom, who had given me the gum on my second day, and whose son, Jake, was in Grace's group.

"Please tell me there are other shopping options," I said, hoping she didn't spot the trap in my cart.

"Sadly, this is it," she said. "Sometimes we make a group trip to Costco, if you're interested." For a moment I thought about all the veggie puffs one could get at Costco. "I've gotta run, though," she continued. "My nine-year-old has lice, and I came here for the mayonnaise." I was too afraid to ask questions, but my head started to itch uncontrollably. Ella walked off, and I realized it had been weeks since I'd had a real conversation with another adult, let alone another mom.

While Grace and I were standing at the checkout, I heard someone call my name. A woman.

"Agnes?"

I turned around and saw Ruth Moore. She was wearing makeup and a navy skirt suit with matching heels. She looked like a flight attendant.

"Hi," I said, trying to stand in front of the mousetrap. She looked over my head and scanned the conveyor belt.

"Oh no! You have mice?"

"Yeah," I said. "Well, I have a mouse. I'd like to think she's living alone."

"They never are." Ruth smiled. "I'll send someone to have a look around."

"Thanks," I said. "That would be great."

"How are you settling in?" she asked, putting some chicken cutlets on the belt.

I thought about Jack's instructions and wondered if I should be asking Ruth questions, but I had no idea what to ask. I couldn't turn to Jack, because I'd been checking daily and both he and his voice mail were still unavailable. I also didn't know how much Ruth knew about my situation, and I didn't want to talk about it. I moved quickly to the cashier and handed her money for the trap.

"Oh, fine," I said.

"Really?" she asked, reaching into her own cart but still looking at me.

"Yes," I said, not convincing anyone.

"Well, if you need anything at all, you can come to me. Jack and I are old friends. I've been cleaning up after his messes since before you were born."

My face flushed, and the metallic taste in my mouth returned. "It's late," I stuttered, quickly bagging the trap and waiting for change. "I have to get Grace home for dinner, but it was good seeing you." I forced a smile, praying this was the end of the conversation.

"You too, Agnes. And I'll see what I can do about your rodent friend."

~

That night, I put the trap under the table when Grace went to sleep. She was about to start crawling, I was sure of it. I'd lie on the floor, watching her push up to her hands and knees and rock back and forth, preparing to launch. I didn't need her launching straight into the glue trap.

As I took the trap out of its plastic wrapping, I thought about seeing Ruth in the supermarket. Instead of getting information or answers from her, I only seemed to have more questions. How much did she know about Jack? What other messes were there, and why would Ruth be involved with Jack if she knew about them? Why didn't I know about them? Just thinking about it all was exhausting, and I was bone tired. I shrugged off my questions and set the trap.

~

Stacey Figg showed up one morning with some bait boxes.

"These are the best," she said. "They wander into the box and can't get out."

"How did you know I saw a mouse?" I asked.

"Oh, I heard you yelling," she said. I wondered what else she'd heard. I prayed I hadn't also been shouting in my sleep.

"What happens to them inside the box?"

"Same as the glue traps. You just wait for them to die, but with the box you don't have to see it happening," she said. "Or you call me and I can help you drown them."

It took all I had not to throw up on poor Stacey Figg and her bait boxes.

"Want me to make breakfast?" she asked. "I'm already dressed and ready." She held out her arms to show me. She was wearing another wrap dress. This one was purple.

"Sure," I said hesitantly. As much as I relished the mornings with Grace, because she was the easiest right when she woke up, it was good to have help with her while I got myself ready. It would be even better to eat something for breakfast that was not in bar form or mixed with rice cereal.

"Why don't you go up and get dressed and I'll take over down here," she said, walking in and heading back to the kitchen. "Looks like you've unpacked," she said. "Does this mean your husband is coming?"

I pretended not to hear and walked up to my room. When I came down, Stacey Figg had proudly scrambled some eggs. She slid a plate toward me.

"So what was breakfast like in California?" she asked.

"Huh?"

"Oh, I dunno. What did you eat for breakfast?" I did not want to talk about California. I especially did not want to talk about California with Stacey Figg.

"My mother was a great cook," she said, not waiting for an answer. "Breakfast was her specialty, and she taught me everything she knew. My eggs are pretty damn good, if I do say so myself. But back to you, Aggie. I want to know about your life before you got here."

"There's nothing to know." It sounded like Stacey Figg didn't have a mother anymore, either. I could have asked her about it, but she didn't want to talk about herself, and neither did I. I put my head down and ate quickly, only stopping to chatter to Grace, then hustled the three of us out the door.

Stacey's eggs were good. Later that day, I realized that she must have come over with the eggs in her pocket, because I didn't remember buying any.

~

I was starting to feel a little safer. I still locked and unlocked the door and checked the windows every night, but it was more out of habit. Perhaps after Don's one hundredth text telling me You're safe, it was finally sinking in.

I wanted to talk to Don about my encounter in the supermarket with Ruth earlier that week, so I sat on the brown couch and called him.

"I saw Ruth in the supermarket," I said, not bothering with pleasantries I knew mattered nothing to Don.

"OK..."

"And she told me she's been cleaning up Jack's messes for years." I waited for him to say something. He didn't. "What did she mean by that?" I asked.

"I have no idea," Don said. "Besides, you're the one supposed to be gathering information. Remember?"

"Well, there's not much to gather. Sure, this place is kind of old, maybe even a little run-down, but I don't have much more than that. It's not like I can ask Ruth Moore how the school is doing financially or why she pulled her money out of Jack's fund."

"Listen, Agnes, you're more helpful than you think. Sometimes you hear something that seems unimportant, but it isn't at all. Just keep your ears open."

For old times' sake, I had to ask him. "And I'm safe, right . . . ?"

"Yes, you're safe."

He hung up without saying goodbye.

~

I actually had a more immediate problem than my safety: I was having real trouble figuring out what to wear. On a sunny, crisp Sunday morning, I bagged up all my beach couture, all my high-end Santa Monica boutique wear, and took it into a consignment store in the neighborhood. I was terrified to drive in the Bronx. Cars seemed to drive on top of each other, right up against each other, swallowing up all personal space and honking in protest if some unspoken rules were broken. So instead of driving, I loaded up Grace's stroller, put her in a carrier, and walked fifteen blocks.

I entertained Grace while the women behind the counter pawed through my clothes, chattering to each other in Spanish. I played peekaboo with her (I'd just googled "how to play with an almost nine-month-old") as I watched the women hold up and assess dresses I remembered wearing to romantic dinners with Jack, and jeans I was embarrassed to buy at first, shocked by their price. Those jeans were the uniform of my former life. I thought about Jack and how I'd explain selling all these clothes.

Whatever. I was alone. I needed the money. And why the hell am I explaining why I had to sell clothes for money when you disappeared?

I walked out with a little bit of cash and the promise of more to come. I got home, went online, and ordered some cheap, sensible clothes—button-down shirts and pencil skirts that were snug but not too tight. I also ordered sweaters. Not gauzy, flimsy, beach-at-night sweaters, but chunky woolen things that I'd seen on some of the other teachers. I guess every life has its uniform.

14

In mid-October, I finally discovered the teachers' lounge. One morning, I wrote on the whiteboard, *Memoir: Tell me, in five sentences, something about yourself that nobody knows*. The boys were going to read a memoir, *The Red Scarf Girl*, but before they did, I wanted to see if they could write their own short histories, or at least five sentences about themselves. As the boys shuffled into the room, I sat at my desk, watching them throw down their backpacks and reluctantly get into their seats. After I'd let Gavin take away their recess for a week, they had stopped chatting with me when they came in and just ignored me until I called them to attention.

I waited for the last one to settle in. The last one was usually Davey, who jiggled his way into class without a single supply and often shoeless.

"Davey," I asked, "where are your shoes today?"

He shrugged. "Josh Tapper needed them for gym, so I lent them to him." Josh was a student in one of my other classes.

"Where are Josh's shoes?" I asked.

"Dunno," Davey replied. "It's cool, though, Ms. Parsons. I like being barefoot." He put out his hands, palms down, as if to calm me. I wasn't worried. I saved worrying for the days when he came in wearing only one shoe. Davey made his way to his seat and began the long process of negotiating himself into it. Some of the boys sat right down, but many of them simply couldn't. Davey was one of the latter. He pulled his chair out, moved it around a bit, scraped it along the floor, positioned it several ways, and finally turned it backward. He sat in the chair, leaned against the back with his stomach, and began rocking. If Davey wasn't rocking, he was bouncing, shaking, or standing in the back of the class doing something that looked like a jig.

I directed their attention to the whiteboard and gave them a few minutes to write five sentences.

"Go on," I prodded them. "At least one thing about you that nobody knows." I leaned back in my seat and watched them all start working. "When you're done," I said, "we can put your work up on the smart board." The boys looked down at their keyboards and then looked at each other. I could sense silent communication passing between them. Caleb nodded at Guy and looked down. Art nodded at Davey. And so on. I heard a few snickers from behind screens. I knew something was coming, and I braced myself.

Five minutes later, I called time and asked who wanted to go first. Art raised his hand, grinning, looking around for approval. Once he got what he needed, some silent affirmation from the other boys, he hit a key and flashed his work up on the smart board. I stood up and walked over.

> My name is Gavin Burke and there is something nobody knows. This is the thing nobody knows. I was born without a penis. I just pretend I have one. That's why I yell a lot.

The class erupted in laughter before I even finished reading. I rushed over to my keyboard, frantically hit some keys, and removed the sentences from the smart board. I crossed my arms, looked down at the boys, and stared. Realizing that I was in prime Gavin stance, I shook my arms down by my sides.

"Really, Art?" I said.

"Fart," Guy corrected me.

Art shrugged. My God, these boys did a lot of shrugging. Was he trying to tell me that it wasn't his fault, that he couldn't do any better, or that he just couldn't help himself?

"Fine." I sighed. "Guy. Why don't you show us what you've got?" I knew full well I wasn't going to like it. I turned to face the smart board.

> My name is Gavin Burke and there is something
> that nobody knows about me. I like fluffy ponies.
> All kinds of fluffy ponies. The best ones are the pink
> and sparkly ones. I keep one in my pants all day in
> case I want to pet it.

By then, Davey had reached the point in the class where he had fallen out of his chair and was lying on the floor, shaking with glee.

"Guy?" I asked. "Fluffy ponies? What is that?"

"Hey, you said five sentences, so you got 'em."

"Actually," I said, taking down the sentences, "I said five sentences about you. Last time I checked, you are not Gavin Burke."

"Sad but true, Ms. Parsons," Guy said wisely, looking over at Davey, who was still writhing on the floor.

"Davey," I said, "I think this means it's your turn." By now, I knew exactly where these were going. In hindsight, I probably should have stopped it. In hindsight, I probably should not have agreed to teach at a school for wayward adolescents, so who was I to blame hindsight? I just inhaled and prepared myself for whatever was coming next.

Davey peeled himself off the floor and got up on his knees. His rugby shirt was hiked up over his belly and he yanked it down, although he didn't get the full coverage he wanted. At some point he gave up on the shirt and climbed back into his seat. He fumbled with the keyboard and eventually flashed his words up.

> My name is Gavin Burke and I have a secret. This
> is something I haven't told anyone. Last night I
> dreamed about Stacey Figg. She's so hot. I love
> girls who wear tight stuff and smell like popcorn
> and BO.

He barely got to the end before he exploded into more laughter. "Ooh, Stacey," he mock groaned, closing his eyes and tipping his head back. "You're so hot." Guy threw a shoe at him, and they all screamed with approval. Davey didn't have a shoe to throw back, so he grabbed a bottle of water from his neighbor's backpack and threw that. It missed, hitting the wall and cracking open. I spent the next ten minutes alternating between pretending I didn't care what they were doing and yelling from various parts of the classroom. At some point they must have tired themselves out, because the noise dimmed. I began to talk but was interrupted by music coming from Caleb's laptop. We all looked over at him as Queen sang out the chorus from "We Are the Champions." Before I knew it, the boys were singing along, swaying in their seats, waving their hands above their heads.

"So what you're saying, Caleb," I began, shouting over the music, "is that you'd like to go next?"

He looked at me, his face blank. "I don't think you want me to go next."

"I think I can handle it," I replied, leaning against a wall. "Go for it," I said, almost daring him.

"Fine," he replied, flashing his words on the smart board.

> My name is Agnes Parsons and I have a secret
> nobody knows.

I froze, looking down at my shoes and squeezing my eyes shut, trying to unsee what he had written. What was I thinking, daring this kid?

This kid had probably hacked his way into my phone. I'd overheard the science teachers saying that Caleb had broken through the school's firewall and sent emails from teachers' accounts. How could I be so stupid? Now everyone was going to know that not only was I not in possession of a traveling husband, but that I had basically been abandoned. They would know I was a liar. I looked back at the smart board.

> The secret is that I'm in love. It's a secret love. I love
> Gavin Burke even though I pretend not to. I love
> him because he's strong and manly and makes me
> feel tingly. I love him even though he's a total tool.
> I guess that makes me a tool, too.

I collapsed against the wall in relief, relief that was short-lived. Nobody knew about Jack. But since the Axe-in-the-face incident, when I'd failed to stand up to Gavin in front of the boys, I was just another one of his lackeys. I was no better than Stacey Figg, who quivered with delight at the mention of his name.

"You said five sentences, and I gave you seven. I think that makes me an overachiever," he said.

No, Caleb. That just makes you mean.

He stared at me. I could read right through his stare: *I dare you not to like me.*

I didn't have a response for him. So I just looked past him at the rest of the boys.

"It's that time again, boys," I said. "Do whatever you want." I slumped down into my chair and put my head down on the desk. I sat like that until the bell rang. After class I wandered through the halls, asking for directions to the teachers' lounge. *Jack,* I thought as I stumbled through the halls. *Where the hell are you? Why am I still here?* I walked down to the basement, which I had not known existed, and arrived at the room marked **Teachers' Lounge (No Students)**. Before I went inside, I pulled out my phone and texted Don: Long morning. Please tell me you have some news. I can't do this much longer.

Seconds later I got a response.

Just stay where you are, Agnes. Do your job. Ears open.

Really?

I squeezed my eyes shut and saw the word *Jack* in my head. I breathed slowly and concentrated on his name. If I couldn't have him, or even call him, at the very least I could think about him. I conjured up one of the best memories I could think of—the long weekend we'd spent in Cabo when I found out I was pregnant, the look on his face when I emerged from the hotel bathroom, pregnancy test in hand. I leaned against the door to the teachers' lounge and kept breathing. I didn't need to mark my first entrance by crumbling into a heap of tears.

Eventually, I pushed open the heavy wooden door and was immediately struck by the darkness. The room was void of all natural light. Once inside, I breathed in what smelled like a thousand TV dinners and old, stale coffee. The smell was salty and processed, and it reminded me briefly of the smell of my second foster family's kitchen. In the center of the dimly lit room was a round table and a few chairs that looked remarkably like the institutional chairs around the table in my town house. I identified two larger versions of my lumpy brown couch pushed up against the walls. In the back left corner stood the fridge, in the back right corner, the microwave, and on a dirty counter between the two, a coffeepot.

While I was taking it all in, Stacey Figg made her beeline.

"Agnes!" she shrieked. "Welcome!" All the other teachers awoke from their malaise and looked over at me. I smiled nervously and grasped at my shoulder bag.

"Hi," I blurted back. "I can't believe it took me so long to find this place."

"Yeah, well, we like to be where *they* can't find us," she said, rolling her eyes. "Let me introduce you around." She grabbed my arm and began ushering me around the room, introducing me to teachers whose names I knew I would never remember. I recognized a few faces from day care. I smiled at Ella, who held out a bag of rice cakes. I took one.

"Are you here for the staff meeting?" Stacey asked, ushering me around.

"What meeting?"

"Gavin sent out an email."

"Oh," I said. "I haven't checked email since last night." Stacey looked surprised and pulled out her phone. She showed me the email from Gavin. In the subject line were the words *Middle School Behavior Meeting—Mandatory!*

"Sit here," she said, pointing to the round table. "You can eat with us."

I looked at the table. There was an open bag of desiccated baby carrots that were more white than orange, several packets of soy sauce, one of which had oozed and crusted all over the top of the table, a couple of used chopsticks, and two empty cans of Diet Coke. Jack had banned baby carrots from the house. Something about bleach. I could not even remember anymore. *What am I doing in here?*

"I think I'll grab a cup of coffee," I lied, making my way to the back of the room. Clearly I was not one to be picky. Yesterday I had eaten an expired yogurt for lunch. But this was too much, even for me. I could only be expected to swallow so much grim. I leaned on the counter and watched more teachers file into the room. Finally, Gavin entered, wheeling in a mobile smart board. He scanned the room and stood in the front, arms crossed, legs in a wide stance. He nodded at Stacey, and she passed out handouts entitled BEHAVIOR LOG: NEW ONLINE SYSTEM FOR INPUTTING CLASS DISRUPTIONS AND OTHER INCIDENTS.

"You'll be receiving log-in information this week," Gavin announced. "I encourage you to familiarize yourself with the new format. I think you'll see it's much better than the old, and you'll understand why I spent so much time installing it."

"Tell us, Gavin," muttered a voice next to me, "how much time did you actually spend installing it?"

I hesitated at first, then slowly turned and saw a guy who didn't look much older than the students. He had the shock of dark hair that almost seemed to be a dress code around here. He turned to look at me. "I stand in the back on purpose," he whispered. "It affords me the luxury of making snarky comments."

"Funny," I whispered back. "Some of us stand in the back just so we can hear snarky comments."

"Adam," he said, leaning slightly toward me. "Tech. Which means I spent hours installing this stupid log."

"Agnes," I said. "English." I wanted to say something witty back, but I'd already used up my one witty line. "I don't get it," I said. "What is this, exactly?"

"It's a place for teachers to log behavioral incidents, you know, like classroom disruptions."

I didn't want to tell this guy that on some days, my class felt like one long disruption. If I had to start logging disruptions, I wouldn't even know where to start.

"Teachers have to fill out an online form for each incident. Sometime in the middle of seventh grade, Gavin prints up all the reports for each kid. Some of them are reams long. In the spring, for effect, he walks around to each homeroom class and personally delivers the pile of papers. The kids totally lose their shit." He paused, making sure nobody saw us talking. "Claims he does it to put them on notice—you know, let them know they won't get into high school if they don't see the error of their ways. Problem is, his stunt just makes the kids worse. It's a complete shit show around here come high school application time."

High school application was still a foreign concept to me. "Ugh," I groaned. "Poor kids."

He looked surprised. "You don't hear that a lot around here."

"Maybe not," I replied. "But if he knows this freaks them out, why do it?"

"That," he muttered back, "is the big question."

I sensed he was going to say more, but Gavin stared and smiled right at me. He seemed to be speaking directly to me. "All you have to do now is enter the following," he said, clicking a remote in his hand. On the screen of the smart board were the words *Date/Time Teacher on Duty Behavior Observed Action Taken*.

It looked pretty simple to me, and pretty harmless. What I couldn't figure out was how I would know when something amounted to an infraction. Was flying a paper airplane an infraction? Was sitting on the floor under your desk an infraction? Was playing music in the middle of class an infraction? How about playing catch with a shoe?

"This system has some cool features," said Gavin. "Now you can pull up a student's entire file and see what other classes aren't working for him. It also sends you a weekly summary of the infractions you've logged." Why did it sound like it was a game show and there was a prize for most infractions logged? Gavin did a few demonstrations on the screen, but I couldn't really follow. I must have closed my eyes for a second, because my head dropped down and I quickly snapped it back up again. Not surprisingly, Gavin was looking right at me.

"For those of us who are having a hard time paying attention," he said, forcing a smile in my direction, "I'll wrap this up. Please see me with any questions, and don't forget to download the mobile app." I could have sworn he winked at me.

The meeting ended, and teachers began to file out. Adam held the door for me. Because we'd been standing side by side, staring straight ahead to avoid getting caught chatting in the back, I hadn't really looked at him straight on before. His face was asymmetrical and his nose bent a little to the side. It wasn't an ugly face, necessarily; it was sweet, comfortable, friendly. I needed a friend on campus, besides Stacey Figg, and this seemed like the face of a friend.

"Give me a holler if you have any questions about the log," he said. "Tech support is down here in the basement. You know, underground, where we belong."

"I will," I promised. "Thank you." I smiled. Out of the corner of my eye, I saw Stacey and the teachers' lounge crew gathering around Gavin but eyeing me. Adam turned his head and followed my gaze.

"Gavin's minions," he said. "For some people"—he grinned impishly—"getting to redo middle school every year is a dream come true."

~

There was a note under my door when I got home. An exterminator had come but I wasn't around, so he left me a number to call. The very thought of an exterminator creeped me out, but a mouse population creeped me out even more. I took the number and made a mental note to thank Ruth if I saw her again, but given her comment to me at the supermarket, I was hoping not to see her again. *I've been cleaning up Jack's messes since before you were born.*

Beeks called me that night. We'd exchanged texts but hadn't really spoken since she took stock of my kitchen and found it severely lacking.

"How are the meat sticks?" she asked.

"Beeks!"

"I'm kidding! And I'm sorry, Aggie. The absolute last thing I want to do is bitch snack you."

"Huh? What's bitch snack?"

"Come on, it's gotta happen in LA, too. It's when another mom points out that you've provided your kids with inadequately nutritious food in an incredibly passive way. You know, like, 'Oh, I see Kyle loves those little power bars. Who doesn't love a sugary cookie?'"

"Ouch."

"Or, 'My little Hunter just wishes I'd give him processed cheese crackers like you send with Alec.'"

"That's rough," I said.

"Tell me about it. Seriously, I just can't keep up. Last month I learned that agave syrup is officially bad. I finally remember to buy it, so I can stop using sugar in the cookies I bake for snack day and getting the stink eye from the teachers, and some shitty mom tells me that nobody's using agave anymore. Some crap about glycemic whatever."

I knew all about the agave backlash. I was married to Jack.

"Beeks, I forgive you for bitch snacking me," I said. "I've forgotten about it, anyway. I'm too busy dealing with these kids who hate me."

"I thought they liked you."

"Not anymore. Apparently I'm just as bad as all the other people who let them down."

"I find that hard to believe. Buck up, Aggie. Maybe wear some more of those see-through sundresses. That should totally help your cause."

"I'm not so sure. Thanks to the veggie puff–meat stick diet and the fact that I haven't exercised since July, I'm pretty sure nobody wants to see what's underneath my dress."

"Oh, Aggie, you've clearly never been a middle school boy."

15

At the end of each day, I picked up Grace. Once a week, on our way home, we'd dart off campus to the supermarket. As I walked up to the store, I noticed the sign outside had changed. My heart leaped momentarily. Maybe the supermarket was under new management and would now be an organic wonderland. I probably wouldn't be able to afford much, but maybe, just maybe going to the supermarket would be something other than depressing. I ran through the automatic doors, pushing Grace ahead of me.

The minute I got inside, I knew I'd been wrong to hope. Nothing had changed. The lighting was still bright but grim, a layer of dust still covered everything in here, and the shelves were just as barren. Honestly, it looked like the fruit and vegetables had been grown in a Bronx toilet bowl. *I guess that makes them local.* I grabbed the last avocado on the shelf, a shriveled, black, sad thing, and some bananas and apples for Grace. I found something claiming to be chicken breast in the meat section along the back wall and then walked several aisles over to the middle of the store.

Jack had always warned me about the middle of the supermarket. Even at the best stores, the middle is where the processed crap lives. Stick to the perimeters, he said, and you'll be fine. I walked into the middle curiously, almost defiantly. Other than the baby aisle, the middle was unknown to me.

"Nobody has to know we were here," I said to Grace.

We walked past soda and stacks of disposable plates and silverware, and then I saw it: plastic wrap. Not just one type of plastic wrap, but colored plastic wrap in blue, yellow, and purple. I grabbed the boxes and threw them onto the top of the stroller and headed to check out.

We went home and ate a chicken dish I'd watched Sondra make a thousand times. She never tried showing me how. According to the old plan, I would never really need to know how to make it. But I was hungry. Hungrier than yogurt. Hungrier than rice cakes. Certainly hungrier than toddler fingers and veggie puffs. I heard Beeks's voice in my head and made enough chicken for a few more meals. I put the leftover chicken breast on a plate and pulled out the yellow plastic wrap. I tore off a sheet and spread it across the plate. The chicken suddenly looked jaundiced and wan, and I wondered if there was any food out there that looked better under a sheet of yellow plastic.

~

The next night, as Grace and I were walking home, I thought smugly about the dinner that waited for us in the fridge. Last night's leftovers were the closest I had come to meal planning, and while I wasn't exactly on top of my evenings yet, I was beginning to feel like at some point soon I might be. I threw open the front door and pulled Grace and her stroller backward up into the foyer. This was a New York trick I'd learned for navigating narrow doorways. I felt pleased with myself for the second time in five minutes. Leftovers for dinner and stroller tricks might be small things, but small things got me through the day.

The second I got inside the foyer and pulled the door shut, I knew that someone else was in the house. I froze, my heart thumping, my skin prickly with panic. I quickly yanked Grace out of her stroller and held her close to my chest. She whimpered.

"Hello?" I called, my voice quaking. Had I really been foolish to start feeling safer?

"You know," she said from the living room, "living with a deviant adolescent comes in handy." Beeks walked into the foyer and stood right in front of me. "You see, before kids I never knew how to pick a lock." With one hand she showed me a stretched-out bobby pin. With the other she reached for Grace, scooping her right out of my arms.

"You scared the shit out of me," I said, handing over Grace.

"Apologies," Beeks said as she took a step back to fully assess me. "Well"—she sniffed—"it certainly didn't take you long." She held a confused but surprisingly quiet Grace in her arms.

"Huh?"

"Your outfit. What did you do? Rob Ann Taylor? You look like the poster child for middle school teaching."

"I kind of had to. I couldn't keep wearing yoga gear to class."

"And your hair . . ."

"Yup," I said proudly. "Here it is." I pulled my hair out of its perma-bun and let it fall past my shoulders.

"Zees," she said, breaking into her first real, full-faced Beeks grin. She walked behind and picked up the back of my hair with her finger-tips. "Zees is good, Anyes." *Anyes* was how she pronounced my name when she spoke, as she was doing now, in the voice of Madame LaFolle, a character she'd created in college to assess our outfits before we left our dorm room. She continued to paw my hair, pulling strands closer to her face for examination. "What is zees, though? Zees color, it is . . . um, how you say it . . . a mouse?"

"Oui, madame," I said, taking her other hand in mine. "This is not just any old mouse. This is New York mouse. I thought you might like it." I looked at Beeks, my Beeks, and could not understand how I could ever be mad at her.

We both stood there staring at each other. Beeks turned, and she and Grace started walking into the living room. We all sat on the little brown couch, with Grace in between us, looking at each of us, like she was following a tennis match.

"You know," Beeks began, "you look healthy."

"Just say it, Beeks," I said. "By 'healthy,' you mean fat." I never thought I'd miss exercise, but I had forgotten what it felt like to want to move just for movement's sake. Everything I did now had a purpose.

"No. By healthy, I mean *healthy*. Besides, I like you better this way. This is how I remember you. This is the old you."

"Beeks, the old me is long gone. This is the New York me, the temporary me. This is the me that is waiting."

"What are you waiting for?" Beeks turned her full body to me, tucking her right leg underneath her.

"Jack." I sat up straight, determined not to be ashamed.

"Aggie, don't you think that there's a tiny bit of this version of you that's the authentic you?"

"The authentic me? Whoa, that's very LA of you." I smiled at Beeks. I needed to keep this conversation light, and accusing each other of being LA was an old, favorite pastime of ours. "The old me is . . . old. I'm not going back to that. I look like this because I have to. I don't have money to look any different, and honestly, I just want to fit in. But I am waiting for Jack. The authentic me is still married to Jack."

"So you're sure he's coming back?" Grace had climbed into Beeks's lap and was pulling at her coconut-flavored curls, jamming her fists into her mouth to taste them.

"Yes, I'm sure. I mean, I don't see him coming here, but at some point he'll send for me, and then I'll go home." I shifted on my couch cushion. I was relieved that I hadn't told Beeks that Jack had asked me to come here to try to get information for him. That was a whole line of questioning I wasn't sure I could handle.

"How do you know that?"

"I just know. Until I hear otherwise, I'm going with that. End of story." I hoped my firm tone would put her questions to bed.

"And you're not mad?" Beeks's questions, or so it seemed, were insomniacs.

"What do you mean?" I knew what she meant.

Beeks paused. I could see her thinking before she spoke. I got nervous. As a rule, Beeks did not think before she spoke.

"Listen, you can tell me you didn't marry him for his money, but you can't tell me it wasn't part of the attraction. You're telling me now that it's all gone you're not even a little bit angry?"

I looked at Beeks because I could not think of anything to say to her that I hadn't already. Turns out, Beeks didn't need me to respond, because she kept talking. She leaned back into the couch and let Grace sit in her lap. "I dunno, Agnes. When a woman marries a guy *partly* for his money and the money vanishes, usually she's a lot more pissed off."

I was breathing through Beeks's words. I was breathing so loudly I could hear myself, but she just kept talking.

"This guy promised to look after you, and he goes and steals some money, sends you here, goes AWOL, and you don't seem to be angry. I just don't get it. I get madder when I lose a parking spot."

I sat in silence, grateful that Grace could not yet understand us.

"Of course I'm angry," I said, looking down and plucking at the thread on the hem of my shirt. "At first I was a little angry, and with each day that I don't hear from him, I just get angrier." I forced myself to look at her. "I hate what he did, and I hate that I don't really know what he did. There's so much I hate about this, Beeks. But I don't want to hate Jack. I just can't." I looked back down at my shirt, which began to unravel. "I have a job to do, and I have Grace, and if I start hating Jack, I'm gonna fall apart. I can't fall apart, Beeks."

We sat in silence for a few minutes, both staring at anything but each other. I mumbled something about dinner and leftovers, but Beeks would have none of it.

"Tonight," she announced, standing up, "tonight, we dine out."

I hadn't eaten in a single restaurant since I'd arrived here. With Jack, restaurants had been part of our everyday lives, part of our currency. He'd book restaurants weeks in advance, planning our vacations around our reservations. The idea of someone else making food and putting it in front of me, only to clear it all away at the end, nearly drove me to tears.

"Brian has a pub up here he loves," Beeks said. With her free hand, she pulled me off the couch, and the three of us walked out into the darkening autumn.

~

The walk to the pub took us through the North Riverdale neighborhood surrounding St. Norbert's. Like campus, the area was hilly. Until that evening, I had only ventured up and down the main street. I didn't know there were houses so close by. The houses were small and boxy, most of them attached row houses like mine. It was hard to see the houses, though, because nearly all of them were plastered with Halloween decorations. When I was growing up, Halloween decorations had been a pumpkin, just one, and never carved. It was always a sad sort of affair, a last-minute, marked-down purchase.

Halloween was the closest Santa Monica came to an official religion. People who believed nothing believed in the sanctity of hiring a decorator to turn their house into a gothic wonderland from October 1 to November 1. People who shunned organized, formalized worship of any kind whipped themselves into a dogmatic frenzy of outdoing their neighbors by transforming already impressive homes into movie sets. I am not exaggerating when I say I once saw a house with singing, mechanized butlers, all dressed like extras from an *Addams Family* movie.

Never to be outdone, Jack hired a team of decorators to hang fake yet lifelike bats, gossamer cobwebs, and electric candles. But Jack had his Halloween limits. He refused to hang anything that suggested death or decay, or possibly even advanced age. My first year in the house, I thought it might be fun to hang skeletons or turn our porch into a graveyard, but Jack would not hear of it. No hollowed-out faces or RIP signs came near our home. Jack did order several pumpkins to arrive, precarved. Although the decorations were up for a full month, the pumpkins arrived on October 29 and promptly disappeared on November 1. Precarved pumpkins rot quickly, and rot screams decay.

North Riverdale also embraced Halloween, although in a far more DIY manner than Santa Monica. Weather-beaten witches perched precariously on rooftops, presumably saving the spot for Santa, who would replace them in a few weeks' time. Thick, gauzy, cottony cobwebs coated the bushes and hedges, and gravestones popped up in all the small, boxy front yards. The few trees in front of houses had ghosts, plastic skeletons, and bats hanging from thin, aggravated branches. It was getting dark, but I could have sworn I saw a grim reaper in a window and blood oozing down the side of one of the bigger houses. The decorations were fun, almost joyous in their creepiness, and I would have missed them completely if not for that walk with Beeks.

I also would have missed this Irish pub. I'd never been in any kind of pub before. Pubs weren't Jack's thing, and frankly, I'd heard the pubs in Santa Monica were full of British expats (there were many of them) who wanted to eat their fish and chips, watch their soccer, and still be able to walk out into the sunshine, something they could not do "at home." One of the baby-group moms was from London. She loved those pubs but never invited any of us to go. Those pubs didn't do outreach. They were comfort for people far from home. I was far from home now. I wondered where I was supposed to find comfort.

Beeks could see that I had drifted off into self-pity. She could see it right on my face and maybe read it in my slouch. She hooked her arm through mine. "Buck up," she said. "Let's go eat some greasy food together."

Greasy it was. She ordered a side of something called shepherd's pie for Grace, which was, as far as I could tell, mashed potatoes on top of ground beef. Grace sucked down the entire plate in five minutes. The pub was dark, and there was music coming from somewhere. It didn't sound live, but I wasn't sure. Beeks ordered a beer. I'd never been much of a beer drinker, and I'd been dying for a glass of wine that was not from a dusty bottle with little pieces of floating cork. I ordered a glass of the house red and almost hugged the waiter who brought it to me. I nearly leaped out of my chair when he brought our food. I couldn't remember the last time anyone had brought me food. Beeks and I ate burgers. I didn't even know if they still sold hamburger buns in LA anymore—all our burgers had been in wilting but defiant lettuce wraps.

Over dinner, we talked about everything but Jack. We talked about school, and Beeks filled me in on her life. Work was hectic; her boss was threatening to make her share an office with a younger colleague whose boobs allegedly stood up on their own. Brian was working long hours, and Beeks got yanked into school at least once a week to sit in the principal's office with one of her boys. While she was resigned to all of it, the balancing was weighing her down. But here's the thing—for the first time in a long while, I actually had something to match Beeks's struggles. Before, when she'd talked about the balancing, I sat in my enormous staffed house with my one child and no job other than to look cute, stay thin, and show up, and felt inconsequential. Now I actually had something to talk about—I had day-care stories, sleep issues, and job drama. True, I'd have traded it all in for Jack and my old life. But for the time being, it felt good to be able to return fire.

I told Beeks about my boys, Gavin, and the ever-present Stacey Figg, and sure enough, as we walked up the stairs to my house after dinner, Stacey emerged from her own house.

"Uh-oh," whispered Beeks. "I believe I am about to meet the Figg."

"Stacey." I smiled. "Everything OK?"

"I was about to ask you the same thing," she said, closing her door behind her. "It's not like you to go out at night, and I wanted to make sure everything was all right."

"Did you now?" Beeks muttered under her breath. I shot her a look. Beeks's mutter was never as quiet as she thought it was.

"All good here," I said. "Just having dinner with a friend."

Stacey's eyes fixed on Beeks. I had no choice but to introduce them. "Stacey, this is Beeks. Beeks, this is Stacey. Stacey Figg."

"No shit," Beeks said through her teeth. I elbowed her.

"We work together," Stacey announced proudly, raising her chin and crossing her arms over her chest. "Do you live around here?" she asked, walking down her steps and coming over to us.

"No," said Beeks. "I live in the city. Just visiting."

"How do you guys know each other?" She took another step closer to us so that she was almost standing between us and my front door.

"Old friends," said Beeks. "Old, tired friends." She looked at me. "I think I need to be getting home. Brian is away, and last week Stevie took the sitter's phone and messed with the autocorrect. Every time she tried to type 'Hi,' it corrected to 'Bite me.'"

Stacey's eyes grew wide in disbelief and disgust.

"Nice meeting you," Beeks said, cutting off any further questioning. She ushered Grace and me into my foyer. As soon as we were inside, before Stacey was out of earshot, Beeks declared, "Wow, you weren't kidding about the Figg."

"Beeks, hush. She hears everything."

Beeks laughed and followed me upstairs to put down an overtired Grace. She was asleep before I had even rolled her down into the crib. I bent down to kiss her forehead.

Before she left, Beeks reached into her giant purse and handed me a package. "For Grace. Get it?" she asked as I opened the plastic bag, releasing a pair of pink fairy wings. Glitter flew out of the bag and onto the floor. I tried not to think about cleaning it up. "She's a Fairy Freeze employee!" Beeks yelled, very proud of herself.

"I get it, Beeks," I said. "And I love that you bought her these." She must have known I'd completely forgotten about a Halloween costume for Grace.

"And with that," Beeks said, opening the front door, "I must be on my way. Happy early Halloween."

"Happy early Halloween," I replied, returning her hug and locking the door behind her, unlocking it and locking it again.

Halloween. I did not know it then, but on Halloween, Jack would finally reach out.

Just not to me.

-16-

Halloween was on a Saturday this year, so in-school festivities took place the day before. On the morning of October 30, Gavin announced the middle school candy policy: there would be none.

"This is Principal Burke," he declared that morning over the loudspeaker.

"He doesn't need to announce himself," said a voice from behind me in the hall. "Nobody else uses the loudspeaker."

I turned around. "Hey, Adam," I said. "Happy almost-Halloween."

Gavin's amplified voice continued: "Just a friendly reminder that any costumes are subject to approval by the administration. Also, any candy found on a student today will be confiscated."

"That man . . . ," I said.

"Tell me about it. I'm assuming you skimmed his forty-page trick-or-treating manifesto?"

"Um, I saw it," I said, shaking my head. "But no, I never read it. How does trick-or-treating work for the kids?"

"They can go chaperoned up and down Main Street, and there's a party for them in the gym. Other than that, only faculty families trick-or-treat on campus."

"All of which I would have known had I bothered to read the manifesto," I joked.

"Listen, tomorrow night some of us are going out for a drink," he said as kids wove around us in the hall. "Wanna join? No costume required."

"Oh, I wish I could. But I can't miss Grace's first Halloween. Besides, I don't have a sitter," I said. "Maybe next time."

"Sure thing, Agnes," he said, checking his phone for the time.

I glanced at my watch. Class started in two minutes. "I gotta run, but thanks—another time!" I called as I ran to class.

~

"Principal Jerk sent out an email with a long list of rules about costumes," Guy said from behind his laptop. "He does it every year."

"He's a total dick," said Caleb.

"Caleb," I said, warning him. It was one thing for me to overlook the "Principal Jerk" comment. I had to draw the line somewhere.

"Yeah," said Davey, who had just walked into class, both shoes on but untied. "We call it the why-bother email, because, you know, why bother with Halloween if we can't eat candy and he has to approve our costumes?"

"Let's do something fun today," I said, hoping to distract them from their Halloween misery. "We have a lot to cover in the memoir unit, but I want to warm up with a couple of prompts. Today you're asking the questions, and I'll do my best to write five sentences for each one. I want you to see what it's like to be the one asking, because writing a good memoir is about asking the right questions. OK?" I did not wait for their approval. "Guy, you go first."

Guy looked nervous. He shifted in his seat. "What about rules?" he asked. "What's off-limits?"

"Sexy stuff," giggled Davey. He blushed and looked down.

"Just the usual," I said. "I think you guys know what's off-limits, but I'd like to thank Davey for giving us some parameters." He blushed harder.

I sat for a few minutes and then called on Guy again.

"Here is something that nobody knows about me," he read from his screen and then looked up at me.

"OK," I said. "Give me a minute." I typed something out on my own laptop and then read it aloud.

"There is something that nobody knows about me. I am addicted to veggie puffs. Veggie puffs are technically a baby food, but I can't eat enough of them. I love the light, puffy airiness and the way they melt in my mouth as the flavor explodes. I especially love the sweet potato and the kale-strawberry puffs. Combining kale and strawberry is nothing short of genius."

I realized I probably had some puffs in my bag. Sure enough, when I reached down into it, my hand fell upon a can. I fished it out and held it up high. "Behold, veggie puffs!" I cracked open the can, stuffed a handful in my mouth, and passed them around.

Davey jammed a large portion of puffs into his face and was the first to gag. "Ms. P., these are gross," he said, choking.

"No joke," said Guy, who was picking at the puffs one at a time.

"They may be gross at first, but after a few cans, they start to taste good. Really good. And then, after about ten cans or so, they are all you can think about."

Art was throwing puffs directly into Caleb's mouth. "These things suck," he said, "but thanks for sharing your food with us."

"Yeah," said Caleb, chewing. "They may be nasty, but they're better than the popcorn we steal from the teachers' lounge." All the boys nodded in approval.

I knew I had to move quickly to get in as many boys as possible, so I called on the boys in the front row one by one. Davey asked me to write about my earliest memory, which I thought was pretty insightful for a boy who was barely capable of dressing himself.

"My first memory is of my parents pushing me in a swing," I said. "The hard part about living in Southern California, if there is a hard part, is that you can't place a memory in a time of year. I remember the flat wooden seat of the swing, and I remember sunshine. But sunshine could have been at any time of the year. I remember I was wearing shorts and sandals, but that could have been in June or November." I stopped for a moment. I hadn't thought about that swing in a long time, but it was there, right atop my memory pile, waiting for Davey's prompt.

I answered as many of the boys' questions as I could. I worked my way through the class, saving Caleb for last, in case he decided to derail the assignment. "Caleb?" I asked, looking right at him.

"Well, I was gonna ask why you smile at us so much," he said. He wasn't smiling. I read the familiar expression on his face: *I dare you not to like me.*

I stared back, and this time I was ready with my own expression. *You can't make me not like you. So stop trying.*

He looked at me, confused. Guy filled the awkward silence. "Yeah, how come you smile at us the way the other teachers smile at Johnny Stark?"

"Yeah," said Art. "Even when we're getting into trouble."

"Dude," laughed Davey. "When are we not getting into trouble?" He reached out to his friends. High fives all around.

Johnny Stark was a student of mine in another class and one of the few fully functioning middle schoolers at St. Norbert's. He was, from what I could tell, a sweet, compliant, uncomplicated boy. He was, above all else, a personal favorite of Gavin's. In fact, he was a member of a group of five or six boys on whom Gavin seemed to dote and constantly praise, often in earshot of as many teachers and students as possible.

"Anyone can smile at Johnny Stark. It's pretty easy to smile at a kid who does exactly what he's asked to do, when he's asked to do it, who makes you feel like you're succeeding every day." The boys in the front row squirmed in their seats. "If you ask me, teachers are supposed to smile at all the kids, but especially at the kids who are sometimes harder to smile at." I was nervous. By answering this way, I was being more honest with the boys than I probably should have been. I was acknowledging that sometimes they made it hard to like them. I thought about smiling at little Ronan at Sunny Day every time he peed under the slide right in front of me. "I think it's important to smile bigger at you guys, so I do. I smile bigger."

The boys grinned, even Caleb, despite himself. At the end of class, I said to the boys, "Happy almost-Halloween. Have fun. Eat candy when nobody is looking."

I was feeling oddly celebratory.

17

The next evening, I put Grace in her fairy wings, stuck my tongue out to make her smile (worked every time), and took a picture to send to Beeks. I'd stocked up on candy, which I hadn't bought in years. Jack handed out gourmet lollipops to the trick-or-treaters who came to our door in Santa Monica. Some of them were kid friendly—vanilla bean, chocolate, caramel—but not all. I was never really sure that little kids could appreciate a latte-flavored lollipop, but it was not for me to comment. The pops, like so much else, were a tradition that preceded me.

After an early dinner, I put on the porch light and Grace and I waited for trick-or-treaters. We lay on the floor in front of the brown couch. Grace turned to face me, then rolled my way, over and over until she got to me. We rolled together until we hit the wall, then we rolled all the way back across the room, this time with Grace in the lead, both of us giggling. At some point I got winded and rolled Grace onto my stomach. "That was hard work," I said. "I definitely need more exercise." She put her head down and rested on my chest. We lay like that until she got antsy and began rolling again, this time on her own.

When nobody arrived by five thirty, I tore open the bag of Butterfingers and ate three. But three is an odd number, so I ate a fourth to even things out. At five forty-five, I ate four more, to be truly even. But eight is an odd sort of even number, so at 5:50, I jammed two more in my mouth. Two families of trick-or-treaters showed up, so I reluctantly parted with a handful of Butterfingers. At six, by the time the rush of trick-or-treaters finally arrived, I had finished the Butterfingers as well as half a bag of mini Twix. A few faculty families with middle schoolers, some of whom I taught, came. I also recognized some day-care families. It was jarring to see the husbands who went with the moms I knew. Ella's husband had a goatee and tattoo. I wondered if they were real or part of a costume. I handed out what little candy I had left. I then tore open a sack of Junior Mints, which was easy because I never liked Junior Mints. No one does. I dumped the little boxes into the plastic pumpkins of about twenty kids who showed up.

As the kids left, Stacey Figg came running up my stairs. She was wearing a black unitard and had wound yellow crepe paper around herself. A headband with two black fuzzy balls attached to springs was clamped down over her hair.

"A bumblebee!" she announced. With each step I worried that she'd make a sudden wrong move and tear the crepe paper. "Did I miss anything?" she asked, breathless.

"No, so far there have only been a few trick-or-treaters," I said.

"You should have just left a bowl of candy out so you could have come to the faculty happy hour," she said.

"Maybe next year," I muttered, secretly praying that this time next year I'd be handing out gourmet lollipops in Santa Monica.

"Never mind," she said, straightening the crepe paper that had bunched around her midsection. "I'm home now, and we can keep an eye on each other." She wasn't wrong. With each knock on the door, I knew I'd be seeing her outside, doling out enormous candy bars from a giant pillowcase covered in pumpkins, as she eyed my diminishing stash of bite-size candy. I felt my phone buzz in my pocket. When I got back inside, I saw a text from Adam.

Happy Halloween!

He had texted me a picture of three math teachers dressed as three different kinds of pie, with the numbers three, one, and four on their chests. I texted him a picture of my pile of candy wrappers.

At seven, when what appeared to be the last of the trick-or-treaters left, I looked over at Stacey, who was standing on her doorstep holding a handful of enormous Butterfingers. I felt queasy looking at them.

"Good night, Aggie," she said.

"Good night," I replied, hopefully for the last time. I had consumed a frenzy of sugar. Exhausted but jittery, I carried Grace upstairs, put a clean diaper and a pair of warm pajamas on her, and rolled her down into her crib. I congratulated myself on getting her down without her crying and left her room.

I walked down into the kitchen. Maybe a glass of wine would undo the sugar damage and help me unwind. Before I'd filled the glass to the top (don't judge), my phone buzzed again.

Don.

Call me.

My hand trembled, and I picked up the phone to call him but was interrupted by a knock. I opened the door to a pirate, a prisoner, and three Batmans. Stacey jumped out of her house. She had abandoned the crepe paper and headband and was just wearing her unitard.

"Hey, boys," I said. One of the Batmans took off her mask.

"Not a boy," she said.

"Oh. OK then, hey, kids," I said, without a trace of enthusiasm. "I don't have much left, but you can take what I have." My hand still trembling, I reached behind me to what remained of my candy stash and handed it to the girl. "You can divvy it up or go next door," I said, looking over at an expectant Stacey, her pillowcase in hand. "Happy Halloween." I closed the door before they could respond. I had things to do that did not involve small people, candy, and confusing costumes.

I called Don. He picked up after one ring.

"Agnes," he said.

"What is it?"

"I have news from Jack."

I fell back onto the brown couch. "Is it time?" I asked. I could hear myself breathing.

"Time for what?"

"Time for me to come home, Don. It's almost November. I've been here for two months."

Now it was Don's breathing I could hear, not mine.

"Don?" I asked. "What's going on?"

"You are not going back to LA in the immediate future." He was breathing loudly but speaking quietly, more quietly with each word, so that by the time he got to the end of the sentence, I could barely hear him.

I sat upright. "What do you mean?"

"Jack is coming to New York," he said.

"Really?" My voice jumped an octave. "That's great!" As soon as I said that and the words hung over me in a bubble, I wondered just how great it would be to have Jack living with me, the brown couch, and the mouse population.

"Actually," he began, "there's a little more to it."

"Don." I sighed. "When is there ever not?" Silence. Rhetorical questions were more than Don could handle. "What are you trying to tell me?"

"Jack is coming to New York, he's just not coming to you. Not yet. He'll be somewhere in Manhattan. Soon." He completely ignored the second part of my question. I can't say I was surprised.

"How soon is soon?" I asked.

"I don't know. He just said soon."

I closed my eyes and saw the word in black: *Soon*.

"What else? What else did he say?"

"The money trouble," he said. "He owes a lot of it. More than I thought. Agnes, if I hear more, I promise to call you."

"Thank you," I said. "I guess this is better than nothing."

"One more thing," he said, sounding like he wished he didn't have to say anything at all.

"What?"

"He wants me to tell you he loves you. He loves you and he misses you both."

Although this was Don's voice, these were Jack's words. They were the first words I'd heard from him since I spoke to him from the road. I let the words sink in and sat back on the couch, trying to find something to say. Luckily, I was rescued by a knock on the door. Then the bell rang. Then it rang again. I ran to the door and pulled it open, hoping Grace hadn't woken up.

"No. More. Candy," I barked at a group of three kids who looked too old to be asking strangers for candy. I started to close the door, and then Barack Obama took off his mask.

"Ms. Parsons, it's us," Davey said. "Something happened."

Art took off a Darth Vader mask to reveal a tuft of red hair and a panicked face. "It's Guy. We don't know where he is." His voice was shaking.

Don's voice spoke out from my phone. "Agnes, what's going on? Are you there?"

I put the phone to my ear. "Don, I have a . . . situation here. I'll call you soon."

Before I hung up, Don said, "Keep your phone with you at all times. Jack may be calling."

The boys were staring at me. I looked around, double-checking Stacey Figg's front door and bay window. When I didn't see anything, I pulled them in as quickly as I could, breaking about a million rules. I ushered in the three boys, the third of whom was a terrified-looking

Caleb, holding a brown paper bag with eyes cut out. He saw me looking at it.

"Oh, yeah," he explained. "It was the first thing I could find."

I closed the door behind them, and we stood huddled in the foyer. I heard a door slam outside. I prayed it wasn't Stacey Figg.

"OK, boys. Why don't you tell me what's going on."

Art and Davey looked at Caleb, their eyes begging him to take charge, or at the very least, to talk first. "Guy is missing," he said. "He got into trouble at the end of the day yesterday and was thrown out of math. The Jerk called him in today. Last time we saw him, he was in the Jerk's office."

I looked at the boys and tried to think of how to help. I couldn't call Gavin and ask him where Guy was, because then Gavin would know that he was missing, and he'd want to know how I knew. "Boys, do you think it's possible that he is still with Principal Burke?"

"No, definitely not," Caleb said. "We saw the Jerk in the dining hall, and we ran by his office on our way here. It was dark and empty."

"Think!" cried Art, his voice cracking. "Where is he?" I put my hand on his arm and squeezed it lightly.

"OK," I said. "Art. You have younger sisters, right?"

"Yes." He sniffled.

"Great. Grace is asleep. She won't wake up. But if she does, sing 'You Are My Sunshine' and rub her back. We'll be home soon." Art looked like I had just slapped him, but he nodded and didn't move when I led Davey and Caleb out the front door. I grabbed my coat off a hook. "Masks on, boys. We don't want to raise suspicions." I realized I didn't need to be spotted, either, so before he could object, I snatched the Darth Vader mask from Art's hands and put it on my head. Davey and Caleb did the same, and the three of us made our way out into the night.

I stuck my head out over the threshold, and when I was sure Stacey was not at her window, we left, walking quietly. Every so often one of the two boys would whisper, "Over here," and we'd check out another potential hiding spot. We looked in all the places I'd think to look— near the benches in the rose garden, behind the giant glacial rocks that dominated the lawn that ran the length of the campus.

"I think we need to check the Virgin," said Caleb.

"Excuse me?"

"The Virgin Mary. She's up at the entrance, near the pond and the bridges." I'd often walked the bridges with Grace and thrown stale veg-gie puffs (yes, it happens) to the bulging, nuclear goldfish in the pond below. Inside a small alcove was a statue of the Virgin Mary, surrounded by tall glass candles that always seemed to be lit. I had never gone in. It was too intimate, and frankly, a little creepy. Clearly I was not alone in this.

"Ugh, really?" asked Davey. "That place gives me the creeps. I don't think he's there. Besides, it's Halloween. That place is gonna be even more scary tonight. What if the drowned kid is there? Huh? What about the drowned kid?"

Caleb looked back at me. "Back when this was a Catholic school," he explained, "they say there was a boy who drowned in the pond. On Halloween. A priest was hurting him, and he drowned himself." He stopped to look around. "But it's probably not true."

"I'll go with you," I told them. I walked quickly and made sure I stayed in between the two of them. We walked along the main road until we came to the bridges. I could feel Davey faltering beside me. I grabbed his hand. Another rule down. "Davey," I said, "I can go ahead, and you guys can stay here. Would that be OK?"

"I wanna go, too," said Caleb. "If he's here, I wanna find him. Davey, you don't wanna be alone here. Come with us." Davey nodded his assent, and the three of us walked over the first bridge and turned into the alcove. All the candles were lit. The Virgin Mary stood among them, her arms outstretched, her smile wan and expressionless. Behind her, an imposing shadow version of herself took up the entire back wall.

I leaned in and looked behind her but didn't see Guy. We backed out and walked over the second bridge. From the middle of the bridge, we heard crying.

"It's him," whispered Caleb. "I hear him. That's Guy." We stopped on the bridge and looked down into the water.

My God, I thought, leaning over the edge. *Virgin Mary, if you have any power here, please let me not see Guy down in the water.*

We still couldn't see Guy, but we heard him. We walked across the bridge and down under it, toward the water. There, sitting on his knees, rocking back and forth, was Guy, tiny and shivering in a T-shirt and basketball shorts. He looked up. Caleb ran over and sat down right next to Guy, wrapping his arms around him. Guy was small, so much smaller than Caleb that he seemed to almost disappear in Caleb's arms. Davey and I stood back.

"Dude, Guy. It's OK. We're here." But Guy kept rocking and crying. He spoke finally.

"My dad's gonna kill me this time. He's really gonna kill me."

I walked down to the two boys and knelt right in front of them. I took off my coat, threw it over Guy's scrawny shoulders, and put my hands on his knees.

"Why?" I asked. "What happened?"

"Principal Burke," he said in between sobs. "Last week he said that if I got another detention, he'd call my dad. As soon as he said I shouldn't get another detention, I just couldn't help myself. It was like I just *had* to go and do something dumb. He's calling my dad on Monday."

"And what happens when he calls your dad?" I asked. Davey had now walked down and was sitting cross-legged beside me. I had never seen him so still. He was almost unrecognizable. The four of us huddled together, to avoid the wind that had picked up and to keep from being seen.

"Principal Burke calls a conference and tells my parents what a loser I am. Then my dad goes nuts." He cried more, even harder.

"His dad is tough," Caleb said. "Really tough." He looked at Guy, and I could see him thinking. Guy's eyes grew wide, and he reached up to wipe away tears. I saw light bruises on his arm. Without thinking, I put my hand on them.

"Guy, what is this? What's going on? Did your dad do this?"

"No, those are from his growth hormone shots," Caleb answered. Guy was still staring at Caleb, letting him do the talking. "His dad makes him take them a few times a week. He thinks he's not growing fast enough."

"His dad is pretty tall," added Davey. "But his mom is short. His dad is worried he'll be short, too."

"It got worse after I started taking the other medicine." Guy paused. "The doctor gave me something for my ADD. I stopped being hungry and my dad said the ADD pills were slowing my growth, and that's when I started the hormone shots." He looked down at his knees, my hands still on them. I was getting stiff kneeling, so I rocked onto my backside and put my hands on my own knees.

"What if I talk to Principal Burke?" I said. "What if I ask him not to call your dad?"

"He won't listen," said Caleb. "He loves conferencing with our parents. They do anything he says as long as he doesn't send us home. They don't want us at home. None of them do."

"That man," groaned Davey, "is a total bag of douches."

Caleb, Guy, and I laughed. "Let me try," I said, waiting for our giggling to die out. "Maybe I can sit in on the meeting. I can make an excuse. You know, I'll tell Principal Burke I want to learn from him." The boys looked at me. "Would that be OK?"

Guy nodded, and the four of us stood up.

"I promise I'm going to help you," I said, looking down at Guy. "Trust me." He nodded and smiled through his tears.

"You better watch out or people are gonna think you actually like us," said Guy.

I smiled and wrapped my arms around myself. Feeling useful was still so new to me.

"Let's rescue Art from babysitting duty and get you boys back," I said. We crossed back over the bridge, and I nodded as we passed the alcove, in a secret thanks to Mary and her candles. *Thank you for keeping Guy safe.*

I needed to get us all home. I'd deal with Gavin on Monday.

18

On Monday morning, the boys were still jittery. I was sure some of them had eaten candy—and only candy—all weekend. When you ban Halloween candy in school, you just have to assume that your students are going to spend every second they can, both in school and out, scarfing it down with abandon.

Of course, my four boys had reason to squirm. Caleb and Guy stopped by my desk after class. Caleb's green eyes were darting around, looking at the door, at me, then the door again.

"Any news, Ms. Parsons?"

"I'm going now," I said. "The meeting hasn't happened yet. Before class, I went to see Principal Jerk—I mean, Burke"—the boys smiled—"and he was in his office meeting with the math team." I stood up. "I'm going to find him now."

I left the boys and walked down a flight of stairs to Gavin's office. The office was empty and the lights were off. I panicked. Could he be meeting with Guy's parents now? Had I missed my chance to find him? When I could convince my feet to unroot themselves from the floor, I spun around and ran straight into Adam. I stumbled backward.

"Hey," he said. "You OK?"

"I need to find Gavin," I said. "It's important."

"I just saw him setting up for a meeting in the conference room on the ground floor," Adam said. "Everything all right?"

"Kind of." I didn't think the meeting would be happening so soon. I thought I'd have time to plan for it, to think about what I was going to say. Hell, I at least wanted to be wearing a clean shirt. I looked down and saw a clump of Grace's cereal clinging to the hem of my blouse.

"He's meeting with some parents now, and I think I need to be in on it," I said.

"Word of advice," Adam warned me. "Try not to interrupt him. Even if he is saying literally the dumbest shit you've ever heard, let him finish. He goes nuts when someone cuts him off."

"Good to know," I said. "I'll try to keep that in mind. Wish me luck," I called as I ran down another two flights of stairs to the ground floor. Sure enough, I looked through the wall of glass along the conference room and saw Gavin sitting with a couple who could only have been Guy's parents. I wanted to stand and stare for a few minutes, but I didn't have a few minutes to spare, so I reached into my bag, grabbed a handful of sweet potato puffs, swallowed them whole, and charged into the meeting.

Gavin looked up as I pushed myself through the door. "Agnes, can I help you?"

"Hi," I said, trying to give myself time to think and swallow the puffs. I looked at the couple at the table and addressed them directly. "I'm Agnes Parsons. I teach your son." I ran my tongue over my teeth to remove all traces of food.

"Agnes," said Gavin, with far less patience in his voice, "I don't know what you're doing here, but this meeting isn't open to teachers. Why don't you and I talk later?" He said the word *later* through clenched teeth. I noticed he was wearing a long-sleeved shirt. His eyes were the same, though, mismatched and intense. It was hard to look at them but harder to look away.

"I'd really like to sit in, Gavin." I used the neediest voice I could muster, the voice I used when I wanted something from Jack that he didn't want to give me. It was the voice I'd used for the If-I-Die folder. Hopefully I'd have more luck this time.

"Fine," he said, his teeth still clenched, a forced smile on his face. "Let me introduce you to Mr. and Mrs. Martin." He motioned to the impeccably dressed couple sitting next to each other on one side of the table. Mrs. Martin looked so much like Guy—small and thin, with dark, shiny hair and big brown eyes. She wore a gray cashmere sweater set, her hair in a neat twist, a gold lariat around her neck, and an enormous pair of diamonds in her ears. I momentarily thought about my own diamond studs and wondered who was wearing them now. Mr. Martin was tall and broad, and his hair was lighter, a thick sandy brown. He wore a sports jacket over a checked shirt and thin navy cashmere sweater. Neither of them smiled. Mrs. Martin looked birdlike and terrified, a look I had seen so many times on her son. Her husband stared at me, a look of annoyance crossing his face. I waited for Gavin to introduce me. The less I said, the better.

"Mr. and Mrs. Martin, this is Agnes Parsons, Guy's English teacher. Apparently she would like to join us."

Neither of the Martins said a word or reached to shake my hand. I took a seat opposite them, on the other side of Gavin, who presided from the head of the table.

"As I mentioned to you on the phone, we feel that Guy's behavior has reached a new low. Just to list a few of the highlights," he said, lingering sarcastically on that last word and opening a manila folder in front of him, "Guy frequently skips class, is often found hiding in the bathroom or the lunchroom, and when he does come to class, it's usually long after class has started."

Mrs. Martin opened her mouth, but no words came out. Gavin marched on.

"Honestly, attendance is only one part of the problem, a much larger problem. Let's see," he said, riffling through the folder, "he has a serious problem completing schoolwork. Well, I shouldn't really say problem—it's more like an unwillingness. I've spoken to all his teachers, and it seems he has barely done any work this semester."

I wanted to say something, but I remembered Adam's words and let Gavin finish his sentence. Had he spoken to all—or any—of the teachers? He certainly hadn't spoken to me. It was true that Guy hadn't completed all the work I'd assigned, but frankly, none of the boys had. I'd only just learned that the boys paid Miles Wahler, a quiet kid who sat in the back and drummed on his desk, five dollars each to read *The Red Scarf Girl* and tell them what happened.

"Maybe this is a good time for me to say something," I said.

"Not yet, Ms. Parsons," Gavin shot back through a forced smile. "Not quite yet."

"Then there are the continued disruptions in class," he went on. "When Guy does feel like showing up, he likes to disrupt the class as much as possible. Many teachers report that they have no choice but to throw him out of class for the sake of the other students."

This wasn't true at all. I'd heard from his other teachers that Guy spent many classes on an extended bathroom break, but I hadn't heard a single teacher say he was disruptive. He certainly wasn't the most disruptive kid in class. If anything, on some days he wasn't disruptive enough—he often sat in class sullen, almost catatonic.

"So you see," said Gavin, "we have a problem here. Before we take any further steps, we wanted to fill you in."

Mrs. Martin looked right at me. "What were you going to say?" she asked.

I didn't wait for Gavin's permission to speak. "What I wanted to say was that I really do think he wants to do well. He doesn't want to cut class. He doesn't want to get into trouble."

"Then why is he?" asked Mr. Martin. "Why is he cutting class if he doesn't want to? You're not making any sense."

I had to get back in before Gavin cut me out. "He wants to do well, Mr. Martin. I really believe it. He just may not know how."

Mr. Martin looked at Gavin and silently threw up his hands. Without even looking at Gavin, I knew he was glaring at me. I looked at Mrs. Martin, whose eyes had filled with tears. She began to nod.

"What do you mean, he doesn't know how?" she asked.

I looked at her as if we were the only two people in the room. "What I mean is . . . that for Guy this is kind of like not being able to do math or read well. He doesn't know how to be in class and not be nervous. He goes to the bathroom and hides because he's scared. I think Guy is so terrified of messing up that he slowly falls apart during the day." Mrs. Martin nodded, and I kept talking, refusing to look at Gavin. "The good news is that he wants to do well, which means we can help him do well. Does that make sense?"

She nodded some more and then turned to her husband. "Phillippe," she began, "maybe it's all the medication . . ."

But he would hear nothing from her, or from me. "Laura, we didn't send him all the way up here to be coddled," he said in French-accented English, so that "coddled" sounded like "cuddled." By the look of things, Mr. Martin didn't believe much in either coddling or cuddling. "Soft doesn't work for him. The boy needs consequences, real consequences." He looked at Gavin, who nodded in approval. Mr. Martin had just said one of Gavin's favorite words, and he'd said it twice.

"I agree," said Gavin, "and I apologize for Ms. Parsons." He glared at me again. "She's new."

"What I meant to say—" I started, but Gavin jumped in.

"It isn't just the detentions. Guy applies to high school next year. I don't need to tell you how competitive the admissions process is. This is going in his file, and his file is going to high schools. I don't know any admissions committee who'd take a student with problems like this without serious intervention." He paused and waited.

"So tell us. What do we do?" Mrs. Martin said, leaning in, putting both her manicured hands on the table. She looked tired and desperate.

Gavin sat forward in his chair and clasped his hands on the table in front of him. "There are ways of helping kids like Guy. I have contacts in all the admissions offices. They know me. They trust me. If we do enough work with him, perhaps a deal can be made with one of them." He looked down and then back up again as if an idea had just come to him. "There's a program that I run the summer between seventh and eighth grades for kids like Guy, kids who have had serious behavior problems in middle school. I select children to participate in it, and if they agree to go, I remove all behavior incidents from their transcripts. High schools never need to know any of this has happened."

The Martins were both nodding vigorously, their eyes wide.

"For now, though," Gavin went on, "we need to put him on academic and behavioral probation."

"But that goes in his file, that is something that sticks," said Mr. Martin, his voice rising.

I heard my phone buzz suddenly. I reached down into my purse and lifted it out, holding it under the table.

Darling. Soon.

It took every unused stomach muscle I had not to fall back in my chair. My heart pounding, I stared down at my phone, refusing to put it down, not wanting to let go.

"You can put your faith in me," said Gavin, shooting me an icy look. "There are things we can do to ensure nobody knows about this. Let's reconnect after the holidays. Besides, I'm sure you want to spend time with Guy while you're up here." Both Gavin and I knew full well that Mr. Martin had zero desire to spend any time in the presence of his disappointing child. Mrs. Martin got up and followed her husband out of the room, her head bowed. I realized that in another life we might have been contemporaries. She could be leaving here to meet me in the city for lunch, maybe some shopping. We might laugh about the frumpy, inept teacher who sat in on the meeting. Instead, she looked right through me. I barely registered. She didn't even say goodbye.

When they were out of earshot, Gavin spun to face me.

"What the hell was that?"

"Gavin, I'm sorry." My phone, still in hand, buzzed again.

I promise.

I stared, unable to take my eyes off the screen, as if I were holding Jack right there in my hand.

"Are you texting? Is this not important to you?"

"What? No." I dropped the phone into my bag and stood to face him.

"Then what the hell's going on? Why would you show up and sabotage a meeting like this?"

"Gavin, I wasn't trying to sabotage anything. I just want to be helpful. The kid is terrified. Have you seen him lately?"

"Please don't try to tell me about Guy or any of these kids. These are *my* kids." He banged his fists on the table. "I've known them all for a lot longer than you have. Don't walk in here and act like you're some kind of expert, and never, ever undermine me again." He stared. It was hard to stare back at both of his eyes, so I chose his blue eye and looked into it.

"Don't you want these kids to be successful?" I asked. "Haven't you thought that maybe they aren't doing what we want them to do because they can't, not because they won't?"

"Spare me your West Coast education bullshit, please." He took a step closer so we were only separated by the edge of the table.

"Just because you haven't tried it doesn't mean it's bullshit," I said, now switching to his brown eye.

"Agnes, are you winking at me?"

"No." I blinked a couple of times and settled on his nose.

"So what?" he asked, confused by the disarray of my facial expressions. "You really expect me to believe that these boys aren't behaving because they can't behave, not because they won't behave?"

This was exactly what I was saying, but I realized I needed to dial it back for him if I didn't want his narrow little mind to combust. "I think we're expecting more of them than some of them are capable of doing. That's all." I sighed and crossed my arms, thinking back to Sunny Day. "Kids do well when they can," I said, hearing Marge's words come out of my mouth.

He pulled away. "You're obviously not cut out for the rigors of an East Coast prep school. You need to take this act back to your preschool on the beach." He waved me off dismissively and started walking to the door.

That was when I realized that Gavin didn't want to help these kids out at all. He talked a good game, but he was happy with the way things were. He had no desire to help these boys succeed. I just didn't know why.

"One more thing," I said. "About Guy."

"What about him?"

"I know he had a bad week last week—" Before I could say any more, Gavin cut me off.

"First of all, Guy Martin is having more than a bad week. Let's not downplay things," he said. "He's having a bad year, just like he did last year and the year before. Guy Martin, you could say, is having a bad middle school."

"He's a mess, Gavin," I begged. "Please go easy."

But Gavin just laughed, shook his head in mock disbelief, and walked out. I slumped down into one of the chairs at the table and pulled out my phone.

Jack.

I let my fingers run over the screen, over the words of the texts. Then I texted back.

Jack? Is this you? Where are you? Are you OK?

Within seconds of sending the text, I received a message: The number you are trying to reach is blocked or not in service. I tried calling the blocked number, but the voice mail woman turned me away. Jack was still not in service, so I texted the only person I thought could help me. I texted Don.

Got a text from Jack. I tried to respond. His number is blocked.

A few moments later, Don replied:

What do you want me to do?

I had to hand it to Don, that was a good question. What did I want him to do?

Is Jack texting me?

He could be. And then seconds later, he wrote, Yes.

How do I contact him?

You don't. You wait.

Let me guess—stay put? Do my job? Ears open?

Exactly.

Where is he? What's going on?

Don did not respond. He had no answers for me. He couldn't tell me why this all had to be on Jack's terms, every detail in his exacting control. He couldn't tell me why I'd been reduced to sitting and waiting to hear from a husband who wouldn't even let me text him. Having my texts bounce back to me was a humiliating reminder of just how little control I had.

When I'd told Beeks that I hated everything about the situation—what Jack had done, what he was asking me to do—I'd left out the thing that made me the angriest. I'd left out myself. Because it was beginning to occur to me that not only was Jack the kind of husband who could disappear and return at arm's length and on his own terms, but that I had been the kind of wife he expected to be willing to take it.

19

I know they say that when it rains it pours, but that night it rained so hard I awoke to a puddle of water in the middle of my bed. I slept soundly, so soundly that I didn't hear a single drip. I only realized what had happened when I heard Grace's cry on the monitor and noticed that the bottom half of my comforter was underwater. My first reaction was one of surprise—not at the water itself, but at the fact that I had slept at all, let alone deeply.

When I realized I was literally underwater, I looked up at the ceiling and saw what looked like a puddle suspended over my bed. Outside sheets of rain were falling. I rescued Grace from her crib, ignoring the enormous wet sag of her diaper, and ran to the kitchen to get a bucket. Once I'd taken off all my sheets and positioned the bucket in the center of my bed, I walked around the rest of the house looking for leaks. I discovered that it was only leaking over my bed, so I changed Grace's diaper and put her down on the kitchen floor while I prepared her breakfast.

I mixed up some cereal, grabbed a banana, and went to pick her up. Grace was not where I'd left her. I frantically looked around the kitchen but didn't see her. I ran into the dining room, instinctively looking down. I stooped down under the table and saw Grace, her hand seconds away from the glue trap I'd forgotten to take away. Grace had crawled. She'd crawled, and I hadn't seen it. All I could see was a look of victory and terror on her face. I dropped the food I had been holding and threw myself under the table, right in between Grace and the trap. I lay there, on my back, looking at her, willing her to crawl to me. She obliged and moved toward me perfectly, putting her little hands on my belly. After weeks of rocking back and forth on her hands and knees, Grace had mastered the perfect crawl. *Jack. You're missing this. You're missing all of it.*

"Gracie! You did it! You crawled! You crawled!" I squeezed her to me. Yes, I was under a table. Yes, I was an inch away from a glue trap, which had only managed to trap a couple of roaches and some mouse droppings (how was this possible, and why had I forgotten to call the exterminator?), but I wanted to stay under that table with Grace for as long as possible. The carpet was matted, scratchy, and uncomfortable, the space under the table dusty and confining. But under there I felt safe and happy in an uncomplicated way. Everything else I'd been feeling was so tangled. Grace's crawl was the opposite. It was a perfect, uncomplicated crawl.

I lifted the two of us out from under the table and danced around the dining room with Grace on my hip. Even though life had been on hold in so many ways for us, Grace's life moved on. She'd done what babies her age are supposed to do. I had a wistful moment when I realized I wouldn't be able to march Grace into my pediatrician's office in Santa Monica, with its modernist, pristine furniture and parents who could pay out of pocket for medical care. That office had been replaced by a neighborhood clinic that took the insurance I got through the school, a clinic with no natural light and furniture that looked like it had been picked up off the sidewalk. Dr. Reilly was kind enough, but it was an entirely different level of service—I was a patient, not a client. Nobody in the office was jockeying to show me how well they knew me or Grace. Nobody was trying to make me feel good about my choices as a parent. If I called to tell Dr. Reilly that Grace had crawled, chances were he wouldn't know who I was talking about. I waited for Grace to crawl again, then took a video and sent it to Beeks. I wanted most to send it to Jack, but Grace's crawling was something we'd celebrate without him. For now.

-20-

After dragging the boys through the remainder of the memoir unit, I launched into our first novel, *Roll of Thunder, Hear My Cry*, a book I had actually read as a middle schooler, about which I remembered nothing. I reread it, happy to have something to do in the evenings other than obsess about Jack's texts, or lack thereof.

"Get out your books, boys," I began.

"*Roll of Thunder, Hear Me Snore*," said Art. He announced this at the beginning of each day since we'd started reading the book. I didn't even hear him anymore.

"I'm going to the bathroom," Caleb announced.

"Me too," said Art, looking up at him and grinning.

"Boys," I said. "Remember the rule—one at a time."

That rule was Gavin's, not mine. Apparently when the boys went to the bathroom in clusters, they'd play a game. Whoever was the last one in the stall got pelted with wet paper towels. "That's why we started peeing in the sinks," Davey had explained to me.

"Fine," said Art. "I can wait."

We pulled out our books, and I began the discussion. I was in the middle of a sentence when Caleb came running in. He looked terrified.

"Ms. P., it was only a joke! I swear!" He raced to his seat and put his head down. Gavin ran into the room and stopped at the door, glaring at Caleb.

"What's going on, Caleb?" I asked.

Gavin looked furious. His face was red, his ears redder. "Tell her, Caleb. Tell Ms. Parsons what you did when you were presumably on a bathroom break." Spit was building at the corners of his mouth.

Caleb looked up. He was not crying, but he looked like he might start at any moment. "Something dumb," he said. "I did something really dumb." He bit down on his lower lip. It amazed me that, at times, these boys could look like small men, and at others, like right now, like scared little kids.

"That," said Gavin, "is an understatement." He looked at me. "While he was supposed to be in *your* class"—I could feel the blame being laid at my feet—"Caleb decided to do some mirroring."

Mirroring was when the kids projected images onto a teacher's smart board without the teacher knowing who was doing it or where it was coming from. The kid didn't even have to be in the class to do it. Needless to say, it was a popular pastime for some of my boys.

I looked at Caleb.

"I mirrored a picture of Jabba the Hutt onto Ms. Figg's smart board," he said, cringing.

"Right in the middle of her class," Gavin added.

"This is awful," I said, shaking my head and looking at Gavin. "Just awful. Please let me deal with this, Gavin." I knew he wouldn't leave if he didn't think I was taking this seriously.

Gavin threw back his head and mocked me with a laugh. "How exactly are you planning on dealing with this? The way you deal with everything else? By ignoring it? By pretending these poor little boys can't help themselves?"

I looked at the boys, who all seemed shocked by the standoff. It was one thing for Gavin to berate them publicly. I don't think they'd seen him bully a teacher before.

Gavin kept going. "I think I've seen enough of *your* problem solving. I'll take this one, if you don't mind." He said it like he was giving me a choice. He wasn't.

"Caleb," he said, looking at Caleb with a smile. "Get out."

Caleb looked terrified.

"Where is he going?" I asked. "Your office?"

Gavin laughed. "No. Last time he was in my office alone he went into the attendance system and marked all his absences as excused. Then he sent a bunch of emails from my account. No, Caleb can be the inaugural attendee of the detention room in Dowell Auditorium."

"What?" I asked.

"From now on, kids who get kicked out of class will go to Dowell. No more roaming the halls, no more mischief in my office. I have handpicked detention monitors to confiscate all devices and make sure they do schoolwork."

"But how do we do work without our devices?" asked Guy.

"Oh, I guess you'll have to figure that one out for yourself," Gavin sneered. "I'm sure you'll be in Dowell soon enough." He turned his attention to Caleb. "OK, get up," he ordered.

I started to speak, but Caleb interrupted me. "It's OK, Ms. P. I'll go." He squared his shoulders and bravely followed Gavin.

Gavin looked pleased, which wasn't any more appealing than Gavin looking displeased. "That's right, Caleb," he said. "It's good to know when you've been beaten." Gavin was speaking to Caleb, but he was looking at me.

～

That night I sank into the brown couch and stared numbly out the window, barely able to make out the bleak, bare trees against the dark sky. I could sense that winter was going to be rough—the days were short, the light was dim, and the cold seeped in deep, to parts of me I didn't even know could get cold.

Unlike the air-conditioning, the heat in my house was centralized, but after weeks of trying to get comfortable, I determined that the thermostat was no more than decoration. The heat came on when it felt like coming on, regardless of how much fiddling I did with the dial, and there was no comfortable setting—I either froze or roasted. It was as though the heat were being controlled from an undisclosed location; someone else was deciding how comfortable I would be.

That night, I froze. I was swaddled in layers of clothes—pajamas, a sweatshirt, a vest—and I sat on the couch with a mug of cocoa in my hand. I grabbed a blanket and wrapped it around my legs, then closed my eyes for a few minutes. When my phone rang I jumped, spilling a few drops of cocoa on the blanket. A blocked number.

I grabbed the phone and held it to my ear. Too afraid to talk, for fear it would be someone else, I just breathed like an idiot.

"Aggie, it's me."

Even if I could have spoken, I didn't want to. I just wanted to keep listening. Although Don had been assuring me Jack was fine, and although I'd gotten texts from someone I assumed was Jack, when I heard his voice, I realized that there was a piece of me that hadn't been sure I'd hear it again.

"Aggie?"

"Yes."

"It's me," he said.

"Say it again," I said.

"What?"

"My name. I need to hear you say my name."

"Aggie," he breathed. "Aggie, Aggie, Aggie."

I closed my eyes.

"I've missed you," he said. "God, how I've missed you."

"I've missed you, too. So much." It was hard to get air into my lungs, so I leaned forward and propped a pillow behind me.

"Are you OK?" he asked.

"OK?"

"Yes, are you OK?"

Depends on what you mean by OK. I'm lonely. I'm tired. I'm scared. Once I started, I never really stopped being scared.

"I'm OK," I said. My eyes were stinging. I looked up at the ceiling. "Where are you, Jack?" It hurt to say his name.

"And Grace? Is she OK? How is she?"

"She's fine," I said. "She crawled. Where are you, Jack?"

"That's wonderful. I love you, Aggie," he said. "I'll be with you soon, I promise. I'm sorry it's so hard."

"It doesn't have to be this hard." I swallowed.

I sat in the gaping silence between us, but before I could say anything else, he whispered, "I have to go now. Kiss Grace for me, please."

"Jack . . ."

"Soon, I promise." The call ended. Jack was gone.

I dropped the phone and sat frozen on the couch. I could still hear his voice in my head, and for the first time since I got here, I could almost feel his presence. I was afraid to move. I didn't want to lose him again. Eventually, I let my head drop back and closed my eyes.

I woke up several hours later short of breath and covered in sweat, and the heat wasn't even on yet. I had Jack on the brain. I couldn't remember my dream, but I knew he was in it. I could still feel him in the room.

-21-

All that week, dreaming about Jack kept me awake.

Since I heard his voice that night, my dreams were more vivid, almost Technicolor, and I often woke up in the middle of the night breathless, wanting him more, unable to go back to sleep.

With Jack, sex had always been like restaurants—part of our daily lives, how we measured our week. We ate out on certain nights—if we didn't, if we couldn't get a reservation, or didn't get the right table, Jack would be grumpy. He was the same way about sex. The rules were unspoken, but they were there. There was a four-times-a-week requirement—three weeknights and one on the weekend. If for some reason sex didn't happen, even for a reason out of our control, Jack was surly, grouchy, almost childlike in his petulance.

Some women would have found his demands burdensome. Beeks certainly had a lot to say about it.

"Are you serious?" she asked during one of the first calls we'd had about Jack.

"Very," I said.

"Dear Lord. I don't even brush my teeth four times a week anymore."

I laughed. "Beeks, you know that I wouldn't do it if I didn't want to."

"Well, then," she conceded, "good for you. Have some sex for me while you're at it, because if these kids don't start sleeping through the night, I may never have it again."

I wasn't just not burdened by Jack's demands, I was flattered by them. I never worried about Jack looking around, the perennial fear of an LA wife. I'll admit that there were times, especially in Grace's first months, when I would have preferred a night off. But then I heard some of the baby-group moms talk about their husbands' sudden lack of interest. Jack's interest never waned, and I wore it proudly.

I remember seeing my obstetrician for my six-week postpartum checkup. She gave me the green light for sex but told me that she always advised her patients that they could tell their husbands it was really an eight- or even ten-week waiting period. "You know," she said, "give yourself some time if you need it." But Jack was primed, ready to go, and waiting for me when I got home from the appointment. I remember seeing his car in the driveway, my stomach turning slightly at the worry that I wouldn't be able to give him what he wanted, not just on that day, but ever again. I was worried about the pain, but, truthfully, I was more worried about Jack.

In the days that followed that first phone call, I was more desperate than ever to have Jack back. Whatever he'd done, whatever mess he'd made, I didn't care. I could feel his hands on me. In the middle of the day. In class. It was disturbing, distracting, but it was also fantastic. I'd never had much of an active fantasy life before, at least not one that involved sex. When I was younger, fantasies were more of the get-out-of-Modesto or the live-free-of-roommates variety. With Jack, I didn't have time to fantasize much. I had everything I thought I needed. Now I could feel his hands on the small of my back, on my stomach, his fingers pressing into me, pulling me to him. I could feel his mouth all over me at the least appropriate of times, and I could hear him growling quietly in my ears. Suddenly, we were having sex on top of my desk, in the back stairway of MacReady, even on the brown couch. I found myself shaking my head or blinking frantically to bring myself back to whatever the day was demanding of me, but with each passing day, Jack's hold on my imagination grew stronger.

~

Even though things were heating up inside my brain, on the Monday before Thanksgiving, the temperature dropped dramatically. Once again, my Santa Monica apparel was insufficient. The lined twill jacket that had protected me in a Southern California winter was like putting a Band-Aid on a gaping flesh wound.

Grace was not faring much better than I was. Dot did her best to mention it without actually telling me that I needed to stop sending my child in substandard outerwear. (She pinned notes to Grace's thin fleece jacket: "Maybe something warmer for tomorrow?" or "Little Grace was cold on our walk. Time for her winter coat?")

I knew exactly what I'd be buying if I had been looking for a coat a few months ago, from the comfort of my Santa Monica home, and with the seemingly infinite quantities of Jack's soon-to-disappear money. I had spied Santa Monica moms wearing flattering, fitted Swiss down coats with a large, obvious logo on the sleeve. Some of my friends wore vests festooned with these logos, because while a full coat would have been unnecessary and almost ridiculous in Santa Monica, they wanted the world to know that should they ever need a down coat, this was the brand of coat they would buy.

It was hard to believe that there was ever a time when a coat that cost several thousands of dollars would easily have been part of my uniform. I was now in the market for a coat that came in at well under one hundred dollars. I had far fewer zeros in my arsenal.

Stacey Figg had given me a coupon for 40 percent off at a website that seemed to specialize in mom clothes. In Modesto, my parents had kept our coupons in a plastic pouch in a kitchen drawer. The pouch had two pockets—one for items we used (we were not picky about things like detergent or toilet paper brands), and another for items we didn't but might like (fancy cookies in tins, plug-in air freshener). If we were having a good month, we dipped into the second pocket.

"All outerwear is an additional twenty-five percent off this week." Stacey beamed while standing outside my door one morning. She thrust the coupon at me. "Thanksgiving sale!"

"This is perfect," I said, buckling Grace into her stroller. "Thank you, Stacey," I added.

"Wanna have dinner tonight?" she asked. "I can cook."

I felt bad. This wasn't the first of her overtures, and if her scrambled eggs were any indication, Stacey's dinner would put my one chicken dish to shame, but I just couldn't bear the thought of dodging her rapid-fire questions for more than a few minutes.

"Thanks, but I think Grace and I need an early night. Another time?"

"Sure," she said. "Whenever. I'm always here."

That night I went to the website printed on the coupon and thought of my parents. In some ways I'd come so far from the life they'd tried to make for me, but here I was, shopping for a coat with a coupon, and I felt suddenly tethered to them. *I got myself into this. I became someone you would not recognize, but look—I have a coupon!*

The coats might have been shapeless, but Stacey was right—they were practically free. I scrolled through the options available to me and quickly realized that the less money I spent on a coat, the more likely it would be that I'd look like a walking, overstuffed comforter. I read the reviews, ignoring that most of them came from women who tagged themselves in the forty-five to sixty age range, and saw a coat which got high ratings for warmth. I needed warmth. This mom coat, the outerwear version of the mom-kini, was my only option, and for some reason the coat was even cheaper if I bought it in plum. I also clicked on the children's section and found Grace a pale-blue coat, as well as matching mittens and a hat.

The coats would arrive in a couple of days, giving me time to figure out what Jack would say when he came and saw me here, in this puffy plum comforter, with its detachable hood and removable lining. I hadn't heard from him since that first call, but I could hear his voice in my head. "We'll just have to burn this thing ASAP," I could hear him say, a wicked grin on his face.

"No," I would reply. "Let's keep it. As a reminder." He'd smile more and pull me toward him. The coat and everything under it would come off.

~

Our coats arrived quickly. After a grueling day during which Gavin, on a warpath, had marched into my classes on three separate occasions and sent three boys to Dowell, or as the boys had taken to calling it, "the Bowel," and on which I promised a tearful Guy that his trip home for Thanksgiving was going to be all right even though I had failed to plead his case to his father, Grace and I came home to find an enormous UPS box sitting on the front stoop. I opened the door and kicked the box inside. As soon as I could get Grace down on the floor, I looked around for scissors, but I didn't know if I owned any. What mother, let alone what teacher, doesn't own scissors? I pulled out my house key, slashed open the box, then sat on the floor with Grace to examine its contents.

I'm not ashamed to admit I cried when I tried on the coat. I cried partly because I was so happy to finally dive deep into the embrace of its enormous warmth, but I also cried because wearing it made me feel so far from myself, or at least so far from the self I had been a few months ago. I stood up, pulled the hood over my head, and zipped up the coat. Grace looked at me and clapped for the first time.

"Of course you clapped," I said, looking at her. "I look like a plum Big Bird." I caught a glimpse of myself in the dirty full-length mirror I had leaned on the wall facing the brown couch. Jack was on his way to me. I could just feel it. If I did not recognize myself in this coat, would he?

-22-

We were supposed to be going to Beeks's for Thanksgiving, but on Thanksgiving morning, I woke up tired. It seemed that most mornings I woke up tired. Grace was teething, and when she wasn't teething, she was having teething flashbacks. Every time a new tooth came in, I had only a matter of weeks until a new one would start to force its way out, tearing at Grace's little gums and keeping us both awake for nights on end. On some nights she would cry so loudly and for so long that at some point she had no choice but to puke all over the two of us, finally quieting when she had left me wearing a day's worth of her food. On those nights I joined her and cried. She'd cry for her pain, and I'd cry for Alma. Oh, Alma, how I never fully appreciated all those nights you'd be willing to sleep over (for a price) and take Grace while I slept soundly in a nearby room, eye mask and earplugs in place. Oh, Alma, how I never thanked you enough for those mornings when you'd come early (for a price) and let me sleep late, feeding and playing with Grace until I felt rested enough to emerge from the cocoon of my bedroom. Alma was on the other side of the country, and anyway, I couldn't afford to pay her more than an hour a week. I wasn't paying the baby-group moderator her retainer anymore (yes, that's a thing), so she wasn't returning my emails. Believe me, I'd tried. I was on my own, so I did what people who can't pay experts or hire help have to do—I went online and tried to find some free answers to this never-ending teething nightmare.

At first, I bought some homeopathic teething remedy I'd heard about in baby group. My God, baby group felt like a lifetime ago. Grace easily took the small, sugary tablets, but they did nothing for her pain. I could have sworn they made the nights longer, and when I finally got around to reading the ingredients and saw caffeine listed among them, I threw out the rest of the package.

The night before Thanksgiving was particularly bad. Something else had to be going on—there was no way this was the work of a tooth. We spent most of the night awake, both of us screaming in agony, and after I'd given her a morning bottle and sucked down my own pitcher of coffee, I called the pediatrician. Because of the holiday, the office was only open for a couple of hours in the morning. I made an appointment for 8:30 a.m. and bundled us both up before we headed out.

Stacey stuck her head out of her door as Grace and I emerged.

"You OK?" she asked. "I heard a lot of crying last night. I would've come over, but I didn't want to intrude." Jeez. At some point, I was going to have to have dinner with Stacey Figg and get her off my back, but now was not the time.

"I don't know. It may just be teething, but I can't do another night like that. I made an appointment with the pediatrician, and I don't wanna be late." I left before Stacey had the chance to ask any more questions.

On frigid November mornings like this, I was glad for the lack of space in New York City. Things were close enough that I could be at the pediatrician's office in less than fifteen minutes. I was still too afraid to drive here, let alone park, so we moved quickly through the streets on foot. I felt powerful when we walked like this. It felt remarkable to be able to get your child somewhere just using your own two feet. We walked up and down the hills of Riverdale, past a smattering of old, stately homes, nondescript row houses, and block after block of storefronts.

Dr. Reilly quickly diagnosed Grace with an ear infection—her very first. I quieted my inner voice, which told me that this would never have happened if she weren't in day care, and gladly accepted the prescription for antibiotics. Another dubious milestone.

The pharmacy was a block away. If I had thought the sad supermarket was grim, I was not at all prepared for the pharmacy. I walked through the front door, dragging the stroller backward over the threshold, and was greeted by a blast of hot air. I tore open my jacket and froze as a large black cat ran in behind me and took refuge in the deodorant aisle. The store was tiny—I could see the whole place from where I stood. I grabbed a bottle of baby painkiller (the last one), wiped off the layer of dust, and walked back to the pharmacy. I heard Jack tell me to check if the painkiller had any dye in it. I told Jack to quiet down.

I stood in line behind six people, none of whom were filling prescriptions and all of whom were buying lottery tickets. Grace was crying again. I poured some purple painkiller down her throat, dripping half of it on her coat. The pharmacist motioned for me to come forward. I cut the line, annoying the string of future lottery winners.

"Can I help you?" the pharmacist asked, while chewing what seemed like an entire pack of gum.

"Can you please fill this?" I handed her Grace's prescription. "Right now, while I wait?"

The pharmacist looked down at the prescription and tapped her nails on it. Each nail was a different shade of turquoise, with a mermaid decal on each ring finger. She nodded and continued tapping on the counter. "Sheila," she called, looking back.

"Yeah?" came a voice from the pharmacy.

"You free?" asked the hair and nails.

"Shuwa," replied the voice.

"Huh?" I said, not meaning to say it aloud.

"She said sure," explained the hair and nails, smiling at me. "Give us five minutes, OK?"

I nodded and took Grace to the front of the store. We sat on a dusty folding chair in front of the heating vent. Every time the door opened (it seemed lottery tickets were popular this morning), a gust of freezing wind hit us and provided a few seconds of relief from the blasting heat that was coming from behind the chair. I was about to take off my sweater when a voice from the pharmacy called my name.

I grabbed the antibiotics and gave Grace the first dose in the store. Then we got out as soon as we could and made our way home. Once we were safely installed on the brown couch, I texted Beeks.

Grace has an ear infection. Have to cancel. Sorry xxxx

Seconds later she replied.

Like hell you do. Ear infection? Please. Text me when you have Ebola.

I had been foolish to think that an ear infection would scare off Beeks, and it certainly wasn't going to get me out of Thanksgiving dinner. I wanted to see Beeks and her kids. But I wasn't quite ready for Brian, who possibly liked Jack even less than Beeks did. Plus, Brian's sister Lindsey and her family would be there as well. If I wasn't ready for Brian, I most definitely wasn't ready for Lindsey, the recipient of all his family's less fortunate genes.

I also wasn't ready to spend Thanksgiving without Jack. I had no idea how much he'd spent on the organic, grass-fed, free-roaming turkey he'd ordered each year for Sondra to prepare, but I was sure I wouldn't be eating one at Beeks's house. But it wasn't Jack's turkey that I was missing. I missed the feeling of sitting down to a meal with him and not needing anyone else at the table. I kept staring at my phone, waiting for a text or another call. A few hours later, after I'd given Grace another dose of medicine, the two of us boarded the subway for a long, slow ride down to Beeks's Upper West Side apartment. We'd been on the subway a couple of times before, but this time it was emptier and Grace and I practically had a whole row to ourselves. I wiped down our seats with the sleeve of my coat before we sat. Grace sat up in her seat and leaned into me. She was sleepy—we both were. As the train rocked and swayed, so did Grace. Before I knew it, her head dropped to its side and rested on me. Asleep. Not just a catnap on my chest or in a sling, or even the stroller. But a real sleep, a sleep that lasted all the way to our stop—a full forty-five minutes.

There were moments like this that caught me by surprise. Moments when it was just the two of us out in the world. Grace and I were on the subway, making our way down into Manhattan, the rhythm of the city rocking her, her soft little body pressed into mine. These were not moments I had expected, and when they came, when it hit me that we could do things like this—treat an ear infection, ride the subway—I was knocked backward. In those moments, I was reminded not only of how alone we were, but also of how all right we were, and how much I could actually do for Grace. I could take this cosseted, previously overnannied baby on the subway and she would be fine. These moments were not frequent, at least not yet. But they were mine, and I was happy for them.

Needless to say, I was feeling pretty confident when I climbed the stairs to Beeks's cramped prewar walk-up apartment, glad that I'd remembered to leave the stroller at home. Before we walked in, my phone buzzed with an incoming call. My hands were full, but I managed to pull it out of my coat pocket.

"Jack?" I asked, without even looking to see where the call was from.

"Happy Thanksgiving, darling."

"Happy Thanksgiving," I whispered, leaning against Beeks's door.

"Why are you whispering?" he asked.

"Oh, I'm outside Beeks's apartment. She says the walls are paper-thin."

"Beeks?" he asked. "You're there?"

"I'm spending Thanksgiving with Beeks and Brian."

"Oh."

"Oh?" I said, sounding more hostile than I wanted to. I corrected my tone. "Jack, what's wrong?"

"Nothing. I'm just alone right now, and I thought you would be, too."

"Jack, I am always alone. All I am is alone." I realized I had no idea where he was. I had so many questions for him, but the last thing I wanted to do was scare him off the phone. "Are you here? Do you want to spend Thanksgiving with me? Just say the word, and I'll tell Beeks I can't come. It's not too late."

"It's too late. Besides, I can't, Aggie, not yet," he said.

"OK, then let's just talk," I said. "I don't have to go in now." I heard the desperation in my voice. "I can stay out here for as long as you want."

"It's fine," he said. "Enjoy your meal."

"Jack, please don't be upset."

"I told you, it's fine," he said, sounding not fine. "Go. Enjoy. Happy Thanksgiving."

Jack had screwed up, disappeared, sent me to New York, and for the first time since we'd met, he'd forced me to have Thanksgiving without him because he wasn't yet ready to see me, whatever that meant. He had done all this. So why did I feel so guilty?

When Grace and I walked into her apartment, Beeks was already hiding in her tiny kitchen with a large glass of deep-red wine. She pulled us in before any of the other guests could see us.

"Please," she begged. "Let me have you to myself for a moment before she descends on us."

"Lindsey?" I asked.

"Ugh. Who else?" moaned Beeks.

"How bad is it?" I asked, peeling off the baby carrier and carrying Grace on my hip while I took off our coats. At some point Beeks took notice of my acrobatics and swept Grace up into her arms while I disrobed. She buried her face in the folds of Grace's neck.

"This is just what I need," she said in a muffled voice.

"Not so fast," said Brian, who walked into the kitchen and put his hand on my shoulder. "If you let her hold a baby for too long, she'll ask for more."

"Too late," said a muffled Beeks from underneath Grace's neck.

"You forget," said Brian, taking our coats with one hand and pouring me some wine with the other, "that our babies grow into messy, disobedient toddlers of the male variety."

"So true," said Beeks, emerging. "Still, it's hard to hold a baby and not want one."

"Speak for yourself," said another voice. I turned to see Lindsey walking into the kitchen. "What? I can't have wine? You guys are hiding it all in here?"

And that, ladies and gentlemen, is Lindsey in a nutshell. Lindsey is healthy. Lindsey has three children and a husband and a nice apartment in the city. From what Beeks tells me, that apartment is full of nice things. I think Lindsey may even have a trainer. But Lindsey never has what she really wants, and what Lindsey really wants is whatever someone else has. At that moment it was wine, and if she didn't have a glass when other people did, it was because we had intentionally kept it from her.

"Seriously?" she asked. "What does a girl have to do to get some wine around here?" She shoved an empty glass under Brian's chin. Oh, another thing Lindsey does not have—social graces. "Hey, Agnes," she said. "Guess Jack is a no-show, then?" She chugged the newly poured wine and handed Brian her glass. "Refill," she ordered, stifling a burp.

I looked at Lindsey. She was thinner than I remembered, and she looked more tired. Her hair was a light brown, streaked with highlights, and she wore it long—too long. She continually ran her fingers through it, maybe a nervous habit. As for her other features, I could never really describe them because Lindsey's predominant physical feature was anger—she wore it permanently and with gusto. I was about to answer her question when Beeks, still holding Grace, chimed in.

"Yup, no Jack tonight. We get Aggie and Grace all to ourselves," she said and then pushed us all out of the kitchen, turning to give me a grimace. "Let's move to the table and get this started."

Beeks's five-year-old twins, Kyle and Alec, and her three-year-old, Jimmy, sat under the table and were holding down Pesto, the family cat. Lindsey's three children—a boy and two girls—and her very quiet husband were all huddled around various handheld devices in the den, which lay off to the side of the dining room.

"It would be easy for me to judge," whispered Beeks. "But if I had to live with Lindsey, I think I'd be permanently glued to my phone, too." We sat next to each other at the table, and I put Grace down on the floor so she could have a front-row seat to whatever was happening to the poor cat. Stevie, Beeks's thirteen-year-old stepson, walked in, grunted, and took a seat at the table.

We managed to avoid talking about Jack for most of the meal. This was mostly because Lindsey, draining glass after glass of wine, dominated the conversation. I heard about her son, who had made it to the finals of a chess tournament ("very tough, lots of competition"), her youngest daughter, who was a semifinalist in the citywide geography bee ("She was robbed. The parochial schools cheat like hell"), and her middle daughter, who didn't seem to have any accolades of which to brag and whose main talent appeared to be rolling her eyes and picking at her food.

After she had finished ritually bragging about her own children, she moved on to grilling Beeks. Beeks maintained that between all four of her kids, the accomplishments were too few to name, but I knew better. Downplaying things was Beeks's thing, and it was how she managed to be in the same room with Lindsey without strangling her.

At some point Lindsey turned her drunken sights on me. "Your hair," she said. "I don't remember it being so dark."

"Yeah," I said. "Trying something new."

"What's the estranged husband gonna say when he sees you've let yourself go like this?"

"Who?" I asked, instinctively putting my hands to my hair. I'd heard Lindsey, but I couldn't believe I'd heard her.

"Your sugar daddy? The guy who has disappeared with all your money? The reason you had to move east to teach frickin' middle school to rich kids in the Bronx?"

I moved my mouth but could say nothing at all. I just stared. I didn't know what Beeks was doing, because I couldn't look at Beeks. I didn't know if she'd told Lindsey everything, but she had laid me bare at that table with the one person who could not resist shaming me. If Lindsey could read the panic on my face, she didn't let on. She kept going.

"What's he gonna say when he sees that his hot Santa Monica trophy wife looks like a librarian from Queens?" She drank some more wine and said, "I mean, to think there was a time when you were the hottest one in the room. To think you were thinner and blonder than me."

"Lindsey!" Beeks finally snapped from across the table.

"What?" Lindsey said, looking around for support.

"Frank," Beeks said to Lindsey's silent husband, who sat at the head of the table with his head down, wincing like a terminally shy student, begging not to be called on. "Do something about your wife. Please."

Frank did not raise his head. He would not be called on. Lindsey was on her own, and so, then, were we.

"Brian!" yelled Beeks. "Do something about your sister."

"Lindsey," he began, but she cut him off.

"Oh, please, Brian." Lindsey snorted. "The only person who ever liked that husband of hers is Agnes. Don't pretend you didn't think he was a complete tool. You too, Beeks," she said, looking at a horrified Beeks. "You guys hated him. Right from the beginning. Don't pretend you're sad he's not here. Hell, she wouldn't be here if he hadn't left her. From what you told me, Agnes didn't jump until he told her to. No way in hell she'd be slumming here if Jack hadn't gone AWOL with all their money."

I knew Beeks didn't like Jack. I knew Brian didn't like Jack. I knew nobody really liked Jack. But I always thought Beeks loved me enough not to talk about Jack, least of all to Lindsey, the least discreet, most uncouth person we knew, and I never imagined, not for a minute, that Beeks would betray me to her like this.

Just then, Kyle, who had given up on the cat and joined us at the table, grabbed a spoon of mashed potatoes and flung them right at

Lindsey. Before she knew what was coming, her face was covered in creamy white mash. The other boys hooted and hollered their approval. Alec stood up and spat his water out at Kyle, who knocked over a glass of wine. Jimmy banged on the table in support. Lindsey jumped up, screaming, wiping the potatoes out of her eyes.

"Jesus, Brian! Get ahold of your kids, will you?" she barked, running into the bathroom. The cat followed. More potatoes followed the cat.

I was not there when Lindsey emerged all cleaned up, because as soon as I could, I got myself and Grace out of that apartment. I couldn't look at Beeks. She tried to stand between me and the door, but I pushed past her.

"Aggie, please," she said. "I'm sorry. I'm so sorry."

I wanted so much for her to stand up at that meal and tell everyone that Lindsey was making it all up, that she'd never discussed me or Jack with her. But she couldn't, and I couldn't be in that apartment a moment longer.

-24-

Beeks's betrayal left me with no choice: I broke down and had dinner with the Figg.

In the days that followed Thanksgiving, I moved in a fog. I was avoiding Beeks and calling and texting Jack's blocked number with reckless abandon. One night, when Grace was already asleep and I'd spent half an hour crying and yelling at Jack's unresponsive voice mail lady, Stacey Figg knocked on the door. I thought back to my first days here, when a knock on the door would send me into a full panic. I was so miserable now, I might not have noticed or minded if a serial killer had shown up at the door. I was so focused on my own misery that I might even invite the killer for a glass of dusty wine.

"You're sad," she said, wearing her jumpsuit and presenting me with a casserole dish.

"It's that obvious?" I said, letting her in, taking the large warm dish in my hands. It took all I had not to hug that dish.

"It's hard to miss, Agnes. But don't worry, the answer to your problems is now in your hands."

I looked down. "What's in here?" I asked.

"Only a heavenly blend of pasta, cheese, and spinach," she said, leading me into the kitchen. I stood by dumbly as she grabbed knives, forks, and plates and put them on the dining room table.

"Sit," she said.

I sat.

"Is it your husband?" she asked, sliding a spoon into the casserole and serving me a heaping piece.

"No," I said. "It's a friend. My best friend." I should have said "my only friend," but I didn't think I could say those words without crying. I didn't want to give the Figg more information than I needed to, but it felt good to talk to someone, especially because both of my someones were unavailable. I shoveled in a bite of food.

"Is it Banks?" she asked.

"Huh?" Damn, this food was good. It was warm and salty and I wanted to grab the dish and hide with it upstairs.

"Banks. Your friend?"

"Yeah," I said. I thought about correcting her, but I couldn't bring myself to say Beeks's name. I wanted to be alone in a small dark room, making my way through this casserole. I did not want to be sitting here discussing Beeks with the Figg.

"What happened?" she asked, taking her own bite of food.

"We had a fight," I said.

She leaned back in her chair, folding her arms over her chest. "What'd you fight about?"

"My husband," I said, exhaling. "She doesn't like him."

"Really?" Stacey said, her eyes suddenly widening. "What doesn't she like?" I got the distinct impression that Stacey Figg was suppressing the urge to rub her little hands together. This was getting uncomfortable.

"Oh, she doesn't like that he travels so much." I felt bad watching the Figg deflate. She had been hoping for something better. I could see it on her face. The truth was better, much better, but it was also worse.

"Is that all?" she asked.

"More or less," I said.

"Which is it?" she asked.

"Huh?"

"More or less? What else doesn't she like? Don't you want to talk about it?" Her eyes were shining with anticipation.

"No," I said. "I don't." I might have wanted to, but I couldn't bring myself to talk about it, so I switched gears. "I'm also worried about the boys in my class."

Stacey poured us both some water. "Why?"

"I don't know. Gavin keeps walking in and sending boys to Dowell, presumably because he doesn't think I'm throwing them out of class enough."

Stacey leaned in. "You need to trust Gavin more. He knows these boys. He knows they need boundaries and consequences." There were those words again.

"Really? I'm not so sure he knows them. Besides, it's not like all his boundaries and consequences actually work. The boys don't respond to him at all." I had also overheard Caleb and Davey talking about Gavin's summer program, the one he had mentioned in the meeting with the Martins. Apparently, he'd told them they would be "invited to attend" if they wanted to get into high school.

"That program is gold," Stacey said when I told her about it. "It works. The boys get into the high school and they all do well there, or at least they do better."

"Isn't it possible that they do better in high school because Gavin isn't around terrorizing them?"

Stacey wasn't buying any of this. "He knows what he's doing, Agnes."

"What about Ruth?" I asked, as nonchalantly as I could.

"What about her?"

"What does she do?"

Stacey looked at me, confused. I tried to clarify. "I mean, what does she do here? Is she involved in school administration, or does she just fund-raise?" I really wasn't sure what I was asking, but I wanted to stop talking about how wonderful Gavin was and I thought I should probably have some info on Ruth for when Jack finally showed up.

"Beats me," she said, taking another bite. "We don't see her much, especially because Gavin does such a great job."

I couldn't hear any more. "This casserole is delicious, Stacey. I didn't know anybody could do this with pasta, cheese, and spinach."

"Oh," she said proudly, "I'm full of surprises."

-25-

Beeks's betrayal didn't just drive me into the arms of the Figg. In the days after Thanksgiving, I couldn't stop thinking about Lindsey's words. Maybe she was right. Maybe I had gone from the hottest person in the room to the person you'd be most likely to overlook. Jack was close now, and I could hear his voice in my head. I decided to take Lindsey's words to heart and went in search of some highlights.

My search took me three blocks down Riverdale Avenue. I needed something close, and I needed something cheap. I knew better than to test my luck at a salon in Manhattan; I just didn't have that kind of money now. I'd asked an art teacher with decent highlights where she got her hair done, and she sent me to a nearby salon called Tropical Escape. It felt strange to be going somewhere other than class without Grace. After I had overheard some day-care parents mentioning that Dot offered extended hours, I signed Grace up for a longer day. Less than one week after Lindsey had shamed my overgrown highlights, I walked into Tropical Escape and into the arms of Evon, a tall Honduran woman with straightened brown hair.

I tried to explain to Evon what I had in mind. I talked about highlights and lowlights. I didn't show her any pictures, as I'd been trained to do in Santa Monica, but she nodded and I felt safe. I wasn't sure why. It wasn't like me to trust a complete stranger with my hair. Colorists needed to be recommended, approved, and heavily vetted, and on the basis of one recommendation, I walked into this place and put myself at Evon's mercy. I was just so happy for someone to be taking care of me that I think had Caleb and Davey been the ones doing my hair at Tropical Escape, I would have been fine with it.

I closed my eyes and rested while Evon went to work painting on highlights and wrapping my hair in foil. I read mindless magazines while I sat in the foil. In LA, celebrity news was city news. I could turn on the morning news and get weather (almost comic in its lack of variation), traffic (ditto), and celebrity gossip, delivered with the seriousness of a stock-market update. It had been months since I'd read a shred of gossip, and I devoured the stack of magazines on the Lucite coffee table.

I paged through the magazines and thought about Jack. It was hard to picture our reunion, because it was near impossible to see Jack here. I pictured our first moments together and wondered what I would wear, knowing that none of my current outfits would suffice. Then I realized that my outfit was the least of my worries: Jack had asked me for information, but I still had nothing. I had no idea why Ruth had pulled her money out of Jack's fund. I'd had so little contact with her, and it wasn't like I could barge into her office and demand answers. Don had said that sometimes information that seemed unimportant could be useful, but there was nothing I had seen here that I could even report as useful. What had I learned? That the middle school was launching an online behavior report system? That detentions had been localized in the Bowel? Jack had said that some parents had invested with him, but the only parents I'd met were the Martins, and as far as that went, I still had nothing. Jack had given me one job, and I'd failed to do it. (OK, maybe he'd given me *way* more than one job.) Still, I wanted something, anything, to show him that I could be useful, and possibly even helpful.

The timer rang and Evon led me to the back of the salon and washed my hair in the sink, slowly massaging my scalp. My goodness, was this really something I had done almost monthly in Santa Monica?

I couldn't remember the last time someone other than Grace or Beeks had touched me. Evon's hands were soft and strong. The large pads of her fingertips dived deep into the grooves of my scalp. I groaned with pleasure and looked around sheepishly when I realized what I had done. Evon did not mind. She smiled at me.

"Long day?" she asked.

"Long year," I said, closing my eyes.

"Year's almost over," she replied, sitting me up and wrapping a towel around my head. Evon led me to her chair, and I plopped down into it. I'd forgotten how much I liked sitting in a salon chair. The soft seat, the footrest, and the knowledge that I'd soon be leaving with a fresh set of highlights and a spring in my step. I kept my eyes closed for as long as I could, savoring every minute I had free of work or Grace. It was hard to believe I'd had so many of these moments before, so much time free of obligation. Now I had nothing but obligation.

Evon went to work blowing out my hair. The heat of the dryer almost put me to sleep. How I missed my Thursday blowouts. I closed my eyes again and drifted off. I heard the voices of women walking in after work for their hair appointments. I kept my eyes closed so I wouldn't have to talk.

When I opened my eyes, I almost fell out of the chair. I had walked into the salon hoping to mask the dark roots that had grown halfway down my head. Now the roots seemed even darker, and it looked like just the tips of my hair had been dipped in a bowl of bleach. I closed my eyes, squeezing them, willing myself not to cry. I heard Beeks's voice in my head. *What the hell did you expect? When you get your hair dyed in the Bronx, you'll end up looking like Jenny from the Block.* Thinking about Beeks, my Beeks who had betrayed me, made me want to cry even harder. I was desperate to call her immediately and tell her what I'd done, but Beeks was not available to me. I squeezed the armrests, grabbing control of myself, and smiled.

"I love it," I lied.

Evon grinned proudly. The other women in the salon came over and clucked around me.

"So pretty!"

"Your husband will like!"

Both could not have been further from the truth. When I picked up Grace, she and Dot both gave me a similar quizzical look. "Oh," said Dot. "You've made some changes."

"Uh, yeah," I said. "You could say that." I scooped up Grace and headed home.

I kept away from mirrors for the night and fought the urge to call Beeks. For the first time, I secretly prayed Jack would take his time returning.

~

Not surprisingly, the Figg had a lot to say about my hair. She showed up that night with a bottle of wine and two glasses. I heard a jingling sound, looked outside, and saw her standing at my door. I stared at her, speechless. Her trunk was red, her short arms Kelly green, and her entire torso was covered in tiny bells, which jingled each time she moved.

"Christmas." She beamed, shimmying. "I start wearing my sweaters as soon as I open my advent calendar." Before I could say anything, she looked up at my hair. I was hoping our height difference would protect me.

"Wow!" she said. "That's bold."

"Yeah," I said. "Bold, and kind of an accident. I went in for highlights."

"You certainly did," she said, grinning.

"I know, I know. I just needed a pick-me-up. I guess I got a little carried away."

"Still haven't made up with Banks?" she asked.

I shook my head.

"Whatever," she said. "I have wine."

"Yes. You do." I blinked back some tears. She smiled at me sympathetically.

I opened the door and let in the Figg and her bottle of wine.

"Beeks," I said, closing the door behind her. "Her name is Beeks."

26

I dragged myself to class the next day, burying my hair under a woolen cap. I arrived before the boys, hung up my coat and hat, and prayed that nobody would notice.

Caleb was the first one to arrive. "Whoa!" he exclaimed, skidding to a halt in front of my desk. "Ms. P., you look awesome!"

Before I could answer him, Art and Guy ran in with a handful of other boys, including some students from my other classes. Davey was chasing them all with a spray bottle. When they got into class, the boys all ducked under their seats. Davey kept spraying relentlessly. The boys who had somewhere else to be quickly left when the bell rang.

"Good morning, boys," I said, calling to them from the front of the class. "Davey," I said. "What are you doing?"

"We found this bottle on the stairs!" he said, facing off with Guy.

"What's in it?" I asked.

"No clue," he said. I walked over, grabbed the bottle, opened it, and sniffed.

"Bleach," I said. "You've been spraying your friends with diluted bleach."

Davey didn't seem fazed. Instead, he looked at me and said, "Ms. P.! You look hot!" As he said it he put his hand over his mouth, realizing that he may have gone too far. "I mean hot in an appropriate way."

"No worries, Davey," I said, taking the bottle from him. This wasn't so bad after all. I might have looked like a skunk in reverse, but to these boys I looked fabulous. Not one of them failed to compliment me. It was easy, therefore, to overlook the fact that they were shooting each other with a bottle of bleach that they did not find on the stairs, but rather, that they had stolen from the janitorial closet. Upon further examination, I found a Dustbuster in Art's backpack.

None of them could settle into class that morning. It was always hard for these boys to come back after a break. Hell, reentry from recess was tough—a few days off from this place must have been an impossible transition.

"Boys," I pleaded, standing in front of them. "Any chance you can settle down, just for a few moments, so I can give you the day's prompt?"

"Please," said Art, "no more prompts. No more writing. We were all up late working on our social studies essay." He looked at Caleb and said, "Well, most of us were." Caleb blushed and looked down.

"OK then," I said. "I promise no writing in class today. We can just talk about the book."

"*Roll of Thunder, Hear Me Snore*," Art announced on cue.

"Really," I said, taking his bait for once. "What's so boring about it?"

"All of it," said Davey. All the boys nodded in agreement.

I knew they weren't connecting with the book. The night before, I'd searched my mind for something I remembered about reading this book in middle school. I thought back to my seventh-grade teacher, Mr. Sharkey. He wore Hawaiian shirts, sang in an Eagles cover band, and played a lot of music in class. Then I remembered how I'd connected with the book—it wasn't by just reading it.

"OK, boys, listen to this," I said. I didn't want to look like an idiot in front of them, so I'd had Adam show me how to sync my phone up with the smart board. I pressed play on my phone, and as the music began to play, lyrics appeared on the large screen over my head.

I watched the boys listening to Billie Holiday crooning "Strange Fruit." The boys looked confused. I played the song again.

"Her voice is weird," said Davey. "Real weird."

"It sounds like she's singing underwater," said Guy.

"Look at the lyrics," I charged them. "What's she singing about?"

"Fruit," said Art. Some other boys laughed nervously.

"Good," I said. "What kind of fruit?"

"Ms. Parsons," said Caleb, "if she's just singing about fruit, then why is she so sad?"

I smiled. He was leading me right there. "Look at the lyrics," I said, pointing at the smart board. "How does she describe the fruit, Caleb?"

"The eyes are bulging and the mouth is twisted," he said. I played the song a third time. Before I could say anything else, he went on, "the smell of flesh burning."

"Yes," I said. "What's the fruit? What's really hanging from the tree, Caleb?"

"Bodies," he said.

"What kind of bodies? Think about the book. What kind of bodies are hanging from trees?"

"Black bodies," whispered Guy.

"Right again," I whispered back. "I know this is a tough read, a lot of these books are, but there's a reason you're reading them. Think about the kids in your book having to walk past these bodies hanging from the trees." They all looked at me. Actually, they all gazed at me. One or two of them actually nodded. As tough as it was being here, I'd never forget how good it felt to be looked at this way, like there was nothing I could not make better.

～

On my way to pick up Grace, I called Beeks. She'd been calling and texting since Thanksgiving, but I hadn't responded. I still wasn't sure

I was ready to forgive her, but I was tired of avoiding her. It had been over three weeks, and I was ready to hear her voice again.

"Crap," she said before I could say anything. "They're freezing their pee again."

"What?"

"Yup. You heard me right."

"The boys?"

"Who else? Stevie got the twins to do it on a dare. Hell, those two will pee anywhere. It's not like they need to be dared. Now my freezer is full of baggies of pee. I know this because I just defrosted one thinking it was chicken stock."

"Oh no!"

"Oh yes. Guess what? You can't make soup with pee."

We both laughed and then paused in awkward silence.

"Thank you for calling," she said.

"Beeks, I don't like being mad at you," I said. "It doesn't feel right."

"Listen—my stupid indiscretion aside, I love you and I'm sorry. I'm so, so sorry, Aggie."

"I know."

"I want you to know that I didn't tell her everything."

"What do you mean?" I knew what she meant.

"I just said Jack had gotten himself into some trouble, money trouble. I left out the rest. Listen, I know that I violated your trust. It was really only once, and I felt terrible as soon as I said anything, but I know that it doesn't make it better."

"You're right," I said. "It doesn't. How could you do it, Beeks? How could you talk to Lindsey about me, about Jack, about any of this?"

"I don't know. I think I was worried about you and I was blowing off steam. I just blew it in the wrong direction. I'm sorry, really I am."

I didn't say anything.

"Listen," she said, "you don't need to really forgive me yet. Just don't not talk to me. I know I deserve the cold shoulder, but I just don't think I can handle it."

"It's fine," I said. "I'm not going to stay mad at you. Certainly not because of Lindsey. I know how you feel about Jack. I've always known. You have a terrible poker face."

"I'll be a better friend," she promised. "I can do better."

"OK," I said, "I'll hold you to it."

"New subject," she announced, less than a second later. "What you are you making for dinner?"

"Seriously?" I asked.

"Yup. I want to make sure you two aren't still eating like runaways."

"Actually, I haven't had to cook much lately. I've been eating with my neighbor."

"*No* way!" said Beeks. "You're eating with the Figg?"

"I am indeed."

"How did that happen?" she asked. "Do I need to start yelling?"

"No, you don't. It happened because she found me feeling sorry for myself," I said.

"Now I really feel bad," she said. "I drove you to the Figg."

"Yes, you did. Right into the arms of her Christmas sweater."

"No WAY!"

"Yes way. And if you don't start being nicer to me, I'm gonna ask her if I can borrow one."

27

Jack called me again that night. The heat had not yet kicked in. I was sitting in a hot bath, listening to music, when the music paused and the phone rang. I dried my hand on a towel and reached for it. Blocked number.

"Jack?"

"Hello, darling."

"Hello."

"It's really good to hear your voice again," he said.

"Where are you, Jack?" I asked, sitting up, pulling my knees into my chest.

"What?"

"Where are you? Are you still in LA? Are you in New York now? Are you somewhere else?"

"Aggie, I . . ."

Maybe if he'd called me in the morning I'd have been more patient, but it was late, and I had used up all my patience over the course of the day. "Jack, where are you? Are you just going to keep calling so we can hear each other's voices? Don't you need more?"

"You know I need more," he growled.

I leaned back and knocked a shampoo bottle into the bath.

"What's that noise?" he asked.

"Oh. I'm in the bath," I said.

"You take baths?" he asked.

"I do now," I said. "The heat isn't on yet, so I'm warming up old-school."

He paused. I heard him breathing.

"What do you look like?" he asked.

"What do you mean?" Did Jack know about the ombré fiasco? "Um, I'm kind of the same as I was when you left. My hair is a little darker . . ."

"No, Aggie. Tell me what you look like. All of you. Right now."

Really?

"Aggie . . ."

"OK, OK. I'm naked in the bath . . ." I looked down. This was not going to be pretty.

"Surely you can tell me more than that," he murmured.

Sure, Jack. If you must know, I don't really bother shaving anymore and I haven't seen any hot wax since I got here, so my bikini line has grown down to my very hairy knees. My skin is the color of milk, and thanks to my toddler diet, my thighs now officially touch.

This wouldn't work. Jack didn't want to hear that. Hell, I didn't want to say that. I needed to describe myself to him the way I was, the way I used to be, the way he wanted me to be. "Sure," I said. "I can do that." But just as I was about to describe my toned, bronzed, hairless legs of yore, I got a text.

MS P I AM IN TROUBLE

And then:

U THERE?

I texted back immediately. Who is this?

CALEB.

"Aggie, what's going on?" Jack asked while I texted Caleb, Where are you?

"Oh, one second, Jack."

NEED YOUR HELP. OUTSIDE IN BUSHES.

I texted him back: Wait there. Don't move. I need to check coast is clear.

"Aggie?" I could hear his growing impatience.

"Jack, I have to go. Can you call me later?"

No answer.

"Jack, I'm really, really sorry, but something came up."

"Something came up?" he asked, almost mimicking me.

"A problem with a student."

"Now? At night?"

"Yes, now. We can do this later, I promise," I said.

He didn't respond.

"Goodbye. I love you." I waited for him to say goodbye, but he was already gone.

I jumped out of the bath, dried off, threw on some sweats, and raced downstairs and into the foyer. I stuck my head out over the threshold and checked to see if Stacey Figg was keeping watch. Her downstairs lights were off.

OK, I wrote. Coast clear. Meet me at the door.

Caleb emerged from the bushes and flew up the stairs. I held the door open, motioned for him to come inside, and we stood in the foyer. So much happened in this tiny, cramped, seemingly inconsequential space.

"What's going on, Caleb?"

"I did something stupid," he said, staring down at his large feet, which were shuffling back and forth, mashing dirt into the tile. He wore a winter coat and a red hoodie underneath, the red hood pulled up over his head, almost covering his eyes.

I waited. I found that the boys talked more if I asked less. (In moments like this, I often wondered if I'd remember any of this when Grace was an adolescent. Perhaps I should have been taking notes.)

He spoke. "The big essay for social studies."

I waited some more.

"I got an essay online." He looked up at me, his eyes full of tears, his face full of panic. "I cheated and Ms. Creek knows it."

Caleb was a boy who didn't need to crib an essay online. His work for me was sporadic and often rushed, but it was good. I wanted to know why he cheated, but I didn't ask, the same way I knew not to ask how Caleb got my cell phone number: I really didn't want to know the answers. I didn't want to know that he cheated because he could, or because it was easier, or that he got my phone number because he'd hacked into the teacher directory. These kids made stupid mistakes and bad decisions with shocking, almost reflexive regularity. All I could do was help clean up.

"How do you know you got caught?" I asked.

Caleb removed his hood and looked at me squarely. "Ms. Creek sent me an email. She wants me to meet with her tomorrow. I'm sure Principal Jerk will be there, too. I'm toast, Ms. Parsons. They're gonna throw me out." With each sentence he grew more hysterical, his voice cracking.

"Let's just take this one step at a time," I said. "I'll talk to Ms. Creek tomorrow. Would you be willing to write the essay yourself? Can you have it done by the weekend?"

"I can't do it!" he cried. "I don't know how! I haven't taken a single page of notes all year. I don't know where to start!"

"Caleb, I'm going to get someone to send you some notes. Read as much as you can. Read all night if you have to, and tomorrow you and I will start work on the essay. Let me deal with Ms. Creek."

He exhaled loudly. "I knew you would help," he said.

"Of course. And Caleb . . ."

"Yes?"

"When this is all said and done, you and I are going to talk about making sure that it doesn't ever happen again. All right?"

"All right." He nodded, reached for the door, pulled his hood up over his head, checked both ways, and ran into the night.

I closed the door and tried calling Jack back, but the phone went straight to the voice mail lady. At least she had replaced her out-of-service cousin. I wanted desperately to hear Jack's voice again, but I was annoyed. I tried him one more time, and when I heard the voice mail lady's voice again, I threw my phone down onto the couch and went to bed.

-28-

The next morning I waited for Mona Creek, the boys' social studies teacher, in front of her first-period class. She was tall and rail thin, with dark hair she wore in a tight bun, giving her a permanently pained, pinched look. She always looked surprised, but she seemed especially surprised to see me.

"Mona," I began. "Have you got a minute?"

She blinked her assent, her large brown eyes quickly shuttering.

"It's about Caleb and his essay," I said. "He's really panicked. He knows what he did was wrong, and he wants to make it right. He wants to write the essay himself."

Mona stared at me. "You mean he wants you to write it for him?"

"No, Mona. I mean, he wants me to help him write it. I'm supposed to be teaching writing, so I'd like to help." I smiled at her. I really wanted her to smile back at me, but I wasn't sure Mona smiled.

"Fine," she said. "Good luck to you."

"One more thing," I said, still smiling. "Would it be OK to wait on bringing Gavin into this?"

Finally, Mona shot me something that resembled a smile. It wasn't a happy smile—it was a smile of relief. "OK," she said. "I can do that." I thought about it for a moment. Was Mona happy because she got to avoid Gavin?

"Gives me more time to grade papers," she said. Poor Mona Creek. All she wanted was more time to grade the many, many papers she was assigning and receiving.

~

That night, Caleb and I got to work on his essay.

"I hate social studies," he said, shivering in the foyer.

I made two cups of hot chocolate and brought in two chairs.

"Sit," I said.

"Fine," he agreed, shoving his hands in his pockets and sitting down. He slumped all the way down in the chair so that his legs took up the whole foyer. He gazed down at them. I really wanted to tell him to look at me while I was talking to him, but I heard Marge's voice in my head from my days at Sunny Day. *Boys don't want to look at you while they are talking to you. Many of them can't do two things at once, and if one of the things is looking at you, you can kiss the conversation goodbye.*

"Let's talk about this essay," I began.

"I can't, Ms. P." He looked up. Some hair fell onto his forehead. "Really, I can't write a whole essay. Not about the frickin' American Revolution."

I was getting tired of hearing the same thing from the boys. I needed to prove to them that they could do this, that they could in fact write an essay. I handed Caleb a small wire-bound notebook. He looked at it like it was papyrus.

"For real?"

"For real. We can use this to help us. I grew up in California, which means I didn't spend a single day learning about the American Revolution. I'm in worse shape than you are."

"Unlikely," he said.

"No, I think you have a head start. How many years have you spent learning about colonial America?"

Caleb looked at his hand and started mumbling to himself and counting on his fingers. "OK," he said, "you win. But just because I've spent five years learning about this stuff doesn't mean I can write about it."

"Caleb, writing is thinking. If you can think, you can write."

He did not look convinced.

I asked him questions about the notes I'd sent him. I told him to write down his answers, each on a separate page. I ripped out all the pages and organized them into three piles.

"Here," I announced, now sitting on the floor of the foyer. "This is your essay." He looked baffled but amused.

"What do you mean?"

"Each pile is a paragraph," I said. "Each pile is a different effect of the revolution. One pile is social effect, one is political, and one is economic. They are in your own words. You wrote on those pages. I just helped organize them. We grouped them together and made an essay. All you have to do for now is outline what's on these pages."

He looked at me blankly.

"Once you've outlined, then you can write an essay. I can help, but seriously, writing is just thinking. You can do this."

Caleb eventually reached down and picked up the piles. He laid them on top of each other. "How do you know how to do this?"

"How to do what?"

"How to help us like this. How do you know what to do?"

My own competence was still a total shock to me. "Honestly, Caleb, I have no idea."

-29-

I woke up early to the sound of my phone. I opened one eye and checked the time—2:00 a.m., 11:00 p.m. on the West Coast.

"Hello," I breathed, still half-asleep.

"Hello, darling."

I pushed myself up in bed, leaned on my elbows, and clutched the phone to my ear.

"Are you lying down?" he asked.

"What?"

"Please, Aggie," he begged. "Just tell me. Are you lying down?"

"Sort of," I replied. "Not really."

"Then lie down, Aggie. Lie down and tell me what you're wearing." I heard his breathing grow heavier. "Please."

Describing my pale, hairy body in the bath was bad enough. Did I really have to do this? Making a mental note to start some sort of exercise as soon as possible, I ran my fingers across the sweatshirt I wore to sleep, the sweatshirt from college that I'd stashed in the back of my closet when I moved in with Jack. I don't think Jack even knew about this sweatshirt.

"A sweatshirt," I said, moving my hand up the neckline I had cut years ago in an effort to look cool.

"Take it off," he said.

"Really, Jack?" I asked.

"Really."

This was the last thing I wanted to be doing. But Jack wanted it. Jack wanted me. Maybe if I gave him what he wanted, he'd come back sooner. I sat up a little and peeled off the sweatshirt. Still holding the phone, not wanting to put Jack down, I yanked the sweatshirt over my head with the other hand and tossed it onto the floor. I lay back down. The phone and Jack were gone.

"Aggie?" I heard him call. I looked around.

Shit. Shit. Shit. The phone was trapped in the sweatshirt. I tried to reach for it on the floor but fell out of bed and landed with a thump. I scrambled for the phone. In a sweat, I reached for it.

"I'm back," I heaved, on all fours. "I'm here."

"Now what," he breathed. "What's left?"

If only you knew how many layers were left. I climbed back into bed, lay flat on my back, closed my eyes, and tried to concentrate.

"What else?" he said. "What else are you wearing?"

"A long-sleeved T-shirt," I said, my eyes closed.

"Take that off, too." I put the phone down next to me, hit the speaker button, and pulled the waffle-knit shirt up over my head. I yanked my arms out and threw it down.

"What else?"

"An undershirt."

"Take it off." What was he panting about? I was the one doing all the heavy lifting.

"Sweatpants."

"Take them off, Aggie." I shimmied the pants down to my ankles and kicked them off, all without the use of my hands.

"Leggings," I said. "Leggings are next."

"Jesus Christ, how much are you wearing to bed?"

"If you must know," I said, opening my eyes and sitting up again, "I sleep like a bag lady. I layer up because it's freezing when I fall asleep, even after I take a bath in a very old tub. Jack, George Washington could have bathed in this tub. At some point, usually around five, the heat kicks in. Full blast. I don't want to boil in my bed, so I need to start peeling off layers. By six, when Grace starts to call for me, I'm in a T-shirt and underwear. Really big underwear. Turns out really big underwear keeps you a lot warmer. You've caught me just before the heat wave. It's about to get pretty damn hot, Jack. You don't wanna miss it." I didn't recognize my own voice.

"I can wait, Aggie," he said, refusing to mirror my anger. "I can wait for you to peel off all your layers."

"Yeah, well, we're only halfway there, so I'm just not sure it's worth it, Jack."

"Don't you want to feel my hands on you?" he asked. "Don't you want me, Aggie?" The growling had returned, and it was hard to resist. I felt myself getting warmer.

"My God, yes. I want it more than you know. I want your hands on me, Jack. I just don't want to spend thirty minutes getting undressed only to feel *my* hands on me." I paused and squeezed my eyes shut. "If you don't want to answer any of my questions, then fine. But if you want me, Jack, if you really want to touch me, then you're going to have to come and do it yourself."

Fantastic, I thought, looking at the pile of clothes next to me. *Now I have to put all this shit back on again.*

Beeks called first thing in the morning. She called to ask what Grace wanted for Christmas. While she was reeling off a list of ideas, I told her about Jack. I thought catching Beeks off guard would keep her from losing her mind. It did not work.

"He wanted you to do WHAT?" She launched immediately into her yelling portion. "MY GOD, AGGIE, THAT GUY DOESN'T QUIT. The only thing Brian and I ever do on the phone is fight." She then proceeded to ask me all sorts of sordid questions.

"Tell me again," she said. "What do you have to do to yourself?"

"Beeks!"

"And what's he doing while you're doing the flannel-pajama strip-tease? Do I even want to know?"

"Beeks!"

"And how does he know you're actually doing it and not just faking it while you watch TV on mute? Do you have to take pictures? Do you need to send him proof?"

"Beeks. Please. Must I?"

"I don't know, must you? How many times have you had to do this?"

"Never. I've never done it before. Besides, how do you know I didn't want to do it?"

"Oh, I just know," she said.

"Beeks, please. Exactly how humiliated do you need me to be?"

"Fair enough. No more questions," she relented. "As for my day, I'm about to make you really jealous. I will be spending the morning in the principal's office . . . again. Kyle spent last night writing a letter to his teacher. *Dear Miss Sonia, I am sorry I burped in your face.* That letter took three hours to write. Ask me how excited I am about this."

"Why didn't you let me write it for you? I'm adept at sounding like a misbehaving boy."

She laughed and then said, "OK, back to the subject at hand."

I groaned.

"Seriously, Aggie. I'm glad he's back. I'm happy for you."

"Thank you." *I think.*

"Just promise me you'll draw the line somewhere?"

"What do you mean?" I asked.

"If he asks you to FaceTime, just say no. Feeling yourself up over the phone is one thing, Aggie, but holding up a camera to it, that's just wrong."

"Thanks for the advice, Beeks."

"Listen, Aggie . . . one more thing," she said in a tentative tone I rarely heard from her.

"What?"

She paused. "Nothing. Like I said, I'm happy for you." It was so unlike Beeks not to say every last thing on her mind (and then some), but I gladly took her reticence. "I think this is a good development," she said.

"Thanks."

I hope you're right, Beeks. I really hope so.

PART THREE: WINTER

I was sitting in the living room examining the contents of a large fruit and cheese basket Ruth Moore had sent to my house that day. Jack's imminent return had sent me in search of some exercise. Given that I'd been describing my body over the phone as completely unchanged from the days when I spent two-thirds of my time taking care of my appearance, if I didn't do something soon, when he finally saw me in the flesh, Jack might decide I needed a little less . . . flesh. I naturally thought about yoga, but I couldn't find anything nearby, and I didn't have the money for classes. I needed something free and flexible. I'd seen people running past me on campus and up and down the streets of Riverdale—and they all seemed so happy and pleased with themselves. Why couldn't I be a smug runner, too? I knew Jack didn't approve of running, that he thought runners looked stringy and unsexy. "Nobody wants to see a runner naked," he'd often say when a runner ran past us on the beach. That might be true, but I was willing to bet that Jack would happily take a runner's body over mine.

I had just come back from a run across campus through something called freezing rain, and the absolute last thing I wanted to do was go anywhere. I pulled Grace out of the plastic bubble protecting her, grateful that my ridiculous stroller had a running feature, even if I'd only just started using it. My feet were so cold and wet that my toes had frozen together. I was defrosting them on the radiator, eating cheese (take that, Smug Runners!), and reading Ruth's note.

Happy holidays, Agnes! We're happy to have you here with us this year. Hope you've settled in and haven't seen any more of your little "friends." Best, Ruth.

It was hard to believe Christmas was so close. Frankly, I only realized we were weeks away when the boys started talking about Christmas trees in class.

Guy had said that the only thing he liked about Christmas was the tree, and Art looked at me and said, "Ms. P., did you get your tree yet?"

"Huh?"

"A Christmas tree? Do you have one?"

"Crap," I blurted. "No. I guess I need to buy one. I've never bought a tree before."

"Really?" Davey asked, looking shocked. "You never bought a tree in LA? Even a pink one?" He laughed at his own joke, a joke I'd heard many times.

"No. My husband bought our trees."

"Oh," he said, looking at the other boys. I saw Guy mouth the word *husband* to Caleb, who quickly looked at me.

"Yeah, I've never even had a real tree," I added. The boys looked shocked.

I didn't tell them that as a child, my family could never afford a real tree. I grew up with a small fake affair my parents bought before I was born and that I inherited after they died. With Jack, I had a large, gallant, but also artificial tree. It smelled like a real tree and it looked like a real tree—or at least I thought so until I first smelled a real tree at Beeks's house—but Jack didn't like needles. He didn't like the way they invaded and then lingered for weeks after the tree had gone.

Jack's tree came decorated and was delivered by men who manicured it yearly to fit the living space, even though artificial trees don't grow. (The same men removed the tree and presumably stored it somewhere for the following year.) The next day a different team, this time of women, would arrive at our house to decorate the tree. They would string lights, add garlands, and, finally, hang ornaments. All of it, the lights, the garlands, the ornaments, it was all monochromatic—and all a neutral color—gold, silver, chrome, or ivory. An exception was made for occasional ornaments, so each year I ordered anniversary ornaments for us, and then last year I ordered one in anticipation of Grace.

"You can't control a real tree," he said on our first Christmas together, a couple of months after we'd met and just after we'd gotten engaged.

"Why would you want to control a tree?" I asked, almost laughing at the idea.

"For the same reason you'd want to control anything," he said, pulling me closer. God, that man smelled good. I hadn't spoken to him since our botched racy phone call, but I could still smell him. "If you can control something, make it fit your specifications, get it just the way you want it, why not do it?"

I remember feeling his hands slide under my shirt. I don't remember what happened next. Actually, I do. But I couldn't risk drifting into fantasy in front of the boys, so I shook the memory from my mind.

The doorbell woke me at five the next morning. I leaped out of bed, grabbed a sweatshirt, and flew downstairs. Before I opened the door, I checked my reflection. If this was Jack, he was going to be sorely disappointed when he saw me.

I opened the door. Not Jack. Instead, I saw Caleb, Art, Guy, and Davey, and a patchy and very harassed-looking evergreen tree.

"Surprise!" they yelled. I shot a panicked look toward Stacey's house, but it was too dark and too early for her to be up and lurking. I pulled the boys into the foyer.

"Here's your tree," Guy said proudly, trying to drag the tree in behind them. All four boys got together and gave the poor tree one final yank into the foyer.

"Boys? What is this?"

"A brother of one of the security guards sells trees. We pooled our money and got this delivered to the guard gate this morning," Art announced proudly.

"You can't not have a Christmas tree," said Guy. "Everyone needs a tree."

I looked at the plucked tree, many of whose branches were likely strewn across campus. What branches remained had been bent and twisted in the journey. It was a little pathetic, but it was trying hard not to be. Kind of like the boys.

"So true," I said. "Everyone needs a tree."

I let them help me install the tree between the brown couch and the bay window, and we all stood back to admire it.

"Looks good," said Davey.

"Looks perfect. Thank you, boys." I smiled at all four of them. "I appreciate that you did all this for me." In just a few short months, I had gone from being someone who had everything done for her to someone who had to fight back tears when anyone helped at all.

"Oh, we forgot!" said Art, grabbing his backpack and opening it. "We have these, too!" He pulled out a garbage bag and handed it to me. "They threw in some ornaments because we said you probably didn't have any."

"You guys are the best," I said. "You're so awesome that I'm giving you something in return." I ran into the kitchen and came back with some cans in my hand. "Kale strawberry and my new favorite, plum carrot." I handed the boys the cans of veggie puffs, and they all laughed.

"I'm not so sure this is a fair trade," said Caleb.

After I ushered them out, I went upstairs to get dressed. I checked my phone. I had five missed calls from a blocked number. Jack seemed only to be calling me when I couldn't talk, as if he knew, somehow, that I'd be unavailable. I was happy and proud of my boys. I didn't want to be, but I was annoyed. I sighed and threw down the phone.

~

Grace and I went to a day-care winter holiday party, which had the double distinction of being both potluck and nut-free. I signed up to bring an entrée, then completely forgot about it. I texted Beeks in a panic.

Potluck emergency. Need a dish to bring to day-care party in an hour.

She replied quickly. Easy. Boil some pasta, then melt cheese over the meat sticks. Put it in a dish and call it a casserole.

Really?

Yup. Just shove the dish in the middle of the table and act like you've never seen it before. No one will suspect a thing.

I made some pasta, then opened four jars of meat sticks, drained the viscous goo, and dumped it all into a yellow casserole dish that must have belonged to the previous tenant of my town house. I tossed some shredded mozzarella on top and nuked the dish for thirty seconds.

When I walked into the day-care building, I was immediately greeted by a table of food, complete with signage—FUDGY GLUTEN-FREE BROWNIES BAKED BY JAKE'S MOM, ELLA, and BROCCOLI BITES BAKED BY JORDANA'S DAD, LUKE. I'd be damned if I was going to let someone write CHEESY PASTA WITH MEAT FINGERS MICROWAVED BY GRACE'S MOM, AGNES. I skipped the signage and hid my plate at the back of the table.

Grace seemed completely comfortable in her surroundings, which put me quickly at ease, even though I'd held back from so many of the parents so far. While she crawled in and out of a plastic climbing structure, I sat on the play mat alongside her and talked to the parents, some for the very first time. We played a game I would soon learn was incredibly popular at day-care gatherings: "I was so tired, I . . ." We went around and said the worst thing we'd each done that week while in the throes of parental exhaustion. Tom, a dad of twins, said he was so tired he brushed his teeth with his wife's face wash.

"Big deal," said Ella. "I'm so tired that I've given up face wash. I just swab my cheeks with a baby wipe."

"I can one-up you," chimed in Gabby, whose daughter, Lyla, was also in Grace's day-care group. "I was so tired I cleaned Lyla's butt with a Clorox wipe." She was soon bested by a dad who accidentally put hand sanitizer on a diaper rash. We all laughed. Everything about this group was different from my Santa Monica baby group, and at the same time, everything was the same. Only the diamond earrings were smaller. OK, there were no diamond earrings. I felt more at home than I had in a long time.

~

Later on, I opened the boys' bag of ornaments and tinsel and dumped it out onto the floor in front of the tree. As if on cue, Grace crawled right into the mess and began shoving things into her mouth. I scooped her up and carried her on my hip as I hung the ornaments. I hummed Christmas songs and we held the tinsel together, my hand guiding hers as we threw it onto the tree. She watched closely as I hung the ornaments on the few branches strong enough to hold them—the drag across campus had taken its toll on the tree. Each ornament was a little off—chipped, cracked, missing a hook—and no two were alike.

This small, understated tree took me back to Modesto and to my parents. Back then, a decorated tree also meant one with a handful of mismatched ornaments clinging desperately to branches and a few scattered strands of tinsel. If we needed new ornaments, we'd wait until the day after Christmas to buy them from the local drugstore, when they were stashed in discount bins by the cashier.

I hadn't thought to bring any ornaments with me. I wasn't thinking about Christmas when I left California in August. I expected to be back in Santa Monica by now, hanging Grace's first Christmas ornament, putting her in an expensive, highly impractical dress she'd wear once—twice if you count the Christmas picture.

There was no Christmas picture this year. There was no first Christmas ornament. There was no Christmas dress. This year, on Grace's first Christmas, she wasn't going to see Jack's tree in all its monochromatic glory. I couldn't call him, and I kept missing his calls. No, we weren't going to see Jack's tree, and barring some surprise, I was pretty sure we weren't going to see Jack, either.

-3-

Beeks called me on Christmas morning. I could smell the tree all the way up in my bed. I sat back against my pillow and inhaled the pine. Grace was watching *Rudolph the Red-Nosed Reindeer* on my phone and picking at a bowl of multicolored goldfish crackers I'd discovered in the inner aisles of the supermarket. It was quiet and I had nowhere to be. I was planning on spending most of the day in much the same way.

Grace looked puzzled and showed me the phone when Rudolph was interrupted by Beeks's face and contact info.

"Merry Christmas," Beeks said as I put the phone to my ear.

"Right back at you, Beeks," I replied.

"I wish we weren't going to my in-laws'," she said. "I really wish you were coming here."

I didn't. The memory of Thanksgiving was still too fresh. Even if Beeks could promise me a Lindsey-free Christmas in her apartment, I didn't think I was ready to go back.

"Don't feel bad," I said. "This is the first time in a few years that I don't have to spend Christmas with Don, Cheryl, and their ungrateful children. Honestly, the thought of watching Christmas movies in my pajamas with Grace is glorious."

"I get it," she said. "I'd rather be on the couch with you, Grace, and that reindeer." Beeks knew that I'd been watching the Claymation

Rudolph on Christmas mornings since I was a kid. "Instead, I'm here making sure the boys don't throw Christmas cookies out the windows again."

"Again?" I asked.

"Yup. Last year, they opened a bathroom window and threw a whole batch down at people on the street, one at a time, like pretty little bombs."

"Could have been worse," I said. "Could have been a fruitcake."

Beeks laughed. "Listen," she said, her voice modulating to the key of serious business. "There's something I've been wanting to say to you." She paused. "I know what I said to Lindsey was wrong, but Aggie, it was hard."

"What was hard?" I asked, straightening up in bed, readying myself to hear what Beeks wanted to say but couldn't last time we spoke.

"It was hard for me to see you with Jack. Not because I didn't like him. I did like him. He's a likable guy. You were the hard part, Aggie. It was hard to see you."

"I'm not sure I understand what you mean," I said.

"I mean that it was hard to watch you with Jack."

"Why, Beeks? Was it so hard for you to see me happy?" I felt my heart beating faster.

"That's not fair. Think about it, Aggie. Think about how we met, right before we both got out of Modesto. When I think about you, I think about that feeling, that ticket in my hand, that ticket out of town. I think about how it felt that summer before college. We thought that anything was possible, even if it wasn't. It wasn't hard to see you happy and married, Aggie. It wasn't even hard to see you not working. It was just really hard to see you stop trying."

"Trying what? What had I stopped trying to do?"

"You stopped trying to be the person you wanted to be when we met, when we left Modesto, the person who couldn't wait to be in charge of herself and her own life. You could have still gotten married and been that person, Aggie. You could even have stopped working and been that person. But you didn't even try. You just stopped. And I can't help but wonder how Jack let you."

Grace was trying to climb off the side of the bed. With one hand I clutched her; with the other I held my phone.

"Honestly, Beeks, I don't think Christmas morning is the best time for us to talk about what a disappointment I've been to you."

"That's not fair," she said. "That isn't what I'm saying, and you know it."

"Then what are you saying?" I charged, clinging to Grace.

"I'm saying it's more complicated than me not liking Jack or not liking the fact that your life changed," Beeks said quietly. "It's not as simple as that."

"Well, you got your way, Beeks," I said, sounding angrier than I'd intended. "It's Christmas and I'm alone. We don't need to talk about the person I was with Jack, because like it or not, he's not here." I looked up at my dusty ceiling, throwing my head back and blinking away angry tears. "Oh, and there are cobwebs growing in the corners of my room. So later today I'll grab a broom, stand on my bed, and take a whack at them. Good enough for you? Is this the me you prefer?"

"Aggie . . ."

"No, Beeks. I don't want to spend Christmas morning defending my choices to you."

"I love you, Aggie," she said before I could say anything else.

"Merry Christmas, Beeks. I'll call you later," I said, which was code for *I can't talk about this anymore.* We hung up, and I handed the phone back to Grace so she could resume her reindeer watching. I took some deep breaths, willing myself to calm down.

Grace gave me another puzzled look as her program was interrupted for a second time. She showed me the phone.

Merry Christmas, darling.

I pulled the phone up to my nose and smelled it. God, I was desperate. I closed my eyes and waited for a response. *Please let him be close.* I had some Jack memories I kept in the front of my mind so that I could access them whenever I needed. I flipped through them and landed on the story of how we met. I'd been walking down the street when I saw Marc Owen, an ex-boyfriend from college, walking toward me. I desperately wanted to avoid Marc. It had been a couple of years since I'd seen him, and our breakup was messy—so messy that Beeks referred to him as "stalker boy." Before Marc got too close, I ducked into a sushi restaurant. Marc followed. I looked around frantically and immediately spotted Jack at the sushi bar. He was hard to miss. It's hard to overlook thick, wavy, dirty-blond hair, strong cheekbones, and enormous hazel eyes. His was an older, distinguished, and not just handsome but beautiful face. Beeks always said that Jack looked like an actor who could easily play the president of the United States on TV. I stared at his handsome, presidential face, and I made a beeline. He looked up at me, and I spoke to him as if we knew each other, as if he'd seen me before, as if I wasn't a complete stranger.

"Please," I said. "Pretend we're together. Just for a minute."

He furrowed his brow, but the corners of his mouth were raised in amusement.

"Please," I said again. With my head, I motioned to Marc, who was not far behind me.

Jack looked over my shoulder at Marc entering the restaurant and, with one hand, pulled me into the chair next to him. He wrapped his other arm around my waist and leaned in to me. His broad, square shoulder touched mine as he whispered in my ear, "I'm going to pretend I'm saying something really sexy right now. So you need to look like you just heard it." I looked at him, our faces so close, and he took my breath away. Just like that. Just like they say it happens. Marc took a few steps in and looked at us and stopped. He stared at us huddling for a moment and then walked out of the restaurant. Jack kept his arm around my waist.

"Hungry?" he asked, still staring at me.

I was a lot of things in that moment, but I wasn't sure one of them was hungry. Mostly, I was scared. Not scared because I thought Jack was dangerous, but scared because I would have sat for hours if Jack had asked me. Hell, I would have done just about anything if he had asked.

"I can't," I said. "I have to go."

"Do you? Do you really have to go?" He dropped his voice even lower and leaned forward.

Oh yes, I really do. I nodded because in order to speak, you need to be able to breathe.

Jack took his arm off my waist. I looked down to where it had been, and then I looked back at him. I pushed my chair away and got up, slowly. "Thank you," I said. He didn't take his eyes off me.

"How would I go about finding you if I wanted to see you again?" he asked.

"Me?"

"You," he said, smiling and raising an eyebrow. He put his hand on his chest and said, "My name is Jack Parsons."

There seemed to be less and less space between us, even though neither of us had moved.

"Agnes," I stuttered. "Agnes Riley."

"Anything else you can tell me about yourself?" he asked.

"I'm a preschool teacher," I said. "In Santa Monica."

"OK, Agnes Riley, who teaches preschool in Santa Monica. I'll see you around."

I wasn't looking to be consumed, and I certainly wasn't looking for a man almost twenty years older. But Jack came looking for me. One week later, he was waiting for me as I got off the bus in Santa Monica, two blocks from Sunny Day. And that is the story of us—at least, it's the story of how we started.

I texted him back.

Merry Christmas.

The text did not bounce back. I was officially unblocked. I handed the phone to Grace and rolled onto my back.

Grace looked at me again, and I saw another text had come.

Darling. Look outside.

I shot up in bed, almost knocking Grace off the side. I grabbed her, my heart beating in the back of my throat. I shivered again and picked her up. I shot a look out my bedroom window, but the overhang on the porch was blocking my view. I ran down the stairs with Grace in my arms. I raced into the foyer and stared at the front door. I don't know how long I stood there staring at it, but at some point, I reached out and touched the handle. Before I turned it, I grabbed my hat off a hook. *Good thinking*, I thought to myself. *If this is Jack, if it's really him, better cover up the ombré fiasco.* I pulled the hat down over my hair, twisted the handle, and pulled the door open. Jack was standing on my doorstep, leaning on the frame, inches from me.

"Merry Christmas, darling," he whispered.

I gasped, swallowed the lump in my throat, and felt my eyes grow hot with tears. I reached to touch him, to make sure he was real. I put my hand on his arm and left it there, resting on the thick, buttery leather of a coat I had never seen.

"You're here," I said. "You're here." He looked so out of place in New York, on campus, on my doorstep.

Jack leaned toward me and looped his other arm around my waist. He pulled me to him so that our faces were almost touching. "I am," he said. "I couldn't not see you today. I couldn't not see you both on Christmas."

His lips touched mine, and we stood there like that. Our lips touching. I felt his teeth tugging on my lower lip and then I felt more. Jack could kiss me like it was the most intimate thing. Like there was nothing else left to do.

I felt dizzy and stumbled. When he held me tighter, steadying me, I said, "It's cold. Come inside."

"I can't stay, Aggie," he said, our faces close. "Not yet."

"What?"

"I can't stay now. I have work to do today. I just wanted to see you." He reached down and kissed the top of Grace's head, breathing in her scent as he kissed her.

"What kind of work could you possibly have on Christmas?" I asked, pulling us both away.

"Aggie . . ."

"How?" I asked, resisting as he reached for me. "How can you be here in New York, but not be with us? How can you miss Thanksgiving and now Christmas?" Everything I had been holding in came pouring down my face.

"I'm still fixing things, and the kind of work I'm doing doesn't necessarily stop for Christmas." He reached out and pulled me back to him, this time more forcefully. "Soon, though. Soon I'll be back for good."

"That's not good enough," I sobbed, wishing I had an extra arm to wipe away the tears that were suddenly pooling in the neck of my sweater. "I'm all alone, Jack, and it's so hard."

"I know," he said, "and you've been so good." He pulled me even closer, so that our noses touched. His hand moved up my back, and he leaned in and kissed me. The kiss was tentative and careful, and when we stopped, our foreheads still touching, I felt his hot tears mixing with mine. The air was biting and it felt good.

"Soon," he whispered.

This time he kissed me with the even deeper urgency of someone saying goodbye. He gasped at the end and then moved his mouth to my ear, whispering, "I promise." Maybe if I had a tidbit of information for him, anything, I could lure him inside, but I didn't, and frankly, if

Jack could touch me, after months of being apart, and still walk away, then info about Ruth Moore wasn't going to persuade him to stay. He let go of me, took a step back, and before I could say anything else, he turned and walked away. He got into a car that was parked and running, a car that I hadn't even noticed was there. Out of the corner of my eye, I saw something rustle.

I instinctively looked next door and saw Stacey Figg's figure behind her blinds. I even caught a glimpse of the fabulously bright sweater she had saved for Christmas Day. I'd watched the sweaters until they had reached a crescendo of tackiness. Today she wore a neon-green number with a 3-D Santa face. Each time she raised her arms, Santa's left eye winked and "Ho, Ho, Ho" rang out from the mouth. I had never seen (or heard) anything like it before. I shuddered to think what Jack would have made of the Figg and her sweaters, but I never found out. I turned back to the car and watched him drive away.

~

With Jack's voice in my ear, Grace and I spent our week alternating between doing very little at home and making brief but hectic forays into Manhattan. As much as I wanted to stay home and rest, being at home was hard. I had too much time on my hands to replay our scene on the stoop. When I began to wonder where Jack was and felt myself growing despondent and angry, I used running as a distraction. Because I was so new to it, I had to pay close attention to my form and where I was going, which kept me from spiraling into obsessive Jack thoughts.

One day, I ran down to the water and was about to turn back when I saw Adam at the trailhead of a wooded path that ran alongside the Hudson. He was turning to head down the path when he caught sight of me and my enormous stroller.

"Agnes!" he called, pulling out an earbud. "You run?"

"Sort of," I huffed.

"Wanna run together?" he asked, jogging in place.

I had just about enough gas to make it home, but I was curious where this wooded path led. I knew if I tried it myself I'd likely get lost and end up somewhere in the next state, so I nodded and pushed the stroller over to the trail. A gust of wind whipped off the water and smacked me in the face. I was running in yoga pants, a wool sweater, and a down vest. Adam was wearing a long-sleeved shirt and running tights that stopped midcalf. I wondered how he kept so warm, then noticed that he had the hairiest ankles I'd ever seen on a man.

"I'm pretty sure I can't keep up with you," I panted as he broke into a jog. "You can run ahead at any point."

"No worries," he said, pulling his hat down over his ears. "I'm glad to have the company."

So was I. I knew it was something of a charity run, as Adam didn't seem to be working hard at all and was happy to chat while I huffed and puffed alongside him. Turns out that if you're not in great shape, you can't run and talk at the same time. I managed to ask occasional pointed questions, ones I knew would inspire long answers. I learned Adam was into gaming and was more than happy to talk about it. I also learned that his dad died when he was a baby, and he grew up a few miles away in Yonkers.

"So I grew up with a single mom, too," he said, motioning to Grace, who was thankfully still asleep in the stroller.

I wanted to correct him and tell him that I wasn't a single mom, not really. I had a husband who was on his way back to me. But that would have required more talking than I was capable of.

"But my mom never ran," he said. "How long have you been running?"

"Not too long," I said, using all the breath I could muster. "I'm a new runner."

"Well, you've gotta start somewhere, no matter how old you are," he said, reminding me that he was probably a decade younger than I was.

Over the break Grace and I also saw the large tree and even larger crowds at Rockefeller Center. We walked past decorated shop windows through hordes of tourists. We stopped to pet the horses pulling carriages in the park. I can't say I didn't look for Jack around every corner, but I was glad for the distraction and the throngs of people. We drank a lot of hot chocolate, or at least I did; Grace licked off the cream. I even cooked food that week—lentil soup, meatballs, lasagna—that the two of us ate. We were both graduating to real food at the same time.

In the ten months since Grace had been born, I don't think I had spent as much time with her as I did during winter vacation. When we moved to New York, I didn't know Grace. I didn't know what made her laugh, what scared her, what soothed her; Alma was the one who knew all that. But now that she was growing into herself, now that she was becoming her own person, I got to discover her likes and dislikes as she did. I got to learn Grace as she became Grace. It was a paltry season for gifts, but learning Grace was my Christmas present.

-4-

On New Year's Day, Jack texted me for the first time since we'd stood on my doorstep.

Happy new year, darling. This year will be better. I promise.

This was getting ridiculous. I mocked the boys endlessly for texting each other while sitting about two feet apart, sometimes closer, and for having no idea how to talk on the phone. (Art called me once when the boys had gotten into trouble off campus. Like a visitor from a nearby planet who had never before made a phone call, he just shouted his name into the phone—"Art! Art!"—to let me know he was calling.) I was no better now, reduced to texting my own husband because while he had unblocked my texts, he was still not taking my calls. I could mock all I wanted, but thanks to Jack, I had been reduced to a middle school communicator.

"Screw you," I heard myself say, jumping off the brown couch. "Screw you for promising me that things will get better without telling me what that really means."

As soon as the words were out of my mouth, I momentarily panicked, wondering if someone had heard me. Alas, I was, as always, alone. With the words out of my mouth and off my chest, I texted Jack. Happy New Year. I can't wait for better. Xxxxx

His texts came more frequently over the next few days.

Can't get you out of my mind.

Woke up with you in my head.

One afternoon, while Grace and I were at the supermarket, Jack wrote, Missing you, darling. So much.

I leaned on the cereal aisle, grabbed my phone, and texted back a string of x's, instead of texting what I really wanted to say: "If you miss me, come and get me. I'm pretty much where you left me. At the shitty supermarket."

I hadn't spoken to Beeks since Christmas Day, which meant I hadn't told her I'd seen Jack. I was desperate to talk to her, but I just couldn't, not yet. I knew what she'd say, though. I could close my eyes and hear the yelling portion. ("You waited days to tell me that you saw your missing husband? You text me when you get your period! Last week you texted me a picture of plastic wrap on sale! How could you hold out on me like this?")

Because I couldn't call Beeks, I had no choice but to knock on the Figg's door.

"Agnes!" she said, surprised to see me.

I had a baby monitor in one hand, a bottle of wine in the other, and my phone in my coat pocket, just in case. "Grace is asleep. Wanna drink?"

"Sure," she said, not sure at all what to make of my offer. I had never shown up on her doorstep unannounced before. She held the door open, and I walked inside and sat down on her couch. It was not brown. It was red brocade and covered in a swath of floral fabric.

"What's up?" Stacey asked, opening the bottle of wine I'd brought with me.

"My husband," I said. "I saw him."

"I know," she said, sitting next to me and filling our glasses. "I saw him, too. I was here when he came on Christmas."

I knew that. I'd seen her and her sweater. What I didn't know was why she was here on Christmas and not somewhere else. I didn't really know anything about her. Stacey Figg didn't talk about herself. She was too busy asking questions.

"Yeah, well. He's gone now," I said, my voice cracking. "He's gone and I'm alone again."

She looked at me. "It's hard being alone," she said. "Really hard." We looked at each other for a few long seconds.

"He'll be back," I said. "It's not like I'll be alone forever."

Stacey looked away, and I wished I'd said something else.

She then moved into her kitchen and started to season a bowl of fresh popcorn with spices. I followed her in.

"Stacey, I . . ."

"You know, I haven't always been alone," she began, her back to me. "It's not like I was born a thirtysomething single woman living in a town house at a boarding school. I have a history."

I bit my lower lip, waiting for the awkward moment to pass, when my phone vibrated with an incoming text. I looked at it.

What are you wearing?

Stacey turned around and saw me checking my phone.

I slipped it into my sweater pocket, ignoring Jack's words.

"It's fine," she said. "We can change the topic. My life is boring anyway." She sat down on her couch and put the popcorn on the coffee table. I sat down next to her and officially dropped the ball. I should have shown an interest in Stacey's life, but Jack's text threw me off.

Later that evening, when I was back in my own house, safely ensconced on the brown couch, I opened up my texts and responded to Jack. What was I wearing? It was January in New York and I was wearing just about everything I owned. I texted him back, Too much.

His texts were coming faster now, and I could feel him growing hungrier for me. I kept being as coy as I could, which wasn't easy for me, especially because even though I was frustrated, I was equally hungry. I was sure it wouldn't be long now, but it was still up to Jack to decide when I'd see him again. I was willing to let this happen on his terms—after all, I was well practiced at that—I just wasn't sure how much longer I could take the waiting.

5

Beeks was not wrong about February. She had called a few times since our conversation on Christmas morning, and one evening after Grace was asleep and I was alone with half a bottle of wine, I answered one of her calls.

"I'm calling to warn you about February," she said.

"What do I need to know about February? It's short."

"February may technically be the shortest month of the year, but in the Northeast, it's by far the worst," she said. "It's cold and depressing. Twenty-eight days will feel like a lifetime. You'll never be so happy to get to March as you will be here."

"Got it," I said. But I really didn't get it. Not yet.

"I'm also calling to apologize. Again. I just need to learn not to say everything I'm thinking," she said.

I couldn't imagine a Beeks who didn't say everything she was thinking, but it hadn't really been a problem until now. In all the years we had known each other, Beeks and I had never really fought. Now all we did was bicker and make up, only to bicker again. It was going to take some time for us to relearn how to be best friends in the same city, and I wasn't sure if I was going to be sticking around to find out if we could do it. Although the days were supposed to be getting longer, they felt short, dark, and mean. The cold was brutal even with my comforter coat. One particularly cold day, I made the rookie mistake of going for a run in the comforter coat. Five minutes in I started to bake. I ran into Adam near the library.

"Agnes?" he called. "Is that you?"

"It definitely is," I said.

"Where's Grace?" he asked. "We never run without her and the giant stroller."

"I'm dumb enough to run in this weather, but not dumb enough to drag her along." I laughed. "She's still in day care."

"About that coat . . . ," he said.

"Yeah," I interrupted. "There's a reason I never see anyone running in a down coat. I'm broiling."

The February chill seeped deep into my bones, and once it got inside me, it stayed there, taking up residency all day long. Each night I sat, steeping in the tub, thankful not to be paying the water bill.

Then there was the snow. Halfway through December, I wondered where it was. None fell on Christmas. By New Year's Eve, I thought we were in the clear. Like so many other things, I assumed New Yorkers had been exaggerating about the snow.

One Friday night in early February, I noticed a cold, metallic smell in the air when I went outside to take out the trash.

"That's snow," chirped Stacey, who appeared as I stood on my stoop, sniffing the air around me like a curious puppy. "You can smell it the night before it falls."

"For real?" I asked, looking at her. Although it was only five, it was almost pitch-black. We were both in sweats, robes, and shearling boots.

"Oh yeah. Trust me, you're waking up to snow tomorrow. Is this your first time?" she asked.

I wanted to tell her about my real first snow, the year Jack had taken me skiing in Tahoe. I wanted to tell her about the alpine lake and how it changed from sapphire blue to emerald green and then back again each time I looked at it. I wanted to tell her about the mountains of soft, fluffy, powdery snow that went as far as I could see. For a moment I thought about our hotel, the wooden beams in the ceiling, the fireplace in the bedroom, the sleigh bed that hung over the lake.

"No," I said. "I saw it once before." It wasn't that I didn't trust her. Some memories were just too painful to revisit.

Stacey saw right through me. "What's wrong?" she asked.

I needed somewhere to unload this memory, and Stacey Figg was standing right there. I was vulnerable and she could smell it on me.

"My husband," I said. "I first saw snow with him."

"No word yet?" she asked. Oh, I'd had plenty of words—I just didn't have Jack.

"Nope."

"Wine?" she asked me.

I grabbed the baby monitor, and we resumed our positions on Stacey's couch. She brought out something white and bubbly. I could just hear Jack's voice in my ear. "What is this?" he'd drawl. "Soda?"

"Thanks, Stacey," I said, trying my best. "This is perfect." I drank the soda wine. It was sweet and lifted me, so I quieted Jack's voice in my head. Besides, it felt good not to be alone. Stacey asked about my students.

"I think half my job is just convincing them that I actually like them," I said.

"We do like them, don't we?" she asked.

"Not everyone does," I said, looking down into my wine.

"Gavin likes the boys, Agnes. He really does." I didn't trust myself to make eye contact. "He has their best interests at heart," she said.

"I guess he has a funny way of showing it," I said.

"Well, this is a safe place," she announced, holding out her hands. "You can come here and talk about anything, even Gavin."

I looked up. "Thanks, Stacey," I said.

"Oh, honey," she said, beaming, "it's my pleasure."

~

Grace and I woke up the next morning to snow. By the time she called out for me at six thirty, it looked like snow had been falling for hours, because there was already more than a foot on the ground. I was giddy. I ran in and scooped up Grace, hastily changed her diaper, and threw coats, hats, gloves, and boots on both of us, right over our pajamas. The snow felt different than it had in Tahoe. It was icier and wetter, but seeing it spread out across the campus, watching how a landscape that had once been so familiar was now transformed—that was glorious. I held Grace's hand. She was able to toddle if she grasped a few of my fingers. She shuddered when the snow hit her cheek, and when her mitten fell off and her hand plunged deep into the snow, she wailed. I picked her up and wiped her off.

We walked across the fields. Kids were sledding down the snow-covered glacial rocks. Teachers were out walking or playing with their kids, as though everyone had temporarily come out of hibernation. I saw a couple of Smug Runners wearing what looked like snowshoes. I was pretty sure I wouldn't be joining them today. Adam waved at me from across the field, and I even got a wave from Ruth Moore, who was walking across campus in enormous furry snow boots. I found a quiet spot and put Grace down on her feet. Then I dropped down onto my back and made a snow angel, just like I'd seen on TV. I stood up and showed Grace my design in the snow. Then I laid her down and had her make one. She liked that a little less. A bunch of kids sledded past us.

"Wanna ride?" It was Caleb, Art, and two students from my other classes.

"Sure!" I yelled out at them.

The boys trudged over with a long black sled.

"Let us take her, Ms. P.," begged Art. "Remember, I have sisters."

"Sure thing," I said. "Just bring her back." I watched Art carefully put Grace in between his legs and Caleb ran, pulling them along. I could hear Grace shrieking with joy, and by the time they brought her back to me, she was finally sold on the snow.

It snowed through most of February. When the snow fell it was white and pristine, full of light and possibility. Days later, when the snow stubbornly refused to melt because the ground was frozen solid, it turned gray and ominous. It piled higher and higher by the side of the road and stared at me, menacing, as I maneuvered Grace's battered stroller through it. Poor stroller. It had been purchased for walks on the beach, not for the filthy slush of February in New York.

With each fresh snowfall, I knew I'd see the boys sledding. Grace had become a middle school mascot, and they fought for her attention. She was more than happy to oblige. I didn't invite the boys in on snow days; too many people were out. But I often made hot chocolate with marshmallows, and we drank it on the steps in front of my door. We even used the time to work on the boys' first big essay for me. I was using the notebook method I'd devised for Caleb, and so far it was working well, even if Art kept moaning about his dysgraphia (I had to google that) and Davey had lost three notebooks in two weeks.

On a particularly snowy day, I gave them an impromptu lesson on thesis statements.

"Yeah, what do you want ours to be?" Art asked me.

"Sorry, boys," I said, taking a sip of cocoa. "You guys are coming up with your thesis statements."

"But what if we're wrong?" asked Guy. He lobbed a snowball at some kids walking by but missed and hit the bushes.

"You won't be," I said. "And the essay will be easier to write, because it'll be about what you think, not what you think I want to hear."

Guy did not look convinced.

"It's true," said Caleb, grabbing a fistful of marshmallows from the bag. "Writing is just thinking," he announced, and when he was sure nobody was looking, he smiled at me.

6

Grace would soon turn one. She was slowly making moves to walk on her own and was moments away from being a full-fledged toddler. The night before her birthday, Stacey dropped off a glittery pink party hat for Grace to wear at breakfast. "Every girl should be a princess on her birthday," she said, her voice falling slightly. I thanked her and put the hat on Grace's high chair so I wouldn't forget.

That night, I spent a long time putting Grace down to sleep. I hadn't anticipated it being so hard to let go of this year, the year in which we'd been abandoned, the year in which we'd been forced to move across the country and to live in a way I had not planned. As hard as it had been, it wasn't easy to watch Grace's first year slip away. I sat on the floor in the corner of her room, singing her to sleep.

I ran my fingers along the soft, nubby carpet, the carpet where I'd sit and change Grace's diaper, sing her to sleep, fold her laundry, and, lately, where I wrestled her into her clothes.

I'd had a patch of carpet in Modesto, not in my first foster house, or my second, but in the house I lived in for my last two years of high school. It was the carpet under the windows in the corner of my bedroom. If I closed my eyes, I could still smell and feel that worn patch of carpet and the netting underneath. I sat on that patch of carpet and filled out applications for jobs, not just summer jobs, but spring jobs and fall jobs. I sat there and worried about paying for class trips to Disneyland and new clothes. I sat in that spot and filled out financial aid forms and scholarship applications, and I sat there wondering if I'd be able to go to college at all.

I did not want Grace to need a patch of carpet.

~

Beeks called first thing in the morning.

"Happy birthday, Grace," she said, on speakerphone. I told her I'd tried to bake a cake and failed. The cake seemed to be cooked on the outside but was completely raw on the inside.

"It looks like a Boston cream doughnut," I said. "And I know what those are, because I don't live in LA anymore."

Stacey dropped off cupcakes she'd baked for Grace, each one perfectly iced and bejeweled. My birthday cake was sinking deeper into itself by the minute, and I was never so grateful for Stacey and her ornamentation. I fed one to Grace and two to me. I packed another in my bag, just in case. Once we were cleaned up and ready to go, I sat down on the floor and faced her.

"Happy birthday, sweet girl," I said. "I love you so very much." She crawled over and pulled herself to standing while holding me. I squeezed her tight, and in honor of her birthday, I let her hold my keys all the way to day care.

~

On my way to class, I got a text from Jack.

Happy birthday to Grace. Dinner tomorrow?

Before my brain could process the text, my fingers typed, Yes! I'll make sure she gets a good nap so she's awake for it!

. Sorry, darling. Adults only.

Of course. What had I been thinking? We had never been the kind of parents to take a baby to dinner, but I still couldn't help but feel uneasy. I knew this day meant nothing to Grace, but was it possible that it also meant nothing to Jack? I wanted to say something to him, but I also wanted to see him.

Will find sitter.

My first thought was of Beeks. I could drop Grace off with her on my way to meet Jack, but even though she was trying her best, I knew Beeks and I knew myself. I wasn't strong enough for her questions or her withering glare, and honestly, I still didn't think I was ready to step back inside her apartment after Thanksgiving. I wondered if I'd ever be ready to go back. Once I had dropped off Grace at day care, I texted the Figg.

My husband wants to have dinner tomorrow night. Would you be able to watch Grace?

She responded immediately.

Of course. With pleasure. I can even watch her at your place— easier that way.

My next step was to do something about my hair. The next day, I taught my morning class and took the rest of the day as a personal day. My online search led me to Mark Anthony on the Upper East Side. It was the salon with the combination of the highest ratings and the fewest dollar signs. Still, Grace and I were going to have to spend a month or two eating mac and cheese to pay for this. A very blonde, wiry receptionist took my coat and led me back to Kirstin, my even thinner, blonder colorist. (Apparently all the thin blonde people had been hiding here on the Upper East Side.)

I took off my hat and ran my hands through my hair. "Fix this," I begged. "Please."

She laughed and her eyes widened. "Whoa! What happened to you?"

"Don't ask," I said, putting the hat back on again. "Just tell me. Can you help me?"

"You know," she said, directing me to her chair, taking off the hat, and running her fingers through the disaster on my head, "the best way to fix ombré like this is to just cut it out. Marco can give you a really cute bob." She raised a toned arm and pointed to a very tan man in the skinniest jeans I had ever seen on a male. I tried not to think about my own once-toned arms, which now resembled flabby strings of spaghetti. My sporadic running was doing nothing to help matters.

"My husband has a thing for long hair. I think I'd better not."

"They all do." She shrugged. "Have you thought about extensions?"

Of course I had. Who in LA hasn't? I thought back to a particularly insufferable mom from baby group who wore them. She religiously tossed her hair—or whoever's hair it was.

"Aren't they pricey?" I asked, wondering how much longer I was going to have to worry about how much things cost.

"There are tricks," she said. "You can start out with a small amount, and we can add more later."

I agreed to the extensions and sat in Marco's chair, letting him cut off all the bleached-out ends. Then I moved back over to Kirstin, who colored my hair a beautiful "Upper East Side blonde," as she called it. When she was done she wove in some extensions. She kept lemony-blonde extensions in stock because there was never a day when someone didn't walk in off the street and ask for them.

I gasped when I saw myself, and not in the way I had done in Evon's chair. My hair seemed to be lit from within. I just stared, taking in the new-old me.

I walked out of the salon many, many hundreds of dollars poorer. It hurt to think about the money I had spent. So I didn't think about it. Instead, I pulled out my phone, did some quick research, and went in search of something to wear, as well as something to wear underneath. The single thong that had made the trip from California had been eaten up in the washing machine months ago. I went straight to a well-reviewed boutique near the salon and found a black dress. I walked into a boutique next door and bought a replacement thong in a soft, creamy nude and a matching push-up bra. I held them high and imagined Jack's face when he saw them.

Beeks called while I was paying for the clothes I could not afford.

"Wanna meet for dinner?" she asked. "Brian is taking the kids to a hockey game. I can come up to you."

"Um, I can't."

"Why do you sound that way, Aggie?"

"What way?"

"Like you're afraid to tell me something," she said.

"Because I'm afraid to tell you something." I listened to her silence. "Beeks, I'm meeting Jack for dinner."

"Really?" she asked. "In the city?"

"Yup."

"Alone?"

"Yup."

"Want me to come up and watch Grace?"

"Actually . . . ," I began.

"There goes that sound again," she said. "Let me guess. The Figg is babysitting."

"She is indeed," I admitted, squeezing my eyes shut in preparation for the yelling portion, which never came.

"You don't have to be afraid to tell me this stuff," she said in the nicest voice she could muster. "I can handle it, Aggie. I'm a big girl."

"I know."

"Anyway, have fun sexing it up tonight," she said over the growing background noise of her life.

"It's just dinner, Beeks. I am not staying over. I don't think much sexing up is going to happen." If that was true, then why had I just shelled out for underwear?

"You'd be surprised what happens in the bathrooms of swanky New York City restaurants," she said.

"Really?"

"So I've read. I have to go. Alec has thrown the cat down the trash chute again. I have to go down to the basement and rescue it." She did not wait for me to say goodbye.

I used a dressing room in the boutique to assemble myself. Stacey was picking Grace up from day care, so I didn't have to go home.

Grace. I was desperate to see Jack, to be alone with him, so desperate that I had just shelled out for clothes and hair that I could not afford, but I still couldn't understand how Jack didn't want or need to see Grace when it was so hard for me to be away from her. I shoved down any bubbling resentment and got to work on the rest of my appearance. My hair was already done. I pulled a makeup bag out of my purse and then put on the new underwear and the black dress. I yanked a pair of heels out of my bag and dusted them off. These heels hadn't seen the light of day since LA. Sadly, even though spring was technically days away, it was freezing and I still needed to wear the comforter coat. The coat aside, I was ready for Jack.

- 7 -

In LA, sushi had been one of our mainstays. At least once a week—usually on Tuesdays—we'd eat at either our local sushi restaurant or one of the famed *omakase* bars in town, where a short-tempered sushi chef would decide what we'd eat, the order in which we'd eat it, and with which sauces, if any. I couldn't even remember the last time I thought about sushi, let alone *omakase*, but I found myself in a dark downtown sushi restaurant looking for Jack. I wondered who had recommended this place to him, or where he'd read about it. I pushed open a heavy oak door and inhaled the smells of raw fish and vinegar. I walked up to a willowy hostess and gave her my name. "Agnes Parsons," I said. "I'm meeting my husband." I swallowed the last words, letting them rest in the back of my throat.

I handed her the comforter coat, and she motioned for me to follow her to the back of the restaurant. I was surprised. Jack didn't like the back of restaurants, and he always preferred the sushi bar. Was this intentional, or were we in the back because Jack was a fish out of water, in a city without his arsenal of connections to get him a good table around Valentine's Day? I walked back and saw Jack sitting, wearing a light-blue shirt and a dark jacket. He looked up, saw me, and stood immediately, smiling tentatively. Maybe he was as nervous as I was.

"Aggie," he said as I drew nearer.

"Jack," I breathed, taking a few big gulps of air to prevent myself from falling over. Despite my last-minute makeover, I felt unrecognizable from the person I was in Santa Monica, but Jack was completely unchanged. I'd been too stunned to take stock on Christmas Day, but Jack was just as I'd left him, or just as he'd left me—lightly bronzed, rested, thin, his cheekbones just the right amount of pronounced. He was also close enough that I could smell him, which only made matters worse. I breathed in his scent and clutched the back of my chair. We stood and stared at each other until Jack moved quickly and wrapped his arms around me. He pulled me close and kissed me, running his hands through my new hair. I did my best to kiss him back without fainting in the restaurant.

When he had finished kissing me, he kept his face close to mine and smiled. "Hello," he whispered. I felt his breath on my cheek.

"Hello back," I murmured. He held my chair as I stumbled into it, taking his time to push me in, then kissed me again while I sat there. When the waitress returned, Jack ordered sake for both of us and the *omakase*. She asked if we had any food allergies or restrictions, and Jack told her that any wasabi should be freshly grated, no powdery stuff for us. Other than that—he smiled—*we're easy*.

Easy. Nothing about this was easy. I had so many questions for him. I didn't know where to start.

"Jack . . . ," I said, taking a sip of water, keeping an ice cube in my mouth.

"Not yet," he said, knowingly. "Let me look at you first." I felt his eyes on me, appreciating me. Jack could do that. He could just sit and stare at me forever. He never got bored, never looked over my shoulder for someone more exciting. Even Beeks noticed that. ("I think Brian only looks at food that way.")

"You look beautiful, Aggie," he said. "Breathtaking."

I was pretty sure I looked anything but breathtaking, but after all these cold, lonely months, I wanted to bask in his adoration for as long as he'd let me. Apparently after all these months, I also had questions, and eventually, they got the better of me.

"Where are you staying?" I asked.

"The Baldwin," he said. "It's on the Upper East Side."

Of course it is.

"How?" I asked, feeling my heart race. "How are you staying in a hotel on the Upper East Side?" *How are you staying in a hotel on the Upper East Side with all the thin blonde people and their worked-out arms, when I am living in a dusty town house with roaches, mice, and the brown couch?*

"Aggie," he began, "I have to. I need to raise money, and to raise money, I have to stay in the right places."

He didn't say "alone," but he might as well have. He needed to stay in the right places, and he needed to do it without me and Grace. My heart thumped in the back of my throat. "No, Jack. I was the one who didn't have a choice. I had to leave my home. I had to drive Grace across the country and take a job at a middle school. I have to live in a drafty, pest-infested house. You have choices, Jack. You just seem to be making all the wrong ones."

He pushed his chair away and stood up, looked around, and then sat back down, composing himself. "I get it," he said, leaning in, his voice low. "You're angry, and you have a right to be." He swallowed and moved his chair around the side of the table, so that we sat right next to each other. "I made a mistake. But you have to believe me when I say that I am fixing it, and that I need for things to be this way for a little while longer."

"How much longer is longer?" I asked, trying not to be distracted by his hands, which were under the table and then under the hem of my dress. I felt the warmth of his fingers, and when they pressed into my skin, I had to take a breath to steady myself.

"I don't know," he said. His hands moved higher, pushing down as they climbed up my thigh. "But if you give me a little more time, I can make things better, even better than they were before."

"I don't want better than before, Jack." Without thinking, I scooted my chair back, away from him and his hands. "I don't need better. Don't you get it?"

"Aggie," he whispered. "I'm sorry. My God, all I am is sorry. You have to believe me."

"Why?" I asked. "Why should I believe you? You promised me that I'd never have to worry again. Jack, I've spent months doing nothing but worrying."

"I screwed up. I know that."

"Why?" I asked.

He cocked his head to the side, furrowing his brow.

"Are you going to tell me why you did it?" I explained.

Jack stared at me. He didn't seem to be blinking or breathing.

"I don't know," he said. "I don't know how I got so lost. I wanted to give you and Grace all the things I thought you needed. I wanted to be the provider I promised I'd be." His eyes filled with tears and he looked away.

"But I didn't need all of it. You have to know that," I said, now reaching out and taking his hands in mine. "Look at me," I said. "I didn't need all the glitter. I still don't."

He met my eyes. I lifted his hands to my lips and kissed them. We both leaned in, our foreheads touching. "Just let me fix this," he whispered. "Please, just give me some more time."

He looked up at me. His eyes were desperate, and a little bit of something else—I couldn't tell what. But I knew these eyes, this man. Jack had given me a second chance at a family. Why couldn't I give him another chance, the chance to make things right?

"OK," I said, nodding, convincing myself as well as him. "I get it. A little while longer. I can do that."

We ate dinner, and I didn't ask another question. I wasn't sure if I wasn't asking because I thought he'd get up and leave, or because I just wanted to enjoy dinner with my husband, without the tense back-and-forth of my interrogation. But there was also something else. Although there was so much I wanted to ask, there was so much I didn't want to know. I was still afraid of the answers. So I shut my mouth and opened it only to eat, drink, and answer the few questions Jack tossed my way. He asked about the weather, a little about my job, if I'd found a place to work out (I mean, really), but most of his questions were about Grace.

I described the past few months as best as I could. I knew Jack liked a good milestone, so I showed him some videos of Grace clapping, crawling, and waving, making sure to avoid the many pictures I had of her shoving fistfuls of veggie puffs in her mouth. Mostly, though, I ate.

Eating was easy. Each time our server brought out a new dish, we'd look at the sushi chef and nod our approval. I made sure to give the chef an extra large nod, letting him know that not only did I approve of each dish, but I was really grateful that someone else had prepared my dinner, and that dinner didn't involve pasta, chicken, and a bag of frozen vegetables. I noticed people pulling out phones and taking pictures of their food, but I knew I wouldn't forget this food. Many of the dishes were the same as ones we'd eaten in California, yellowtail with a jalapeño puree, seared crab cakes, oyster with scallions, but not all were familiar. At one point our server brought out something spiny and held it on a plate before us. The spiny creature, a sea urchin, jumped. It returned some minutes later, dead and on a pillow of rice.

At the end of the meal, as we got up to leave, Jack slipped his arm around my waist, right where he'd put it years ago, the very first time we were in a sushi restaurant together. I closed my eyes as he leaned in to me, his mouth on my neck, in my ear. "Wait," he whispered. "Wait until you see the hotel. I promise, it'll make up for all those nights you had to spend in the Bronx."

I thought about my fabulous underwear. I thought about texting Stacey and telling her I'd be there in the morning. She'd take Grace, and I could be up at school in time for first period. But I couldn't. I pulled away, removing his hand from my waist. "I can't," I said, holding on to his fingers. "I have to be home for Grace. I don't think the sitter can stay over, and I have to work in the morning."

He looked surprised. "What, you don't have sick days?"

I did have sick days, but I'd used most of them for the days Grace was sick. Turns out day-care kids really do catch everything. What I couldn't tell Jack, what he'd never understand, was that I wasn't ready to spend the night away from Grace. I felt an ache in my chest when I thought about it. If I couldn't tell him this, I certainly couldn't tell him that the other reason I couldn't run away with him for a night of hotel sex was that I was nervous to leave the boys alone with Gavin. I needed to be around to protect them; I was their buffer.

"No," I lied. "I don't have any more sick days." I looked at my watch. "I really have to get uptown."

Jack looked like a small boy who'd gotten a toy for Christmas only to have it whisked away. "I wish I'd known," he said.

"Why? You wouldn't have taken me to dinner if you knew I couldn't spend the night?" I had spent all that time trying to stay calm, and there I was, firing up, my heart pulsing.

"No. Don't be silly." He reached out and put his hand on my face. "I've missed you. I just wished I'd known that I have to wait a little longer."

I got it, or at least part of me did. I was wearing fantastic new underwear, and I wasn't wearing it to eat sushi. Hell, I'd even shaved above my knees.

Jack walked me outside, hailed a cab, and handed the driver some cash. I thought briefly about getting out of the cab in a block or so, pocketing the cash, and taking the subway home. Before I got in, Jack said, "One more thing, Aggie."

I knew where he was going. I'd been waiting for him to go there all evening. "Ruth Moore?" I asked, picturing her waving to me from across campus the morning after the first snowfall.

"Yes."

"How do you even know her?"

"She was at USC with me and Don, but that's not important. I want to know what you've learned here. I want to know what you know."

"I don't know anything. I don't even know what I'm looking for."

"If you pay close enough attention, you can find dirt on *anyone*," he said.

"Dirt? I thought I was just looking for information on why she pulled her investments. What are you asking me?"

I never found out. Jack planted his hands on my waist and leaned in to me as I fell back on the taxi. Before I could ask any more questions, he kissed me, hard. When he pulled away, he kept his hands on me and said, "Just keep your ears open for something we can use to convince her to help us." He stared into my eyes and spoke slowly. "You know what I'm asking you, right, Aggie?"

He was gone before I could answer.

- 8 -

The next morning I was staring up at the ceiling in my bedroom, replaying the conversation with Jack over and over in my mind, trying to make sense of his last words to me, when I got my first text from Gavin.

We have a situation. Be in my office as soon as you can. —Gavin

I knew that if I was being pulled into a "situation," my boys must be involved. I texted Gavin back and moved as quickly as I could, trying not to think about what was happening in his office.

Gavin was waiting for me just outside his door, his hands in position across his chest, his legs firmly planted in a wide stance, as though he were a bouncer guarding a nightclub.

"They're inside," he said.

"Who is?" I asked, hoping my suspicions were wrong.

"Who do you think? This time they've gone too far."

I wanted to see the boys to make sure they were all right, but I also needed some information, even if it was from Gavin's perspective.

"Why don't you tell me what happened," I said. I tried to emulate his stance, to show him that I was just as tough as he was, but I had so much in my hands—my water bottle, my purse, some papers—that it was hard for me to cross my arms across my chest. I tried but dropped everything I was holding. As I bent down to pick it all up, Gavin took a step closer to me, so that when I tried to stand, my head almost hit his crotch. I looked up at the crease of his pants and felt queasy. I shuffled back, on all fours, and slowly righted myself to standing, bringing all the fallen objects with me. Gavin just sneered while I maneuvered, shook his head in disgust, and led me into his office.

I followed him in and saw a very guilty-looking Caleb, Guy, Davey, and Art all squeezed into two chairs. It was not a pretty sight. As soon as he saw me, Guy began to cry, his tiny frame quivering. Davey was not far behind, blinking back his tears.

Art was the first to speak. "Ms. P., we really didn't mean to—"

"Art." Gavin held up his hand and spoke in a sickly-sweet tone. "Art, before we get ahead of ourselves, why don't you tell us what you didn't mean to do? You didn't mean to break into the kitchen last night? Or you didn't mean to steal all the ice cream for today's merit club party? Or perhaps you didn't mean to lock Mr. Higgins in his room?"

"OK, *that* was an accident," chimed in Caleb. "We really didn't know he was in there."

"The other stuff, that stuff we did," said Guy, looking at me and breathing in between sobs. "We did it. It was dumb, I know. But we never get invited to the merit club parties, and we just wanted some of the ice cream."

The merit club parties were invitation only. Students who got an eighty-five or above on a test (quizzes didn't count) or who performed an act of "notable responsibility" were asked to join Gavin for ice cream one morning each month. Needless to say, my boys had never seen the inside of a merit club party. The whole thing baffled me. The ice cream was terrible—cheap, off-brand stuff that came in enormous tubs, neon colors, and only a few uninspired flavors, all of which tasted the same. (Yes, I'd tried it all. It had been a long year.) These kids regularly sneaked off campus to eat better ice cream. Why risk it to steal from the crappy merit club?

"Yeah," said a pathetic-looking Guy. "We just wanted someone to ask us."

Caleb spoke next. "On our way out, we accidentally locked Mr. Higgins in his office. We thought we were being good by locking doors. We just locked the wrong door." Mr. Higgins was a security guard with an office near the kitchen. He genuinely liked all the kids, which made the whole thing worse.

"Because these are *your* boys," Gavin said, looking right at me, still smiling, "I think it's up to you to write this up."

"What do you mean?" I asked.

"You're going to write your very first discipline log entry, Agnes. That's what I mean. You've done nothing to bring these boys in line, and it's about time you started." He was still smiling.

"Gavin, I don't even know how," I started.

"Oh, I've thought about that," he said. "I am well aware of your limitations." He lingered over that last word, sounding out each syllable, Figg-style. "Caleb can help you. He knows the ins and outs of our system." He paused and smiled at Caleb. "After all, you can't fake an email from a teacher if you don't know how to hack into her account. Isn't that right, Caleb?"

Caleb's face sank. "You know about that?" he asked.

"I know about everything," he said. "Nothing goes unseen by me." He walked to the door and turned to us. "Make it a doozy, Agnes. I want to include it in the behavior reports I deliver to the boys at the end of the month. You know, the packets I'll be sending to their parents in a few months and to high schools next year." He spoke to me, but he was glaring at the boys. When he had finished speaking, he walked out.

"Dude, I cannot believe he left us alone in here," said Davey, suddenly perking up. "What should we do first?" He looked right at Art, who was nodding vigorously. "Wanna take the exclamation point off his keyboard? He loves that thing."

"Boys!" I yelled, waving my arms and dropping more papers. "Are you guys really serious?"

I had more to say, but Art cut me off.

"Hey, Ms. P.! What did you do to your hair?"

The boys looked at me as if for the first time. I ran my hand through my highlighted extensions and smiled apologetically. Why did I get the feeling Art did not approve of my new look?

"I just kind of liked it better before," he said, reading my mind.

Davey chimed in. "You look like my mom." He put his hand to his mouth as soon as he said this and gasped slightly. "I mean, no offense." I knew exactly what "no offense" meant for a middle schooler. It was code for YOU SHOULD TAKE HUGE OFFENSE.

"You do smell super good, though," said Guy, always trying to smooth things over. "You start wearing Axe?" I could see that as soon as he said this, he wished he hadn't.

"Boys!" I snapped. "You cannot mess with Principal Burke's keyboard! You just did something dumb and got caught. Why are you planning the next dumb thing before the paint is even dry on your first dumb thing?"

They just looked at me.

"Do you just assume I'll keep bailing you out? Don't you care that you're making me look like a fool?" I was met with a sea of blank stares.

"I don't know why we're doing this stuff," said Caleb. "It just feels good when we're doing it." I knew there was a larger conversation I needed to have with these boys, a conversation about impulse control and all sorts of things they didn't want to hear, or weren't ready to hear, but for now I just wanted to complete the task and get out of Gavin's office.

"Caleb," I said, "here's my laptop. Let's get this done. My code—"

"Yeah, I know your code," he said.

"How do you know it?" I asked. Getting my cell phone number from the teacher directory was one thing, but how had this kid gotten my laptop code?

"It's easy," said Guy. "He just watched you type it in a few times."

I wanted to bolt, to get as far away from the boys and their misdeeds as possible, but I just glared at Caleb and looked away while he logged on as me. He opened up a new report and titled it ICE CREAM FIASCO AT MIDNIGHT.

"I'll leave you to this, boys," I said, sitting in the corner and slumping into a chair. "Do not submit until I have reviewed it," I warned.

"Got it," said Caleb. The other boys gathered around him while he typed. They added comments and suggestions. Guy corrected his spelling. Davey bounced around the office, touching as many things as possible, almost determined to knock over as much as he could. When they were done, they called me over to look at it. I stood behind them, my hands resting on the desk.

> Feb. 15—Agnes Parsons: Caleb Fisher, Guy Martin, Davey Heath, and Art Dunlap stole high-quality ice cream from the kitchen, depriving the hardworking, rule-following kiss-asses in the merit club of their delicious treats. Oh, and they also locked Mr. Higgins in his office, which was a total accident. Gave the boys detention and made them polish Principal Jerk's shiny head.

"Just take out 'kiss-asses,'" I said flatly. "Everything else is fine."

"Really?" Caleb whipped around to look at me.

"Really," I said, raising an eyebrow. "Looks fine to me." I wanted to know if they could stop themselves, or if they really had no self-control at all.

"Dude," said Davey. "Do not submit the form." He looked back at me. "We were just playing," he said.

"I know," I said. "You're always just playing. You tell me you're worried about getting thrown out of school, about not getting into high school, but you spend your days doing things to get yourselves thrown out, to make sure you never get into high school."

Caleb hit some keys. "It's fixed, Ms. P., but I wanna have a look around while I'm in the neighborhood. Don't worry—I'm gonna log on as Principal Burke."

Before I knew it, a long list of entries appeared on the screen, all under a heading with my name on it.

"What the—?" said Art. "Ms. P., did you write these?"

I leaned in to get a closer look. "What? No! You heard Principal Burke! This was my first entry."

Caleb began reading each entry aloud.

> Oct. 1—Agnes Parsons: Caleb Fisher and Guy Martin made inappropriate comments about "my time of the month" during class—detention.

> Oct. 14—Agnes Parsons: Caleb Fisher flashed a pornographic image of several women on the smart board during class—detention.

> Oct. 16—Agnes Parsons: Davey Heath and Guy Martin played football with a bottle of soda in class. Soda exploded all over back wall—sent boys to Principal Burke's office.

One thing I could say for sure was that I had never thrown a student out of class, and certainly not since Gavin created the Bowel. (The boys said it was awful. He'd handpicked the most miserable teachers as monitors.) I noticed the entries picked up in both frequency and severity in November, after I had challenged Gavin in front of Mr. and Mrs. Martin.

Nov. 18—Agnes Parsons: Art Dunlap and Guy Martin plagiarized homework assignment from internet—gave detention and assigned extra work.

Nov. 23—Agnes Parsons: Caleb Fisher and Art Dunlap caught cheating on test—DOUBLE detention.

Nov. 30—Agnes Parsons: Guy Martin referred to me as "dumb bitch" when I asked him to stay after class to discuss missing assignments—DOUBLE detention.

We read as many as we could stomach, and then the boys turned to me.

"I don't know," I said, meeting their baffled gazes. "I don't know what these are or how they got here."

"You sure about that?" asked Art. "Because it looks like you wrote these."

"Yeah," said Guy. "Why should we believe you?"

"Boys," I said. "This is not me. I didn't even know how to use the system before today."

We sat silently while Caleb tapped on the keyboard. The boys would not meet my eyes. "It's the Jerk," he said. "He did this. They're from his account."

"This douchebag has it coming to him," said Art, quickly transferring all his anger from me to Gavin. He put his hands on his hips and jumped out of his chair. "Let's get him back!"

"I've got it! How about we have him sext Ms. Figg?" Davey suggested. "We can get gross pictures online and pretend they're him!"

"Or maybe," I said, "you can take actual pictures of him. I mean, why stop there? If you really want to get him, hide out in his house and get pictures of him in the shower!" They looked bewildered. "I mean, why not? If you really wanna screw up your futures, you might as well go for it!" I was doing so much hand waving that my arms were beginning to get tired.

"You don't get it," Caleb said.

"Oh, I get it," I said. "I get that you feel powerless, because he has all the control, and that it doesn't matter what you do. But you're wrong, because I know what he did. I know these are faked. I can help you."

"That's a lie," said Caleb. "You keep telling us that you're gonna help us. But you haven't. You didn't help Guy even though you said you were going to." He looked over at Guy, who nodded meekly. "He got grounded over Thanksgiving and wasn't allowed to go skiing with his family over Christmas break, all because of the Jerk."

"Is that true, Guy?" I asked.

Guy nodded. Caleb went on.

"Pretty soon, all our parents are gonna see these reports. Next year, high schools are gonna see these reports. Who's gonna want to take losers like us when they see this stuff?"

"The Jerk told our parents they have to send us to his stupid summer program if we want to get into high school next year," Art added.

"Just let me try to help," I begged. "Give me some time."

"Go for it," said Caleb as he got up to leave, signaling for the other boys to follow. "But I don't think anyone can stop the Jerk, especially not you."

Before I could say anything else, I was alone in the room.

9

I wasn't sure where to go next, so I left the building and started walking aimlessly across campus. A light snow began to fall, and I looked up at the gray sky and let the flakes fall on my face. I needed to do something other than confront Gavin and tell him I knew what he was up to. He'd only dismiss me, tell me to go back to the beach. Besides, if I wanted to help the boys, if I really wanted to make sure they were safe, then Gavin had to get caught. If I confronted him, he'd delete the entries he'd forged before it went any further. I opened my eyes and looked out across the field. I had only one option: I had to go to Ruth Moore and tell her what I knew.

Ruth's office was clear on the other side of campus. I trudged across the frozen ground to Granger Hall, a large brick building with spires and an imposing copper roof. I walked in and presented myself to Ruth's secretary, Esme. Esme had short gray hair and a very lazy eye. I introduced myself, trying not to stare. She looked both shocked and terrified when I told her that I didn't have an appointment. She picked up the phone, whispered into it for a few moments, and began nodding.

"It's all fine," she murmured, more to herself than to me, straightening papers on her desk. "Fine, fine."

"Excuse me?"

"It's fine," she said, not looking up. "She can see you."

Esme stood and showed me back to an imposing wood door, which swung open to reveal an even more imposing office, complete with stained-glass windows and dark wood paneling. In the middle of it all, sitting behind an enormous mahogany desk, was Ruth Moore. She stood as I walked in.

"Agnes," she began, "it's good to see you again."

"It's good to see you, too," I said, taking a chair opposite her desk. "I've wanted to come see you for a while, to thank you for your help and for the Christmas basket, but I wasn't sure . . ."

"Of course," she said. "And I kept my distance for that very same reason. Teachers are funny creatures, very sensitive, you know. If it got out that you were here because of a connection to me, well, that wouldn't bode well for you. Would it?" She smiled at me, a smile that was hard to read.

I tried smiling mysteriously back at her, but I apparently don't do mysterious very well.

"Are you all right, Agnes?" she asked.

"Oh. Yes. I'm fine." I fiddled with the zipper on my coat, sliding it up and down.

"Why are you here?" she asked. "Is it because of Jack?"

At the mention of his name, I heard Jack's words: *If you pay close enough attention, you can find dirt on anyone.* I felt uncomfortable, almost itchy. I unzipped my coat again and scratched at my collar.

"I'm here because of my students," I said as quickly as I could, silencing Jack's voice.

"Oh," she said, her voice rising in interest.

"Well, it's not really the boys I'm here about," I said. "It's Gavin."

"Yes?" Ruth asked, sitting forward.

"He's been entering fake discipline reports in the online system," I said, all in one breath. I watched her eyebrows rise and kept going. "I saw pages of reports I'd allegedly written, reports about my students. But the thing is, I hadn't written any. Someone else wrote those reports."

I paused to catch my breath. "Gavin wrote those reports." The words tumbled out, and I let them sit there.

"Agnes, I don't need to tell you that you're making a very serious accusation."

"I know," I said. "There are pages and pages of faked reports that came from Gavin's account."

"How do you know?" she asked, putting her elbows on the desk and resting her chin in her clasped hands.

"I can't say."

"You can't say?"

"No." I clasped my own hands together on my lap and took a breath. "I can't."

She stared at me for a few long seconds.

"Gavin is ambitious, Agnes. If what you say is correct, and I want to be clear that I'm not sure that it is, maybe he's doing it to inflate his own importance."

"How so?" I asked.

"Well, the worse the boys appear to be, then the better he looks when he's able to help them."

"*If* he's able to help them," I said. Hell, I was already in here making pretty serious accusations. I might as well give it all I had.

Ruth narrowed her eyes, as though she had to think about what I'd just said. "Leave this with me, Agnes. I promise to get to the bottom of it."

"Thank you, Ruth."

"Agnes, it goes without saying that if you can get your hands on any actual evidence to back up your claims, you should bring it to me immediately."

"Of course." I nodded.

Ruth stood up, so I did the same and we walked to the door. As she opened the door, she said, "Please remember that I am here for you." On cue, Esme shuffled over and escorted me out.

~

After my classes, I walked toward Blackwell, hoping to get Grace early. My meeting with Ruth had put me at ease a little. I wanted to call Jack and tell him that he was barking up the wrong tree. If he wanted Ruth's help, whatever that meant, he just had to ask her, as I'd done. In the meantime, I needed to get Ruth more information, possibly even proof that Gavin was faking reports. I could print out what Caleb had shown me, but then she'd ask how we logged in to Gavin's account. No, to really nab Gavin, I also needed an explanation—why was he faking the reports? I didn't buy Ruth's "inflated importance" theory. There had to be something else. The problem was I didn't have anyone to ask. I couldn't go to Stacey, because as far as she was concerned, Gavin was the patron saint of the middle school. As I walked up to the icy front door of Blackwell, I thought of the one person who might be willing to dish on Gavin, and who might have the kind of information that usually stays hidden, underground—Adam.

I retrieved Grace, and we walked home as the snow got heavier. I pulled out my phone, took off my gloves, and texted Adam.

Adam. Do you have a sec?

Sure. What's up? Wanna run?!

I started to text him but was nervous about writing down my suspicions.

Can I call you?

Sure.

"Hey," he said.

"Hi. I know this is a little out of left field, but I've found something in the behavior log. I think Gavin is forging entries."

"What?"

"I'll tell you more in person, but the boys were in his account and they saw entries he'd written . . . in my name." I lowered my voice. "Can you meet me at my house? I'll be home in twenty minutes."

"Of course. I'll be there in thirty."

And that was how Jack walked in on me and another man in my home.

10

I got home, released Grace from her stroller and winter wear, found somewhere safe for her to play, and tried to straighten up the house. Nobody other than the Figg had seen the inside of this place recently, and looking at it with fresh eyes, I saw what a mess it was.

I started with the brown couch, which had wrappers and socks wedged in between its cushions. I picked up books from the floor, more food wrappers, and found a bra I swore I'd lost as well as a glove I thought I'd never see again. I moved into the dining room and spotted Grace under the table. I surveyed the tabletop, which was just a glorified storage spot for books, papers, and, apparently, old rice.

"Gracie," I said, "what I wouldn't give for an hour or two of Sondra." She raised her arms and whined at me. I picked her up and shuffled around, moving piles to other, less visible locations. When she started to moan louder, I realized she hadn't eaten yet. "OK, OK, we can eat now, clean later."

By the time Adam showed up, Grace and I were halfway through dinner. She was reluctantly eating some chicken, corn, and rice, all of which I'd proudly prepared myself. She could tell I wasn't paying much attention to her, because whenever I turned to talk to Adam, she jettisoned a fistful of food onto the floor. I tried not to think about vacuuming it all up.

"You're right about the reports coming from Gavin's account," he said. "I checked quickly, and he wrote them all."

"The real question is why," I said, wiping a lump of corn from my shoe.

"I think I may know," Adam said. "There's this program, a summer program that Gavin runs."

"Yeah," I said, airplaning chicken into Grace's open mouth. "The boys said they all have to go. Gavin told their parents they won't get into high school without it."

"Sounds about right," he said. "Gavin's minions jockey for jobs with him over the summer. Stacey Figg launches a campaign each year to make sure he hires her." I laughed at the thought of Stacey Figg taking out full-page ads in the student paper, begging Gavin for a job.

"So what's up with the program? How is it connected?" I asked, still trying to trick Grace into eating more. I was playing peekaboo with one hand, and whenever she laughed, I would use the other to jam in some food.

"The program is a complete cash cow. The school gets a cut, but so does Gavin. He pockets a lot of the money—at least half of it."

"What?" I asked, almost dropping the spoon. "How do you know?"

"I have access to the school's accounting because I installed the systems for it. Last year, I also worked part-time in the accounting office. Your boys aren't the only ones with mad hacking skills."

I stopped trying to feed Grace and turned to face Adam. "So Gavin prints up these fake discipline reports, gets the parents to sign the kids up for this program, and the boys have to spend their summer with him?"

Adam nodded.

I looked back at Grace. She was done, her mouth sealed shut. I tried to coax in more food, but she turned her head. I was learning that one of the first rules of parenting is to know when you've been beaten, so I stood up and lifted her out of the high chair, holding her away from me. Grace was one step ahead of me. She reached out for my hair and wiped a clump of chicken and rice into it. With her other hand, she smeared corn mush on my left cheek.

"Are you OK?" Adam asked, trying to help me but clearly unsure how. He handed me a paper towel.

"Follow me upstairs. I need to put her in a bath before she makes this worse."

The three of us folded into the small bathroom. I wasn't sure two adults could even fit in here at once. I dropped down and knelt in front of the bath. I scooted all the way forward, my knees pressed against the tub, giving Adam room to sit on the toilet seat. My back was practically resting on his knees.

I poured warm water over Grace's body and thought about Adam's comments. A school with a cash cow might not be having money troubles. Or maybe the school was so hard up, it needed the summer program. Did Ruth know anything about this? Was this the dirt I'd been looking for?

"Ruth has to know that he's pocketing a lot of cash from the program," I said. "She must realize the school doesn't get all of it."

"She's pretty hands-off when it comes to the middle school. From what I hear, she'd rather look the other way," he said as Grace splashed me. "But who knows. It's hard to know where the money is going—it's just not all going to the school. Maybe she doesn't care."

I tried to sound as casual as I could. "I think that's something we need to find out. If she knows what Gavin's up to, that's pretty bad." *If you pay close enough attention, you can find dirt on anyone.*

Grace splashed me again. I needed this bath to come to an end. I rinsed her off and lifted her out of the tub. While holding her with one hand, I wrapped her in a fuzzy hooded towel with the other. I only had one bath mat, and it was in the laundry. I didn't see the pool of water next to the bath, and I slipped with Grace in my arms right onto the toilet, right onto Adam's lap.

"Whoa!" he laughed, holding on to me and the toilet so that all three of us didn't end up on the floor. I laughed, too, and Grace squealed with delight. This was much more fun than she'd ever had in the bath.

We were all laughing when Jack walked in.

I say "walked in," but there was no way to fit another human into that bathroom. Jack stood in the doorway, his hands by his sides, staring. He just stood there, silently, and looked at me, laughing and sitting on another man's lap, our daughter in my arms.

"Jack!" I scrambled to get up, but I slipped, right off Adam's lap and into the puddle on the floor. Adam saw me struggling. He reached down and took Grace. I leaned on the bath and stood, inches from Jack. Jack just stared, his jaw and fists clenched.

"Jack," I gasped, trying to get air back in my lungs. "Adam works with me. At school. He's the IT guy." I glanced at Adam, who looked confused and terrified. I can't say he was alone. He stood up, pushed his glasses in place, handed Grace to me, and nervously reached out a hand to Jack.

"Nice to meet you," he said, his voice shaking.

Jack stared and then unclenched his jaw and smiled. It was a smile I did not recognize.

"Jack Parsons," he said calmly. "Her husband." He shook Adam's hand and kept smiling that smile.

"Adam was just helping me," I said. "With a situation at school." I tried to slow my breathing down even more, but I felt like I had used up all the air in that muggy little bathroom.

"I think this is a good time for me to go," said Adam, not looking at me. "I'll let you know if I find more, Aggie." I cringed when he said my name like that. Jack didn't like other people calling me Aggie, especially other men. But Adam had no way of knowing that. I smiled weakly at him, but I did not want to. Not in front of Jack. Adam squeezed past Jack, then looked back and said, "Nice to meet you, sir."

Crap.

Another man, a man much closer to my own age, a man on whose lap I had just been sitting, a man who had the nerve to call me "Aggie," had just gone and called Jack "sir," as though Jack were the father of his prom date. The front door slammed shut, and Jack moved. He moved so abruptly that it knocked me back. He came toward me, so close to me that I had to back up against the tile wall. Even when I had nowhere left to go, he kept moving, pressing into me.

"Sir?" he whispered, our faces almost touching.

"Jack," I begged. "I was just . . . he was just trying to . . ." This was going nowhere. I took a deep breath and looked into his eyes. "It was nothing."

"It didn't look like nothing." I could feel his breath on me.

"I promise."

His eyes moved down my body. My clothes were wet and my shirt was clinging to me. He ran one hand along my hip and ran the other under my wet shirt. I could hear my own breathing rushing in my ears. I held Grace to my side, hoping she'd stay calm.

"Jack . . ." Before I could say anything else, he pushed me against the wall, and then his mouth was on mine, his body pressed hard against me. He leaned in and pressed harder, his hand moving up my body. A noise I hadn't heard for a while escaped from the back of my throat. Jack stopped abruptly, pulled back, and looked at me, a small smile on his mouth.

"Can your IT guy do that, Aggie?" he breathed.

I desperately wanted someone to swoop in, grab Grace, and leave me alone in that room with Jack.

"I'm going," he said, taking another step back.

"Please, Jack, don't." I reached and put my hand on his chest. He shrugged me off.

"I'll leave you to bath time," he said, raising an eyebrow and looking down at Grace.

"Stay," I begged.

"Why?" he asked. "It looks like you're doing just fine without me."

"Jack, it's nothing," I said. "He's helping me get information on the school. I promise. There's absolutely nothing happening between us."

He didn't seem to hear me. "Funny," he said, smiling but not smiling. "You really didn't wait long, did you? And tech support, Aggie? You hook up with tech support?" He had backed up toward the bathroom door, but in two steps he was back on me, leaning in, his lips on my ear.

"Jack, I'm not hooking up—" I started again, but he cut me off.

"One more thing," he breathed.

"Yes?" I asked. *Anything.*

"This place is filthy," he whispered. "Get yourself together, Agnes."

11

I spent the night curled in a ball on the brown couch. Every time I closed my eyes, I saw Jack's face as he stood in the doorway. I awoke to a rustling noise from under the couch. I leaned over and leaped. The mouse had returned and was burrowing in a bag of chips I had left open. My sudden movement scared her, and she ran into the corner of the room and disappeared through a crack in the molding.

For a brief moment, I was happy to see her. Maybe she knew I needed the company. Or maybe she just liked barbecue potato chips.

~

In the days that followed, I sent dozens of texts to Jack's new number but got no response. I knew that I was not the one who should be feeling guilty, but I did. Jack's silent treatments could do that. I felt terrible. I felt so terrible that I told Stacey Figg about it while we were drinking wine, this time in my house.

"*No* way!" she squealed, her hands making small, rapid-fire claps. "He just walked in?"

"Yup, and there I was, right on Adam's lap. It could not have looked worse."

"Well, it could have," she said, laughing. "It could have looked a *lot* worse."

I frowned, and she said, "No worries, Agnes. Your secret is safe with me."

"What secret?"

"Your Adam secret."

I jumped up off the brown couch. "There is no Adam secret. There's no Adam. We're just friends." Stacey didn't look convinced.

"Stacey," I said, sitting back down, doing my best to look unruffled. "Adam was only here to talk about the boys, nothing else."

She perked up, her ears twitching. "What about the boys?" she asked, putting down her empty wineglass.

I poured us both a second glass, sucked mine down, and stumbled. "There's something going on. I met with Ruth to talk to her about it."

"What?" She went to pour me a third glass, but I held my hand out to stop her.

"Oh," I said, realizing that I'd slipped up. "Nothing."

"No," she pressed on. "What did you say to Ruth?"

I felt my face burn, with the wine and with the realization that I might have revealed too much.

"Oh, nothing," I mumbled. "I'm just a little worried about the boys. I went to Ruth for some guidance, that's all."

I heard Grace's voice on the monitor. I jumped and ran up the stairs. Grace didn't need me. She often cried out in her sleep. But I hovered upstairs for a few minutes, finally walking down when I heard Stacey open the front door to leave.

"Getting late," she said. "See you tomorrow. Same time, same place?"

"Sure," I said. "This is my week to host." I smiled at her. She gave me a very large, very toothy smile in return. It was yet another smile I could not read.

~

I woke up on what I thought was the first of March only to look at my phone and learn that it was still February. Beeks was right. This month was endless.

I dragged myself to school, still half-asleep. I walked into class a few minutes late and saw the boys sitting in their seats. They'd barely made eye contact with me since the behavior log incident. They sat complacently, almost languidly, in class while I read or lectured to them. It was like teaching a room of zombies.

"What's up, guys?" I said, dropping my bag onto my desk chair. "What's going on?"

Caleb hit a key and the Funeral March played from his laptop. "Today's the day," he said, speaking over the low, solemn music. "It's happening."

"What?"

The music kept playing, so he spoke over it. "Principal Burke's handing out the behavior reports. Andrew Dyson already got his. So did Clay Miller."

"You know what that means," said Davey, fidgeting with a ball of yarn he'd presumably stolen from the arts and crafts room. "Our parents will be getting them this week."

The music stopped. "I thought you said you were gonna fix this," said Caleb, closing his laptop and staring at me. "You said you had this. You lied."

"I didn't lie, Caleb. I said I would help and I meant it. I just need more time."

"We don't have more time," moaned Guy. "Our parents are gonna read these. You know what that means!" I did know. I knew exactly what that meant for him.

"And these reports," said Caleb, "they're just gonna prove to our parents that the Jerk was right about us all along. It also means if we want to get into high school, we have to do the stupid summer program."

Art stood up and banged on his desk. "And if we don't spend all summer in the Jerk's reform school, we're gonna have to go to public school!"

"Public school!" wailed the boys in the front row.

"Boys," I begged. "Just give me a little time."

"Why not today?" charged Caleb, his voice growing more agitated. "What's wrong with today?"

"Because today is still February," I said. "And around here, I'm not sure anything good ever happens in February."

12

When March finally arrived, I woke up . . . tired. I had hoped to be able to spring out of bed, full of purpose. But I was still spending night after night playing out the bathroom scene in my mind. It was there whenever I closed my eyes, ready for a replay—the look in Jack's eyes as he stood on the threshold, his breath on my ear, his hands on my skin. I ignored the nagging exhaustion and drank an extra few cups of coffee, sucking down the grainy sludge at the bottom of the French press. I needed all the strength I could muster if I was going to storm into Ruth's office, unmask Gavin, and expose the summer program charade. Once Ruth knew why Gavin was faking the reports—that he'd been cashing in on the summer program—she'd have no choice but to shut it all down.

As I walked toward MacReady before first period, I saw Gavin near the entrance of the building. I was deciding whether to pretend I hadn't seen him when he called out to me.

"Agnes," he drawled, speaking to me without moving his lips. "You're early. Ready for another day of complete uselessness?"

"Excuse me?"

"Let's pretend you don't know what I'm talking about." He smirked. "I always knew you were a complete waste of space, and after I schooled you in front of your boys, they know it, too."

"Really?" I spat. "*You* schooled *me*?" I looked around for somewhere less public and walked into MacReady, leading Gavin to a dark corner under the stairs.

"What else would you call it? I made you sit down and write a behavior report, your first ever, for a class full of walking behavior problems. I forced you to do it, and they all watched."

"Actually, Gavin, I didn't do it. They did, and while they were writing themselves up, they discovered something interesting."

"What's that?" he asked, the shadow of the staircase falling across his face.

"Your faked reports," I said, talking quickly, before I could change my mind. "Pages and pages of your faked discipline reports."

His expression betrayed nothing. He just kept staring at me as if I'd told him I was thinking of buying a slipcover for the brown couch.

I pressed on. "I know you've been doing it to get kids to sign up for the summer program, the program that lines your pockets." I crossed my arms over my chest and took a step back. I hadn't planned on revealing all I knew to him, but it felt so good to unload it.

"You know nothing, Agnes," he spat back at me. He leaned in, putting his hand on the wall behind me, cornering me. "You know nothing at all. You're just a trophy wife from California whose husband needs to hide her for a while because he's gotten himself into trouble."

I gasped and immediately wished I hadn't.

"That's right. I know who you are. Ruth told me everything."

"Ruth?" I asked, unable to say any more. My knees were starting to buckle. I leaned back on the wall and gripped it to steady myself.

"Yes. Ruth," he said, raising the eyebrow over his brown eye.

I looked at his eyes, both of them, each seemingly operating in its own orbit. I closed my own eyes and said quickly, "Ruth knows, Gavin. She knows what you did."

"Oh, does she now?" he asked, not missing a beat. "I'm *so* glad you mentioned her, because there's something I've been wanting to share with you." He slid his hand into the pocket of his Dockers and pulled out his phone. "I wasn't sure I was going to need this so soon, but hey, I'm flexible."

"What . . . ?"

"Oh, you're quite the detective, aren't you, Agnes? Did you think this was your big moment?" He waved his hands above his head, mocking me. Before I could say anything, he turned up the volume on his phone. Immediately, I recognized Ruth's voice.

"Agnes is ambitious, Gavin. If what you say is correct, if she's been meeting privately with students in her home—maybe she's doing it to inflate her own importance. Maybe she's doing it to make her seem indispensable to these boys. Let's just assume it's that and not something more sordid. At least for now."

If my knees were buckling before, now they completely gave way and I began to slide down the wall. I gripped harder, but my palms were so sweaty that I got no traction. Gavin didn't wait for me to compose myself. He pressed play again and came in for the kill. I heard his voice.

"Thank you, Ruth, and thanks for your support with the summer program and my creative recruitment. Our boys deserve a little summer school anyway, and I know the program is only going to keep bringing in students from other schools. Once they see what we can do with troubled boys, it'll just be a matter of time before we're turning them away from the high school. The extra cash doesn't hurt, either."

Creative recruitment? Ruth knew. She knew and she didn't mind. She didn't mind because the school made money and the program made the school look good. It made boys who couldn't function in middle school seem completely reformed for high school, when all most of them really needed was a fresh start and time away from Gavin. I kept staring at him, unable to speak. Then I heard Ruth again.

"I agree and I appreciate all your work, especially your creativity. Remember, you can come to me whenever you like. I am here for you."

Those were the words she'd used with me. A salty, rancid juice was working its way around my mouth. I let go of the wall, thrust my hands into my pockets, and willed myself not to throw up.

Gavin shut off the recording. If I had no words before, I had fewer now.

"You see, Nancy Drew, this is what you don't know. Ruth Moore's greatest gift, the secret of her success, is that she agrees with whoever she is talking to, with whoever is in the room. You never really know if she's on your side."

I could not breathe, let alone speak. He was right. It was like Ruth was reading from a script—the same script she had used with me.

Gavin went on. "Actually, if I'm being honest, the real thing you should know about Ruth Moore is that the only side she's really on is hers. She'll say whatever she has to say to keep her job. Hell, that's how she got the job in the first place."

"But how did she know? How did you know—about the boys, in my house?"

"Oh, that?" Gavin threw his head back and laughed. He pulled out his phone again, and I heard a different voice.

"I didn't want to be the one to tell you this, Gavin, but really, we're friends, and I thought you'd want to know. It's Agnes and those boys of hers. I'm sure it's nothing, but some of the teachers are murmuring about how closely she is working with them."

Stacey Figg.

She whispered the word *closely* as if it were *cancer*. *"Gavin, I've also seen her let them in her house . . . at night. I could be wrong, but I'm worried. What if she's doing something in-a-pro-priate?"* Stacey lingered over every syllable, like she could taste each one.

I stumbled forward, as if I'd been hit from behind. Because really, I had been. I'd been sucker punched—first by Gavin, then by Ruth, and finally by Stacey Figg.

"She can't possibly think . . . ," I mumbled at Gavin. I grabbed the banister and staggered up the stairs. Everything was starting to fall down around me, like a poorly constructed house of blocks. I thought I could help the boys, but I had made things worse, and in the process, I'd probably lost my job. This stupid job that I didn't even want at first. This stupid job that I still needed. This stupid job that I had to keep until Jack got himself out of whatever mess he was in.

Then there were my boys—my poor, sweet, hapless boys. I'd wanted them to feel like someone here was on their side, but all I'd done was screw everything up. I was crying before I even got into class. The boys were walking in, and I raced to my seat and dropped my head to my desk. I help up my hand, motioning for them to stop barraging me with questions.

"Ms. Parsons, are you sick?" asked Guy. "What's wrong?"

"Should we get the nurse?" asked Art.

I couldn't pick up my head until I had composed myself. *I shouldn't have come here.*

I raised my face so they could see my red, puffy, blotchy eyes. "I'm OK," I said. "Rough morning."

"What happened?" asked Caleb. "Did someone hurt you?" The boys all sat up as he said this, as if they were ready to line up behind him and fight for my honor. My heart melted, and I felt even worse.

"Boys," I said. "I just can't. Not now. Here's your assignment. Each of you write one really funny thing. As funny as you can. When you're done, just start reading. I need a good laugh this morning."

13

I wasn't looking for Stacey Figg, but she found me two days later, walking out of MacReady as I was pulling on my hat.

"Going to day care?" she asked, putting on her coat. Stacey knew exactly where I was going. She knew all my movements.

"Yes," I said, a little too forcefully. "Why don't you walk with me?" I knew Stacey didn't walk and usually waited for the campus shuttle. Something about shin splints and low muscle tone.

"Sure," she said, taken back by my request. I saw her weighing the inconvenience of walking against her piqued interest in my overture. "I can walk." She zipped up her enormous silver coat and pulled its giant furry hood over her head. She looked like something out of a space fantasy. We started walking. I took large strides, moving as quickly I could.

"What's up?" she huffed.

"Oh, I don't know. Maybe you should tell me. You seem to know everything that happens here."

Stacey stopped walking and caught her breath. "What do you mean?"

I wanted to keep going—I needed the movement—but Stacey couldn't walk and talk at the same time, so we stood in the middle of the path. "I wanted to think that you were a friend, Stacey, I really did."

"What are you talking about?"

"How do you know the boys come to see me in the evenings?" I charged. "Have you been spying on me?"

"What? No," she said, laughing nervously.

"You sure about that? Because Gavin played me a recording."

"A recording?" she asked. There was a bench nearby. She looked at it longingly.

"Yes, Stacey. Gavin apparently likes to record conversations. I heard you telling him the boys come to my house . . . at night."

Stacey reached out and put a mittened hand on me. "Honey, you have to know that I did it for you . . ."

"For me, really?" I pulled back so hard that her hand fell.

"Yes, for you. I didn't want things to go too far, you know, for your sake. Agnes, people are talking . . ."

"Exactly which people are talking, Stacey? If you were so worried about me, why didn't you come to me? Why go to Gavin?"

"Because Gavin relies on me. He needs me to let him know when these things are happening. I am his eyes and ears." She shrugged and lifted her palms to the sky, as though she couldn't help herself from being so incredibly useful.

"I don't think that's the reason, Stacey," I said, taking a step closer to her, using my height advantage and staring her down. "I think you did this for you, not for Gavin, and definitely not for me. I'm such an idiot. All this time I thought you were a friend. But you're not a friend. You're a parasite. You sucked up all the information you could get about me and you used it to make yourself look indispensable." All the anger I'd been pushing down, my anger at Gavin, at Don, hell, even my anger at Jack, it was spilling out, all over Stacey Figg and her giant silver coat.

I could feel the anger on my face, but Stacey was smiling. "A parasite?" she said. "I wasn't such a parasite when I was pouring you wine. I wasn't a parasite when I was cooking you dinner and watching your kid. Besides, do you really expect me to believe that you thought I was a friend? I know you tolerate me because I'm next door and I let you cry on my couch and eat my food. You talk about yourself the whole time; you never ask about me. Besides, I know what you say about me, how you ridicule me to your *real* friend." She stopped and took a breath and then spoke more slowly, as if this part was really important. "I know that you call me the Figg, like I'm a thing, a thing that doesn't even deserve a real name." Her voice quivered.

I didn't know anything about Stacey Figg. She spent hours trying to extract the details of my past, and I didn't even know where she'd lived before she occupied the house next to mine. Still, I wasn't sure I deserved this.

"So you sold me out," I said.

"I did what I did because you have to watch your back here. If you don't get on board with Gavin, you're gone . . . and I don't have a rich husband and a house on the beach. I need this job."

I wasn't sure if I still had a rich husband, and I knew I didn't have a house on the beach anymore. But I thought it better to keep that to myself.

She was right. At best, I had simply tolerated Stacey Figg; at worst, I'd used her. While I hadn't expected her to rat me out to Gavin, I had no right to expect her loyalty. I put my hands in my pockets, looked down at the ground, and walked away, watching my boots break through the layer of ice that had formed on top of the dirty snow. I was no match for the Stacey Figgs of the world. I was in way over my head, playing against people who were much better at this than I was. I just wanted to pick up Grace and go home. So I did, leaving Stacey and her silver jacket behind.

-14-

That night I lay in bed determined to make peace with the mess I'd made. The boys would all be here for the summer. Their parents would fork over money to Gavin, and they'd all get into high school. Maybe it wasn't so bad. Maybe that was the way things were done here in New York, or at least in last-stop private schools.

I stared at the popcorn ceiling. As discouraged as I was, I couldn't stop thinking about the boys. How eager to please yet how quick to screw up they were, and how badly they felt about themselves. It was one thing to be tricked into paying to get your kids into high school; it was another thing to let these kids be continually demoralized in the process, broken down slowly, day by day. I had no idea if or when things would get better for these boys, but I wished that I could have been the one to help them.

I rolled over on my side when my phone buzzed. An incoming call. Jack. He was finally reaching out to me again. As much as I wanted to hear his voice, I was scared, worried about what he'd say to me.

"Jack?"

"Yes. I'm sorry, Aggie. I'm sorry I lost it. I just couldn't bear to see you with another man, not like that."

"I told you, it was nothing."

"You don't know how hard it is for me to see you with anyone else, to even think about you with another man."

"You don't have to think about it. Nothing happened, and nothing's going to happen. I'm yours. I never stopped being yours."

"Show me, then. Tomorrow night," he breathed.

Tomorrow was Friday night. I didn't have to worry about school the next morning.

"Your place or mine?"

"Mine," he said. "Unless your place has room service?"

Room service? All my place had was a mouse and inconsistent heating. "Yours. Definitely yours. Let me see what I can do about Grace."

~

I called Beeks and asked if Grace could spend the night with her.

"What, the Figg is busy?"

"Long story. Let's just say the Figg isn't available."

"OK, but this time you can't tell me you won't be sexing it up."

"Fair enough," I said.

"And you have to promise you will come to me for Easter."

"Beeks . . ."

"Actually, make that the Sunday after Easter. I have already promised Easter to Brian's family, where we will all be eating his mother's tasteless ham and listening to my father-in-law regale us with bird-watching stories."

"It's a deal," I said.

"You know that I would have taken Grace anyway," she said.

"I know. Thank you, Beeks. I mean it. I don't know what I'd do if you weren't here."

"Me either," she said. "But let's not think about that."

~

I'm not sure why I spent so much time riffling through my closet, looking for something both clean and sexy, with the added benefit of still fitting me. The hotel room door had barely closed behind me when Jack started to remove my clothes. As soon as I was over the threshold, he pushed me up against the wall, and while kissing the base of my throat, he started working on my blouse with one hand, running the other under my skirt. As he made his way down the buttons (Why? Why had I chosen so many buttons?) I pushed him away, not because I wanted him to stop—my God, I didn't—but because I wanted to see him, to watch him. It was still so new to have him inches from me, to be able to look at his face, to smell him, to feel his hands, that I wanted to make sure it was really happening.

"Let me see you," I whispered.

"Fair enough," he said and managed to take off all my clothes while fixing his eyes on mine the entire time.

He stared at my naked body for what felt like a week. I stood before him, my clothes in a pile on the floor, and he just stared, as if he could not believe he was seeing me.

"You're here," he said, as though I was the one who had gone missing.

He took a step closer to me, his hands still by his sides. His not touching me was dizzying. Finally, he leaned in, his mouth seconds from mine. *Oh my God, just do it. Just put your hands on me.*

"You know I nearly died without you," he said, his breath on my neck.

"Jack . . ."

"I couldn't think, couldn't sleep, I couldn't even breathe without you," he said.

"Jack . . ."

"I need you, Aggie. Tell me you need me, too," he said, his hands now on my hips, pulling me even closer to him. "Tell me."

"I need you," I breathed. "I need you, Jack."

He took my lower lip between his teeth. He moved his hands slowly up my body.

"Say it again," he murmured.

"I need you, Jack."

~

A few hours later, while we were waiting for room service (room service!), Jack pulled me to him and ran his fingers up the length of my body. I looked down at my white, slightly less wobbly thighs. Still, I wondered when Jack was going to say something about the extra flesh I'd accumulated here in New York. He didn't.

"You're so beautiful," he said, tracing the outline of the mass of flab where my flat stomach used to be. If I inhaled and held my breath, the small hill of stomach would disappear, but I couldn't hold my breath for hours on end, so there I was, in all my convex glory.

When his hands were somewhere south of my belly button, he said, "Let's talk about what happens next."

"I think I know what happens next," I said, rolling on top of him.

He laughed. "That's not what I meant."

"Wow," I breathed. "That's a first."

He moved me off onto my side. We lay facing each other again. I looked at Jack, his hazel eyes softening at the edges, his cheekbones, his still-bronzed face inches from mine. I'd spent all these months away from him, and yet we could slip right back into each other this way, as though we hadn't spent more than a day apart. Muscle memory is a funny thing.

"No, Aggie." He smiled. "What I mean is what happens next for us. How we're going to get it all back."

"Does this mean we're going home?" I asked.

"Not yet. I still need to raise a little more money," he said.

"That's fine," I said. "It's only March. I probably wouldn't want to leave my boys in the middle of the year anyway."

"You have boys?" he asked, pulling me closer. It was easy to make Jack jealous. Too easy. Within seconds he rolled back on top of me and pinned my arms by my sides.

"Oh yeah," I whispered as his mouth worked its way down my body. "You should be really jealous. There's nothing like the attention of a middle school boy to make a woman feel good about herself."

"I'm hardly jealous of middle school boys," he murmured. "But if anyone gets to be around you all day, it should be me."

His lips were on my stomach when room service knocked on the door.

"They can leave the tray," I panted.

He looked up at me. "Hold that thought," he said, jumping up and wrapping the sheet around himself. *Just last night I was sleeping in about eight layers of clothing, and now here I am, lying completely naked on a hotel bed.* I pulled up the covers as the food was wheeled in, trying not to make eye contact with the guy doing the wheeling. I saw that he had a short ponytail and goatee, but then I quickly fixed my eyes elsewhere. Jack signed the bill and walked back over to the bed.

"Ruth Moore," he said, climbing back in.

"Yeah, that's someone I really want to picture right now," I said, running my hands up his back. I kissed the base of his neck. "Let's table her for later."

Jack propped himself up on his elbows. "I need your help, Aggie."

"*My* help?" I asked, playing dumb.

"Yes, *your* help. I don't just need Ruth's money back. I need more."

"More?" I looked past his face at the enormous TV mounted on the wall. "Why do you need more?" I asked.

Jack took my face in his hands. "Because I lost more than I thought, Aggie. To pay everyone back, I need Ruth to help bring in new investors. She's connected to everyone here."

"New investors?"

"Yes," he said, leaning closer. "To replace the ones that pulled out, and to pay people back."

"To pay people back," I repeated, staring right into his eyes.

"Exactly." He stared right back. "And I've explained that we need some . . . information on her. We can't just ask her. We need her to have no choice but to help."

I suddenly got very cold. I rolled over, out from under Jack, and stood up. I pulled the comforter off the floor, wrapping it around myself. Thoughts of Ruth, Gavin, and the summer program ran through my mind. If Ruth did know Gavin was faking reports to get kids to sign up for the program, that was the kind of information that could really help Jack.

"I have nothing," I said, not looking at him. "I barely know anything about her." I started to get a little dizzy. "Besides, I don't want to get into trouble."

"What?" he asked. He pulled me down so we sat facing each other. "Aggie, why do you think you're here? Why do you think I sent you to that school?"

"Oh, I don't know," I said. "For my safety? For your daughter's safety? Because we had no place to live while you're sleeping in a five-star hotel?" Damn, it was freezing in here. Why wasn't this blanket warming me up?

He softened and ran his hands up along my thighs under the blanket. "Darling, you knew you were also sent here to be a listener. I could have moved you to a number of places to keep you safe. St. Norbert's is where you send your kids if you're rich and desperately want them in private school because certain families do not send their children to public school. All 'your boys' come from very well-off families that give generously to the school and to its endowment, just to get their boys in. They are all beholden to Ruth. With one word, she can bring in more people and more money. That is why you went."

"So, what? We threaten her and she tells them to invest with you? And they do it because they want their kids in school?"

"That's not exactly how it works," he said. "She can mention me in passing, enough to make it seem like she may be looking for people to invest. The trick is to make me sound exclusive, as though they'd be *lucky* to invest with me, with the added perk of being in Ruth's good graces."

I shuffled back in the bed and rested against the headboard. I looked down at the sheets, with their ridiculous thread counts, and thought about the sheet on the massage table. I thought about the moment I realized something bad had happened to Jack, that feeling I first got when I was lying on that table with my face wedged in the doughnut pillow. It had been over seven months since then. All I wanted, each and every moment of these seven months, was to go back to things being the way they were before, before all this happened. In all that time, I would have given anything to be alone in a hotel bed with Jack. But now that I realized how orchestrated these months had been, I couldn't process it all. I needed to clear my head. I could do a lot of things in bed with Jack, but thinking was not one of them.

"I need to go," I said, getting up. "I have to think about this."

Jack walked over to me. He pulled me close.

"Don't you want to help me, Aggie?" he whispered.

"Of course I do. I just need to think."

"Do you understand what I'm saying? I'm in trouble, real trouble. If you don't help me, if I can't get the money, then I'm going to jail. Is that what you want?" His shoulders crumpled and he looked small and desperate.

"What? How can you say that?" I asked. "Of course I don't want you to go to jail."

"Really?" he asked, an eyebrow raised. "You don't want to move on?"

Without thinking, I threw his hands off me. "What kind of question is that? You were the one who disappeared, remember? I didn't move on. I waited. I waited for you, Jack."

"No, Aggie," he said, stepping away from me now, his voice cracking. "I waited for you."

"What?"

"I waited for you, Aggie. All those years. I was waiting for you. I could have gotten married, settled down, so many times, but I never did. I was waiting for you," he said. "That day in the sushi restaurant, I knew it. I knew it as soon as you sat down next to me. *She's here,* I thought. *She's finally here.*"

"What you're asking me to do," I said, "it's a lot, Jack. It's a lot to ask."

"Do you know what the worst part of jail would be? Losing you. I can't do that, Aggie. I can't lose you." His eyes filled.

"You won't," I whispered, moving closer, putting my mouth on his tears.

"Take some time to think, then," he said. He looked away for a moment, then added, "Just remember, Aggie, this isn't just for me. You're also doing this for us, for our family. You're doing this so Grace can have both her parents around, so that she can have all the things you didn't."

He looked back at me and took my face in his hands. We stood there for a while, just looking at each other, and then I retrieved my clothes from the chair Jack had placed them on after he'd folded them neatly. I ran my hands through my new hair and checked myself in the mirror. Jack had saved me—why couldn't I do the same for him? Besides, all the things I wanted were at my fingertips. Jack had given me a job, and if I did it, if I did that one job, I could have it all back.

I didn't owe St. Norbert's a thing. I could blackmail Ruth Moore and then close my eyes, click my heels, and be back in Santa Monica by the beginning of summer, as if none of this had ever happened. That would show Gavin, Stacey, even Ruth how much they'd underestimated me.

Jack came up behind me, and I looked at our reflection in the mirror. "I promise, Aggie. It will all be worth it. Remember, we're doing this for us, for our family."

"For our family," I repeated, looking at Jack in the mirror. I looked into his eyes because I could not look into my own.

15

"You were right, boys. I failed you. I failed all of you."

That's how I started the next class.

"I couldn't stop the program from happening. I couldn't stop Principal Burke, and I'm sorry."

"It's OK," said Guy, breaking the silence. "We know you tried." He forced a smile.

"Did you?" asked Caleb from the back of the class.

"Yes, Caleb," I lied. "Really, I did. I went as high up as I could, but I couldn't stop it from happening. I'm sorry, boys, truly."

"It's fine," said Art. "We just wanted you to try for us. Nobody else does." I looked away. We sat in more awkward silence, and then, with an enthusiasm I did not feel, I said, "Let's get to work. Outside!"

That morning was cold and brisk but sunny, and the boys followed me out. I couldn't look at them, not directly. Maybe it would be easier to teach without eye contact if we were outside.

I had just handed back the boys' essays (all of which I'd graded in a fog of wine and self-pity), and we were still in the poetry unit. I started by reading Robert Frost's "Birches" to them. I couldn't remember his name, but I remembered the hippie middle school English teacher who had dragged my class outside, asked us to hold hands around a tree, and then cried while reciting the poem. But "Birches" was too long for my boys. Ten lines in and they started playing catch with Davey's shoe. Davey, meanwhile, started to wander from the group. Art began pulling leaves off a nearby bush. I saw Caleb glance around distractedly, looking for some trouble.

"New poem," I said. The boys groaned.

"It's a short one. I promise. Eight lines." Still, more groaning. "Come on, guys."

"Fine," said Davey, leaning against the base of the Norbert statue. "Go for it."

I opened my book to "Nothing Gold Can Stay" and started reading. When I got to the end of the poem, I looked around at a sea of blank faces.

"Nothing?" I said.

"Nope," said Caleb, almost proudly. "Not a thing."

"What's happening in the poem, boys?" I asked, looking down at the book, not waiting for them to answer. "I see the word *grief*, so I know there's something sad going on. When Frost says at the end that 'Nothing gold can stay,' I think he means that nothing beautiful lasts forever. Maybe he even means that the prettiest stuff, the gold, that stuff really doesn't last . . ." I heard a choke in my voice. I quickly looked down past the phone at my shoes. Crying was not in my lesson plan.

"I know what Eden is," said Caleb, quickly covering for me. "Adam and Eve. That's a pretty sad story." He looked at me, nodding and waiting for approval, wanting me to see that he was trying.

"Nature's first green," I said, my voice cracking. "The first line of the poem." We looked at each other. "Eden didn't last, did it?"

"Nope," added Davey. "Adam and Eve got sent away. They got sent out of paradise."

They weren't the only ones.

"Wow," said Art. "That's kind of sad."

"Sad but happy, because you know that the leaves will come back," added Guy, always on the lookout for a better ending.

"Not all the leaves," said Caleb. "Maybe the prettiest ones never come back."

"See?" I gulped. "See what you did? You just analyzed a poem."

"Did we get it right?" asked Guy nervously.

"There is no right." I looked up. The trees were still bare, but the sky was a brilliant blue. I looked back at the boys. They had done good work today.

"Class dismissed," I said.

I wondered if the boys would remember anything about my class. I wondered if they would remember this poem, or their hippie California teacher who dragged them outside and cried because she had failed them.

16

There were words tugging at the back of my brain that night. After tossing, turning, and shifting positions more times than a yoga instructor, I stood up and started walking around the bedroom.

I thought back to the day in Santa Monica when I'd gone through Jack's desk, or at least I'd tried to go through it. I hadn't seen anything because I hadn't wanted to see anything. It's hard to see clearly when there's sand in your eyes.

I ran downstairs into the living room and stared at the stack of boxes behind the TV, the ones I still hadn't unpacked—the boxes with the framed photographs, my useless books, and the contents of Jack's desk. I moved the boxes around and smiled when I saw Sondra's handwriting—"*Jack office*"—and ripped off the packing tape and opened the box.

I removed the familiar Lucite cubes and paged through the same client reports I'd seen in Santa Monica. I looked at the bottom of each one to the section marked GAINS AND LOSSES. I felt my eyes glaze over, but I blinked and forced myself to look closely at the pages. I looked through thirty or so reports, and in each one, the client had gains, big gains. At some point, I even began to read the charts. I kept looking and could not find a single report with losses. If this was the case, Jack had made his clients a ton of money. Had he really taken all of it? And if this was a onetime mistake, wasn't he still making money for them? Why did he need to raise more money to pay them back?

I felt a little light-headed and leaned against the wall. Jack had sent me here for one reason—to get money for him. Jack wanted new investors, new investors to pay back the old ones.

I was past the point of going back to sleep. Grace would be up in a few hours, and three hours of sleep was almost as bad as no sleep at all. So I did what no wife should do when her missing husband returns and tells her that he needs her to help raise money to pay back his old investors—I went online.

It didn't take long for me to find what I was looking for, even if I hadn't known I was looking for it. I found an article about a guy in LA who was doing time in jail for promising high returns on people's investments, but instead of investing people's money, he'd used the money to buy himself boats, houses, and cars. He paid his old investors with money he raised from new ones. Every time he needed new cash, he would go out and raise more money. The problem was, he never invested any of it. The words were right there on the screen—black, on a white background, just as the words *No Money* had been in my head when I sat in Don's office in August. This time the words spelled out *Ponzi Scheme*. This wasn't a onetime mistake that Jack was trying to fix. Jack hadn't taken money he'd made for his clients, because Jack hadn't made money for his clients. He'd just made it look that way. Jack was running a Ponzi scheme.

I read through pages of stories about Ponzi scheme operators who had defrauded people—all kinds of people, rich and poor—into investing in funds when they weren't investing at all. They were only paying back other defrauded investors. The schemes were all sizes—some taking down universities, others defrauding individual investors, regular people. The cycle was never-ending, only coming to a halt when the operator was caught or the money dried up—when the amount of stolen money got too big.

When I had read just about all I could stomach, I closed my laptop and called Don. I was on the brown couch. I picked up a bag of almonds I'd bought earlier in the week, but the mouse had beaten me to it, chewing a hole in the top of the bag. I briefly contemplated eating the rest of the nuts, those the mouse hadn't touched.

Even though it was the middle of the night in California, Don picked up on the first ring.

"I know," I said before he could ask me any questions.

"What?"

"I know what Jack is really doing."

"And what would that be, Agnes?"

"I know that he's running a Ponzi scheme," I said, stumbling over the words, hoping he'd tell me I was losing my mind.

He didn't.

"This time he's in way over his head," he said. "People wanted out; they wanted to withdraw their money. He almost had the money to pay everyone back, but the number was just too big. He's in serious trouble, Agnes. This time he needs your help."

"This time? What do you mean this time?" I pushed away the almonds, spilling them all over the floor. I got down to pick them up and found myself eye to eye with the mouse who had hidden under the couch. I stared. She stared back.

"What do you mean, Don?"

"This is not the first time Jack has gotten himself into trouble like this." *I've been cleaning up his messes since before you were born.* The mouse blinked first and ran away, scurrying under the molding in the wall, presumably back to her multiple children and many cousins.

"Don," I said, pushing myself up. "How is this a surprise to me? How the hell did I not know this?"

"Who was going to tell you?"

I could think of a person or two who should have told me that this was not the first time my husband had to go into hiding because he owed money or that his whole business was built on a lie. But I knew I couldn't yell. Don didn't do yelling. He liked yelling even less than he liked crying. So I took a deep breath and told Don that Jack wanted me to talk to Ruth. I didn't use the word *blackmail*, but I didn't have to.

"Makes sense," he said flatly. "We all have a function for Jack. I've always been his fixer. I guess you're his Hail Mary."

"I'm what?"

"You heard me, Aggie. Listen, it's the middle of the night. I have to go."

I sat back on the brown couch and eyed the almonds, still unsure whether I'd eat them or not. Could I do this for Jack? Could I be his last, best hope? I wanted to be. I wanted to have a function for him, a purpose, something other than staying thin, having scheduled sex, and showing up to restaurants on time. I certainly didn't have a function here anymore.

I thought about the boys sitting under the tree and reading the Frost poem. I thought about the looks on their faces when I told them they'd actually read and understood it. It might have been the first time all year that I'd seen them feel successful as a group. But as much as I wanted them to feel that way every day, I didn't see how I could help them. I was up against something here at St. Norbert's that felt too big, or at least too big for me. No, I couldn't help my boys, but I could help Jack.

I thought about Jack breaking down that night in the hotel room. I pictured his teary face and heard him telling me how much he needed me. Before Jack, nobody had ever needed me, not like that. I heard him saying "for our family" over and over again in my head, and I thought about all the things I'd needed growing up, all the things I didn't have.

I thought about my patch of carpet and about being painfully alone. Jack had given me so much. Maybe it was my job to help him be better, to get him out of trouble and show him that things could be different, to show him the person he could be. Maybe this was just what I'd have to do for the sake of Jack, for the sake of Grace, for the sake of my family.

I abandoned the almonds and called Don back. His phone went straight to voice mail, so I left a message. "I'll do it, Don," I said. "I'll be his Hail Mary."

PART FOUR: SPRING

-1-

I called Beeks and told her. I couldn't tell her everything—I didn't want to implicate her—but I told her enough to let her know what I was doing was risky. She knew that it involved Jack and some money and me sort of blackmailing Ruth Moore so that Jack could get some money. Before I told her, I had made her swear to say nothing until I was done.

"Fine," she said.

"And no yelling portion," I said.

"That's a lot to ask, but I think I can do it," she promised.

Turns out, I didn't have to worry about a yelling portion, because Beeks was speechless.

"You there?" I asked.

"Yes."

"Well?"

"I don't really know what to say," she said.

"That's it, Beeks?"

"Yes, Aggie, that's it. OK, maybe one thing." I should have known. "Listen, I get that you can forgive anything once. Really, I do. But this doesn't sound like it was a onetime thing. You know that, right?"

"I know that."

"OK then, that's all I have to say."

I did not know if Beeks withheld the yelling portion because she was too shocked to yell, or because yelling would have been the death knell of our friendship. I didn't stick around to find out which it was. Just saying the words to her made me ashamed. It was a horrible feeling.

The next morning, on the first day of April, I awoke to a text from her. The text had no words, only an attachment. I clicked on the attachment and was directed to a website. I read the words on the screen:

> APRIL FOOLS' DAY: April 1. In some cultures, April Fools' Day is known as Fool's Errand Day. A fool's errand is a task that is known to be unwise and against a person's better judgment, yet is still carried out.

I texted Beeks back.

Message received. Feeling foolish all the same.

2

Ruth Moore was not expecting me, but she didn't look surprised to see me. Poor Esme just shrugged and waved me back.

"Agnes," Ruth said, looking up.

"Hello, Ruth."

"What can I do for you?" She pushed her chair back and crossed her arms.

I sat in the chair opposite from her, my hands in my lap. I picked at my cuticles and bit my lower lip.

"Are you OK?" she asked.

I did not meet her gaze. "The thing is," I began, almost midsentence, "I know all about the summer program. I know that Gavin uses his faked reports to get kids to sign up for it and that he pockets some of the money, and I know that you know about it."

Her eyes narrowed. "What do you want?"

"It's not really what I want. It's what Jack wants," I said, swallowing. "He needs new investors, and he wants you to get them for him."

Ruth assessed me for a few very long seconds, and then she laughed. "Really? You came into my office to blackmail me?"

My cheeks burned. There it was again. The shame. I mechanically parroted back Jack's words, feeling like a robot with a dying battery. "Jack needs new investors, and he wants you to get them for him."

Ruth pushed herself up to standing. She walked over to the chair next to me and sat down. I looked at her large feet and thought about sitting next to Don in his office. Ruth leaned in toward me. She spoke very quietly.

"Is this really what you want to do?" she asked.

"Yes," I whispered, my face searing, my armpits now moist.

"You have a silver bullet here. Do you understand that?"

I blinked my approval at her, like a hospital patient in full-body traction.

"So instead of, oh, I don't know, having me fire Gavin and letting him take the fall, you'd rather have me find people to invest with Jack even though I pulled out my money, even though I don't trust him myself?"

When I didn't say anything, she went on. "This is it? You have a chance to make me fire Gavin. He's a perfect fall guy for this, Agnes." She narrowed her eyes again. "I could even give you his job."

My own eyes flickered when she said this. I wished they hadn't. I didn't want her to know that I was having second thoughts. She read me and kept going. "This is what you want? You want me to convince people to hand over their money to a man with a shady history of money troubles and just hope they see some of it back?"

Damn you, Jack. Damn you for putting me in this position.

I gave Ruth the weakest nod I could muster. "I have to go," I said. "Jack will contact you." My feet finally free, I ran out of her office, grateful for the cool air on my face. I ran across campus and did not stop running until I got to Grace.

3

In the days following my visit to Ruth, that feeling of shame returned. I was never ready for it, but when it sneaked up on me, I felt my cheeks warm, my skin prickle, and my stomach turn. I knew I couldn't let it get the better of me, but I also knew that I hated it. I'd burned through the gamut of emotions since Jack left—panic, fear, desolation, irritation, even anger—but shame, that was the worst. I'd have taken any of the others in its place. The weather was slowly improving, and I ran more, as though pounding through the shame could push it away. Nothing worked.

Jack sent Grace an Easter dress, maybe to make up for the Christmas dress she didn't have. The dress was taupe silk with ivory organza flowers around the neckline. I tried not to think about all the food that would get caught in those pretty little flowers. I also tried not to think about the dry-clean-only tag inside the dress. Jack had also sent a matching ivory cashmere cardigan. How could he know that I'd shrunk all Grace's cashmere in October when I tried to wash it on what I thought was the cold, delicate cycle in my antebellum washing machine?

On the Sunday after Easter, I got dressed for our post-Easter brunch with Beeks and tried not to think about Beeks, Brian, and Jack in the same room. I dressed Grace in her silk dress as she stood, holding on to her crib.

"This is for you," I said, staring into her blue eyes. "It will all be worth it. I promise." The words caught in the back of my throat, but Grace just smiled and stood on the floor next to her crib, gripping the bars. "Do you think you could sit now?" I asked. I pulled the dress down over her knees and slid a matching bow in her hair. She didn't have shoes to wear with it. Other than her snow boots, I had one pair of shoes for her. They had once been white but were now a dark, scuffed gray, and they hardly went with silk and organza. I knew Jack would notice the shoes, but I didn't have time to buy her a new pair.

Grace made a funny noise, then let go of the crib and clapped her hands, as I'd seen her do many times. This time, though, she did something more. She clapped her hands, stared at me, and then she took her first steps. She took six steps, perfectly, as though she'd waited fourteen months to walk just so she could skip the awkward drunken-dwarf stage. She walked and then collapsed onto the floor. I moved to her quickly and folded myself over her. I thought about crying, but crying ruins silk and organza, so I squeezed my eyes shut and ran my hands over the carpet.

~

Jack was meeting us on the corner of Ninety-Sixth and Broadway. Beeks lived a block away, but I knew Jack would want to walk in together. I also knew he had no desire to come all the way up to the Bronx to get us, so I told him to meet us at the entrance to the subway.

You take Grace on the subway?

Yes, Jack. I take Grace on the subway because you cannot take taxis in Manhattan on a teacher's salary. My own thoughts aside, I texted back:

Lots of children ride the subway.

I walked up the subway stairs on Ninety-Sixth Street. Jack was always early and I was ten minutes late, so I assumed he'd be waiting for me. When I got to the top of the stairs, I looked around but didn't see him. Grace was in my arms, the stroller too much for me to handle on the subway. I scanned the four street corners for him. When I didn't see him anywhere, I turned and looked into the window of a coffee shop. Jack was at the counter, looking down, reading the paper. I walked to the window and knocked. He looked up and his whole face smiled at me. I just wanted to stand there and bask in it for a few uncomplicated minutes, but he stood up and walked out to us.

"Hello, darling," he said, kissing me and holding me to him so his chin rested on my temple.

"She walked, Jack." I beamed, pulling away so I could see his face.

"She walked," Jack said, looking right at Grace, running his hand down her leg, letting his fingers linger on her feet. I was grateful that he said nothing about her shoes.

We walked a block to Beeks's apartment. Jack held Grace and I linked my arm through his. We looked like a family. A Sunday best family. A Sunday best family that goes to no church but finds it necessary to procure a silk-and-organza dress for a one-year-old who will, in a few short hours, be covered entirely in yogurt. I had always wanted to be a Sunday best family.

-4-

Beeks was not home when we arrived. Neither was Kyle. Turns out, if you keep throwing things down the trash chute, at some point you'll get stuck and break your arm. The two of them were in the emergency room. Brian nervously promised they'd be home within half an hour. None of us wanted to be there without her. Brian took our coats, and I went into the kitchen to see if there was anything I could do for Beeks. The men sat in the living room, while Stevie and the other boys played a video game behind them.

Jack and Brian had met a few times, but those times had been awkward, bordering on unpleasant, so Beeks and I had an unspoken agreement to keep their encounters to a minimum. Jack never understood why someone who went to Harvard, and then to Harvard Business School, would want to work in a green energy company, when he could, as Jack put it, "name his price." I knew from Beeks that Brian loved his job, even if he wasn't making hedge-fund dollars. We sat uncomfortably on the dark-gray tufted couches in Beeks's living room, and I put Grace down to walk for us. Like a wind-up doll, she performed on cue, saving us from having to do any talking at all.

Beeks walked through the door, escorting a beaming Kyle, who sported a bright-blue cast. We all jumped up to meet her as though we'd been waiting days for her arrival. She laughed. When she pulled me close to her she whispered in my ear, "Don't be so nervous, Aggie. No drama. I promise." She pulled back a little. "But I do want to talk to you before you leave," she whispered. She hugged Jack and made an enormous fuss over Grace. Poor Kyle was completely ignored until his brothers realized he was home and pounced on him.

"Get off!" screamed Beeks. "Get off him! He's in a cast, you guys! Do you want him in another one?" The boys just looked at her, completely surprised by her outrage. One by one they peeled themselves off their brother, who could not have looked happier with their attention.

Beeks was right. Lunch was uneventful. There was no drama. She made her famous ham with Pepsi. She'd texted me a picture of herself the day before, pouring a bottle of Pepsi over a pink ham studded with cloves. As promised, it was delicious, and thankfully Beeks followed my advice and didn't mention anything to Jack about soda being a part of the recipe. She steered the conversation to interesting yet safe topics. We didn't discuss Brian's job, and we obviously couldn't talk about Jack's work. So for the first time ever we talked about her work . . . and mine. I told funny stories about my boys. I even told a few about Stacey Figg. When the meal was over, I was grateful—both that it had ended, but also that it had ended without a bang.

Beeks asked me to follow her into the bedroom to get our coats. Once we were in there, she closed the door behind us.

"Aggie," she began. "I'm not going to ask you any questions. I know you love him. I see that. But if whatever you do for him gets you into trouble, I want you to know that Grace will always have a place here with us."

Suddenly, my ears buzzed loudly, and for a moment I could not see. The room spun around and I heard the words again. *She will always have a place here with us.* They were Beeks's words, but I'd heard them before. My first foster mother had said them when the social worker came to visit me, a few weeks after my parents had died. "Agnes will always have a place with us," she said, standing in the living room talking to the social worker. It didn't turn out to be true. By the middle of eighth grade, I was with another family. And then another.

"I have to go, Beeks," I said. I grabbed our coats, staggered out of her room, and motioned to Jack to pick up Grace. I bolted out of the apartment and didn't bother to wait for the elevator. With Jack behind me, I ran down the stairs two at a time to the small, dark, mirrored lobby. I never thought I'd be so happy to breathe Manhattan air, but once outside I took in huge gulps of it.

"Are you OK?" Jack asked as I heaved on the sidewalk, the spinning in full force.

I crouched down and gripped my knees and tried to slow my breathing. My eyes watery, I looked up at Jack and nodded, but I could not yet talk.

"Aggie," he asked, Grace in his arms, "what's wrong? What happened?"

I took a huge gulp of air and brought myself up to standing. I exhaled slowly, opened my eyes, and looked at him. "What you're asking me to do, Jack. It's a lot. It's a lot to ask."

"What did she say to you?" he asked through his teeth.

"Who?"

"Don't play dumb, Aggie. What did Beeks say to you when you went into her room? Why did you run out?"

"Nothing." We stood in front of Beeks's building, and although people were moving around us, I kept my eyes on Jack. The wind was picking up and tousling his hair. *Breathe.*

"Nothing? You expect me to believe that?" he asked. Grace started to whimper in his arms. I reached for her, but Jack took a step back.

"Jack," I pleaded. "Jack, you're asking me to break the law." I side-stepped a small dog that had started to sniff my leg. The dog's owner yanked at the dog's leash and kept walking.

"Does Beeks know?" he asked, pulling his caramel-colored blazer tightly around him as a gust of wind came barreling down the sidewalk. Grace put her head on his shoulder and played with the lapels of his blazer.

"No," I said, shivering. "She just knows that I'm conflicted about something."

"Conflicted?" He laughed. "That's rich. What are you conflicted about? Do you really expect me to believe that you never wondered where all the money was coming from?"

"What?" *Deep breaths.*

"You heard me. You never asked where it was all coming from—the cars, the house, the jewelry, the vacations, all the restaurants. You never asked."

"Why would I?"

"You sat in the armchair in the office and watched me pore over the numbers night after night and you never asked a single question."

"What was I supposed to ask?"

"Oh, I don't know," he said, almost amused, but not. "'Can we afford all this, Jack? Where's all the money coming from?'"

"What would you have told me if I'd asked? Would you have said, 'Sure, Aggie, it's all coming from people who think they're investing with me but really aren't'? Besides, we both know you wouldn't have wanted me to challenge you like that." The wind was blowing harder and my hair was flying around.

He took a step toward me, and with his free hand he grabbed my arm. He spoke in a low but clipped voice. "For a poor girl, you took to it very well. You took to all of it, and now that I'm asking you to help pay for it, you balk. Ask yourself, Aggie, are you willing to give it all up? Do you want this to be your life?" He looked disdainfully at the New York around us—the dirty gray buildings, the weather that started out clear and sunny but was now cold and blustery, the pigeons, the dogs, the people walking right into the middle of our personal space. I thought about my New York, which also had a brown couch, a leaking ceiling, and hulking window air-conditioning units. "Is that what you want for yourself, for Grace? Because if you don't help me, Aggie, *this* is your life." Jack was right. I hadn't known what was going on, not because I'd asked and he wouldn't tell me, but because I'd never wanted to know. I'd made a calculation and plunged my head deep into the sand. I was happy to live that way, and I'd still be living that way had none of this ever happened.

"I thought you were my life," I said. "You and Grace."

He let my arm fall. "Just help me now and I promise this will never happen again."

"You'll never rip people off again? Or you'll never get caught again, Jack?"

We stood staring at each other as people maneuvered around us.

"I need you," he begged. "Please help me, Aggie."

"That's what I thought. I have to go," I said, reaching out and taking Grace from his arms. I let my hands linger on him.

I heard Jack calling out for me as I ran down to the subway with Grace in my arms. Grace. *She will always have a place with us.*

That night I walked outside to take out the trash. It was cold and I wasn't wearing enough. I rushed down the stone steps of my stoop and tripped on the bottom stair. I came crashing down, my lower back slamming into the stone. The trash flew into the air and exploded when it hit the ground. I lay on the ground, my back throbbing, the smell of trash in my nose. It was a cloudless night, and I lay there looking up, trying to find a single star in the city sky. I found a small cluster and squinted through my tears.

This is what I have become. This is who I am now. I am cold and covered in trash, and other than a one-year-old who likes to play with her food, I am the only living descendant of Maureen and Bob Riley of Modesto, California. I am the only person who remembers them, and I know that there is nothing about my situation that they would like. My parents taught me to be honorable and self-sufficient and to look after my family, and for the first time since they'd died, I really hoped they couldn't see me.

-5-

Later that night, hours after I'd cleaned up the mess, I returned to the stoop. I couldn't sleep and I couldn't be inside. The walls of the house seemed to be inching toward me. I bundled up and opened the front door, hoping to sit on the front steps and clear my head. I didn't expect to see Stacey Figg doing the same thing.

"Hey," she said, turning to face me. She looked awful. Circles ringed her eyes, and her hair, which I'd never seen down, was enormous—angry and unsubdued.

I didn't say anything, I just sat down on my steps.

"I'm a bad person," she said, looking away.

"Let's not get carried away," I said, hearing my voice but Jack's expression. "Besides, you aren't the only one." I ran my hands through my hair and leaned back against the step, letting out a deep breath. "I think I just made a huge mistake."

"What did you do? Sell out your students? Rat out your neighbor? Oh no, that was me . . ." She looked down at her feet, which were in a pair of silver clogs. Stacey Figg loved silver.

"I sold them out, too," I said. "To Gavin and Ruth. I could have helped them, but instead I decided to help myself."

"Huh?" she asked.

I didn't want to go into details. So I just shrugged and hoped that she'd get the message and not push me.

"Would you go back and undo it?" she asked, sensing my reticence.

"I think I would." It helped to say the words out loud.

"Then it's not too late to help the boys. Is it?" She leaned toward me and lowered her voice.

I thought about it and wrapped my arms around my knees, resting my chin on them. "No, it's not."

"Then how about this," she said, sitting up straight and flexing her feet. "Tell them I'll talk."

"What?"

"You can use my name. You can tell them I'll talk."

"Stacey, I think I'm gonna need actual proof, or at least more than your word against theirs."

"Then tell them I have emails. From both of them."

"What if they drag you down with them and you get fired?" I asked.

"Then I'll find another job. It's not hard. Nobody wants to teach middle school."

"I do," I said.

"Yeah." She smiled. "You do."

We sat outside in silence for a while, neither of us saying much. At some point, a tray of Stacey's carrot muffins surfaced. I think I ate six. Before she headed back inside, Stacey looked at me and said, "I'm sorry, Agnes. I really am."

"I'm sorry, too. For never really trying to be a good friend. And I get it," I said, swallowing a bite of muffin, because I did get it. Stacey had done something pretty crappy and was trying to undo it.

Now it was my turn.

~

Early the next morning, I barged into Ruth's office with Grace in my arms. I expected to find Ruth alone, but she was sitting at her desk talking to Gavin. They both looked surprised to see me.

"I'll take the deal," I said to Ruth, hugging Grace to me for fortitude. "I'll trade what I know for getting Gavin fired, and when he's gone, I'll help hire his replacement." Out of the corner of my eye, I saw Gavin's jaw drop to the floor. "And the summer program," I added. "You agree to shut it down."

"What about Jack?" Ruth asked.

The words were caught in my throat, but finally I spat them out. "Jack's on his own," I said, ignoring Gavin, who was silently gasping and flailing. Using one of Jack's favorite expressions, I said, "I'm letting the chips fall where they may."

"And what if Jack's chips end up in prison?" Ruth asked.

"Then they end up in prison. They're his chips, not mine."

Gavin put his jaw back together and jumped out of his seat. "What's going on, Ruth?" he asked.

With Grace in my arms, I pivoted and took a step closer to him. Now it was his turn to back up toward the wall. "Ruth didn't tell you?" I said, looking at Ruth out of the corner of my eye. "You were right, Gavin. Ruth does agree with whoever she happens to be talking to."

His face fell again, his jaw landing right between his feet. "She agreed to fire you and suspend the summer program if I stay quiet about what I know."

"Is this true?" He looked at Ruth but didn't wait for an answer. "What if I talk?" he gasped, his voice cracking.

"Stacey Figg will talk, too, and if that's not enough, she's got emails . . . from both of you." I looked over at Ruth, then back at Gavin again. "Besides, what would you tell people, Gavin? Would you tell them you forged hundreds of behavior reports just so parents would sign their kids up for a summer program, which is your meal ticket, all while demoralizing the students you're supposed to be educating?"

He looked at me, then at Ruth, and then back at me again. "Demoralizing?" he asked, looking truly confused. "Why are you fighting for these boys?"

"Someone has to." Grace was making noise, so I pulled a baggie of puffs as well as my keys out of my coat pocket. I put her down at my feet and let her have at them.

"Nobody has to fight for these boys. These boys will all be just fine," Gavin said.

"How do you know they'll be fine, Gavin? Because they're rich?"

He laughed. "It's not just that they're rich, Agnes. It's that they're rich and mediocre. Do you know what that means?"

I wasn't sure I knew at all what he meant, and Gavin read it on my face. He crossed his arms and kept talking. Grace toddled over to a bookshelf and started pulling off books one by one. I let her.

"It means that these boys will inherit enormous family businesses, or they will marry into enormous family businesses. It means they can go to low-level colleges, barely graduate, and still live lives most of us could never dream about. It means they will have cars and homes bought for them, and then bigger cars and bigger homes." He talked quickly, spit flying out of the corners of his mouth. "Don't pity these boys, Agnes. When you're rich and mediocre, nobody expects you to cure cancer. Hell, no one even expects you to go to medical school. These boys will be handed everything, all of it. They get the keys to the kingdom, and they get them without ever having to work."

For a moment, I felt sorry for him. Maybe it was hard to watch these kids barely make it through middle school but know that it didn't matter, that none of it mattered. Then a light passed over his face, as if he had just had a realization.

"Oh, but that's why, isn't it?" he said, nodding his head.

"What are you talking about?" I asked.

"That's why you like these boys. You like them because you got the keys to the kingdom and you never had to work." He paused and then smirked. "I mean, until you did."

I felt heat rise up through me. "You don't know anything about me."

"I know enough," he said.

"I'll tell you why I get these boys," I said, my voice rising and shaking at the same time. "I get them because everyone else underestimates them. Everyone underestimates them the same way you underestimated me." By the time I had finished, I was shouting. I had scared Grace, who had taken a break from unshelving all the books and started to whimper. I scooped her up and kissed the top of her head.

"Enough." Ruth spoke from her seat behind the desk, startling me. I'd forgotten she was in the room. "Gavin, go home, pack up, and be gone by graduation." Ruth looked at her hands, assessing her long, tapered fingers. "Agnes, you stay. We have a few details to iron out." She smiled warmly at me.

"Ruth," I said, not smiling back, "let's just be clear. Nobody may ever know that you sold out your students to make yourself look good, but I will."

She didn't miss a beat. "Then I guess we'll both know things about each other, won't we?"

"I have to go," I said. "I have one more thing left to do."

Gavin was just the warm-up. Now I had to confront Jack. I pulled out my phone to text him.

Meet me. Now. My house.

Really? Right now?

Yes. Grace is in day care. We have the place to ourselves. Come find me.

I knew this wasn't exactly fair, but I also knew Jack wouldn't make a trip this far uptown if he didn't think sex was involved.

See you in 30. Can't wait.

Yup, see you in thirty. I now had half an hour not to lose my nerve.

-6-

A few minutes later, while I was shoving socks and books under the brown couch, I heard a knock on the door. I took my hair down, walked into the foyer, and checked my reflection. I opened the door and Jack walked in. His hands were on me before I even closed the door behind him.

"My God, it's been too long." It was like he'd forgotten all about our conversation in front of Beeks's apartment and could only think about how long he'd gone without this, if he was even thinking. His lips were on my ear, neck, my chest. He forced me back into the living room, and I bumped into the back of the couch.

"What's this?" he murmured, his mouth still on my neck, his eyes behind me.

"This?" I said, looking down. "This is the brown couch."

"How about we christen it?" he murmured in my ear. He untucked my shirt and ran his hands underneath, his fingers quickly working to unhook my bra.

"Jack . . ."

"Shh. We can talk later," he said. He ran a hand down my waist. It landed on an especially large pair of underwear that came up well over my belly button.

"Jesus, Aggie, what the hell are these?" he said, pausing momentarily.

"These are the underwear version of the brown couch," I said proudly. "Ugly but extremely comfortable."

"I'm sure it's comfortable wearing something you could camp in," he said. "But those things are coming off." He kissed me again, hard, and worked to unbutton my skirt.

What's the hurry? I thought to myself. *This could be the very last time we do this. What's the harm in waiting?* But then he slid a hand down into my underwear and I fully understood the harm in waiting. It took all the strength I had to push him away.

"What?" he asked. "You don't want this? Tell me you don't want me." His hands and mouth were back on me, still working, his breathing hard.

I pushed him away again and said quickly, "Of course I want you. But I can't help you, Jack. I'm not doing it." I was breathing so heavily it was hard to get the words out.

He fell back, as if I'd hit him. "You can't do that."

"I have to."

"You can walk away from me, from us? What about Grace? You don't want her to have her father at home? You don't want her to have a real family? You want her to grow up like you did?"

"If I help you, if I do this for you, I could also get into real trouble, and then Grace will have neither of us."

"Nobody will know." He moved toward me and put his hands back on my waist.

"What about next time?" I asked, steeling myself. "When this happens again, and we both know it will, because that's how a Ponzi scheme works . . ."

He let go of me and looked shocked, as though he'd never heard those words before.

"What do you know about a Ponzi scheme?"

"I know that you faked it. You faked all of it. If it comes out that I knew and that I helped you raise funds from new investors just to pay off old investors, then I could go to jail, too, and then Grace will really have nothing."

Jack opened his mouth, but I cut him off. "If you want to earn the money back the right way, I'll help you," I said. "We refund your investors and we're done. We get a fresh start."

"But then we'd have nothing, Aggie."

"We'd be a family, Jack." I took a step toward him.

Jack took a step back. "You say that, but you're terrified of that life, aren't you?" he said. "Never having enough, always needing more."

"I am scared of never having enough. But not scared enough to break the law."

He smiled a sad smile. "Wow. Some trophy wife you turned out to be."

"You're right. I had nothing before you," I said, my voice breaking, my eyes suddenly stinging with tears. "But you're also wrong. I wasn't the trophy, Jack. You were. You were *my* trophy."

"What?"

"You were my trophy," I said, wiping my face with my sleeve. "You were my trophy for all those years I lived without family, for all those years I worked so hard. *You* were the trophy." I was suddenly crying so hard I couldn't breathe. I felt hollowed out. "You were right. I didn't ask any questions. I didn't care what was happening to me or who I had to become. I just wanted the prize."

"Wow," he said. "I guess I underestimated you."

"That seems to be a theme," I said in between sobs.

"It wasn't supposed to happen this way," he whispered.

"Tell me about it," I said, looking into his beautiful eyes. Could I really do this? Would I be OK if I never saw those eyes again?

"Really, Aggie? You're OK with Grace having a father in jail?"

"I'm not OK with it. But I don't have a choice. She should at least have one of us, and if I help you, she could have neither."

I thought he was going to speak, but he grabbed me hard, pushed me down on the couch, and kissed me. He grabbed my hair and pulled at it lightly, gasping when his hand came away with a clump of long blonde strands. "What the hell is this?" he asked, pushing himself off me, holding his hand for me to see. "Why is your hair falling out?"

"It's not my hair."

"Then whose hair is it?"

"Someone else's."

"Aggie, why are you wearing someone else's hair?" He stared at me, his mouth wide open. I can't say I blamed him. I was pretty disgusted with the extensions, too.

"Because I cut my hair, Jack. I cut my own hair when I got here, and I was terrified that you wouldn't approve. That's what I did, or at least that's what the person I was did."

"What happened to that person? Did you leave her in Santa Monica?"

"No. She left Santa Monica. She even came here to New York. At some point, though, I lost her."

He threw the extensions to the floor, tucked in his shirt, and buttoned his pants.

"Jack, I'm sorry." I began tucking my own clothes in.

"Not as sorry as I am. I have to go. I love you, and I love Grace. I always will. Goodbye, Agnes," he said, and without waiting for me to respond, Jack was gone.

PART FIVE:
EPILOGUE

THE LAST DAY
OF SCHOOL

I'd like to say that my boys shone at the last-day-of-school ceremony. I'd like to say that each of them won an award—even if it was for hours accumulated in the Bowel or number of late passes stolen from Gavin's desk. But at the tented ceremony held outside on one of the lawns, my boys were largely invisible. I watched Caleb, Davey, Art, and Guy slink into their alphabetical seats and wriggle and squirm through an interminable ceremony. One by one, awards were handed out to the same small group of boys, who, by the end of it all, seemed almost embarrassed by their riches. Afterward, I hovered near the buffet with Stacey and Adam and watched my boys with their parents. Davey was right—my hair did look like his mom's. It also looked like Caleb's mom's and about two-thirds of the hair on all the mothers there. The boys waved to me. I waved back.

Gavin had left in the middle of an early May night. I'd heard he'd gotten a position in Connecticut. "It helps that nobody wants to teach middle school," grumbled Mona Creek one morning as she heaped creamer into her coffee.

After the ceremony, I walked home and called Beeks.

"I made it," I said, stopping to sit on a wooden bench. "I made it to the end of the year."

"And in two weeks, you'll make it to the Cape with us," she said with a laugh. "You'll love it. Nothing but ice cream and pale New Englanders as far as the eye can see."

"Sounds delightful," I said.

"I dunno. I think the adjustment to East Coast beachgoers may be a little rocky. It was for me."

"I think that's an adjustment I can handle," I said. "In the scheme of things."

"I really can't talk," she said. "I have the twins' end-of-year play. I agreed to be snack mother. Again."

"Now it's my turn to yell!" I hollered. "Why do you always have to be snack mother?"

"To save the kids from black-bean brownies and kale chips. Nobody wants to eat that shit."

I laughed. I didn't even bother waiting for Beeks to say goodbye.

I'd been calling Don periodically to check on Jack. The pieces were falling around him. Lawsuits had been filed, and whatever he still had was sold to pay back his investors. I thought about calling Don for a new update, but I slid my phone into my pocket, got up, and kept walking.

Grace was in her final hours of day care, and I took advantage of my final hours alone before the summer. I had packing to do. Ruth had offered to let me move into a better-heated, centrally cooled house on the other side of Stacey Figg, and I agreed, on the condition that I could bring the brown couch with me. I also lobbied hard for a new coding program for the boys—to be run by Adam. If anyone could put their hacking skills to good use, it was him.

I walked up the front stairs, put my key in the lock, and pulled open the door, releasing several hundred empty canisters of veggie puffs.

They spilled out of the foyer and onto the steps, tumbling all around me. I stumbled back, hopping over the cans, and turned around to see my boys standing in the bushes.

"Surprise!" screamed Davey, throwing up his arms, bringing his snug shirt with him and revealing a stripe of white belly.

"We wanted to do balloons," said Guy. "But Caleb thought this was funnier."

I looked at Caleb, who was grinning sheepishly. "Yeah. Don't ask us how long it took to collect all these," he said. "We've been hitting your recycling bins at night." He pulled a can from behind his back. "We brought you a full can of your favorite."

"Plum carrot!" I said, taking the can and making a note of the duct-tape bow.

I laughed and reached out to hug them. "You guys always go one step too far, one step into crazy-land," I said. "I'm going to miss crazy-land. It'll be a long summer without you guys." I inhaled sharply to avoid getting teary.

"We'll miss you, too," said Guy, who was never above a few tears.

"Is it true that you're gonna be the middle school principal?" Art asked.

"No," I said. "But Ms. Figg and I are going to help hire the new principal. So you're still going to be dealing with me next year, even though I may not be teaching you."

"What about after that?" asked Davey. "What about high school?"

"What do you mean?"

"We've been talking," said Caleb, looking at the others. "We think that next year you should apply for a job in the high school here. That way, if we go, you'll go with us."

I sniffled sharply again, but this time, my tears got the better of me.

"Boys, even when you're in high school, I'll still be here for you. *Mi foyer es su foyer.*"

"Huh?" said Art.

Maybe it wasn't such a surprise that one of these boys didn't get the Spanish award.

"Nobody likes middle school," said Caleb. "That's what all the teachers say when they think we're not listening. They say the only people who want to teach middle school are the ones who couldn't get jobs in high schools."

"That's not true. *I* want to teach middle school."

"Why?" sniffled Guy.

"I like it here."

"Really?" he asked.

"Yes, really. I like it that you guys are in between. I like it that you're still boys in some ways but that I get to see glimpses of the men you'll be. I like it that you're middling." They weren't the only ones middling, teetering in between the people they were and the people they could be. I knew exactly why I'd found a home in the middle school. "Besides," I added, "I've kind of gotten used to the Wall of Axe."

"OK," said Caleb, nodding at the others. "We get it."

"Can we take a picture?" Art asked. "Before we go?"

"Sure," I said. We took a selfie in front of the house, veggie puff canisters underfoot. The boys looked at the picture and sent it to each other. Then they gave me one last awkward hug and ambled off, bumping into each other as they walked. I wondered how different the boys would look when I saw them again in the fall. Summer wreaks havoc on the adolescent body. I watched them move across campus until they were out of sight. Then, turning to face the house, I climbed the steps, walked inside, and sat down on the brown couch. I popped open the canister of the plum-carrot puffs and tossed a handful into my mouth.

ACKNOWLEDGMENTS

Thank you to Danielle Marshall for taking a big chance on me and this book, and to Alicia Clancy for deftly guiding me through the process. I would never have written *Trophy Life* had I not walked into the Sarah Lawrence Writing Institute and met Eileen Palma, my teacher and dear friend, whose advice made this book better at every turn. I'm grateful to my other Sarah Lawrence teachers, Annabel Monaghan and Pat Dunn, as well as my classmates, who cheered me on from the very first draft. Everyone should have a first reader (and a friend) like Johanna Shargel, who read every draft I sent her way and often texted me first thing in the morning with new thoughts on the book. Thank you to my other readers—Eleanor Menzin, Adina Shoulson, Sarah Josephson, Dahvi Waller, Lexy DeVane Tomaino, Shami Shenoy, and Emily Holsinger Butler, and to the real Beeks, for lending me her name as well as her ear. I'm eternally grateful to David Naggar, who told me to write a book and then championed me when I did.

To my children, Bennett, Efram, Frances, Fiona, and Sidney, who were calling me a novelist when I only had a rough draft in hand. A special shout-out to my boys, who were both in middle school when I wrote this book and taught me that the antidotes to the middle school years are a sense of humor and a healthy dose of empathy.

Mostly, though, I thank my husband, Michal, who gave me everything I needed to write this book, including every type of space I needed—the actual physical space, and the mental space to hole up inside the story and ignore everything around me. Thank you for not letting me name our children Wolf or Satchel, but especially Agnes.

ABOUT THE AUTHOR

Photo © 2017 Jason Roth

Lea Geller is a recovering lawyer who lives in New York with her husband and children. She began her writing career by blogging about her adventures in the trenches of parenting, and got the idea for *Trophy Life* when her two sons were in middle school.

When Lea's not eavesdropping on her children, she can be found running, drinking diner coffee, and occasionally teaching middle-school English. She enjoys embarrassing her family by posting pictures of her vegetable garden on Instagram (#IgrewDinner). You can follow her at www.leageller.com.